GREENMANTLE

CHARLES DE LINT

ORB

A TOM DOHERTY ASSOCIATES BOOK
NEW YORK

GREENMANTLE

Grateful acknowledgment is made to:

Tanith Lee, for the use of the quote from her short story "Blood-Mantle" which first appeared in *Isaac Asimov's Science Fiction Magazine,* Nov. 1985, copyright © 1985 by Tanith Lee.

Jane Yolen, who introduced me to the poetry of Joshua Stanhold in her book about his daughter and their relationship, *The Stone Silenus* (Philomel/The Putnam Publishing Group), copyright © 1984 by Jane Yolen.

Robin Williamson, for permission to use a portion of "Song of Mabon" from *Selected Writings 1980–83,* copyright © 1984 by Robin Williamson. For further information on Robin Williamson, and Pig's Whisker Music, write to: Unique Gravity, P.O. Box 114, Chesterfield, Derbyshire S40 3YU, England. Website: http://www. thebeesknees.com

This book was originally published by Ace Books in February 1988.

An Orb Edition
Published by Tom Doherty Associates, Inc.
75 Fifth Avenue
New York, NY 10010

Tor Books on the World Wide Web: http://www.tor.com

Library of Congress Cataloging-in-Publication Data

De Lint, Charles
    Greenmantle / Charles de Lint.—1st Orb ed.
      p. cm.
    "A Tom Doherty Associates book."
    ISBN 0-312-86510-4
    I. Title.
    PR9199.3.D357074   1998
    813'.54—dc21   98615
                                  CIP

Printed in the United States of America

0 9 8 7 6 5

GREENMANTLE

By Charles de Lint from Tom Doherty Associates

For
Joanne & John Harris

CONTENTS

PROLOGUE

Io Pan! Io Pan!
Come over the sea
From Sicily and from Arcady!

—ALEISTER CROWLEY,
FROM *"HYMM TO PAN"*

Pan? Pan is dead. Or is that a
pun—Pan—*du* pain—*bread*—
peine—*pain*—*the body of Christ?*

—TANITH LEE,
FROM *"BLOOD-MANTLE"*

MALTA, August 1983

By the time Eddie "the Squeeze" Pinelli was five hours dead, Valenti was on a Boeing 747 halfway across the Atlantic. He sipped the beer that the steward had brought him and stared out the window into the darkness. He usually felt an honest regret that things had to get as far as they did before he was called in, but not this time. Pinelli had been a *capo* in the New York City Cerone Family, one of Don Cerone's special boys, but now the sonovabitch was dead and the only thing special about him was that those famous fingers of his weren't going to put the squeeze on anyone anymore. That suited Valenti just fine.

Don Magaddino had called the hit—Valenti's own boss. "It's personal," he'd told Valenti. "That's why I called you, *capito?* It's between you and me, Tony. Okay? I want that *pezzo di merda* dead and then we don't talk about this no more."

Eddie had got a little itchy and a lot crazy and put the squeeze on one of the girls the Don kept on the side. Valenti understood. It had been personal for him, too. Not so long ago, Eddie had tried to make a little time with Valenti's woman, Beverly Grant. Only Bev wasn't going to get up and walk away like the Don's girlfriend had when Valenti had walked in on her and Eddie earlier tonight. Bev had taken a twelve-story drop and what was left of her you wouldn't *want* to see walk away.

Valenti had wanted to take Eddie down so hard then that it hurt, but the Don wouldn't give him the word and a soldier didn't take down a *capo* without an okay from way up. *Così fan tutti*—that was the way of the world. But Valenti was patient. He'd known that sooner or later Eddie, being the asshole he was, would lose it. All Valenti'd had to do was wait.

After the sweltering oven that was a New York City summer, the Maltese weather was glorious. The air was so clear that he could see for miles across the low hills with their tiered fields being readied for the fall harvest. He had the taxi drop him off at the end of the lane and walked the rest of the way to the villa, taking his time. When he reached the door, he took off his sunglasses and brushed his thick dark hair with his fingers. Then he knocked. Mario opened the door himself.

"Jesus, Tony," he said, his gaze darting nervously behind Valenti then back to his friend's dark features. "What the hell are you doing here?"

Valenti smiled. *"Ciao,* Mario. That's some welcome. Drop by anytime, you tell me, so here I am and—"

"You're a dead man," Mario cut in. "You know that?"

"What're you talking about? The sun down here driving you a little crazy?"

Mario grabbed his arm and propelled him into the house, slamming the door behind them. "I got a woman here," he said. "I got kids. They come looking for you here, what's going to happen to them, 'ey?"

"You got some problem, Mario?"

"The only problem I got, Tony, is you." He stood back and studied Valenti's face. "You don't know, do you?"

Valenti frowned. "All I know is I came a long way to see you, but you don't look too happy to see me."

"You know the Squeeze is dead?" Mario asked.

"Sure I know that. I'm the one that hit him."

"*Madonna mia!* You *are* crazy."

"But not that crazy," Valenti said. "Magaddino called the hit."

"Oh, yeah? And who called the hit on him?"

"What?"

"Your *padrone* is dead, Tony, and the word is you hit him. You hit him, you hit that girlfriend of his—the one with the red hair—and you hit the Squeeze. And let me tell you, a lot of people, they're not too happy about it, *capito?* They want your balls, Tony. They called me. I'm retired—what? Five years now? But still they called me, asking if I've seen you. Asking if I want to make a little money. You know what I'm talking about?"

Valenti stepped away from the door and moved slowly into the villa's spacious living room. He sank into a canvas chair and regarded his friend.

Mario Papale was fifty-eight now, but he wore his years well. His hair was a silvery gray—had been since he was thirty—his dark skin even darker than Valenti remembered, tanned from the Mediterranean sun. He was wearing a pair of white cotton trousers and a short-sleeved shirt that was unbuttoned. Watching the way he walked across the room, Valenti knew that the old Fox hadn't lost a thing, retired or not. Maybe you never lost it.

"They called you?" he asked. "That quick?"

"What did you think, Tony?" Mario replied as he sat down in front of him. "This is a *cane grosso*—a big shot we're talking about. Not just a soldier like you or me."

"I didn't hit him. Eddie—yeah. But it wasn't personal. No matter how I felt, I had orders."

"We're talking a *padrone* is dead here, Tony. Your orders don't mean shit now because Magaddino's dead and you're buying the rap for the hit."

"I've been set up."

Mario didn't say anything for a long moment. He studied Valenti, taking his time about it, then slowly nodded. *"Chi lo sa?"* he said finally. Who knows? "But I believe you. You never could lie to me, Tony. So what're you gonna do? You need anything? You need money? A piece?"

Valenti shook his head. "I've got a place in Canada—a safe place. Clean. No one knows who I am."

"Too close," Mario said. "These *bastardi*'ll smell you out like dogs after a bitch in heat. You got to go someplace where when you say you're a *soldato* they ask what army; not what family, *capito?*"

"This place I set up years ago, Mario—just like you told me to, remember? Even in the *fratellanza* a man needs a place where he doesn't have to worry about his family. I've got money there. And guns."

"They're never gonna stop hunting you down."

Valenti shrugged. "I was getting tired anyway."

"Bullshit."

"Okay. So it's bullshit. You think I should turn myself over to Ricca's justice?" Ricca Magaddino was the Don's oldest son and stood to inherit his empire.

Mario laughed humorlessly. "This afternoon you're staying with me," he said. "Tonight I drive you to the coast and smuggle you off the island. I know people with a boat. You need papers?"

Valenti shook his head. "These men with the boat . . . ?"

"They're friends—not cousins."

"Okay. *Grazie,* Mario. I wouldn't have brought this down on you if I'd known."

"You think I don't know that? Now let's forget this shit. *Come vai,* 'ey? It's been a couple of years. Talk to me, Tony. Maybe we don't meet again, so we take what time we got, okay?"

Mario's wife was half his age, a shy, dark-haired woman named Maria who spoke only Maltese. Mario had grinned when introducing her to Valenti. "Mario and Maria—how you like that, 'ey?" She and the children were staying with her sister in nearby Marsakala when the two men made ready to leave the villa.

"The nights're quiet here," Mario said. "And dark. Just follow me and don't get lost, *capito?*"

He went into his bedroom and unlocked a chest from which he

took a pair of American .38 calibre handguns. Valenti accepted one and nodded his thanks as he thrust it in his belt.

"I hope we don't need these," he said as they went down the hall.

Mario nodded. "My car's got no shocks and the road's the shits," he said, "so maybe you better watch the family jewels, 'ey?"

"Sure," Valenti said with a grin.

Mario hit the lights, throwing the hallway into darkness. Valenti opened the door and the night exploded with sound. The first shot hit Valenti in the shoulder and spun him around. The second and third spat into the doorjamb, showering both men with splinters. A fourth bullet took Valenti's right leg from under him and he fell to the floor.

"*Bastardi!*" Mario roared. He got off a couple of shots, then slammed the door shut and bolted it. "We're in deep now," he muttered as he glanced down at his friend. Thrusting his gun into his belt, he hoisted Valenti up in a fireman's lift and headed for the back of the house. By the time the *soldati* broke in the front, the only thing left in the hallway was Valenti's blood.

"Check out back!" one of the dark-suited men ordered, but they already had men out there and he knew no one was going to get through them.

The intruders fanned out through the villa, shooting into closets, then ripping the doors open, kicking apart the beds, checking any place where a man might hide. But they didn't find a thing. Then word came from the back of the villa that both Jimmy Civella and Happy Manzi were dead and did Fucceri want them to check the fields?

"Sure, sure," Louie Fucceri said. They didn't call Papale the Silver Fox just because of his hair. It wouldn't surprise Fucceri if they were halfway to Milan by now. He found a phone that his men had mercifully left intact and put a call in to his *capo* to report their failure.

LANARK COUNTY, FEBRUARY 1985

The tire blew on Lance Maxwell's pickup about a half mile past the Darling/Lavant township line. The truck skidded in the slush as Lance brought it to a halt on the side of the dirt road. He got out to check the damage, cursing under his breath.

"Stay, Dooker," he told the big German shepherd that was on the passenger's seat.

He hunkered down for a look, then stood, hitching up his pants. Christ on a cross! You'd think the sucker'd hold out for just a couple more miles till he got home.

"Okay, Dooker," he called to the dog. "Come on down, boy." The German shepherd jumped down from the cab of the pickup and pushed his nose into Lance's hand. "Yeah, yeah. Okay. Go catch yourself a squirrel or something. I got work to do."

He fetched the spare from the back of the pickup, leaned it up against the side panel, then dug out his jack and tire iron from under a mess of cord, tools and canvas. Glancing to see where the dog had got to, he spied Dooker sniffing along the side of the road, back toward the turn-off that led up to French Line. The blow-out had stranded him in front of the old Treasure place. Frank Clayton's weather-beaten "For Sale" sign was still out on the snow-covered lawn. Sure, Frank, he thought. The day somebody buys this craphole from you's the day I stand you for a case of two-four.

Dooker returned to see what he was doing as he got the jack under the back of the truck and started to hoist the vehicle up. "Get outta the way," he told the dog when it got too close.

He hadn't been the one to find old man Treasure—that joy'd been reserved for Fred Gamble, who'd driven up to collect on a grocery bill but had trooped right into the place along with everybody else after the cops had hauled the body away. You never saw such a thing. Buddy Treasure mustn't have thrown out a newspaper since before the war.

They were piled ceiling-high along the walls of every room and hallway. Thousands of the suckers, all yellowed and stinking the way newspaper does when it gets wet. There were magazines too. Old copies of the *Star Weekly*—he hadn't seen them for some time. *Life*. *MacLeans*. *Time Magazine*s going back to when most of the cover was just a red border. All kinds. But that wasn't the worst.

It seemed that in the last year Buddy'd decided to stop throwing out his garbage or using the upstairs can when he had to go for a crap. The kitchen had more refuse in it than the town dump. There was mold and shit you didn't even want to think about growing over every- thing. And talking about shit—Buddy'd taken to dropping a load in the corner of the living room and wiping his ass with a piece of old yellowed newspaper.

Weird fucker—no doubt about that. No wonder the missus took up the kids and beelined out of there without a word to nobody.

That was nine, ten years ago now, Lance thought as he removed the blown tire. Longer since the missus took off. Willie Fuller had bought the place from the bank and tried to fix it up but he just couldn't get the stink out of it. He sold it to some out-of-towner who had started to take down the walls, really getting ready to give the place a good going over. But he quit halfway through the job and the place'd been up for grabs ever since, listed with Frank's agency. And the day Frank sold the sucker . . .

"Shit," he muttered as he studied his spare. The tread was worn as smooth as a baby's ass. Well, it'd get him home. He finished up in a hurry, tossed the old rim with the flaps of tire hanging from it into the back of the truck. The jack and tire iron followed it with a clatter.

"Dook!" he called, looking around for the big shepherd. "Hey. Dooker! Get your ass back here—double-time."

He spotted the dog over in the field behind the Treasure place. Dooker had his head lifted high like he was listening to something, his broad head tilted to one side as he studied the woods beyond. Lance started to call out again, but then he heard it, too. A quiet sort of pip- ing sound, low and breathy. It made him feel a little strange—hot, like the way you get when the weather warms up and springtime grabs you by the balls, telling you it's time to make babies.

He took a couple of steps in the direction that the sound was com- ing from and started to get all sweaty. He was getting hard, his penis pushing up against his jeans. Lanark County, like most of Ontario, was in the middle of one of those February thaws that come up for a few days, then buggers off with a laugh, but that was no reason for him to be feeling the way he was. His penis was so hard it hurt. His chest was all tight and it was hard to breathe. His ears buzzed with the piping sound that came drifting across the fields—not loud, but it pierced him all the same.

He thought maybe he was going to come right there, right in his pants on the side of the road, but then as suddenly as he'd become aware of the sound, it left him. He staggered to lean weakly against the side of the pickup.

Christ, he thought. That's it. My first honest-to-Jesus heart attack.

He was still weak. It took all of his energy to lift his head and look across the field. He could see Dooker, still listening, still watching the woods though there was nothing there that Lance could see. Then suddenly the big shepherd shook himself, looked around and came bounding back across the snow toward the truck. By the time Dooker was pushing his nose up against Lance's hand, Lance was breathing easier again.

Gotta see the doc, he told himself. No more farting around. He says diet, I'm dieting this time. Jesus.

He called Dooker into the cab, slowly settled in the driver's seat and started the engine up. Giving the fields behind the Treasure place a final considering look, he put the truck into gear and pulled away.

TORONTO, MARCH 1985

The music was contemporary Europop, but the dancer's moves were pure bump-and-grind. The MC had announced her as Tandy Hots: "And Tandy's always randy, boys—you know what I mean?" Sitting at his table, nursing a beer, Howie Peale figured he knew just what the MC meant.

She couldn't be more than seventeen tops, and that body. Oh, she had the moves down all right. Teasing little moves that made him want to shout along with some of the other guys in the joint, but he held back because he didn't want to look like an asshole to his new friend. Earl Shaw wasn't even watching the show. He was just sitting there, his bull-neck hunched over the table as he leafed through a day-old *Toronto Star.* He was drinking whiskey—straight, with a beer chaser.

Howie'd met Earl in the can—they were both in the Don Jail on drunk and disorderly charges at the time. Right off, Howie knew Earl was his man. Howie wasn't too big and he wasn't too smart. He had survived the street scene by latching onto someone who was both. He'd run errands, do a little of whatever, just to keep on the good side of whoever was his main man at the time. Right now that man was Earl.

Earl was the kind of guy you could really respect. Smart and tough and he didn't take shit from nobody. Even the screws in the can had been a little leery of him. First night they were out, he and Earl hit a gas bar and made off with a clean $243 plus change just by sticking a gun in some pimply-faced kid's nose. Earl'd even split fifty-fifty. No way he was letting go of this gig, Howie thought.

Tandy Hots was down to her G-string and pasties now, moving slowly across the stage until she was right in front of their table.

"They really get off on being up there, huh, Earl?" Howie said. He licked his lips, looking up into the dancer's crotch.

Earl grunted and glanced at her. "Who gives a fuck what they like," he said. "Just so's they do what they're told."

Howie nodded. The dancer moved further down the stage and he tried to imagine a woman like that being his, doing just what *he* told her to. If they were in a hotel or someplace, just the two of them, instead of this strip joint on Yonge Street . . . His dreamy mood left him as he sensed Earl stiffen across the table.

"Look at this," Earl said.

He turned the paper around so that Howie could see. There was a photograph of a good-looking woman accepting a check from a Wintario official. She wasn't built like Tandy Hots, Howie thought, but she wasn't bad at all.

He read the caption. Her name was Frances Treasure and she'd just won two hundred grand in the lottery. He shook his head slowly. Jesus. Two hundred grand! And all she was planning to do with it was buy back the place where she'd grown up and fix it up.

"I tell you, Howie," Earl said, "somebody's looking after me."

"What do you mean?"

Earl put his finger down on the photograph. "See this broad?"

"Yeah. Lucky bitch."

"She's my ex," Earl said.

Howie looked at the photo again. "No shit?"

"No shit," Earl said. He looked Howie in the eye. "And you know what I think, Howie, m'man?"

Howie shook his head.

"I figure she owes me," Earl said. "Course, first we got to find her. That could take a little time. But then . . ." He grinned, a slow and wicked grin that gave him a crazy look. Howie grinned back. Sonovabitch had a weird streak in him a mile wide, no doubt about it, but there was no *way* Howie was letting go of this gig. Not when the good times were just starting to roll.

"What're we gonna do then?" Howie asked.

Earl's grin grew wider. "Then we're gonna party."

THE RIDDLES OF EVENING

Pan pipes a tune but once
And all the forests dance.

—JOSHUA STANHOLD
FROM *"GOATBOY"*

And suddenly they knew that the mystery of the hills, and the
deep enchantment of evening, had found a voice and would
speak with them.

—LORD DUNSANY,
FROM *THE BLESSING OF PAN*

1

Frankie followed the moving van down the short driveway and watched it head off down the road; then she turned to look at the house. The difference between the half-gutted structure that had stood there when she bought the place and what was there now was phenomenal. In the bright sunlight of a perfect day in late May, the site of all her childhood nightmares had been transformed into the house of her dreams. A little smaller, perhaps, but cozy enough for her and Ali.

There was still a lot of work to be done. The workmen had left their typical battlefield of litter and debris behind them, but Frankie was looking forward to doing some work around the place with her own two hands. If anyone had told her that she'd be here now, even a day before the Wintario draw . . .

She found herself grinning foolishly. It was still hard to believe that she'd won. $200,000. Even after the $26,000 she'd paid for what was left of the house and its land, and the $60,000 or so she'd had to put out for renovations, she still had over $100,000 in the bank. Any day she expected someone to come up to her and tell her it was all a mistake, that she had to give it all back, but it wasn't going to happen. She wouldn't allow it to happen. Not now.

She made her way slowly back to the house. Opening the front door, she almost ran into her daughter who was carrying a stack of empty boxes down the stairs.

"Watch where you're going, kiddo," she said.

Ali poked her head around the boxes. "Are the movers gone?"

"Yup. We're on our own now—out in the backwoods of Lanark County where few men dare to go."

"Oh, Mom!"

Frankie laughed and took the boxes from her. Ali had her curly blonde hair but wore it short instead of in a long spill down her back as Frankie did. She also had Frankie's strong Teutonic features—the broad nose and brow, the wide mouth—and eyes such a dark blue that the pupils sometimes got lost in them. They were often taken for sisters, which delighted Frankie who was thirty-four, at the same time as it embarrassed her fourteen-year-old daughter.

"Are you finished with your room?" Frankie asked.

"For now. I thought I'd give you a hand in the kitchen and then maybe we could explore a bit."

Frankie tossed the boxes into the big screened-in porch that led off from the kitchen's back door. "Tell you what," she said. "Why don't you let me finish up in here and you go ahead exploring. Then when I'm done, we can have a bite to eat and you can show me all the hot spots."

"You sure you don't mind?" Ali asked, obviously torn between wanting to get out into the sun and feeling it unfair to leave her mother working alone.

"Trust me."

"Okay." She gave Frankie a quick kiss, then scurried out the back door before either of them could change their minds.

Frankie leaned against the sink and watched her daughter go swinging through the knee-high weeds in the backyard. She'd found a stick and was whacking the heads off of dandelions, stirring up clouds of parachuting seeds in her wake. She looked happy. Frankie just hoped it would last.

When they'd driven out for the first time, Ali's only comment about the house had been "Gross-o." But she seemed to enjoy sitting in when Frankie went over the blueprints with the contractor and it wasn't as though she wasn't used to moving. Poor kid. They'd been in a different apartment for almost every one of Ali's years. They were both looking forward to some stability.

When Ali moved out of sight behind a screen of trees, Frankie turned back to the kitchen, chose a box and began to arrange its contents in a cupboard.

Ali was happy, just walking along and swinging her stick. Whack. She watched the seeds explode at the impact, then slowly drift toward the ground. Some made it. Some got tangled up in the weeds and grass. Some caught the wind just right and went floating off. Whack. She knew her mother was worrying and she wished she wouldn't. Moving out here was the first good thing to happen to them in a long time.

Not that the fourteen years of her life had been bad. It was just that living out here, away from other kids her own age, she didn't have to go on pretending that she was into all the things that they were. Whack. If her mother knew how she really felt, she'd have some justification to worry, but Ali wasn't about to let that cat out of the bag.

How was she supposed to explain that she didn't like her peers, that she wasn't into hanging around, drinking, smoking cigarettes *or* dope, running after boys, groping in some backseat or on a living room couch when the parents were out . . . Who needed that stuff? Whack. Maybe she couldn't yet put into words what it was she did find important, but at least she knew what wasn't.

Out here she could do what she wanted. Go for walks. Read. Find out who she wanted to be without the pressure of other kids, or the pressure of her mother desperately hoping that her daughter was fitting in, that all the moving around from neighborhood to neighborhood wasn't messing up her underdeveloped psyche.

Ali grinned and whacked another weed. Underdeveloped. That was something else the other kids liked to rag her about. The fact that she was still skinny as a beanpole, not filling out like the rest of them.

Whack. Who needed that? She'd seen what a good figure had done for her mother.

She lifted her stick to hit a tall weed—that was one thing she was going to have to do right off: learn the names of all the plants and trees and stuff around her—when she paused, stick frozen high in the air. Looking at her from the side of the road was a rabbit.

Ali didn't dare breathe. It watched her with liquid brown eyes, nose twitching. Jeez, it was cute. She lowered the stick slowly, not wanting to appear threatening, but as soon as she moved, the rabbit turned and bounded off into the woods. Wow. There were probably all kinds of animals right in their backyard. Rabbits and raccoons, deer . . . maybe even foxes.

She had a couple of Tom Brown Jr. wilderness guides back in her room and she could hardly wait to get them out of whatever box they were in and put them to some use. This was going to be a great summer.

Whack, whack. She hit a couple more weeds and started to hum as she followed the road again, wondering where it led. It took her around a bend and she could see buildings about three-quarters of a mile further on. The road seemed to go on into the woods beyond them and she decided to go that far and maybe have a peek at the buildings. She wouldn't go too close—she didn't want to end off her first day by having some cranky old farmer getting pissed off at her because she was trespassing—but she did want to see what the place was like. *Please* don't let them have any kids.

The road just sort of piddled out as it got to the forest. It looked as though it had continued once, but now it was overgrown and only a footpath went on through the trees. It'd be fun to see where it went to, she thought as she turned her attention to the buildings.

The set-up was much like what she and her mom had—a renovated farmhouse with an old gray-timbered relic of a barn towering up behind it and a few out-buildings. But unlike their own place, here the grounds were neatly tended with a hedge running alongside the road, some apple trees up by the barn and flowerbeds in front of the house, filled with multi-colored blossoms. The forest closed in around the landscaped lot on three sides, dense and darkly mysterious to Ali's city-wise eyes. The smell of cut grass hung in the air. She moved a little closer, her stick scraping in the dirt by her sneakers.

"What can I do for you, kid?"

The voice startled her, lifting goosebumps on her skin. She turned to see a man standing up on the other side of the short hedge and she wondered where he'd popped up from. She hadn't seen him as she'd walked up. He was dressed in jeans, with a red bandana around his head like a sweatband. His hair was thick and black and his muscular body was darkly tanned except for a number of white puckers and lines that stood out against the dark skin. His eyes were a pale blue and reminded her of Paul Newman's. She'd just seen *Butch Cassidy and the Sundance Kid* for the umpteenth time on the late show last week. As he moved closer towards her, favoring his right leg, she realized the marks on his body were scars. Lots of them.

"I said, what can I do for you?"

"Uh . . . nothing," Ali stammered. "I'm just, uh, walking—you know?"

"This is private property," he said. "Maybe you better go hiking somewhere else instead—okay?"

Ali nodded quickly. "Sure. I'm sorry. I just . . . that is my mom and I just moved in down the road. I was just checking out the neighborhood. . . ."

Something changed in his eyes as she spoke and he didn't look quite so menacing anymore. "What? The place they were working on this spring?"

Ali nodded again. He studied her for a long moment, then smiled. "I was just gonna have some lemonade, kid. You want some?"

Ali didn't like the idea of going off into some strange guy's house, but he was going to be their neighbor and she didn't want to get off on the wrong foot with him right away. With that bad leg, she thought, she could always outrun him.

"Sure," she said at last.

"C'mon." He led off, limping, and she fell in beside him. "So what's your name, kid?"

Ali glanced at him. "How come you keep calling me 'kid'?"

"I don't know." They'd reached his front steps. "Take a seat. I'll bring the lemonade out. You want it on the rocks?"

"What?"

"With ice."

"Sure. Thanks."

"Hey, wait'll you taste the lemonade first. Betty Crocker I'm not."

He disappeared into the house and Ali sat down on the steps. What a weird thing to say, she thought. But it was a good line. She'd have to try it out on mom the next time she made dinner. She was still trying to remember the little swagger he'd put into his shoulders as he'd said it when the screen door banged open and he was back.

He'd put on a white shirt while he was inside. It made his tan seem darker. The ice clinked in the glasses as he handed her one. She was about to thank him when she remembered what he'd said and decided to taste the drink first. He grinned, as though reading her mind, and then she had to giggle. She covered it up by taking a sip.

"Thanks," she said then. "It's good."

He took a sip himself and set his glass down on the steps between them. "Yeah, it's not so bad. So what's your name?"

"Alice Treasure—but everyone calls me Ali."

"You don't like Alice?"

"They might as well've called me Airhead, don't you think?"

He shrugged. "I don't know. I kinda like Alice. My name's Tony Garonne."

"Have you lived here for a long time, Mr. Garonne?"

"Tony. Call me Tony, okay? And I'll call you Ali. Yeah, I've lived here for awhile. Not steady, you understand, but I've owned the place maybe fifteen years."

"My mom grew up in the place we just moved into."

"No kidding? What happened? Did she inherit the place from her old man or something?"

"No. She didn't get along too well with her parents. She took off when she was pretty young, but her mom had already left her dad by then and . . . well, we just got some money so she bought the old place and had it fixed up." Why am I babbling like this? she asked herself.

"Yeah, well, they did a good job." There was a moment's silence and they both worked at their lemonades. "So it's just you and your momma living there?"

Ali nodded. "Yeah. My dad . . . we don't talk much about him."

"Hey. I'm sorry."

"It's okay. I don't really remember him. He took off when I was just a kid. But he was . . . pretty rough on my mom."

"Guy like that . . ." Tony began, a frown creasing his face, then he paused and found a smile. "So where'd you move from?"

"Ottawa."

"It's gonna be different for you up here. I mean, it's not that far from the city, but it's quiet—you know? Evenings, it's just really quiet. And dark. Takes some getting used to for some people."

"I think I'm going to like it." She finished her drink and set the glass down. "I've got to be going, Mr . . . ah . . . Tony."

"Mr. a-Tony. I like that. It's got a ring to it, don't you think?"

Ali laughed.

"Listen," he added. "You're welcome to come round here any time you want. The reason I wasn't so friendly earlier is I get kids joyriding up this road all the time. I mean, who needs it? And sometimes they want to mess around in my yard and I don't like it. I just want some quiet. But you're a neighbor and you seem okay. Bring your momma up sometime and I'll cook you up some pasta. I make a mean spaghetti. What do you say?"

"I'll ask her."

"Good. I'll walk you to the road."

"You don't have to," Ali said, thinking about his limp.

He caught the glance she gave it. "No, it's okay. I gotta give it a lot of exercise. I don't move so quick like I used to, but I can still get around."

Ali wanted to ask him how he'd hurt it but she decided to wait for another time. She'd already been pushing her luck as it was. He seemed friendly enough now, but she was sure he'd be happier without some gawky teenager like her hanging around.

"You come back for another visit now," he said as though reading her mind again. "And if you or your momma need anything, you just give me a call, okay?"

"Okay. Thanks . . . Tony."

"*Ciao,*" he replied.

"What's that mean?"

"It's like 'so long' or 'take care.' But it means 'hello,' too."

Ali smiled. "*Ciao,*" she said and headed off down the road.

She looked back as she neared the curve to see him still standing at the end of his lane, so she gave him a wave. When he waved back, she continued on her way.

"And he's got a limp," Ali said over a supper of hamburgers, "and he talks a little funny, like . . . oh, I don't know. As if he doesn't know his grammar all that well."

"Ali, that's not nice."

"Well, it's true. But I'm not saying it to make fun of him. I like him."

"Make sure you don't bother him too much."

"He wants us to come for dinner sometime. He's going to make spaghetti."

"What else?" Frankie asked with a laugh. Then she put her half-eaten burger on her plate and leaned closer to her daughter. "Ali," she began. "He didn't seem the kind to . . . you know . . . make trouble for you?"

"Well, you never can tell, can you?"

"Ali!"

"Okay, okay. No, he seems all right. And besides, I had my trusty stick with me."

"Yes, but—"

"And besides *that,* I could outrun him any day of the week!"

Frankie shook her head. "You're incorrigible."

They cleaned up the dishes together, then spent the evening arranging and rearranging the furniture in the living and dining rooms. By the time it was ten-thirty, they were both so tired they could hardly keep their eyes open.

"G'night," Ali mumbled as she shuffled off to her bedroom.

Frankie tousled her hair and kissed her on the brow. "See you in the morning, kiddo."

It's going to be okay, Frankie thought as she undressed in her own room and got into bed. Thank God, it was going to be okay. She had the feeling that everything was finally going to work out for them. She looked around at the unfamiliar shadows in her new bedroom, then rolled over and fell asleep with a smile on her face.

As the last light went out, a figure stirred in the woods behind the house. It lifted its head as though to test the wind for scents and slowly crept forward. When it reached the house, it ran its fingers along the paneling of the porch door, its nails making a slight rasping sound, then it backed away.

Starlight glinted on what might have been tiny horns pushing up from amidst its hair, or it might just have been reflecting from bone ornaments that the figure wore in its dark curls. An observer, had there been one present, would have been hard put to tell in that poor light.

Nodding to itself, the figure pulled a hat from its belt and pushed it down over its hair. It returned to the forest where it put the house behind it and bounded away through the trees, as graceful and quick as a deer.

2

After Ali left, Valenti went back to raking his lawn. He worked slowly, thinking about the girl. He didn't know what it was about her, but she was the first person he'd been able to relax around since all the shit went down a couple of years ago. She was a cute kid—skinny, sure, but he wasn't in the market for kids anyway. He just liked her. There was something about her that drained away the constant tension he felt around other people. He went back over their conversation, smiling when he remembered her "Mr. a-Tony." He hoped she'd come back, hoped her old lady wouldn't think he was some kind of *pervertito* looking to put the squeeze on her little daughter.

Yeah, he thought as he finished loading the cut grass onto his wheelbarrow. He'd like to see her again. He was usually passably friendly with whomever he ran into in the area, but it was all putting on a show. He had to be careful—the *fratellanza* had their fingers in everything, everywhere. He should know. And if word ever got out that he was up here . . . But you couldn't just hide out—being a recluse caused just as much talk as flash did. You had to balance it, play the game of fitting in, but never let your guard down.

"Don't go for flash," Mario had taught him. "Nobody likes a big shot, you know what I'm saying? But don't be humble either, or you get no respect. Be clean and polite and everybody's going to like you, nobody's going to talk about you too much. In our business, Tony, that's the way of the world. *Così fan tutti.*"

Which was okay when you had your family around, but it got lonely for a guy in his position. Sometimes you just wanted to sit down with someone and take it easy—not shoot off your mouth or nothing, but just relax. And if it had to be with a skinny little kid, well, that'd be the way it was in his world.

He dumped the grass out by the barn, stowed the wheelbarrow and rake inside, then went into the house to take a shower. When he was done, he cleared the fog on the mirror and studied himself. He'd seen the kid's eyes on his scars. He should probably be more careful, but what the hell. If he had to walk around the place in a three-piece, he might as well be in the slammer.

The word on the street was that the feds had taken him in on their Witness Protection Program, that they were letting him cop a plea so long as he fingered a few of the bosses. Anyone who believed that didn't know Tony Valenti. He had no fight with the *fratellanza*. All he wanted was the guy who'd set him up and when he got hold of that *pezzo di merda* . . .

Valenti sighed and unclenched his fists. He was working to forget that and getting pretty good at it. What good was remembering? He couldn't do anything about it, anyway. Yet when he tried to forget, he could feel himself changing, could feel the hardness inside going soft, and he didn't want to hear nobody saying that Tony Valenti'd gone soft. Thinking about it, about what had been taken from him—that was all he had left. These days it all just confused him. Sure, the *fratellanza* was only providing services to people, giving them what they wanted, but the longer Valenti was outside the family influence, the more things didn't seem so cut and dried.

The brotherhood was a system of *sistemazione,* giving order to chaos. It had its roots in the *compagnie d' armi* of eleventh-century Western Sicily—small private armies set up by the landowners to defend their families and estates from marauding bandits that eventually became the *cosche* that still rule the area today. The original men of honor were a rough peasant version of the knights of chivalry; the present-day Sicilian *cosca,* or family unit, took its name from a corruption of the dialect term for artichoke: a composition of separate leaves forming a solid unit. The similarities between them and their ancestors were only surface ones now, while the gap between the modern *cosche* and their counterparts in North America was immense.

It was a media fiction that the criminal families of North America were overseas branches of the Sicilian Mafia, that they were all directed by some *capo di tutti capi,* a boss of bosses who ruled from the island homeland. In order for the *fratellanza* to exist on such an international level it would have to be disciplined and centralized, which would make it easy for police organizations to discover, penetrate and destroy. The true reason that the brotherhood could not be effectively fought was that it was many things at the same time, a many-headed beast that could live for some time without any head at all.

The roots of the brotherhood in North America stemmed rather from some few Sicilian immigrants who had been small-time mafia in their homeland. They brought with them the *cosche*'s unique ability to move in and out of written laws, a capacity to grasp situations immediately, to invent solutions to intricate tangles, to gauge exactly the relative strengths of contending parties, to work amazingly complex intrigues and coldly control their smallest acts while, at the same time, allowing themselves to abandon all those controls to generous enthusiasms when it was safe to do so.

Few ancestors of those original immigrants survived in the American *fratellanza,* but there were still some, such as the Magaddino family that Valenti had belonged to. Don Magaddino had been interested only in protecting his family, his property and business, remaining successful without having to resort to handling either prostitution or drugs.

Valenti was taught from the cradle that he must always help his family, first by his uncle—his own father being deceased—and then by Mario, who had sponsored his membership. He was taught to side with the friends of the family and fight their common enemies, even when the friends were wrong and the enemies right; to defend his dignity at all costs and never allow the smallest slight or insult to go unavenged; to be able to keep secrets—*omertà,* the law of silence— and always beware of official authorities and laws.

This he had always done, but now in the eyes of the *fratellanza* he had turned on those who had respected and worked with him, first by hitting Eddie Pinelli for personal reasons, and then hitting his own *padrone.* Neither was true, but the fact that the *fratellanza* believed it was true had outcast him. There was no court he could go to for justice. He was already sentenced and in the brotherhood the only sentence was death. It was only now, forcibly cut off from all he'd known, that he had begun to question.

A man had to have honor, sure. And respect. But then Valenti thought back to how it was when he got into the business and what it was like now. When he thought of how easily the fear by which the *fratellanza* ruled had turned on him . . . He shook his head. He no longer knew what was right and what was wrong.

"Chi lo sa?" he asked his reflection. Who knows?

The only reason he was still alive today was because he'd worked under Mario Papale.

"You've got to trust in the family," Mario had told him once, "but you got to trust in yourself first, *capito?* You take some of that money you're making, just a bit at a time, and you invest it in a safe place where no one knows you, no one can reach you—not me, not your uncle, not even the *padrone.* You understand what I'm saying?

"Maybe—and I hope to God this is the way it works for you, Tony—maybe you'll never need that place. You can use it for holidays, 'ey? But someday that place might be all that stands between you and being dead, Tony. So you keep it. You cover your ass going to and from it. You keep it under a name you never use for no deals. You keep some artillery there and you keep a lot of cash, and then you'll have something the other *soldati* don't—you got security then, Tony.

"The soldiers that got no place to go like that, they've got to walk around careful all the time. But you, you can be patient. You don't have to kiss nobody's ass you don't want to. You get respect that way, Tony. All the time, you get some respect. You don't talk with a smart mouth to the *capi,* you don't throw your weight around with the other soldiers, but you got something special all the same. *Capito?"*

"Sure," Valenti said to the memory. "I understand all too well now."

He turned away, got dressed and went downstairs to make himself some dinner. Afterwards he sat outside with a strong *capuccino* and watched the sunset. He sat there in the darkness for a long time, not brooding, just remembering.

Thirty-eight now, he'd never married and was glad of it, the way things had turned out. But time was that he should loosen up a bit. Nothing stupid, but he was lonely. If the kid came back in the next few days, he'd see if she and her momma'd take him up on his offer of a spaghetti dinner. Hell, maybe he'd just give them a call.

He wondered what the mother was like, then shook his head. That you don't need, he told himself. Be a bit friendly, okay, but he didn't need to complicate his life by putting the squeeze on a neighbor. For one thing, he couldn't move away when things soured. And things, he thought on the basis of too many short-term affairs, always soured.

He was about to go back inside, but paused as he reached for his empty coffee cup. The sound was so soft that, if he hadn't been half-expecting it, he might never have heard it at all.

It came from the woods north of the house, a whispery piping that set the hairs at the nape of his neck a-tingle. The brooding thoughts that had been plaguing him since Ali left for home dissolved into a wash of quiet pleasure. He lowered himself slowly back into his chair and closed his eyes.

The life that had been his was gone and with it his worries, the music told him, but the strengths that had let him stay ahead of the pack were still there. There was no need to be rid of them. All he had to do was channel them into something different. Peace might never be his, but he could still know contentment of a kind.

He sighed, shifting in the chair. The movement broke his concentration and in the next instant the sound was gone. He opened his eyes to look at the forest.

"One day," he said softly, "this leg's not gonna give me so much trouble and then I'm coming to look for you."

The first time he'd heard it, he'd thought it was some kind of a bird, but that was before he realized that the music was something that a bird could never make. Its melody dipped and shifted, now low and breathy, now high and skirling, but always quiet, always just on the edge of his hearing as it ran up and down the musical scale in shivering lifts and falls like no bird ever sang. Always so distant, so quiet.

Sometimes it was so quiet he couldn't hear it at all. He could just *feel* it out there, calling to him. There was more than a mystery in it. It promised him something if he could ever discover its source. What, he didn't know. But something. And he knew he would never regret finding it when he did.

He stayed listening for a long while after, but it was gone for the evening and at last he went inside. His dreams were full of hidden presences that night, of things that stayed just out of sight, the way the music stayed mostly just beyond his hearing. He'd never been able to remember his dreams before coming here from Malta that last time. Now he often had those kinds of dreams, and he always remembered them in the morning.

3

Lewis Datchery was reading by the light of a kerosene lamp. His lips moved soundlessly as his gaze followed the line of print across the page. His book was propped up on the kitchen table and he was sitting on a plain-backed wooden chair that his father had made. The light of the lamp made a circular spill, leaving most of the one-room cabin in shadow. From the walls, the spines of thousands of books faced out, the lamp light glinting off the titles of those with gilt lettering. A cup of tea, sitting at his elbow, had long since gone cold. Absorbed in what he was reading, it was a moment or so before the scratching at the door registered.

His gaze lifted to the old clock on the mantle as he removed his glasses and laid them on the book to keep his place. It was just past eleven. He rose slowly, the weight of his eighty-six years weighing heavier on his thin frame late at night than it did in the morning, and went to open the door.

" 'Lo, Lewis," his visitor said.

She came in like a cat, taking a few quick steps inside, then paused to study the cabin's shadowed corners. A floppy wide-brimmed hat hid most of her features, and the tangle of hair that spilled from underneath it had twigs and bits of leaves caught up in its dark curls. Burrs and thorny seeds had attached themselves to the bottoms of her jeans. Her jacket was at least a size too big for her.

When she was satisfied that the room was empty except for Lewis and herself, she sidled over to the chair across from where Lewis had been sitting and settled her diminutive form upon it. She immediately looked as though she'd been there the whole night, as though the cabin was hers and Lewis the newly arrived visitor.

Lewis smiled and stirred the fire awake in the cast-iron stove. He added some wood to the coals, then set a kettle of water on top. His visitor showed no sign of impatience at his slow movements, nor any inclination to break the quiet that lay easily between them. Not until the tea was brewed and a steaming mug was set in front of her did she move.

"I found this for you," she said.

From the pocket of her jacket she took a paperback book and offered it to him. He smiled his thanks and turned it over in his hands. The book looked almost new. There was a white wolf in the foreground of the cover. Snow was falling. An almost nude woman, pendulously breasted, stood behind the wolf. Behind her was a satyr and a full moon. The title of the book was *Wolf-winter;* the author, Thomas Burnett Swann. Lewis didn't ask where she'd "found" it.

"It 'minded me of Tommy's dog—that wolf."

"It does look a little like Gaffa, doesn't it?" Lewis said.

She nodded. "Is it a good one?"

"Well, now. I don't know that yet."

"Will you read it to me?"

Lewis smiled. "Sure. But we won't get through it all in one night."

"That's all right."

Lewis put his glasses back on and used a proper bookmark to keep his place in the book he'd been reading. Pushing it to one side, he held the paperback up to the light and cleared his throat. Then he began to read to her.

* * *

"I like it," she said later when Lewis's throat started to get scratchy from reading aloud and he decided to stop.

"Do you understand it all?"

She shrugged. "The names are funny, but I do like it. Will you read me some more tomorrow night?"

"Sure."

She regarded him for a long moment with her unblinking green eyes, her whole body languid and relaxed in the chair, then with a sudden graceful movement, she was on her feet and by the door.

"I've got to go now, Lewis," she said. She opened the door turning before she stepped outside. "I've seen them," she added. "In the dark man's house."

"Did you go inside?" Lewis asked.

He was still facing the table and turned slowly when she didn't answer. By the time he had turned around, the doorway was empty, the door ajar. Shaking his head, he rose from his chair and made his slow way to the door. He stood there for a long time, watching the darkness and listening, before he closed it. At the table again, he picked up the book she'd brought him and turned it over in his hands once more.

She could move like a ghost when she wanted to. He wondered how the new people in the house would feel about being haunted by her.

He stayed there for awhile, thinking of her, about what the new people might be like, then he laid the book down again. He left their mugs in the sink, meaning to clean them in the morning when he'd drawn some more water. Taking the lamp, he went upstairs to his bed in the loft overhead.

4

On Sunday Ali and her mother continued to work at organizing the house. On Monday they went into Perth for the day, shopping and looking around, breaking for a late lunch at the Maple Drop Bakery before they came home. It wasn't until Tuesday afternoon, after spending a couple of hours studying for her exams, that Ali was free once more to follow the sideroad that led up to Tony's place.

When she got there, she followed the sound of hammering to the back of the house where she found Tony putting together a fence for his vegetable garden.

"Hey, kid! How's it going?"

"Okay. I had to study this morning—history." She pulled a face. "But now I can do what I want for the rest of the day."

"What's so bad about history?" Valenti asked. "It's important to know the history of things. How are you going to know what to respect if you don't know where it came from? Everything's got its place and only history's going to tell you how it got there."

"I guess. But this is all just memorizing dates and stuff like that.

I'm probably going to flunk it 'cause I just can't remember anything."

"A smart kid like you? You'll do okay."

If this was New York, he thought, and he hadn't lost his place in the *fratellanza,* she wouldn't have a thing to worry about. He'd just have a talk with her teacher and if her teacher had any smarts, he'd pass her. Who knows? Maybe the teacher would need a favor someday. It never hurt to have connections. But this wasn't New York.

"What are you doing?" Ali asked.

"It's the rabbits," Valenti explained. "Okay, I like 'em, but I'm trying to grow some produce here and I don't like rabbits so much that I want to feed 'em all summer and have nothing for myself, you know what I mean? So I'm building the fence to keep 'em out. Maybe I'll put a little sign on it—you know how to write rabbit?"

"Give me a break."

"Okay. So maybe that's not such a good idea." He shrugged. "How do you like your new house?"

"Oh, it's great. Mom and them put in a floor-to-ceiling bookcase on one wall of my room and I've got all my books in it—you should see it."

"Maybe I will—but with a chaperone. You got to watch who you invite into your bedroom, kid. They might not all be gentlemen like me."

"I'm not worried about you."

Valenti regarded her seriously. "That's good," he said. "Because I like you and I think we can be friends, but we don't want people getting the wrong idea or anything. Five, six years from now, though— maybe we got a problem." He grinned when Ali blushed. "So you like books?" he asked, changing the subject. "What kind of things do you read about?"

"Oh, all kinds. Right now I'm reading this book by Parke Godwin that's—"

"What kind of a name is that, 'Parke'?"

"I don't know. What kind of a name is Tony?"

"It's Italian."

"No kidding?" Ali grinned. "Anyway, it's a really good book. It's all about Guinevere and what happened to her after Arthur died. See, everyone's against her and she ends up getting captured by these Saxons . . ."

Valenti went back to working on the fence, listening to her and smiling, feeling good. The work went more quickly with her helping. When she finished describing Godwin's *Beloved Exile* up to where she'd read so far, she went on to talk about other favorite authors. Diana Wynne Jones. Tony Hillerman. Caitlin Midhir. Orson Scott Card.

"Maybe you should bring one of those up, next time you come," Valenti said when she mentioned her Tom Brown Jr. field guides. "I'd like to know some more about what we got out there in the woods, you know?"

Ali nodded, then pointed to the gap between the ground and the bottom of the chicken wire they were attaching to the wood frame of the fence. "They're still going to get in."

"Only the smart ones," Valenti said. "I don't mind the smart ones coming, I just don't want to feed the whole forest."

Ali laughed. "Tony?" she asked when there was a moment's pause in the hammering. "Remember you told me about those kids that come joyriding up here?"

"Sure. What about 'em?"

"Well, what is it that they do?"

Valenti put the hammer down and looked at her. "What happened?" he asked. "Somebody been bothering you?"

"Not exactly. It's just that I woke up early yesterday morning and when I looked out the window, I thought I saw someone hiding in the trees out back of our place, watching the house."

"What kind of someone?"

"I couldn't really tell. I'm not even sure if I really saw anything or not. I didn't tell my mom because she's always worrying about something or other and I didn't know if this was worth bothering about in the first place. I don't want to get anybody into trouble, but it's a little creepy, don't you think—having someone spying on you?"

Valenti nodded thoughtfully. "Yeah, that's not so good. But it doesn't sound like the joyriders. They just come up here Friday or Saturday night, rev their engines a lot, make some noise. You don't see 'em much during the week."

"Well, who do you think it is that's watching our house?"

"I don't know. When I first moved here I used to think there was something or someone out there watching me."

"And now?"

Valenti thought of the distant piping but he didn't think he was ready to talk about it yet. "Now I think it was just some animal—like a fox or something. Say, I'm getting pretty thirsty. How about you? You want a Coke?"

"Maybe some more lemonade?"

"You got it."

He led the way to the house, going to the back door this time. There were a couple of deck chairs by the door and Ali sat in one, turning it so that the sun wasn't in her eyes. She noticed he had a satellite dish on the side of the house that was hidden from the road and wondered if she could talk her mother into getting one. Although it was only a few days since they'd moved, Ali was already missing all the great late-night movies that were on cable. Tony came back with her lemonade and a beer for himself and sat down in the other chair, favoring his leg.

"What did happen to your leg?" Ali asked. A look passed across his face that she couldn't decipher and she wondered if she'd stepped out of line. "You don't mind me asking, do you?"

"What?" Valenti asked, then he shook his head. "No, no. I was just thinking."

He'd passed out when Mario had hoisted him up and carried him from the villa. The next thing he knew they were on a fishing boat—bound for the north coast of Africa. His shoulder wound was clean. The bullet had just clipped muscle and gone right through. But the other bullet had shattered a bone in his leg.

"We had a doc look you over," Mario said, "and he did what he could, but you probably won't be walking so straight no more, Tony."

"What day is this?"

"Two days since they hit my place. We've been moving around some."

"Fercrissakes! I've been out two days?"

Mario laid a hand on his chest and pushed him back on the rough bunk. "Take it easy, Tony. We're gonna be okay. I've got a connection in Tunisia and everything's set up. We'll be dropped outside of Moknine where a truck's gonna meet us and take us up to Tunis. We've got a place there in a hotel where we'll be comped in style—owner of the place owes me a favor. No one's gonna bother us, you hear what I'm saying? We'll stay low there for a couple of months, then I go home and you go wherever."

"You can't go back, Mario."

"What's the problem? A voice on the phone tells me to hit a man that's like my own son? I gotta do what some nobody on a phone tells me to do? Those people got a problem, that's their problem. They can send out their own talent, but me, I'm not in the business no more, *capito?* No one's gonna bother me when I get home, Tony. I got friends could cause big problems for the Magaddinos, you know what I'm saying?"

"Sure. *Grazie,* Mario."

" 'Ey, what's to thank? But maybe you should think about getting out of the business, too, Tony. It makes you too old, too fast. It's not like the old days no more. Go learn another trade. I mean, what's the family ever done for you? You see what they did to me. They let me take a fall for the *padrone*—God rest his soul—and when I'm out of the slammer, I'm deported. Christ, who do I know left in the old country? I'm ten years old when we land in New York.

"But I played 'em smart, Tony. I banked some money where they couldn't touch it and it was waiting for me when I got out. So now I live on Malta—I've got a woman, two kids, a nice place. It's peaceful now, you know? Think about it, Tony."

Valenti shook his head. "I'm going to nail the fucker that set me up, Mario. I got no other choice."

"Yeah, yeah. Your honor demands it. Well, you tell me: These people, did they treat either of us with honor? I tell you again, it's not like the old days, Tony. I got no respect for them now. You wait—

you'll see. By the time you're up and running again, it's not gonna mean so much to you neither. Trust me. A little time goes by, you're gonna feel different about it."

Maybe, maybe not, Valenti thought now. He'd have to see. He looked over at Ali, took a swig of beer and smiled.

"Between you and me," he said, "I got hit in action." He meant to stick as close to the truth as he could; they were going to be friends, he didn't want to lie to her.

"What do you mean?" Ali asked.

"I was a soldier."

"Really? What army?"

Valenti's smile deepened. He could hear Mario's voice in his mind. *You got to go someplace where when you say you're a* soldato *they ask what army, not what family.*

"I was sort of a private soldier," he explained.

"You mean like a mercenary?"

"Yeah. Pretty much. But I'm retired now. And let's keep this between you and me, okay? You got to make me a promise on this." Christ, he thought. He had to be nuts telling her this much. Except who could she talk to?

Ali nodded solemnly. "I won't tell anybody—not even Mom—if you don't want me to."

"I don't want you to."

"My lips are sealed," she said and pinched them closed with her forefinger and thumb.

"How're you going to drink with your mouth like that?" Valenti asked.

Ali giggled and took her hand away. "You want some more help with that fence?"

"Sure. Did you talk to your momma about you both coming over for dinner? What'd she say?"

"She said fine."

"Sensational. This is a meal you're not going to forget, Ali. We're going to start with some antipasti and—"

"What's antipasti?"

"It's like olives, cold cuts, cheese—that kind of thing, you know? So we start with that and a nice white wine—your momma let you drink wine?"

"With dinner, sure."

"Okay. So how's about this Saturday night?"

Ali nodded and followed him back to where they'd been working earlier. Valenti continued to give her a run-down on what she could expect for dinner as they finished nailing the chicken wire up in place. The afternoon went by quickly and all too soon Ali was on her way home, running because she was going to be late for supper.

Valenti watched her go, hoping he hadn't made a mistake, telling her as much about himself as he had. But he was glad he'd done it. It was good to have a secret between friends.

Collecting up the tools, he put them away and headed for the house. He planned to go down and check out the woods behind Ali's place later on to see if he could find any sign of her secretive visitor. While he got his own dinner ready, he tried to make up his mind if he should bring a piece with him or not. In the end he settled on his cane. Out here, who needed guns?

5

There was a tall, grayish-blue stone on the slopes of Snake Lake Mountain, a pointed finger of rock that lifted skyward in among the cedars and pine, the maple, birch and oak. It looked to be a part of the forest and the backbones of stone that lifted from the rich forest floor, but it was older than either—a lost remnant of something secret. It stood in a small flat meadow, scooped from the slope. Above, the forest climbed on to the top of the hill in a tangle of underbrush and old trees; below it, younger trees trekked on down the slopes to circle the small village of New Wolding and its outlying fields before it wandered off to meet Black Creek and the land beyond.

Stags scraped the velvet from their antlers against that stone. Goats and sheep grazed there often enough to give the meadow the short, trimmed look of a lawn. But mostly it was Tommy Duffin who frequented the meadow and played tunes on his reedpipes to the tall old standing stone. He played in the evenings, as the twilight fell. . . .

Like his father before him, and his grandfather as well, Tommy had the coarse rough features of the Duffins. His face was plump, his eyes somewhat vacant-looking, his hair lifting in an untidy thatch from his head. But when he lifted his pipes and set his breath into them, he changed.

His features seemed to become thinner, more defined, and a fire touched his eyes, a flickering of firefly light that said, I know mysteries, hear them in my music. And then he was no longer the same boy of fifteen who lived with his mother in the cottage closest, but one, to the hill.

That Tuesday evening, Lewis looked up to see Tommy passing by. Lewis was sitting out on the steps of his cabin and lifted a hand in greeting. Tommy nodded, friendly enough, but already that sense of distance was creeping into his eyes and he never broke step as he continued on up to the stone. The wolfish Gaffa gamboled in the fields across from Lewis's cabin, making his own roundabout way to his master's destination.

Lewis continued to sit on his steps. He heard a blackbird's song, the hum and creak of insects, then—lifted above them, sweeter by far—the sound of Tommy's piping.

One by one the villagers began to drift in the direction of Snake Lake Mountain, what they called Wold Hill after the hill they'd left behind in the old country. The Lattens passed by first, William and Ella, both stout and graying now, their son Willie, Jr. and his wife, Rachel, walking with them. Then Alden Mudden, Emery and Luca Blegg, and the Hibbuts sisters, Jenny and Ruth, all in a group. Tommy's mother, Flora, followed, walking arm in arm with old Ailie Tichner, the only resident of New Wolding older than Lewis since her husband, Miles had died last winter.

Peter Skegland came next with his wife, Gerda, and their two daughters, Kate and Holly. Walking with the two Skegland girls was Martin Tweedy. His parents, George and Susanna, were not far behind. Bringing up the rear was Lily Spelkins, who'd be sixty-three this summer, but was still as slender and supple as a young girl, and would sometimes dance with the younger women when Tommy's music grew too gay to resist.

There aren't many of us left, Lewis thought as he fell in step with Lily. There were still representatives of all the families that had first immigrated here, all in a group in the late twenties, but slowly and surely they were dying out. Their lives were long, but Lewis didn't like to think of a time when there would be no one left to follow the old ways.

There were so few children—and none in the past ten years. Many had left the village. Of the twelve cottages that made up New Wolding, four stood empty now. They needed only one of the two big dark-timbered barns to winter their diminishing herds and store their excess crops. The only part of the village that truly prospered these days was the graveyard.

"I love this time of year," Lily said. When Lewis didn't answer straightaway, she laid her hand on his arm and gave it a squeeze. "You think too much, Lewis. It's going to make you an old man."

Lewis gave her a half-hearted smile. "And that would never do, would it?"

"When Jango comes this year," she told him, "I'm going to see what sort of a perk-up tea he can whip up for you, Lewis. Anything to get your nose out of those books and into the fresh air a bit. Remember the walks we used to take?"

Lewis nodded. That was before his wife Vera died, before his son Edmond left the village, not to return, before he realized that the some-thing that had held them all together for so long was fading. It was be-fore Lily's husband Jevon died as well, when the village seemed more alive.

Now New Wolding was filled with memories, rather than vitality. It had an air of imminent disuse about it. Tommy's music let one for-get, but only while it played. It wasn't strong enough to draw new blood to the village anymore. The old haunting mystery just didn't seem to run so deeply anymore. It no longer held the dark hounds at bay. And one day, too soon, it would all—

"Lewis!"

Lily poked him with a sharp elbow, bringing him back to the pre-sent moment, but not before he finished his last thought: One day it would all fade away.

"It's as much what we feel," Lily said, "what we give back, as what we take, Lewis. You of all people should remember that—you told it to me."

Lewis nodded. The music didn't come from a void, nor did it play to one. It was a conduit between themselves and the mystery that lay behind it. What it woke in each person who heard it reflected only what was inside them to begin with.

"You're right, Lily," he said, slipping her arm into the crook of his own. "I keep forgetting—it really is that simple."

Lily leaned over and kissed his dry cheek, then gave his arm a tug. "Come along, Lewis. There's something in the air tonight and I think I want to dance."

Lewis smiled at her. Arm in arm, they hurried after the others, drawn to the meadow of the longstone by the call of Tommy's music. No one quite entered, except for Tommy. The rest sat or stood in a half circle in among the trees, watching him play. The last light of the day washed over him and for one breathless moment he appeared to glow. His reed-pipes woke an exultant music that skirled to meet the approaching night in a rush of breathy notes. Then the darkness stole in and the music turned into a jig.

The two Hibbuts sisters, in their fifties now, were the first to leave the shelter of the trees. They moved to the music, Jenny's graying hair undone and falling across her thin shoulders as she stepped to the tune while Ruth, the years wearing on her a little more, didn't move quite so sprightly. Kate and Holly Skegland were next, both young and limber, though not quite graceful yet, and then Lily left Lewis's side to join them.

To those watching from the trees it seemed that there were more than just five of their own dancing to Tommy's music. The little meadow appeared to be filled with other dancing forms, ghostly shapes that spun in the steps with more abandon and an elfin grace. They danced a May dance that plucked the apples of the moon, silver and cool, rather than the bright apples of the sun.

Lewis looked for and found the small form of his night visitor in among the bobbing forms, her dance feline as a lynx at play, and no less merry. Martin Tweedy had left his parents' side to join the dancers, holding hands with both Kate and Holly as they went round and round. A feeling of gladness swelled inside Lewis. An expectancy. A returned vitality. And then the dance music slowed to become a bittersweet air.

The ghostly shapes faded as the music changed tempo. The dancers returned to sit with the others among the trees—all except for one. Lewis saw her slip catlike into the brush behind the tall standing stone. The breathy sound of the reed-pipes grew more haunting still and a hush settled over them all like a collective sigh.

All nightsounds stilled until the pipes played alone into the vastness of the starry skies overhead. No one moved; no one dared to take a breath. It was into this moment of perfect stillness, with just the thread of a melody reaching up to the stars, that the stag stepped into the meadow.

He was huge, more the size of a small horse than a buck, a Royal by his antlers, having three tops and all his rights—brow, bay and tray tines. His coat was a ruddy brown like that of the red deer of the Scottish lowlands rather than the native whitetails. By Tommy's feet, Gaffa regarded the enormous beast puzzledly because—like a fawn—the stag had no scent. Moving silently, the stag stepped fully into the meadow, then turned to face the piper. Tommy brought the tune to a close and the two regarded one another in the ensuing quiet.

That's where it lives, Lewis thought. Inside the stag. The mystery that called from beyond the music of Tommy's pipes—the enchantment that men had followed through the forests of prehistory, in Arcadia's gentle hills, in the black forests of Europe, in England's tracts of bardic woodland, in the eastern forests of North America. No matter what shape it wore, it was always the same mystery. It was what their ancestors had followed, Lewis realized, when they crossed the Atlantic. The mystery had left the shores of England, moving west, and they had followed.

The music that Tommy played was only a memory of what this creature was. It was something between wizardry and poetry, between enchantment and music. Its antlers were the branches of the tree of life and in its eyes was the beauty of the world, always seen as though for the first time.

That was how Lewis saw it—the Royal stag called from Other-where by Tommy's music, by the memories tied into those tunes—Lewis, with his walls of books and the thousands of pages that had passed before his eyes. The others didn't see it quite the same. To them the stag was a wonder, a gift from Tommy's music and the night. The play of the muscles under its skin as it slowly circled the perimeter of the meadow was an echo of their dancing. It was Tommy's music given form for them to see.

Then, from the distance, a new sound came. A discordant baying of hounds. The stag rose on its hind legs, antlers sweeping the sky. For one moment it seemed to all those watching that a man stood there—a man with antlers lifting from his brow—then the stag dropped to all fours and sprang from the meadow in one long graceful bound, disappearing into the forest without a sound.

The baying drew nearer until Tommy lifted his pipes to his lips once more and blew a new music—fierce and wild, a trumpeting blare. Before the sound of it had died away, the baying was gone and the usual noises of a nighted forest returned.

Lewis closed his eyes and shivered. When he glanced at the long-stone, he saw that both Tommy and his dog were gone. As was the stag. As the villagers soon would be, for they were already going as they'd come, in small groups, or one by one. Lily remained, a question in her eyes, but Lewis shook his head. Not until he was alone did he turn away from the meadow and its tall standing stone to return to his cabin.

Unlike the others, he couldn't simply accept things as they happened. Questions troubled him when others had no need for either the questions or their answers. What brought the stag? What was different on the nights that it came from those nights when it didn't? Tommy played the same music.

There was no answer in his books. No answer from anyone he could ask. No answer from Tommy's music nor the wondrous creature it had called up tonight. He thought of his night visitor, of the gleam he sometimes saw in her slightly slanted green eyes. There was an answer in her, he knew. Only with her, he didn't know the right question to ask. To her, "Why?" was only "Why not?" That wasn't enough for Lewis. It never had been.

He lit the lamp when he got home and sat at the table with the paperback book she'd "found" on his lap, waiting for her scratch at the door and her cheery " 'Lo, Lewis." But when she did come, instead of talking to her, about the stag, about Tommy's music, about who or even what she was, he opened the book and read a few more chapters to her. And then she was gone again, swallowed by the same night that had taken the stag, and he was no closer to unravelling the riddles than he'd ever been.

6

There was still a good half hour of daylight left when Valenti closed his front door and started down the road. The black flies were pretty well gone by now, but the mosquitos were more than making up for their absence. He considered going back for some bug-repellent, then decided he couldn't spare the time. He wanted to be all settled in before it got dark so that he could see who showed up, rather than be seen himself. If whoever was watching the Treasure house was the same person who'd been spying on him when he'd first moved here for good, they'd be coming nightly for at least the first few weeks.

At first Valenti thought that the *fratellanza* had caught up with him, but when nobody made any moves to take him down, he put that fear aside. What had driven the hidden watcher, though, he still didn't know. Curiosity, he supposed. Whoever or whatever it was, it was like a wild animal in some respects. He'd never caught more than shadowy glimpses of it himself and once he'd made a concerted effort to flush it out, the watcher didn't come around his place anymore.

He wondered, not for the first time, if there were some connection between the watcher and the music that came drifting out of the woods from behind his house; wondered as well if he were the only person who heard it. He didn't know anyone in the area well enough to ask. What he didn't need was to start people talking about how he was hearing things. There'd been enough talk when he'd come here to stay for good instead of his usual couple of weeks a year. That talk had long since died down and he wasn't about to put himself into public scrutiny all over again.

But that music did more than intrigue him. He thought about it often—especially during the winter when it was seldom heard. Spring was the best time—spring and the long evenings of summer. It tapered out again come the fall, and after Halloween it was mostly just a memory. Valenti was carrying around too many memories, but thinking of the music always made the others easier to bear.

Close to Ali's house, he slipped into the woods to the right of the road and worked his way around to the trees that looked onto the back of the house. He stood there studying the building and its yard. To his right, the hulk of their ruined barn grew dark with shadows. He could see figures move across the windows in the house. Insects hummed in the air. The twilight grew rapidly, throwing the house and lawn into sharp relief before the shadows merged to become one pool of darkness. Over the western trees the sun lingered for a few moments longer, then dropped from sight. The air was filled with a clean, spring night scent.

Valenti began to move closer to the house, then paused and cocked his head. A whisper of sound . . . It came shimmering through the darkness, a breathy and low music, achingly beautiful. Valenti gripped the head of his cane with a white-knuckled hand and slowly lowered himself to the ground. There was a different quality to the piping tonight.

Hear me, it called to him. *Find me.*

Leaning his head against the rough-barked trunk of a tree, all he could do was listen.

In her bedroom overlooking the backyard, Ali was busy putting her books in alphabetical order. She'd been sloppy boxing them up before the move and now she had to pay for it. Up to the *S*'s now, she was puzzling over her Thomas Burnett Swann books. *Wolfwinter* was gone. She'd searched high and low for it but couldn't find it. It was the only one of Swann's books that she hadn't read yet; she'd only just found a copy—in mint condition—in a secondhand book shop before they left Ottawa and had been looking forward to reading it.

That was the problem with moving, she thought. Every time they'd moved, one or two of her books disappeared—usually the middle book in a trilogy, or something really hard to find like this Swann title. Frustrated, she went to sit by her window and stared through the screen at the darkness beyond. A slight breeze blew coolly on her cheek.

She was listening to a cassette of Hungarian violin music by John Owczarek on her Sony Walkman. That was something else her mother worried about—the fact that Ali's tastes followed her mother's so much, rather than what was current for her age group. It was no use trying to tell Frankie different, Ali had realized long ago. Her mother just liked to worry about things.

The cassette ended and she took off the earphones. Unclipping the Walkman from her belt, she laid it and the earphones on the nightstand by her bed. She was about to go back to organizing her books— incomplete Swann collection and all—when she heard music coming from somewhere.

It wasn't coming from the stereo downstairs; her mother was taking a nap and there weren't any neighbors near enough to be its source, so where was the music coming from? And such music. Distant, quiet, but so immediate you could almost touch it. Something inside her stirred awake as she listened to it.

She stared out the window until she began to feel confined. Then she got up and made her way downstairs and out the back door. She wanted to hear what the music sounded like from outside.

If Valenti rarely dreamed before moving to Lanark County, Frankie was just the opposite. Her nights were like film festivals, the dreams showing back to back until morning. All that was missing were the credits.

Her dreams seemed so real that sometimes she carried the memories and emotions evoked by them over into her waking life. She might dream of Ali doing something horrible to her, then she'd wake up and treat the poor kid like shit. Ali, sweetheart that she was, knew enough to stay out of her way on mornings like that, but it didn't make Frankie feel any less guilty about it.

She hadn't meant to fall so deeply asleep after dinner, but the couch seemed to gather her up and take her away. OD-ing on all the fresh air, she thought as her eyelids grew too heavy to keep open and she drifted off. The nap thickened into sleep. She burrowed closer against the back of the couch, her eyes beginning to move rapidly behind her eyelids as she dreamed. . . .

From a formless place, she found herself standing in the front hallway of the new house. She could hear something moving upstairs, something too heavy to be Ali, but so far as she knew, Ali was up there by herself. There was a heavy clomp, clomp, clomp on the hardwood floors. Biting at her lower lip, Frankie moved slowly toward the stairs.

She mounted one stair at a time, and all the while she could hear the sound of some huge thing moving around on the second floor. When she reached the landing, there was nothing to see. The sound was coming from Ali's bedroom. What was she doing? Moving the furniture around?

She started down the hallway, then caught a glimpse of movement from the corner of her eye. What . . . ? Something that seemed like a little man made of sticks was scrambling up the narrow stairs that led to the attic.

Frankie stared after the disappearing figure, mouth open in astonishment. A cat, she thought. Or a raccoon. Somehow it got into the house, heard me coming. . . . But it hadn't looked like an animal. It had been stiff, and manlike in shape, if not size. Like a little monkey made of twigs.

A crash from Ali's room brought Frankie's head sharply around.

"Now look what you've done!" she heard Ali say crossly.

I'm going mad, Frankie thought. She stepped quickly to the door of Ali's bedroom, flung it open and found herself standing face to face with an enormous stag.

* * *

Just before he heard the door of the back porch creak open, Valenti became aware of the wind. It had been steadily building, stirring the leaves and remnants of dried autumn weeds with a crackling whisper of sound. Years of working the streets had given him an acute sixth sense. As he sat here now, feeling the wind, hearing the fey music that piped low and breathy in the distance, that same intuition began to tickle the nerves along his spine. Then he heard the porch door open and looked across the darkened lawn to see Ali step outside.

She had her head cocked as though she were listening to something. The music. Valenti realized that she was hearing it, too. He was about to call out to her, but that hunter's sixth sense stopped him before he did. Something. There was something . . .

When he saw the stag step silently from the woods not a half-dozen yards from where he sat, the sheer wonder of its presence—its size, its silence—made his mouth go dry. His pulse began a quick tattoo as the huge beast moved slowly out onto the lawn. Ali was out there. Maybe the stag would just be spooked and take off when it caught her scent, but maybe it would charge her instead. Valenti started to stand, but then a voice called out softly from the tree above him.

"Don't move."

He looked up. Slanted cat's eyes reflected the light from Ali's house.

"*Madonna mia,*" he muttered. The words came out in a barely audible rasp.

But he couldn't move now if he'd wanted to. Those eyes had done something to him. Sapped the strength from his legs so that he couldn't stand. Stolen his voice so that he couldn't call out a warning to Ali. The slanted eyes blinked, then dropped toward him. The owner of those eyes landed catlike beside him. Curly hair spilled from under the brim of a big floppy hat, framing a narrow foxlike face. The eyes were very close to him now, inches from his own.

It's just a girl, he thought. Just a kid. But her eyes weren't a child's eyes. They were old and worldly-wise.

"Watch," she said. Sitting back, she pointed out toward the lawn where the stag was drawing nearer to Ali.

* * *

The stag moved out from the trees and onto the lawn. Ali's breath caught in her lungs and she trembled—first from excitement, then with a touch of fear as she realized just how far from the house she was and that the stag was drawing closer to her with each deliberate step.

Jeez, what if it charged her? She started to back away, but suddenly the stag was looming right over her and now she was too scared to move.

"N-nice boy," she said. She swallowed thickly. "Good boy. E-easy now . . ."

The stag dipped its head, antlers bobbing with the movement, then it looked up to where the light she'd left on in her bedroom was spilling out the window. Ali didn't want to take her gaze off the animal, but at length, she, too, shot a quick glance up at that square of light.

Frankie stared at the stag. She was so close, and the light was so bright, that she could make out every detail. The broad black nose, the lighter-colored hairs of its muzzle, the ruddy hair on its brow, the liquid eyes, the huge antlers lifting up to almost touch the ceiling of Ali's bedroom. Ali . . .

The stag never moved. From the attic above she heard the scurrying of what sounded like a dozen rats or squirrels crossing the wooden boarding up there, tiny claws clicking on the wood. Frankie looked up, took a step back from the stag in the doorway.

I'm going crazy, she thought.

She remembered hearing Ali's voice in the room. Ali scolding someone. The stag? Oh, please God, this had to be a dream. Let me wake up. The scurrying of whatever was in the attic grew louder, as though the rats or squirrels, if that was what they were, if they weren't little stick men . . . as though they were dancing . . . Panic reared in Frankie, a sheer terror that dwarfed any fear she'd had before. It took shape as a name that rose from deep in her chest and came out as a wail.

"Alllliiiii!"

* * *

When she heard her mother scream, Ali's fear fled. She looked away from the yellow square of her bedroom window, back toward the stag, only to find the lawn empty. She was out here by herself. But then . . . ? She heard her mother cry out again and bolted for the house.

Valenti blinked. One moment the creature was there on the lawn, towering over Ali, in the next it was gone and Ali was tearing across the lawn back to the house. He turned back to his own unwanted companion only to find that he, too, was alone now.

The piping had stopped. But he heard something else. It sounded like the baying of hounds. Then he saw that the stag wasn't quite gone. It was by the corner of the house, moving in long, springing bounds toward the road and the forest beyond it. It wasn't gone for more than a couple of moments before a half-dozen loping shapes appeared, obviously in pursuit.

They were dogs—big ones, Valenti thought. Then his eyesight betrayed him again. For an instant he thought he saw, not dogs, but men pursuing the stag, men in the habits of monks, or the robes of priests. He blinked and they were just dogs again, lost to his sight as they disappeared into the forest after the stag.

Valenti wiped his brow with the sleeve of his jacket. Fercrissakes, he thought. What was going on here? He had to be going crazy. He looked up to where the girl with the slanty eyes had dropped from the lower branches of the tree, then down to where she'd crouched beside him.

Had there been anyone there at all? The music, the stag, the girl . . . Slowly, he got to his feet and shook his head. He felt like he'd just broken a long fever. Looking at Ali's house, he wondered if he should knock at the door to see if they were all right. He seemed to remember a scream. . . .

A dream, Frankie thought with relief as she abruptly woke on the couch. Her own cries had woken her and it had all been a dream. She sat up and looked around herself. The stag in Ali's room, the little twig men or squirrels or whatever they'd been, scurrying around in the attic . . . She swung her feet to the floor just as Ali burst into the living room.

"Mom!" Ali cried, then slowed to an undignified halt. "Mom . . . ?"

"I'm all right," Frankie said. "I was just dreaming."

"It wasn't about . . . ?"

"It wasn't about you," Frankie assured her. "Or at least not exactly. C'mere and give your mother a hug."

Ali plonked herself down beside Frankie and gave her the hug. "Boy, you really missed something," she said. "There was this deer out in the backyard with horns—"

"Antlers," Frankie corrected automatically.

"Whatever. But you should have seen it. It was *huge!"*

"I did see it."

"But you said . . ."

Frankie laughed. "I know. I said I was dreaming. And what I was dreaming was that you had this great big deer stashed away in your bedroom. I heard it moving around and when I opened the door to your room it was staring me right in the face."

"Is that ever weird," Ali said.

"You're telling me, kiddo. Synchronicity and all that."

"Did you hear any music at all?"

"Music? What kind of music?"

"Sort of like on your Georges Zamphir record—you know, panpipes? Only without the orchestra and not so smooth. More . . . primal."

Frankie's eyebrows lifted. "Primal?"

Ali laughed. "No, really. I heard it up in my room and went out to the backyard to see if I could tell where it was coming from, only then the deer was out there and I guess I just forgot about it. But it was really something."

"Well, I was asleep," Frankie said, giving her daughter's shoulders a squeeze, "and if I'd heard any kind of music, I'm sure it would've been the theme to *The Exorcist* or something like that because I was scared."

"Me, too. He was so big."

"You're telling me." They looked at each other and laughed. "Lis-

ten to us," Frankie said. "You'd think we both really saw your stag . . .
I'm going to make some tea. Would you like some?"

Ali nodded and followed her mother into the kitchen, but something was bothering her. She remembered how quickly the big animal had just . . . disappeared. She couldn't have turned her head for
more than a few moments, but when she looked back it was . . . just
gone. . . .

Scream or no scream, Valenti decided to leave well enough alone for
the night. After watching the house for awhile, he saw Ali and her
mother enter the kitchen like nothing was the matter. Since he didn't
even know Ali's mother and he sure as hell wasn't up to explaining
what he'd been doing skulking around in their backyard tonight, he
might as well just go home.

Besides, he had too much on his mind right now. He had to sort
through what was real and what wasn't before he talked to anyone
about it. For all he knew, he might have been imagining Ali out on the
lawn as well.

After taking a last look around, he set off through the trees, heading for home. The wind that had sprung up just before the stag appeared had died down now and the mosquitos were back. This had
been one helluva weird night, he thought, no question about that.

7

The sound of Tommy's pipes, once heard, was not easily forgotten, even for a man of such limited imagination as Lance Maxwell. He hadn't heard them so clearly again as he had on the day of that February thaw when he'd gotten the flat tire, but the memory of them and their vague sound, carried some evenings like pollen on a high wind, continued to trouble him all through the spring.

Whereas their music awoke a longing deeply held in Tony Valenti—a need to unravel the mystery he heard hidden between the notes of the tunes—they just made Lance horny. He looked for release in his marriage bed, bringing a vigor to his lovemaking that had been absent for years.

"I don't know what's gotten into him," Brenda confided to a neighbor one day, "but I'm not going to complain. It's nice to know I've still got what it takes."

She might not have been so ready to accept it if she'd known what was going through Lance's head when they were making love. He liked to enter her from the rear now; he wanted to rut her like a goat, pumping away like Dooker mounting the Sneddens' bitch when it was in heat. It wasn't a woman under him, but a doe, and he was the buck; a nanny, and he was the billy goat; a bitch, and he was the hound. And afterwards, lying spent and staring up at the peeling ceiling of their bedroom, he'd still be hard, his seed sown, but the release he needed had been stolen away on the strains of a music he didn't even know he remembered.

He'd gone to see the doc a week or so after he'd had what he thought was a heart attack. Bolton put him on a diet, told him to take it a little easier because he wasn't getting any younger, adding, "Lay off the cigars, Lance, because if a heart attack doesn't get you, then lung cancer surely will."

He'd cut down to two cigars a day, followed the diet as much as their budget allowed, but there wasn't a whole lot he could do about taking it easier. He barely made ends meet as it was. If he laid off the hauling and odd jobs he did, they'd be on welfare faster than you could shake your dick dry after a piss. So he followed the doc's advice as he could, and damned if he didn't feel better, but he couldn't explain the wanting in him, the feeling of incompletion, and he couldn't explain his new virility, either.

"What's gotten into you?" Brenda asked him one night as they started to make love for the second time in as many hours.

"Got a need, Boo," he grunted, hands moving quick, maybe a little rough, all over her.

His penis stood at attention, hard as a rock against her belly. Brenda took it in hand. The marvel to her was that after reading about orgasms in *Women's Weekly* and *Redbook* and the like for years and never really knowing what they were talking about, for the first time in their twenty-eight years of marriage she was actually having them. And, Lord, but didn't it feel good. And maybe she was getting a little plump, and maybe there were gray hairs hidden by the regular use of Miss Clairol, but wasn't it something that at her age she could still turn a man on like she did? Wasn't that *something?*

Moving under Lance, pulling him inside her, she had to smile. Lord, but those Maxwells had known what they were about when they were naming their little boy.

* * *

Lance tended to avoid driving by the old Treasure place, though he couldn't have said why. He knew it was fixed up—Buddy's little girl, all grown up, was living there now—but the spot just gave him a shiver. About the only thing that had changed for him when Frances Treasure moved in was that he was out the bucks it cost for a case of two-four.

It had been a private bet that he'd made with Frank Clayton—they were the only two who knew anything about it—but he'd paid up all the same. Hell, he was just glad to be alive instead of lying in the slush, praying someone found him before his ticker gave right out. Frank had nothing to do with him making it, and the Treasure place had nothing to do with his having the attack, but he paid the former and avoided the latter all the same.

Tuesday night he and Brenda were watching *St. Elsewhere* on their old Zenith TV. Lance had a beer in his hand; Brenda was dividing her attention between darning socks and the latest dramas of the St. Eligius hierarchy. Lance lifted his bottle, pausing before he took a swallow.

"Let's get to bed, Boo," he said suddenly.

Brenda looked at him. "But—"

"The darning can wait, and so can that," he said, nodding at the tube. He set his beer down on the scratched coffee table. He was already hard. "Let's *go*, Boo."

That night he was a buck, fourteen points if it had one. There was something chasing him and he had to drop his load, quick, or something bad was going to happen. The hounds were out hunting tonight, looking for him, and maybe he'd stand and fight them off, and maybe he'd just run, but first he had to hide his seed. That was what they wanted. The dogs wanted his seed. But he was going to hide it away so deep and so far they were never going to find it, no way.

When he finally pulled away from her and rolled over, Brenda lay quietly for a long time. Not until she was sure he was asleep did she get up and pad into the bathroom. She started to sit on the toilet, but suddenly Lance was there, filling the doorway.

"What're you doing?" he demanded. "Christ on a cross! What the hell do you think you're *doing?*" He was wild-eyed, a stranger.

"I'm just—"

He grabbed her by the arm and hauled her off the toilet. "You want them to find it?" he roared. "Jesus H. Christ, woman, what do you think I was hiding it for? So you could piss it down the drain?"

"Lance, I . . ."

Her voice trailed off. Lance was slowly shaking his head. He lifted a hand to rub his temple.

"Jesus," he said in a softer voice.

"Lance. Are you okay?"

"Got a headache, Boo. That's all."

Brenda massaged her arm where he'd grabbed her. That was going to bruise, she thought. She looked at her husband, remembering the stranger he'd been for a moment there. For the first time since his ardor had returned, stronger even than when they were teenagers and going at it in the back of his father's car, she was scared. This wasn't natural. There was something happening to him, but she didn't know what to do about it.

"Do you want an aspirin?" she asked.

"Yeah. Sure."

She went to the medicine cabinet, shook a couple out of the bottle. We just got this bottle last week, she thought. A hundred tablets. It was half-empty now.

"Maybe you should make an appointment with Dr. Bolton," she said as she brought him the tablets and a glass of water.

He swallowed the pills. "Maybe I should."

When he returned to the bed, she stood in the doorway, waiting until he was under the covers, then returned to the toilet. Any minute she expected him to come bursting in again, but she finished her business in peace and returned to the bed to find Lance staring up at the ceiling.

"What's the matter, hon?"

He shook his head. "Nothing, really. I just can't sleep sometimes."

She pulled back the covers to get in beside him and saw that he was hard again. She wanted to look away, wanted to hold on to the memory of him standing in the doorway and being rough with her—not because she had liked it, but because it had scared her, and she wanted to remember it as a warning—but she couldn't look away from his hard-on.

What had happened to him? Her breasts tingled, already feeling his hands on them. She was damp between her legs. His ardor wasn't natural, she thought. Nor was what she was feeling now. But she reached over and took hold of his penis all the same.

Downstairs, the television continued to operate for its absent audience. *St. Elsewhere* had long since ended. The news was on now, followed by sports and the weather. . . .

Outside, behind the Maxwell's house, Dooker whined in his sleep. His legs moved as though he were chasing something in a dream. Perhaps his imagination was even more limited than his master's, but the dream was very real all the same.

The stag ran before him, the pack all around him. The night was filled with scents, sharp and biting. The music called them on like a huntsman's horn. It felt so good to just be running.

After Lance fell asleep for the second time, Brenda lay quietly beside him, not wanting to move. She went over that moment in the bathroom, the crazy things Lance had said, and then the way that he didn't even seem to be aware of it right after. Like it had never happened.

She rubbed her arm softly. Well, the bruise was there. It *had* happened. But she didn't know what to do about it. There was no one she could talk to about something like this. Lord, she could just imagine the way people'd stare at her if the word got out. No, she had to keep it to herself, hoard it like a secret and just pray—dear Jesus—that it wouldn't happen again.

It was a long time before she finally fell asleep herself.

8

" 'Lo, Lewis."

Leaning on his rake, Lewis looked up into the branches of the oak tree that stood between his cabin and the small vegetable plot he was working on. A familiar fox-thin face regarded him through the leaves, the morning sun dappled on her brown skin.

"Hello, yourself," he said, moving under the tree. "You're up and about early today."

She dropped lightly from the branches to stand beside him. She looked smaller, thinner, in the daylight, but no less mysterious. The brim of her hat was pulled down low and he couldn't see her eyes until she tilted her head up to look at him.

"I like the night," she said, "but I'm not bound to it. You know that."

As she spoke she edged toward his woodpile. A few quick moves later and she was perched upon it, legs dangling down. Lewis followed her, moving more slowly, and fetched up his chopping block to sit on.

"I saw you dancing last night," he said.

"I saw you too—only you weren't dancing."

"I'm too old now."

"Doesn't stop Lily."

"She's twenty years younger than me. It makes a difference."

The slanted green eyes studied him for a moment, then looked away. "Maybe," she said. Her gaze returned to him, a serious look in her eyes. "You shouldn't have let him run so far last night, Lewis."

"He belongs to everyone—not just New Wolding. I couldn't stop him anyway."

She nodded. "But there's no room for him out there anymore. If he runs too far, he'll be gone, too. A mystery like him wouldn't last too long out there."

"It's Tommy's music," Lewis said. "He's the one who pipes the tune."

"Tommy won't listen to me."

"What makes you think he'd listen to me? Anyway, he's not just Tommy when he's piping. He's part of the mystery then."

She sighed. "I know. There's just not enough of you here anymore. If there were more of you, Tommy wouldn't pipe so wild a tune. He's calling, Lewis, because he knows you need more people, and he's sending the mystery out further and further. One night the mystery won't come back. You've got to bring some people in."

"They don't listen anymore," Lewis said. "I've been out there. People've got too much else going on in their heads to hear properly anymore. The music's just not strong enough for them."

"But there's some that would hear it the way it should be heard," she said. "There has to be. If you could reach them . . . When's the Gypsy due?"

Lewis shrugged. "A week . . . maybe two. They keep time like you do—as it comes."

"Ask him," she said. "There's people out there who *will* listen. Ask him to find some for you. Otherwise things'll change and the changes won't be good. The music's going out to the wrong people. When the echoes come back, they're . . . they're not always good. Maybe you should move again, Lewis—like you did when you came here."

Lewis shook his head. "Where would we go?"

"Deeper."

"Deeper *where?*"

She shrugged. "I don't know, Lewis. Nothing changes for me. I've got the moon and that's all I need." She smiled without humor. "Maybe that's what you should do, Lewis. Drink down the moon and let him run free."

Before he could reply, she jumped down from the woodpile and moved behind him. He felt the light touch of her hand on his head as she tousled his thin hair. By the time he turned around, she was gone.

Lewis sat there for a long time, thinking over what she'd said. Out there, beyond this little pocket of the wild, they *did* hear the music differently, and whether they saw the mystery as a stag or a man or something in between, they understood even less about him than Lewis did. The mystery was their enemy. He was something you had to approach with your heart, but all they had in them was reason. The few folk that still searched for him—not even knowing what they were looking for—probably wouldn't recognize him if they did find him.

I wouldn't wish that on anyone, he thought.

That evening wasn't a gather-up night so only the youngsters went up to the stone when Tommy began to play. Lily was visiting Lewis and together they sat outside his cabin, listening to the soft piping that drifted down from Wold Hill. They sat without speaking, though earlier Lewis had repeated the warnings of his small morning visitor with her green eyes and narrow fox's face.

They both thought about the world losing another of its mysteries. It gave the night a bittersweet air. There were so few mysteries left. The world couldn't spare the loss of even one of them now.

9

On Saturday afternoon, Frankie sat down on the edge of her bed still wearing no more than her bra and panties. She'd spent a fruitless twenty minutes trying on various skirts, blouses and dresses and was no closer to deciding on what to wear for the evening than she had been when she'd come upstairs to take a shower in the first place.

You'd think I was Ali's age, she thought, getting ready for my first date. Except Ali was already dressed and waiting for her downstairs.

She didn't know why choosing what to wear seemed so important tonight. From all Ali had told her, Tony Garonne was a pretty casual fellow. And Frankie certainly wasn't trying to wow him. But she hadn't been out anywhere for a long time, and even if this was just dinner at a neighbor's, it was a chance to get dressed up in something a little more becoming than the usual jeans and workshirt.

She combed her damp hair with her fingers, twisting it into curls so that they would dry in ringlets. I should have gone over to meet him this week, she thought. Then I wouldn't be feeling this jittery.

But the usual one hundred and one things had come up—there was a *lot* that still needed doing around the house alone—and almost before she'd known it, it was late Saturday afternoon and time to get ready to go. What if he asked her what she was going to do, now that she didn't have to work eight-to-four in the government anymore?

She didn't know herself, but it always sounded awkward and somehow self-indulgent when she tried to explain that she was going to use the time that the Wintario money had given her to find out just what it was that she wanted to do with her life. Finding oneself had so many weird connotations in the eighties. It sounded so . . . Woodstock. Never mind that she *was* part of that whole Woodstock generation.

She sighed. And of course that might make things awkward as well. According to Ali, he was about ten years older than her. What if he made a pass? What if they couldn't find anything in common? What if—"

"Mom, what're you doing?"

She looked up to find her daughter standing in the doorway, arms akimbo. Frankie smiled ruefully, feeling like a kid with her hand in the cookie jar.

Ali shook her head. "What're you so nervous about? He's just a regular guy."

"Who says I'm nervous?"

"I do. Look at you. Are you going like that?"

Frankie stood up and did a little pirouette. "What do you think?"

"Well, you're certainly going to make an impression." Ali ducked as her mother grabbed a pillow from the bed and threw it at her. "You want me to help you pick something out?" she asked, sticking her head back in.

"Why not?"

Ali went to the closet and rummaged through the hangers until she came up with a dress. "How about this?"

It was a black evening dress, mid-calf and snug in the bust, with shoestring straps. Frankie shook her head. "Oh, I don't know. . . ." she said.

"C'mon. It looks great on you. You can wear that Sarah Clothes jacket of yours over top if you're feeling modest." She handed her mother the shift and went to the dresser looking for a slip and panty-hose. "Do you still have that rhinestone choker with the single pearl?" she asked.

"Are you matchmaking?" Frankie asked.

"Jeez. Get serious, mom."

Frankie shrugged and studied herself in the mirror. She looked good. A little dressy, perhaps, but it was fun after being such a scruff—especially these past few weeks.

"Shoes," she said.

"I'll get them. Maybe you should wear your walking shoes up, though. The road's not exactly a sidewalk."

"Yes, ma'am."

It was sort of fun having someone else make the decisions, Frankie decided. She gave herself a last quick once-over in the mirror, then hurried after Ali, who was impatiently waiting for her in the hall.

"You're looking nice yourself," she said as she followed Ali down the stairs.

"Yeah, well, it's a dinner, you know? I don't want Tony to think I can't look like a lady when I want to."

"Oh, I doubt he'll think that after tonight."

Ali was wearing a loose print dress that was gathered at the waist. Over her shoulders she had a pale rose shawl that matched the flowers on her dress. She looked very nice, Frankie thought, and then a motherly worry arose. Oh, I hope she's not getting a crush on this fellow.

"Mom? Are you coming?"

"I'm halfway there already—what's keeping you?"

Ali grinned. "Do you have room for this in your purse?" She held up a cassette.

"Sure. What is it?"

"Just some music that I wanted to play for Tony tonight."

Frankie stashed it away in her purse. "Well, Ms. Treasure," she said. "Are you ready?"

Ali rolled her eyes and led the way outside.

*   *   *

Tony Garonne was nothing like Frankie had expected. There was a sense of Old World charm about him that was vaguely at odds with the easy familiarity of his speech patterns. He was wearing a tailored suit—which made Frankie relieved that she'd gone along with Ali's suggestion of the black evening dress—and smiled broadly as he opened the door.

"Ladies," he said. "You look sensational. C'mon in and make yourselves at home."

Now it was Ali's turn to feel flustered. Frankie held out her hand. "Frankie Treasure," she said. "Ali's told me a lot about you."

"Nothing good, I'll bet," he replied as he took her hand. "Tony Garonne. How'd you like a little tour of the place before we eat?"

"I'd love it. This is a beautiful house."

"Yeah, well it's what I've got, you know, so I do what I can with it. Hey, what's the matter, Ali? You got no hello for me today?"

Ali nodded. "Hello, Tony."

Valenti gave Frankie a wink and ushered them inside. The first floor was mostly all one room. A tall stone hearth took up one wall, on another a picture window overlooked the front yard. The furnishings were simple, but expensive. Two couches faced the front window at angles, a coffee table between them. Rugs that appeared to be Navajo weavings gleamed on the hardwood floors. A third wall was taken up with a stereo console and a wall-screen television. The cabinet under the stereo was filled with LPs and video cassettes. A long counter divided the kitchen from the rest of the room. Beside it was a small nook with a table and four chairs.

"There's my bedroom, a guest room and the washroom upstairs," Valenti said. "Go take a look if you like. I just got a couple of things to finish up in the kitchen."

"This is beautiful," Frankie said. She crossed the room to look at a watercolor that hung over the stereo. It showed a county road overhung with trees, heavily boughed and green. Very much a Lanark County scene. Frankie fell in love with it on the spot.

"That's by this guy named David Armstrong," Valenti explained. "I got it at a gallery in Ottawa. Local guy, apparently. And this"—he pointed to another watercolor, this time a winter landscape—"is by a lady that lives just up the road toward Calabogie—name of Tomilyn Douglas."

"It's lovely."

"Yeah. I got a couple more of hers upstairs. Check 'em out while I get the last of this cheese sliced."

Frankie glanced at Ali, who was entranced by the size of Valenti's television screen.

"Look at the size of it," Ali said. "It'd be just like watching something in a movie theatre."

"We could watch something later if you like," Valenti called from the kitchen area.

"That'd be great," Ali said, her sudden shyness wearing away. "C'mon, Mom. Let's go look at the upstairs."

More motherly concerns, she supposed as she followed Ali up the stairs. There was a Richard Gill clay sculpture of a tree in the hall going up, as well as another Douglas watercolor—a barnyard scene in muted browns, grays and greens. The two upstairs rooms were both large and, again, tastefully furnished. But no books, Frankie thought. Lots of magazines lying around. *People, Life, Newsweek.*

"Some place, huh, mom? Wow. Look at this."

Frankie turned away from a Bateman print to look at the little soft-sculptured gnome that was standing on the dresser in the guest room. There was a dusty rose business card beside it that said "Fabric Art by MaryAnn Harris." Frankie smiled at the expression on the little gnome's face.

"I got that up at Andrew Dickson's," Valenti said from the doorway. "It's a little craft place up in Pakenham. You been up there yet?"

Frankie shook her head.

"You should check it out sometime. They've got a gallery upstairs that showcases different artists and craftspeople every month."

"Once we get settled in and the last of Ali's exams are over, we'll be doing lots of exploring," Frankie said. "Right now, everything's still so hectic. But it's starting to come together."

"Takes time."

"You're not kidding. This is a lovely place you have here, Mr. Garonne."

"Tony."

"Tony," Frankie repeated. "There are so many beautiful things."

"Well, I can't do anything like that myself, but I like to support those who can. Sort of like a *patrono,* you know what I'm trying to say?"

Frankie nodded. Actually, the house was almost like a gallery. It was so neat and tidy and all the art was displayed in a professional manner, complete with the business card for the gnome. She also felt, from Valenti's enthusiasm, that he really did appreciate what he had here. It wasn't just for show. Or if it was for show, the show was for himself. With the money she had now, she could do as much herself. Though she'd have to be careful not to go too wild. The money wasn't going to last forever.

"So who's ready for dinner?" Valenti asked.

The meal was a great success, consisting of antipasti, spaghetti with clam sauce and garlic bread, washed down with a white Italian wine. Frankie began to relax; their host didn't seem inclined to pry. The conversation had been comfortably pleasant throughout the meal. In fact, Frankie realized later, while Tony hadn't asked a lot of potentially awkward questions, he hadn't offered much on his own background either. Maybe they all had skeletons in their closets, she thought. As far as she was concerned, they could just stay there.

By the time they retired to the living room, she was on her fourth glass of wine and feeling a nice light buzz. Valenti shooed them away from the dishes. "They'll give me something to do in the morning, you know?" Frankie and Ali commandeered one couch, leaving the other for Valenti, who paused as he walked by the stereo.

"Maybe some music?" he asked.

"Great," Frankie said.

Ali sat up. "I brought a tape," she said as she reached for her mother's purse. She rummaged around in it until she came up with the cassette. She handed it over to Valenti.

"What's this?" he asked.

"It's a surprise. Something I taped up last night. Go ahead and put it on."

The sun had set and the room was lit only by one floor lamp over by the stereo. The night beyond the window was the dark that only a country night can be. Nothing but tape hiss came from the speakers at first. Then slowly the sound of crickets and frogs, the whirr of a June bug could be heard.

After a few moments, Frankie turned to her daughter. "Ali, what—"

"Shhh. Listen."

And then it came, a low breath of sound that whispered from the speakers. Frankie regarded her daughter curiously, but Ali was watching Valenti. He stiffened with surprise at the first hint of the distant piping. Ali thought he was going to say something, but instead he leaned back onto the couch and closed his eyes, hands behind his head.

He knows something, Ali thought. She was eager to ask him about it right away—what was it, who was it, where was it coming from?— but she settled back as well, determined to be patient. They could talk when the cassette was over.

Frankie was puzzled by both Tony's and her own daughter's reactions to this odd cassette that Ali had taped. It sounded like one of those "Environments" records that were so popular in the seventies. The sound of rain falling. Dusk on a lake shore. Morning in the desert. Then she heard the music and that started to remind her of Paul Horn's *Inside,* only this wasn't the sound of a flute. Too breathy. It didn't even sound real in a way. . . .

She leaned back against the couch herself, feeling a little woozy. When she closed her eyes, sparks danced in her vision. She'd never had much tolerance for alcohol, but the high she was feeling now didn't seem related to what she'd consumed. It was like doing mushrooms, she thought, surprised herself at how clearly she could remember that sensation since her days of psychedelia had been a good sixteen, seventeen years ago. Mescaline. MDA—though its rushes had been stronger than what she was feeling now. This was lighter, a floating sensation, just like—

When the cassette machine suddenly clicked off at the end of the tape, she sat up, startled. She reached for her wine glass, then thought better of it. Her head was still buzzing.

"That's some recording," Valenti said softly.

"You've heard it before—haven't you?" Ali asked. "Not this tape, but the music."

"Sure. Lots of times."

"Where's it coming from?"

Valenti made a motion with his hand. "Back there, in the bush somewhere. I mostly hear it in the spring or summer, so I figure it's got to be some cottager who's got himself some kind of flute. It's pretty, isn't it?"

Ali shook her head. "No, it's not just pretty. It's magical. There's something . . . otherworldly about it. Something really spacey."

Frankie found herself nodding, then studied her daughter. Had Ali started experimenting with drugs? God, she hoped not.

"Well, yeah," Valenti said. "It's different, sure. But I don't know about magic." Still, thoughts of the strange girl who'd dropped out of a tree to sit beside him earlier in the week rose to the top of his mind. The eyes in that thin face, they'd just grabbed him and made him sit still in his place until they were ready to let him go. And then the stag . . . and the way the music made him feel . . . Maybe he didn't know about magic, but he knew about weird.

"Don't you feel something inside you when you hear it?" Ali asked.

Valenti shrugged. "I suppose . . ."

"Maybe we should be going," Frankie said. "It's getting on to ten-thirty."

Ali looked from her mother to Valenti, then nodded. "Okay," she said without much enthusiasm.

"We'll talk about it some more—next time you come up," Valenti said.

That made Ali feel better. When Valenti took the cassette from the machine and went to give it to her, she shook her head.

"No. You can keep it for awhile if you want."

Valenti smiled, a curious look touching his eyes for a moment.

"That's great," he said. "Listen, do you want some company going down the road . . . ?"

"Maybe halfway," Frankie said. "Just so's the boogieman doesn't nab us."

"Okay," Valenti said. "I'll just change my coat."

"Ali?"

Frankie stood in the doorway to her daughter's room and looked in. Ali was sitting on her bed, wearing the long T-shirt that passed for a nightie in the summer months. She looked up at her mother's voice.

"Hi, Mom. What's up?"

"I was just wondering. This business with the tape . . . ?"

"Well, I know you didn't hear the music the night I saw the deer in the backyard. When I heard it again last night, I taped it. I wanted to see if you and Tony'd feel the same kinds of things I did when I heard it. You see—you're going to think I'm crazy—but there's something secret about that music, only I don't know what it is." Her shoulders lifted and fell. "It just makes me feel, oh, I don't know. Alive, I guess. Am I making sense?"

"I suppose," Frankie said. She was about to go to her own room, when she paused. "You haven't been trying drugs at all, have you? You know, marijuana or . . . ?"

Ali shook her head. "Come *on,* Mom. I might hear weird things in music, but I'm not that dumb."

Not like I was, Frankie thought.

"What makes you think I'd do dope anyway?" Ali wanted to know.

"Nothing," Frankie said. "It's just one of those things that mothers are supposed to worry about—didn't you know that?"

"You can't fool me. I think you just like to worry."

"Thanks a lot."

Ali watched her mother go down the hall to her own room, then slowly returned to sit on her bed. She looked out the window, into the night. What's out there? she wondered. What's *really* out there? Had she just been reading too many fantasy books?

Although there'd been no answer forthcoming tonight, she was determined to find one.

Much the same train of thought was going through Valenti's mind as he followed the road back home. He'd never thought of taping the music like Ali had. But then, he'd seen the wild girl in the trees behind Ali's house—seen her right up close. Maybe if we put what we know together, we'll come up with something, he thought.

He wondered if the wild girl was watching him from the trees alongside the road right now. There was no warning tickle in the nape of his neck, but he had the feeling that this girl could be standing right smack in front of him and he wouldn't see her until she wanted to be seen.

"But I'm going to find you," he said softly before he went into the house and closed the door on what was left of the night. "Just you wait and see."

Invisible in the shadows of the side of his house, a small figure stirred. A smile touched her fox-thin features. She was drawn to the girl who lived in the dark man's house, but she was drawn to this man as well. There was a fire in them both. When they heard the music, it reflected back from them twice as strong. And tonight . . . hearing Tommy's music coming from both Wold Hill and inside this man's house at the same time!

She remembered seeing the girl with her little machine in hand before. Her curly hair tumbled against itself under her hat as she nodded. She had to get a machine like that and learn how to work it. She hugged herself in anticipation of how surprised Lewis would be when she made the machine work its enchanted mimickry for him. Wouldn't his eyes go big!

Giving Valenti's windows a last considering look, she scampered off into the forest, heading for the dark man's house.

10

It was two months after he ran across the piece in the *Star* before Earl Shaw finally had a chance to go looking for his ex. He'd been seeing to the financing of a deal he was setting up for another Colombia-Miami run, and while he knew where he could get backers, he'd rather put the bread up himself.

He didn't mind using other people's money—preferred it really—except the people who were making the right kind of noises this time around were connected. Earl didn't much care for the kind of interest they'd be expecting when he paid them back. They were an old outfit, working out of New York City, but new to the drug trade. Earl wasn't all that keen in getting caught up between them and the established outfits, but what could you do? The deal was sure as hell right.

Hearing about Frankie's big win was the shot in the arm Earl had needed. He knew there'd be no problem getting the bread out of her, so he'd been renegotiating his deal with the New York boys first, as well as putting the final touches on the Colombian end.

Things had started off dicey in New York. He'd had a lot of meetings with the Magaddino *consigliere,* Broadway Joe Fucceri, but in the end things had worked Earl's way. Hell, nobody was going to give them as sweet a deal as what he'd laid out for them, especially now that they didn't have to put out any up-front money. With the deal set for the middle of June, he flew up to Ottawa only to hit the first snag in his plans. Frankie'd covered her tracks too well and she wasn't to be found.

Earl still had trouble figuring her out. Something about her had changed in the few months before she split and to this day it didn't make sense. Hell, when they had first met, she'd liked partying as much as he had. What did having a kid change?

But it had gotten so she didn't want any of the crowd hanging around the apartment anymore and then she'd picked up on the fact that the job he was going to every night had nothing to do with cleaning office buildings. He'd gotten into dealing in a heavy way. What the fuck—a guy had to live, right? Pushing a broom around some asshole's office wasn't living, not so far as Earl Shaw was concerned. And was it his fault he had to start carrying a piece? The action was getting rough and a man had to protect his shit or the big boy'd walk all over him. Christ, he was bringing home the bacon, wasn't he?

But that didn't cut shit with Frankie. She went all prissy on him. There was no more talk, no more arguments. One morning he came home, and she was gone—heading out west where she started divorce proceedings against him.

He would have followed her—just to show her who was boss— but about that time he got involved in some action that took him down to Colombia for a little business trip. After that he'd drifted . . . Miami, L.A., New York, Van, T.O. He'd put on some meat and didn't look a whole lot like the skinny hippie he'd been when he'd first gotten into the drug scene way back when. By the time he ran across Frankie's picture in the *Star,* he'd been up and he'd been down, but he hadn't thought about her or the kid in years. Had to be an omen, he figured. Things'd been down for so long this time, they just had to start looking up again.

Which was all well and good, except come Saturday night—two weeks away from when he was scheduled to fly back to Bogota—he and Howie had run out of options and were up against a dead end. It was around ten o'clock that night—when they were killing a couple of beers in a William Street bar—that things finally took a turn for the better.

"Earl? Earl Shaw?"

Earl looked up into a drunken face he didn't know. The guy was a geek, long thin face, big ears, big horn-rims, nice polyester suit—if you could believe that anyone still wore those things.

"I'm supposed to know you?" Earl asked.

"It's Bob—Bob Goldman, Earl. I used to live upstairs from you and Frankie back in '73 or so—remember?"

Earl added some length to the geek's short hair, replaced the horn-rims with a pair of round wire frames, and then he had him.

"Sure," he said. "I remember you now. You got time for a drink?"

"Don't mind if I do, Earl. Don't mind if I do. I've had one of those days—you know, those days when nothing, ab-so-lute-ly *nothing* goes right?"

Earl nodded sympathetically. "So what're you up to these days?"

"Well, I moved up from T.O. a couple of years ago. I'm into computers now—working as a consultant."

"How's the pay?"

"Oh, the pay's good. No complaints. I've got a place out in the west end and I'm married now, you know. Joy's expecting our first."

Earl put an enthusiastic smile on his face. "Hey, that's great. There's nothing like a fam—"

"But you see," Goldman interrupted, "I had to work today—work late, too—except Joy doesn't buy that. But what the hell am I supposed to do? Listen to her or to my boss? So I said fuck her, went in anyway and I'm not going home until I'm good and pissed. I figure, if she's going to get on my case, I might as well tie one on and make all the harping worthwhile."

"Well, I don't know," Earl said. "Take it from one who blew it. I still miss Frankie and Alice, you know. I'd give anything to be able to make things up to them."

He sighed heavily, hoping he was playing it right. Having lived upstairs from them in Toronto, Goldman probably remembered some of the fights that had gone down. He'd been pretty tight with Frankie, too—sided with her a lot. She'd probably been fucking him on the side.

Earl met Goldman's gaze now, putting as much sincerity as he could into his face. "You ever run into them?" he asked. "I heard they moved to Ottawa."

Goldman looked uncomfortable and shook his head quickly. Too quickly, Earl decided. He was remembering things about Toronto now, Earl saw. Maybe he'd remember that it didn't pay to fuck around with Earl Shaw.

"I, uh, haven't seen her since you two split up," Goldman said. "Are you looking for her?"

Bingo, Earl thought. He knows.

"Well, I wouldn't mind saying hello," he said, "especially to Alice, but I don't suppose Frankie'd be all that keen on seeing me. It's probably better if we don't get together."

Goldman nodded. "People change."

"Ain't that the truth? So what're you drinking, Bob?"

Goldman looked at his watch. "Actually, it's getting a little late. I should be running. But it was great seeing you again, Earl."

"You bet. Sure I can't change your mind about that drink?" Earl asked as Goldman stood up.

Goldman shook his head and backed away from their table. "Stick to him," Earl told Howie as Goldman made his way unsteadily to the door and out to the street.

"I'll get the car. Ten minutes, I'll meet you at the corner of William and York—got it?"

"Sure, Earl."

Howie left the table and slipped into the crowd. There wasn't much to Howie, Earl thought as he went to get the car, but you had to say this for him. When he tailed someone, he stuck on like a burr.

"Hey, Bob!"

Goldman turned to see Earl's friend running up to him. The

smaller man had his left hand in the air, holding a wallet and acting as though Goldman had left it behind. His right hand was in the pocket of his jacket.

Why the hell had he talked to Earl in the first place? Goldman wondered. Frankie had told him often enough about the kind of man Earl had become—about his violence and the kinds of people he hung around with—and Goldman knew why Earl was looking for her. It was the Wintario prize.

"I think you forgot something," Howie said as he reached him.

"I don't think—" Goldman tried.

Howie moved in close and nudged him with his pocketed gun. "You know what this is?" Howie asked softly.

Goldman nodded.

"So we wait up at the corner for Earl and there's no problem, right?"

"Look, whatever—"

Howie shook his head. "I don't want to hear it. Let's just wait for Earl, okay? We're playing by his rules."

As they reached the corner Earl pulled over to the curb in a metallic blue Chev. Howie motioned Goldman into the back seat, then climbed in beside him.

"Listen," Goldman began.

Earl turned to face him. "Hold that thought," he said. "We're going for a little drive so we can have some privacy and then you're going to tell me everything I want to know about Frankie—am I right?"

Goldman swallowed, then nodded.

"That's my boy," Earl said. He reached over and patted Goldman's cheek, then turned to face front. Putting the Chev into gear, he pulled away from the curb.

They drove Goldman into Industrial Park off Old Innes Road and parked the Chev behind some warehouses. Earl killed the engine and stepped out of the car. He stood, listening to the distant traffic on Russell Road. When he was sure there was no one in the immediate vicinity, he motioned to Howie. Howie got Goldman out of the car.

"Okay, Bob," Earl said. "It's nice and quiet here. There's no one to disturb us. Now I want you to tell me what you know about Frankie. You could start with where she's living now."

"I don't know too much," Goldman began.

Earl hit him in the stomach, stepping back as Goldman doubled over, gasping.

"I'll decide what's too much or too little," he said. "Now talk."

"She . . . she was living on Gloucester when she won the lottery. Joy and I used to visit them sometimes, or she and Ali would come over to our place for dinner. . . ." He glanced at Earl, the fright plain in his eyes. In the vague lighting they had a glazed look to them.

"You're doing good so far," Earl said. "So where's she living now? The paper said something about her fixing up her old man's place, but it didn't say where. Did she ever talk to you about it?"

"It's in Lanark. Her . . . her dad used to own a place just outside of Lanark."

Earl nodded. "I thought it was around that area, though I would've put it further south. You got some details now on how to get there?"

"I don't know the exact address—it's on a dirt road—but I can . . . I could draw a map or something."

Earl gave Howie a wave. Howie dug a ballpoint pen out of his pocket. Looking around for something to write on, he spotted a cigarette package which he tore open, exposing the white inside.

"How's this?"

"It's good," Earl said and handed them to Goldman. "Draw, Bob. You can use the hood of the car."

Hands shaking, Goldman drew out a map of the way to Frankie's place, praying that he was remembering it properly. He and Joy had only been out there once and that was in April, before the place was finished.

"Okay," Earl said as he studied the map. "You did good." He took out his own gun and motioned Goldman away from the car. "On your knees, Bob."

"Please . . ."

"See, we've got a problem now," Earl said conversationally. "You've made us and if you'd spill your guts so quickly to us, what's to stop you from doing the same to the man?"

"No," Goldman said earnestly. "I won't tell the police or anyone. I swear! I won't tell a soul. Please. For God's sake, I'll do whatever you want, just don't . . . hurt . . ."

His voice trailed off as Earl stepped in close, holding the barrel of his gun up to Goldman's mouth.

"Suck on this," Earl said.

"Wh-what . . . ?"

"I said, suck on it."

Tremors ran up and down Goldman as he leaned forward and placed his mouth around the cold metal. Earl put his free hand on the top of Goldman's head. Grabbing a handful of the short hair, he rammed the gun deeper into Goldman's mouth. From where Howie stood, he could see the wild light in Earl's eyes as he pulled the trigger.

The sound of the shot was somewhat muffled, Goldman's head serving as a natural baffle. The bullet took out most of the back of the head when it exited. Extracting the weapon, Earl pushed the body away from where it sprawled in the dirt.

"Bye-bye, Bob," he said.

"Shit," Howie muttered.

Earl turned to him. "You got a problem?"

Howie regarded him for a long moment, then slowly shook his head. "What're we going to do with him?"

"Nothing."

"Yeah, but . . ."

"Look, he had us made. We're not talking nickels and dimes here, Howie, m'man. We're talking about a major slice of two hundred grand. We're talking about what that money's going to buy us in Colombia—you see where I'm heading? Against all that, this guy ain't worth shit. What's the matter with you anyway? Were you queer for him?"

Howie shook his head.

"C'mon. Let's get out of here."

Howie nodded and got into the passenger's side. "What about your ex?" he asked as Earl started up the car.

"What about her?"

"You really think she's just going to hand over the money?"

"She's got a kid," Earl said. "We're going to take the kid, then if she don't pay, the kid goes."

"But it's your kid, too."

Earl shook his head wearily. "Christ, Howie. I haven't seen the little squirt for ten years. What's she to me but a baby version of her old lady, huh? I didn't see her coming to stay with her daddy when Frankie walked out on me."

"Well, when you put it like that," Howie said.

"Yeah," Earl said. "I put it like that. Now keep your eyes open for a new set of wheels. I figure these've got a little hot by now."

"Are we going out tonight?" Howie asked. "After your ex?"

Earl shook his head. "I was thinking more along the lines of a nice Sunday drive. We could pull into her place just about the time the sun's going down so we don't get lost driving in."

"Makes sense."

Earl grinned, eyes on the road. "That's what I like about you, Howie. You know how to push, but you're not stupid, so you know when to settle back and let things slide, too."

Howie didn't bother replying. He didn't have to. Earl was talking more to himself, thinking aloud. Howie settled back in the seat, trying to keep the memory of the look on Earl's face when he pulled the trigger out of Goldman's head. Howie didn't ever want to get on Earl's wrong side, he decided. It just didn't pay.

11

"Mom?" Ali called as she came down the stairs. "Have you seen my Walkman? I was sure I'd left it on my bed this morning, but . . ."

Her voice trailed off as she reached the kitchen and found Frankie on the phone, looking serious. Ali sat down at the kitchen table and tried to remember how long ago she'd heard the phone ring. Whoever it was on the other end of the line, they weren't exactly calling up with good news. At least not from the look on her mother's face.

"Who was that?" she asked when Frankie finally hung up.

"That was Joy. She . . . oh, Ali! Bob was killed last night."

"What?"

"He was shot," Frankie said, still trying to come to grips with the news herself. "The police found his body behind a warehouse last night and got his name from his wallet, but Joy still had to . . . she still had to identify the body. . . ."

"Oh, Mom. That's horrible."

Frankie nodded dully. Had someone asked her, she would not have numbered the Goldmans among her closest friends. She saw them more for old times' sake, for the support that Bob had given her through the hard times in Toronto. But even though they didn't have a great deal in common anymore, she still felt very close to Joy in the wake of this terrible news. The poor woman was five months into her first pregnancy and had lost her parents over the winter. . . .

"I told her I'd go stay with her," Frankie said. "At least until Bob's parents fly in from Calgary. They're due in on a nine o'clock flight."

"I don't have to go, do I?" The last thing Ali wanted was to be a part of this kind of bummer.

"I don't think you should stay here by yourself."

"Aw, c'mon, Mom. I'm not a kid anymore."

Frankie shook her head. "It'd be different if we still lived in town, but out here . . ."

"I'm probably safer out here than I'd be in town."

"Well . . ."

"Besides, I could always go up to Tony's. Maybe he'd let me watch a movie or something till you get back."

Frankie looked at the stove clock. Five past two. She'd promised Joy that she'd be in town by three-thirty at the latest and she still had to change.

"Mom?"

"Okay," Frankie said. "But phone him now while I go change."

Ali nodded. "I'll ask him if I can go up later in the afternoon, because I've still got some studying and stuff to do."

"Fine," Frankie said, already on her way down the hall.

By the time Frankie was back downstairs, Ali was waiting for her by the front door, purse and car keys extended.

"Tony says it's okay," she said. "I'm going up around dinnertime."

"Don't make a pest of yourself," Frankie said as she took her purse and keys from Ali.

"Mom!"

Frankie blinked, then looked at her daughter. "I'm sorry, Ali. I keep forgetting how big you're getting. Look, I'll be back as quick as I can, all right? But things might drag on, so don't wait up for me."

"What time should I come home for?"

"I forgot—you'll be at Tony's. What time does he go to bed, do you know?"

Ali shook her head.

"Well, if it's all right with him, wait for me there," Frankie said, not wanting to think of Ali walking that dark road by herself at night. "Okay?"

"Sure. Don't worry about me. I can always snooze on his couch if I get tired."

Frankie nodded. Thank God she'd met Tony last night. She'd been feeling a little nervous about Ali's friendship with him at first, but she'd gotten a good feeling from him last night. Now she felt that she could trust him, so there was that much less to worry about. She pulled Ali close for a hug.

"Be good," she said.

"I will. Don't get into an accident trying to get there too quickly."

A brief smile touched Frankie's lips. "I won't, Mother."

"You'd better go," Ali said, "or you'll be late."

Frankie nodded and hurried to the car.

An hour of studying her biology was about all that Ali could take. It was one of her favorite subjects, but some days simply weren't meant for studying. She was tired of trying to decipher the handwriting in her notebook, the textbook was written in a style that was about as interesting as having the flu, the house was too quiet, and she just felt too cooped up.

It was time to go outside and see photosynthesis at work, first hand. Time to look at some insects, instead of photographs of microscopic spores. Time to collect leaf samples, bark samples—in short, it was time for some fieldwork.

The first thing she did was turn the earth in the vegetable plot that she and her mother had marked out earlier in the day. Tony had given her all kinds of seeds and she was excited about having her very first garden. She saved the sod she'd dug up to put in around the front of the house where it was needed, but by the time she was finished digging in the garden, she was too hot and sweaty to do anything with them. Tomorrow would be soon enough, she hoped. What she wanted now was a shower.

Once inside, she hurried upstairs to get undressed. She pulled off her T-shirt, standing in front of the window, and looked out, thinking how nice it was to be able to change in front of an open window and not have to worry about anyone staring in at you.

She tossed her T-shirt into a corner of her room and started to take off her shorts when she paused, thinking she saw something move in the trees beyond their backyard. She backed away quickly and put her T-shirt on again. Maybe it's the stag, she thought and brought her binoculars to the window. But when she had them focused and had brought the object of her interest up close, she saw that it wasn't the stag. It looked like a person. Ali frowned as she studied what she could see of the figure in the glasses, remembering the other morning when she'd thought she'd seen someone spying on the house.

It didn't look like an adult, she decided, but it was hard to tell if it was even a boy or girl with that floppy hat on. The long hair didn't tell her anything. Then she saw what the figure was fooling around with. It was her Walkman.

The nerve of that kid! First stealing her Walkman, and then sitting out there, practically in her backyard, mucking around with it. Tossing the binoculars onto her bed, Ali raced downstairs and out the front door.

She circled around to the back by way of the road that went up to Tony's, keeping to the ditch and using what cover she could. Here's where all those late night Westerns came in handy, she thought. She was Ali Wayne, sneaking up on the outlaws. Clint Treasure, closing in on her bounty.

Moving as quietly as she could, she crept nearer. When she finally spotted her target, she realized that she could probably have driven a trailbike in and barely been noticed. The girl—thank God she wasn't some muscle-bound farm boy—had the earphones on and was listening to the tape that Ali had left in the machine the last time she was playing it. From the expression on the girl's face, Ali couldn't tell if she liked the *Flashdance* tape or not. She looked like she'd never heard that kind of music before in her life.

Living out here, she probably never had, Ali thought cattily as she moved in closer still, taking care to keep out of the girl's line of vision.

Ali was just a few feet behind the girl when either the tape ended or some sixth sense made the girl turn around. Before she could take off with the Walkman, Ali ran forward and jumped at her. She bore the girl to the ground, straddling her. The body under her was hard with muscles and moved quick as a cat. A hand leaped up to rake Ali's face with its long nails, then paused, inches from her eyes. The two girls stared at each other—Ali trying to hide her fear, the other girl wary as a wild animal.

Slowly Ali got up from her and backed a step away. "Th-that's mine," she said, pointing to the Walkman. "You stole it from me." She hoped that her trembling wasn't too noticeable.

"I didn't steal it," the girl said. She straightened her hat as she spoke. The earphones which she'd been wearing upside down, where they'd hung like a loose chin-guard, had fallen to her lap. "I found it."

"You found it in my room!" Ali cried, her anger getting the better of her fear again.

The girl shrugged. "I just borrowed it. I was going to bring it back."

"Who are you anyway?" Ali demanded. "You've been spying on us, and now you've stolen something. I should just call the cops."

The girl handed the Walkman back to Ali. "My name's Meggan," she said. "Mally Meggan. And I wasn't spying on you—I was just watching your house."

"That's the same as spying."

Mally shrugged. "I've watched that house since the dark man first built it."

"The dark man? Who's that? My grandfather?"

"I don't know his name. He was just a dark man."

"He was a black man?"

Mally shook her head. "He was black in here," she said, touching her heart with a small hand. "He's the one who unraveled the music and nothing's been the same since. People have moved away and nobody new comes. It was all his doing."

"Is that you playing the music?" Ali asked. "The piping I hear at night sometimes?" She sat down, fiddling with the Walkman in her hand.

"No. That's Tommy. I'm not any part of that." She grinned suddenly. "But I *am* apart from it all."

Ali shook her head, not getting the joke. None of this was making sense. "Do you live around here?" she tried again.

"Back there," Mally said with a wave of her hand. The motion was wide, taking in a great deal of land.

"With Tommy?"

"No. He lives with the others. I live by myself."

"But *where* do you live?" Ali asked.

"In the forest."

"By yourself?"

Mally nodded.

"I guess you've got a cabin or something."

"No. *In* the forest. I'm a secret, you see."

Ali shook her head and sighed. This was getting much too weird for her. "If you're a secret," she said, "how come you've shown yourself to me?"

"But I didn't—you caught me."

"But you're telling me all these things. . . ."

"Listen," Mally said. "You hear the music, don't you?"

"Yes. Well, I've heard it once or twice."

"And the stag came to you, didn't he?"

Ali nodded.

"The music wakes something inside those who hear it. In you, it woke a light. In some, it wakes something not so fine."

"Like your dark man?"

"Exactly."

"But . . ."

Mally stood up abruptly, a silverquick movement that startled Ali. "The stag is one of the world's mysteries," Mally said. "I'm just a secret. The way your name is just a part of mine. So when we met each other, we already knew each other—in part. Isn't that true?"

Ali shook her head. "I don't quite follow that," she began, but Mally cut her off.

"Not now, perhaps," she said. "But you will. Or you might. It all depends."

"On what?"

"On who you learn to be."

Before Ali could ask her what she meant, Mally doffed her hat and gave a little bow. Ali stared at the two small horns that curled up from the tangle of her hair.

"Y-you . . . have . . ."

"Many things," Mally said, "but no longer a machine that mimicks Tommy's pipes. Good-bye, Ali."

She began to back away, a smile touching her fox-thin features.

"No!" Ali cried. "Wait a sec . . ."

Her voice trailed off as the wild girl turned and bolted into the forest. Ali watched her go, stunned at her speed, at her quick feline grace. She seemed to flow between the trees, like the stag, or more like a cat, and in moments was gone.

Ali looked down at the Walkman in her hands, then away to where Mally had disappeared. I'm going crazy, she thought. This didn't happen. I didn't meet some girl with horns, her clothes all tattery and covered with burrs, her hair a thicket, her eyes . . . She got shakily to her feet, half-determined to follow after the wild girl, then slowly turned and made her way home.

When she was inside, she laid her Walkman down on the kitchen table and sat down in a hardback chair, feeling completely drained. This was the kind of thing that didn't happen in real life, she tried to tell herself. Only in stories. Kids ran across magical beings in Alan Garner books, or something written by Caitlin Midhir, not in the here and now.

But . . . She sighed, trying to put it in a more rational perspective. Except for the horns, it had just been a strange encounter, hadn't it? An odd meeting, that was all. Except for the horns. Maybe they were fake. Maybe Mally had just pretended they were real to mess around with her head. Except the wild girl had moved so fast. It was like nothing she had ever seen before. It was—

The phone jangled suddenly and Ali just about leapt off her seat. With a trembling hand, she snagged the receiver and spoke into it.

"H-hello?"

"Hey, Ali. I thought you were coming up for dinner."

It was Tony. She glanced at the clock on the stove. Ten past six. Oh God, it was late!

"Jeez, Tony. I, uh, forgot about the time."

"So are you coming, or what?"

"I'm coming."

"Hey, are you okay, kid? You sound a little funny."

"No. I'm fine. I'm just going to take a shower and then I'll be up."

"Okay. But don't take too long. It's going to be dark in an hour and a half and I'll bet your momma doesn't want you walking the road in the dark."

Ali thought about horned girls and stags, about the music that came at dusk if it were going to come at all, and shivered. Never mind her mother, *she* didn't want to be out there in the dark.

"I'll hurry," she said.

12

On Sunday afternoon, Earl and Howie snatched a Toyota in Nepean and left Ottawa by way of the Queensway. The sun was westering and low, shining in their eyes as they followed Highway 7 through Carleton Place to the turnoff at Highway 10 that would take them into Lanark. By the time they reached Lanark, it was going on seven-fifteen and the sun was an orange ball above the horizon.

"It's starting to come back to me," Earl said as they took Highway 1 out of the village.

Howie glanced up from the rough map that they'd gotten from Bob Goldman. "What is?"

"This place we're going to."

"You've been here before?"

"Fuck, no." Earl shot him a quick glance and grinned. "But Frankie talked about it a few times, about how weird her old man was and this place he lived in. You had to get her pretty high first. I just never connected it until Bobby-boy spilled his guts."

"So he wasn't shitting us?"

Earl grinned. "The only shitting he was doing was the load he dropped in his pants. No, this feels right, Howie, m'man."

"The turn's coming up," Howie said as they passed a sign for Brightside.

Earl grunted an acknowledgement as the turn approached.

"How do you think it's gonna go?" Howie asked.

"Sweet and easy. Frankie's always been good at running away from problems, but when it comes to facing up to something, she just folds."

"What about the kid?"

"The kid's gonna do what she's told or she's shit out of luck. Christ, they call this a road?"

"Sunday drive," Howie said.

"Guess they got some real influential taxpayers living out this way."

Howie laughed. They passed a turnoff to the right. "Better slow down," he said. "We've got another mile or so and then we're there."

Earl slowed the car down a few moments later when a house came into view.

"That's gotta be it," Howie said.

Earl nodded, taking in the building debris that littered the front yard. He cruised on by until a curve in the road took them out of sight of the house and then pulled over to the side.

"What time you got?" he asked.

"Seven-thirty."

"Okay."

Earl turned the car in the narrow road, happy now that they'd picked something as small as the Toyota. He'd wanted a two-door so that the kid'd be easier to keep an eye on. They drove back toward the house and took the first left after it, pulling over to the side of the road again. Stands of cedar and pine screened them from the house.

"Well, Howie, m'man," he said as he killed the engine. "Looks like it's time to go."

Howie nodded. They got out of the car together and walked back down the road.

Earl slapped at his neck. "Fucking mosquitos."

Howie waved them from his own face. He watched Earl play with the butt of his gun that was sticking out of the top of his belt. He hoped things were going to go a little cleaner than they had last night.

Ali saw the Toyota go slowly by the house as she was locking the front door and didn't think twice about it. By the time it returned, she was in the kitchen, looking for a bag to carry her Tom Brown Jr. field guides in as she went up to Tony's place. She found a plastic shopping bag from the Perth IGA, dumped the books into it and hurried out the back door.

She was already running late, but the moment she stepped outside, she paused, testing the air for sound, studying the edge of the woods. There could be anything out there, from Mally with her horns to who knew what? The sun was almost down behind the trees. Shadows were growing long.

Get a move on, she told herself. Bad enough she was late. She didn't want to arrive at Tony's all out of breath from obviously having run the whole way. He'd think she was more of a kid than he probably already did—scared of the dark, or of meeting boogiemen in the woods. Boogiewomen? Do you know how to boogie, Mally?

She shook her head, angry at herself, and started across the lawn, pausing again when she heard car doors slam on the road leading up to Tony's place. She moved quickly across the backyard, then through the weeds in the field between their property and the road, raising a cloud of mosquitos that whined around her face. There, a little ways down the road, was the car. A Toyota. And she was just in time to see a couple of men down at the corner where Tony's road met the dirt one that ran by her own house.

This is weird, she thought. Are they going to our place? But that couldn't be—or at least it didn't make any sense. Why would they park where they had?

A pinprick of worry started up her spine as she headed back toward the house, staying hidden in the trees that bordered Tony's road. The two men were coming up their driveway, but what made her stop again, what made new shivers of fear go catpawing up her spine, was not the men, but the eerie sound of distant piping that floated from the forest northwest of where she was hiding.

That's Tommy, she thought, remembering what the wild girl had told her. Tommy playing reedpipes. Whoever Tommy was . . .

"Here's one for you," Earl said as the house came into view.

"What's that?"

"The one thing we didn't think of—what if nobody's home?"

Howie glanced at him, then at the house. No car, he noted first off. Living out in the sticks like this, everybody'd have a car.

"So what do we do?" he asked.

"Check it out. Wait around a bit."

But not too long, Howie hoped, because that was just asking for trouble. Only try telling Earl that. Howie sighed. He wished they were back in T.O. right now, or even in New York, being wined and dined by Broadway Joe. The showgirl that Joe had provided Howie with had been everything Tandy Hots with her act in the strip club had promised to be. Young. Built. There just to please him. The way she'd wrapped her legs around his—

A sudden uneasiness touched him, killing the memory. He cocked his head, listening.

"You hear that, Earl?" he asked softly.

Earl nodded and turned toward him, his features no longer clearly defined as the night crept in around them. "Yeah," he said. "Some kinda . . . I don't know . . ."

"Music."

"Yeah. But it's not just that. It's like we've been made, you know?"

Howie looked nervously around. "We're being watched?"

Earl nodded. He faced the cedars where Ali was crouched, hugging her knees to keep from trembling.

"I don't know who the fuck you are," Earl said, "but I know you're in there. If you've got any smarts, you're gonna step out here where we can get a nice long look at you, because you don't want to know what'll happen to you if I gotta go in there to get you."

Ali stumbled out onto the lawn and stared at the strangers.

"Well, well, well," Earl said. "Look what we got here. How's your old lady, kid? Better yet, *where's* your old lady?"

"Wh-who are you?"

Earl gave Howie a pained look that was mostly lost in the twilight and shook his head. "Fucking kid doesn't even recognize her own old man," he said. "Doesn't that take the cake?"

Howie brushed bugs away from his neck. "Maybe she's waiting to see what kind of present you brought her."

Earl chuckled.

"N-no . . ." she mumbled.

"Oh, yeah," Earl said. "No matter what that whore of a mother's told you about me, you're still stuck with me as your old man. Now you see, I figure it's about time I took custody of—"

"No!" Ali cried, swinging her bag at him. Her shrill voice startled the men. The books struck Earl's chest, knocking him off balance. Before he could recover, or Howie could react, Ali had turned and bolted back the way she'd come.

She ran to the rhythm of the distant music that was calling to her, speeding across the lawn, sleek and fast like a stag, through the field, then up the road to Tony's place.

Behind, Earl reached for his gun. Howie took a step toward him.

"What the fuck are you doing?" Earl demanded. "Get after her!"

Howie blinked, then nodded and took off across the lawn, following the sound of the girl's footsteps. An ugly smile cut Earl's face as he set after them.

Little bitch was going to pay for that. Where'd she think she was coming off anyway, hitting her old man?

Valenti sat up and checked his watch as the tape of piping finished in his cassette machine. It was getting late. About time he could hear the real thing come drifting from the woods behind his place. About time for Ali to be here as well. Where was she?

He got up and turned off the stereo, then went to the front door and stood out on the steps. There'd been something funny about her voice when he'd called earlier, something he couldn't quite place. He looked across the darkening fields. Like someone suffering mild shock, he thought, recalling the quality of it now. What could have happened?

He turned back into the house, thought of calling her again, then decided he'd go down the road to meet her instead. And just to satisfy the uneasiness he felt, just for insurance's sake—"You can never be too careful, Tony," Mario had been fond of telling him—he crossed over to his stereo cabinet and opened the cupboard on the bottom left.

It needed the key that was always in the pocket of whatever he was wearing to get into it. And then you had to know the right board to push on the side of the cupboard that unlocked the hidden compartment under its floor.

He pulled the false floor away to reveal a cavity that went down into the space between the ground floor and the roof of the basement below. There were rifles in there, a shotgun, a UZI machine gun, some handguns, boxes of cartridges, spare magazines for the automatics and the UZI, and a large fireproof box that held various IDs and travelling money in case he ever needed it. Ten thousand dollars in used American bills. Another couple of grand in Canadian currency.

He looked at the weapons, thought for a moment, then extracted a small .32 automatic. He checked its load, then snapped the magazine back into its grip and slipped the weapon into the pocket of a windbreaker. Putting the false floor back in place, he locked the cupboard once more, then put on the jacket. He picked up his cane by the door and went out into the night, moving as quickly as his bad leg could take him.

When he first heard the piping start up he was already out of his own yard and on the road. The music didn't register straight off. He'd been listening to Ali's tape so often during the day that the piping had almost become a part of his thoughts. But now as he paused to listen, waving bugs from around his head, he heard someone come running up the road. He switched the cane to his left hand, thrust his right into the pocket with his .32. It wasn't just one someone, he realized as he took the automatic off safety.

When Earl hit the road, he turned right instead of following Howie and his daughter. He sprinted for the Toyota, snapped the door open and got in. He touched the wires together that they'd pulled out earlier when they'd stolen the vehicle and the car coughed into life.

Right, he thought. He put the car into gear, hit the lights, then tromped on the gas. The peppy little car roared forward, headlights cutting the night like a dragon's gaze. Earl switched the beams to high and speed-shifted into second gear as the car picked up enough speed.

Ali just about died when the headlights came on behind her and picked out the man coming toward her from the direction of Tony's house. The sound of the car's engine drowned the piping, but she could still hear it inside. She was still the stag, fleeing the hounds. She almost bolted into the bush, then realized who it had to be on the road in front of her.

"Tony!" she cried.

The man pulled his hand from his pocket and the headlights sparked on the metal in his hand. He leveled the weapon in her direction.

Howie heard the car start up and nodded to himself. Good thinking, Earl. The kid was going to outdistance them, but not if she stuck to the road. Then the headlights lit up the scene in front of him. Beyond the girl, he saw a man who seemed to appear out of nowhere. Howie scrambled for his own weapon as the stranger leveled his gun, then realized that Earl was burning up the road behind him.

He lunged for the side of the road just as the car reached where he'd been running. There came a sudden crash, as though another car had plowed into the side of the Toyota. Howie shot a glance in its direction and his eyes went wide with fear.

Move, Howie, Earl thought, or you're dead meat. Maybe he'd just clip the kid. She wouldn't be running anywhere so fast then. And if he miscalculated, well, what the fuck. He didn't need to deliver her in one piece. He just needed her for as long as it took Frankie to cough up the money. And if Frankie didn't know the kid was dead, she was still going to pay up. After that, well, maybe it wouldn't be such a bad idea to waste the both of them anyway, just so's not to leave any loose ends.

Howie jumped to one side and then Earl realized that there was someone else on the road with his daughter. He had long enough to see the weapon in the man's hand, long enough to register the man's features—a dead man's face—then something hit the side of the car and he was fighting the wheel to keep the vehicle on the road while slamming on the brakes.

The engine stalled as he brought the Toyota to an abrupt halt. He turned to see what had hit him, not really registering the shock of the impact, still stunned from seeing a man that he knew was dead on the road ahead of him. Turning, he found himself face to face with an enormous buck deer.

"Jesusfuck," he mumbled and reached for his gun.

The stag lowered its head, backed up, and hit the car again. Earl's gun clattered to the floor. The sidewindow cracked into a spiderweb design. Earl shook his head and put up his hands to protect himself as the deer backed up again.

Valenti had his gun ready, finger squeezing the trigger, when the stag burst out of the forest to hit the Toyota side-on. He eased off the pressure on the trigger as the car slowed to a stop, stalled. The engine went dead. The headlights dimmed but stayed on.

"Ali," he ordered, taking a few steps closer to her. "Get up to my place."

"B-but . . ."

"C'mon, sweetheart. Don't argue."

Ali nodded and took a few steps closer to him. When she reached him, Valenti put an arm around her shoulder and gave her a quick hug, his cane bumping against the side of her leg.

"Go on," he said, never taking his gaze from the car and what was happening around it.

"He . . . he said that he . . . that he's my dad. . . ."

Valenti shot her a quick glance. His gaze snapped back to the car as the stag hit the vehicle again.

"We'll talk about that later," he said. "Now go."

He left her side and walked slowly toward the car as the stag backed up once more. In the silence that lay heavy around them, he heard the distant music return. He wasn't sure what was going on, who the men really were, what they wanted with Ali, but it seemed fitting, *right* somehow, that the stag would show up again to help her. He couldn't have said why. The answer to that was in the music.

He lifted his gun as the man who'd been on the road before the car arrived suddenly stood up from behind the vehicle, leveling his own weapon at the stag. Valenti's finger began to squeeze the trigger of his automatic, but he was too late to stop the man from firing almost pointblank at the beast. He squeezed the trigger anyway.

Howie didn't know if a handgun could stop a monster-sized buck like this, but that wasn't going to stop him from trying. He got off two shots—no way he missed—but the deer just looked at him. There was something in its eyes. . . . And then Howie heard the music again. It was a discordant sound, unpleasant. Like fingernails on a blackboard.

Drop, you fucker, he willed, but the deer merely continued to stare at him.

Howie shivered. He was about to fire a third time when he felt a shock go through his right arm. The whole arm went numb and his gun spilled from suddenly limp fingers. It landed with a thump on the road. Pain exploded in his arm. For a long moment he was stunned by it. He reached up to clamp his left hand to the arm and winced at the pain. Blood trickled between his fingers.

"I . . . I've been shot," he said to no one in particular and leaned weakly against the car.

The entire vehicle shook as the stag hit it for a third time. The impact made Howie grip his arm harder and he howled as a sudden new pain shot down his arm. He looked down the road to see the man there getting closer, using a cane and walking with a pronounced limp. Chewing at his lip, Howie let go of his wound and scrabbled with bloody fingers at the side of the car, looking for the doorhandle. He sobbed with relief when he found it, hit the knob, and tugged the door open. He almost fell into the car in his hurry to get in.

"Let's go," he said to Earl. "Christ, man, let's *go!*"

But Earl wasn't listening. The deer had backed up again, but he wasn't watching it, either. His gaze was locked on the man approaching the car.

"You're dead," he said softly.

When the man Valenti had shot got into the car, the interior light went on and Valenti recognized the man behind the wheel. At the same time he realized that the man must have made him. His name was Shaw. . . . Ernie Shaw? A small-time punk that they'd used once because he'd had a connection in Miami that came in very handy for a deal the family was working on at the time.

Valenti had been the family's spokesman for that deal, working with this Shaw. There was no way Shaw hadn't made him now, and there was no way Shaw wasn't going to spill his guts to the first member of the *fratellanza* he could get a hold of.

As he lifted his gun Valenti was surprised at the feeling that touched him. It wasn't as though this punk didn't have it coming for a lot of other reasons. It wasn't as if Valenti had never killed a man before. But there was a feeling of wrongness about what he was doing now—just as earlier he'd sensed a rightness about the arrival of the stag. The music heightened that feeling. But if he didn't do something right now, he might as well go back to New York and hand himself over to the new Don, because they sure as fuck were going to be coming for him if he didn't.

"Get the wires," Earl hissed.

"Christ, man. I've been—"

"Get them."

Gritting his teeth, Howie bent over and fumbled with the wires. When he had them connected, Earl turned the engine over. Once, twice. He bent low as Valenti fired, the bullet shattering the windshield and whining above his head. The third time he tried the engine, it caught. Foot on the clutch, he rammed the gear shift into first, eased the clutch out again, then floored the gas pedal.

As the Toyota leapt forward Valenti dodged out of the way. Earl checked the rearview, but it was too dark to see where Valenti had gone. Now if they could just get away from that fucking psycho deer . . .

He hit the brakes and pulled hard on the wheel, slewing the car into a 180-degree turn, tires spitting dirt into the underbrush on either side of the road. The headbeams caught Valenti struggling to his feet. Gotcha, Earl thought as he tromped on the gas again.

But the stag stepped out of the woods to stand almost on top of Valenti so Earl had to swerve by him. He heard the pop of Valenti's gun, thought about staying to play this out, but the odds were all wrong. There was that deer, for one thing; the fact that it was Tony Valenti who was here, for another. He'd let the mob boys handle Valenti. For a price, he'd lead them right to him. And then he'd finish his own business with little too-big-for-her-britches Alice Treasure.

"I . . . I need a doc," Howie said from the seat beside him.

Earl shot him a glance. For a moment he felt like opening the passenger's door and just booting Howie out, but what the fuck. He'd done his best. It wasn't Howie's fault he was such a dipstick.

"Just hang in there," he said. "First we need new wheels."

"O-okay, Earl."

"Hang tough, Howie, m'man. Things just look bad. But the truth is, they're turning sweeter all the time."

He grinned, concentrating on the road. When he reached Highway 1, he turned left, heading for the join-up with 511 that would take them into Calabogie. A couple of guys he knew had a cottage out that way who owed him a favor or two. This being the weekend, he figured they'd be up. If they weren't . . . Well, he didn't think they'd complain about him using the place. Not if they still wanted to own their balls after they were done talking to him.

Valenti rose slowly from the dirt and watched the taillights disappear. He didn't know what had made Shaw swerve at the last moment, but he wasn't complaining. He returned his automatic to his pocket and picked up his cane.

Time to go, he thought as he stood up and brushed the dirt off his jeans. He wondered how long he had. Till Shaw reached a phone? Valenti knew he'd winged Shaw's partner. Maybe they'd see to the man's shoulder first. So what did he have—an hour tops? Then he thought of Ali.

He looked up the road to his place, realizing that the music had died away again. That made him think about the stag, which in turn brought him back to his own predicament. He had to be gone—by yesterday—but he couldn't just leave Ali alone. Take her with him? No way.

Still trying to decide what he should do, he limped up the road to the place he'd called home for the past year and a half. He was sure going to miss it.

13

Ali was sitting on a corner of the couch nearest the fireplace when Valenti came in. She was wearing jeans and a white cotton-knit sweater and holding a plastic bag between her legs that she was staring at. When he stepped inside, she looked up with a nervous jerk, then settled her gaze on the floor by her feet once more.

"You okay?" Valenti asked.

She shrugged. "I guess."

"You wanna talk about it?"

She nodded, shooting him a quick glance.

Valenti smiled. "Okay. You just take it easy while I make us some cocoa—how's that sound?"

"That'd be fine. Do you . . . do you want some help?"

That's the girl, Valenti thought. "You bet," he said aloud. "I can never get the cocoa to dissolve properly and if there's anything I hate, it's lumps of cocoa floating up and touching my lips when I'm taking a sip—you know what I mean?"

A small smile tugged at the corners of her mouth.

"C'mon," he said.

He waited while Ali laid her bag of books aside and went into the kitchen, then quickly switched his .32 from the jacket he was wearing to the pocket of a sportsjacket which he then put on.

"The cocoa's in the cupboard on the right there—second shelf up," he said as he came into the kitchen. "Can you reach it?"

"I think so."

"Good. I'll get the milk."

There was a nip in the air that was due as much to what they'd just gone through, Valenti thought, as to the actual temperature, so he built a small fire in the hearth and they sat in front of it, sipping their cocoa and talking. Ali told him all about her afternoon, from why her mother'd gone into town to her confrontation with the wild girl who called herself Mally Meggan.

"She had *horns?*" Valenti interrupted when Ali was describing Mally. "You mean like real horns?" He was remembering the girl who'd dropped out of a tree on him a few nights ago. She hadn't had horns that he could see, but then she'd been wearing a hat. A floppy brimmed hat like Ali's wild girl had.

Ali nodded. "Just small ones—like the kind you see on antelope."

"And she lives in the bush?"

"That's what she said. In the forest itself—not in a cabin or a house or anything. And she told me that the music we hear is played by some guy named Tommy. . . ."

She went on to describe the rest of their conversation, regaining some of her old spirit as she did. It wasn't until she started to tell him about leaving her house and hearing the car doors slam that she began to get nervous once more, her voice lowering. She wouldn't meet Valenti's gaze as she told him about the men catching her spying on them, what one of them had said about his being her father, and then the chase.

"And then . . . Well, you know the rest."

She looked at him finally and Valenti nodded. The stag hitting Shaw's car, Valenti shooting Shaw's partner, the two men escaping . . .

"Do you think he's really my father?" Ali asked.

"You don't like that idea much, do you?"

Ali shook her head.

"Let me tell you something, Ali," he said. "It doesn't matter who your parents were, it's what you make of yourself—understand? You want something bad enough—you want to *be* something bad enough—nothing's going to stop you but you. You can pick stuff up—like habits, or a certain way of saying things—by living with people, but just because your old man's a piece of shit, that doesn't mean that you are."

"Yeah, but why would my mom . . . you know . . . why would she want to marry a guy like that?"

Valenti shrugged. "I don't know. I'm betting he wasn't like that when they first met. People change—not always for the better. When that happens in a relationship, sometimes the only thing you can do is get out. Sounds to me, from things you've told me—and having met your momma, who's some kind of lady—that that's what she did. She's nobody's fool."

"You know him, don't you?" Ali asked. "That guy who said he was my father."

"What makes you say that?"

"Just the way you're talking."

"Yeah," Valenti said. "I know him. He's a punk. A small-time, smart-ass punk. But that doesn't make him any less dangerous."

"If he is my father, why would he wait so long to come after me?"

"Well, I've been thinking about that," Valenti said, "and I figure he heard about your momma winning that lottery. He probably figures there's some bucks to be made—wants his own cut of the action."

Ali nodded. "What happened after I left? I thought I heard some shooting . . ."

Valenti studied her for a moment. She was holding up pretty well. Maybe right now she wasn't exactly the same happy-go-lucky kid that bounced around his place and told him jokes and stuff, but she was holding her own. Spunky kid like her, you wouldn't be able to keep her down too long. He decided to level with her, while he could. Might as well, seeing how after tonight he probably wouldn't be seeing her again.

"They threw around some lead—at me and the stag," he said. "I clipped one of them, but they got away before I could do any real damage."

Ali regarded him a little wide-eyed. "You were . . . were you trying to kill them?"

"Guns aren't toys, Ali, and what happened tonight wasn't a game. If you pull a piece, you'd better be ready to use it. And if you use it, you'd damn well better kill whatever you're shooting at, or it'll up and get you." The rules of the business, courtesy of Mario Papale, Valenti thought mirthlessly.

"Yeah, but . . ."

"Remember I told you I was a soldier?"

Ali nodded.

"Well, that army I was in, they weren't too happy with me when I left. They put a contract out on me that fell through—but only because I disappeared. Now this Ernie Shaw, he used to—"

"Oh, jeez."

"What is it?"

"That was my father's name," Ali said. "But not Ernie. It was Earl."

"Earl," Valenti repeated. Yeah. That fit.

"So he *is* my father."

Valenti nodded. "Anyway. This guy recognized me and he's going to be passing the information about where I am over to the people I used to work for, see? And that means they're going to be gunning for me again."

"Tony, what kind of army were you in?"

For all that he'd told her, for all that at this point it didn't matter anymore, his own vow of *omertà*—the law of silence—wouldn't let him come right out and say it.

"Look, it doesn't matter," he said. "It was a family business—that's all. The thing is, they'll be coming for me. That's why I was shooting at Shaw. Because now that he got away, I've got to hit the road, too."

"But . . ."

"I can't stay, Ali. I'm a dead man if I stay."

She regarded him for a long moment. "You know what this sounds like, don't you?" she asked.

"Like what?"

"The makings of a B-movie. All we need now is for Jimmy Cagney to come walking in your front door."

"It's no joke, Ali."

"I know. I'm not smiling. Can you call the police, Tony?"

He shook his head.

"You were a criminal, weren't you?" When he didn't answer, she shrugged. "Okay. It doesn't matter. It's what you are now that's important, right? So you can't run, Tony."

"Are you nuts? If I stay—"

"If you go, where do you go?"

"I'll make out."

She shook her head. "Tony, I may be just a kid, but I know that nobody can live that way—always on the run. Remember what you just told me? If you want something bad enough, nobody can stop you?"

"Yeah, but it'll be me against a lot of guns."

"So get some help."

Valenti couldn't believe what he was hearing. Here he'd been trying to comfort her and she turned things around and was giving him the advice. And maybe she was an innocent, but there was something to what she was saying.

"You sure you're not some forty-year-old midget with a face-lift?" he asked.

"What?"

"You're some kid, you know that?"

Ali looked away, blushing.

"No, I really mean it. There's not many people could go through all that you've been through today and come up smiling."

They were quiet for a long moment, then Ali regarded him seriously.

"Tony," she said. "That stag . . . it was like it was rescuing me."

"I know."

"It's got something to do with the music."

"I think so."

"Tony, what is it?"

Valenti shook his head wearily. "I don't know, Ali. I wish I did, but I just can't figure it."

An hour or so later, Valenti had tucked Ali into the bed in his guest room and was sitting in the living room, staring at the phone. Ali had started out protesting that she wasn't tired, but by the time he'd walked her up to the room, she was yawning so much that she gave in. He sat with her until she fell asleep, then softly left the room.

Downstairs, the first thing he did was get out his weapons. He checked to make sure they were all loaded and in good working order, then stashed them in strategic places around the house. He'd made plans for this kind of thing before. He'd always planned to run if trouble came, but it was best to cover every contingency. He hid the weapons in places he could easily get at, but where people wouldn't be liable to run across them unless they were looking for them. Then he sat down to stare at the phone.

He sat there for a long time, going over the day, from the piping and the stag and li's horned girl, who he might have met himself the other night, to Earl Shaw and the trouble he could bring down on Valenti with just one phone call.

"Fercrissakes," he said softly. "Make the call already."

He lifted the receiver and dialed a memorized number, then waited until the connection was made and the phone rang at the other end of the line, halfway across the world.

"*Pronto!*" a familiar voice said after the sixth ring. "*Chi va là?*" Who's there?

"Hey, Mario. *Come la sei passata?*" How've you been?

There was a moment's pause, then, "My line's clean—are we using names?"

"It's Tony, Mario."

"Yeah, I'm hearing that. You got trouble?"

"I'm making a stand."

"You're one crazy *bastardo*—you know what I'm saying?"

"I got made—but I don't want to run."

"Okay," Mario said. "I know better than to argue with you by now. What do you need?"

"A couple of unconnected men. Bread's no problem, but I got to be able to trust them. And I don't want to see your face over here, *capito?*"

" 'Ey, you're a good friend, Tony, but *I'm* not crazy."

"That's good."

"When do you need 'em?" Mario asked.

"Yesterday."

"So you want some local talent?"

"You got somebody here?" Valenti replied.

"Depends where 'here' is."

Valenti told him, keeping the directions simple.

"I've got a friend in Toronto," Mario said. "He'll be with you by morning. He'll be driving a white Mazda—two door. The other friend's gonna need some papers—so figure late Monday, your time. Say, Tony, you want I should talk to the family, maybe the *consigliere?*"

"Not much he can do," Valenti replied. "Besides, I've figured it was Ricca put the finger on me—him and Joe. I mean, who else?"

"So? A little talk don't hurt."

"Okay," Valenti said. "But you be careful, Mario."

"No problem. *Coraggio,* Tony."

"*Grazie,* Mario."

The connection went dead and Valenti cradled the receiver. He was committed now—too late to run. He stood up and killed the lights when he heard a car in the driveway. Automatic in hand, he eased open a curtain by the front door, then saw it was just Ali's momma. He thrust the .32 back into his pocket and flicked on the porch light before going out to ask Frankie in for a nightcap.

"Oh, I don't think so," Frankie said. "I'm pretty tired and it's . . . it's not been a good day."

Christ, she was some fine-looking woman, Valenti thought. There was really something going on inside her, too. That was something he never would have noticed if he'd still been in New York, working for the family. What she had was a kind of sensibility that reminded him of the artwork and crafts he'd gotten into collecting after he'd moved up here for good. He wished he didn't have to lay this shit on her.

"I think you'd better come in," he said. "You see, your ex-husband went after Ali tonight and I figure he's still in the area, so it wouldn't be such a good idea for you to go home right away."

"Earl . . . ?" Frankie's face blanched. "Ali. Is she . . . ?"

"Ali's doing great. She came through it like a trooper."

Frankie slumped against the side of the car. "Thank God for that. It's my worst fear. Sometimes I wake up in the night, you know, and I . . . I think she's going to be gone. . . ." She shivered, then looked up at Valenti. "He was really *here?* My ex?"

Valenti nodded. " 'Fraid so. He was down by your place and chased Ali up the road. Luckily I was coming down to meet her, so I scared him off, but he might be planning to come back. You could call the police, I suppose, but by the time you convince them that there really *is* a danger, well . . ." He shrugged.

"I suppose you're right. . . ."

Valenti went down and closed the car door, then took Frankie's arm and led her back to the house. Busy night, he thought. It looked like he'd be sleeping on the couch. He just hoped he wasn't leading them into more danger by having them stay over. Still, it was just for one night. In the morning he hoped to convince them to take a little trip for a week or so until this all blew over one way or another. They didn't have to go too far to be safe. Australia should be far enough.

"Where's Ali?" Frankie asked as she looked around the living room.

"She's asleep in the guest room. You can have my room for tonight."

"No. We can't impose like this."

"You're not imposing," Valenti said. "I'm happy to have the chance to do you this favor, Frankie."

She looked at him, her eyes tired, her face showing the strain of her day and now this. But she wasn't giving in, Valenti saw. He knew which of her parents Ali took after, that was for sure. He resisted a sudden urge to take her in his arms. Christ, what was he thinking?

"Have a seat," he said. "Would you like a drink?"

Frankie shook her head. "Maybe some tea?"

"You got it."

For the second time that night he was in his kitchen with a female member of the Treasure family.

"Can I help at all?" Frankie asked after she'd followed him in.

Valenti smiled. "Sure. Tea's in the cupboard on the right there— second shelf up, beside the cocoa."

"Cocoa?"

Hearing a certain tone in her voice, Valenti put the kettle down and went to the fridge for some milk instead. Looked like both Treasures were chocolate junkies.

A half hour and a mug of cocoa later, Valenti showed Frankie to his bedroom and left her there while he went back downstairs. He sat in front of the dying fire, trying to put it all in perspective.

The immediate worry was Shaw, how soon he'd call in, how soon Ricca would send in his *soldati*. But there was still the strangeness to deal with. The wild girl that both he and Ali had seen now. The music. The stag. There was something happening with all that as well. How much trouble it was going to be, Valenti had no way of knowing. He just had a feeling that the real strangeness hadn't even started yet.

After awhile he lay down on the couch, not sleeping, just lying there with his hands behind his head, thinking, waiting now for either Shaw or Ricca's men to show up, or the help that Mario had promised him. He couldn't afford to sleep.

A little later he got up and put Ali's cassette on the stereo, so low that the sound of it wouldn't bother Ali or her momma. The music relaxed him. He lay there thinking of Frankie, wondering how things might have turned out if it had been him instead of Shaw that had gotten together with her all those years ago.

Trouble was, he wouldn't have been any better for her than Shaw had been. Not that he was into hurting women or anything, but both he and Shaw were in the business, and the business tended to get in the way of any kind of a relationship with someone who wasn't in it.

Even when you tried to get out of it. Christ, look at him now—two years retired, and here it was all happening again.

By the time the cassette had ended, he had a bittersweet feeling inside, but he was alert and ready for whatever might come. When the cassette machine clicked off, he made a tour around the outside of the house. Except for the bugs, nothing was stirring, so he went back inside and made himself a capuccino. Studying the books that Ali had brought up, he chose one, the *Guide to Nature Observation and Tracking,* and started to read.

14

The stag ranged far that night. Originally sent from Wold Hill by the spell of Tommy's piping, something in its encounter with Ali and Valenti, Earl Shaw and Howie Peale, caused it to run further afield than ever before. It wandered Lanark County like an autumn wind, through backfields and up into farmyards where dogs woke from dreams of hunting to bark at its passing like a ghost wind; along Highway 1, up through Hopetown and across the Clyde River, looping back to cross Highway 16 at Middleville; through the marshland between Gillies and Ramsbottoms Lakes, crossing the Clyde again to clatter through Lanark village, before completing its sweep back up toward Snake Lake Mountain.

Where it passed sleepers, dreams were suddenly filled with resonances never sensed before, while those who were awake, paused in their conversations for that one moment it took for the stag to go by, resuming them again then, knowing they weren't quite the same, but not knowing why. The stag was unconcerned with either dreamers or those still awake, for it was following its own need through the night, chasing down the moon. There were few that didn't sense its presence in the night, but fewer still actually caught a glimpse of it—the branch-spread of its antlers briefly outlined against the sky, perhaps, or the white flag of its tail. Nothing more.

It wasn't until it was closing in on Wold Hill once more that it heard the sound of the pack, keening in the night air. They were distant, black shapes that were no more than shadows, running on silent pads, tracking it. And if sometimes they looked like hooded monks, like men running upright behind it, sometimes the stag itself seemed to be a man, too, running on cloven hooves, the stag's antlers shrunken to goat's horns, dirt-brown skin gleaming and sweaty in the starlight.

Two figures stood up from where they'd been sitting under the shadow of the gray-blue stone on Wold Hill. They looked southward.

"He's coming back now," Mally said.

Lewis nodded. "The dogs are right on his tail."

"They won't catch him—not this time."

"But they will?" Lewis asked, making a question out of what could as easily have been a statement.

"Not if you don't let them."

"I've talked to Tommy—but I told you he wouldn't listen to me."

Mally nodded. "You'd better go now, Lewis. I'll see you later."

He looked at her, trying to read the expression on that fox-thin face, but the brim of the hat made a deeper shadow of what the night already hid from him.

"See you then," he said and hurried, as much as his old body could, out of the little glen and down to his cabin.

Mally watched him go, then turned to look at the southern end of the clearing. A man came running out from the trees—half-goat, half-man, then more stag than goat, then fully stag. Mally puckered her lips and whistled softly.

"Come now," she said.

The stag paused before soft-stepping its way across the grass to where she could lay her hand on its flank. She stroked its wet coat, murmuring all the while.

"It's not belief that binds you here," she said, "nor disbelief—no matter what all their scholars say. It's just reason—all those straight lines that they lay on the land and in their minds. . . ." The stag nuzzled her shoulder. "You'd better go now—they're close. Too close."

She slapped it on its rump and it sprang toward the stone. The shadows were thick there. It might have disappeared inside the stone, or changed its course at the last moment and dodged around it, but by the time its pursuers bounded into the glen, the stag was gone without leaving a sign. Mally met the hound-shaped shadows, arms akimbo.

"Too late again," she said softly.

The lead shape moved forward and she doffed her hat, reaching inside. When she brought out her hand, it was full of light—tiny sticks of light, the size of small bones or twigs. The lead shape paused, then they all scattered as she flung the light in an arc toward them.

Where the sticks touched their shapes, they hissed and burned, but most came nowhere near their targets as the shapes fled. In moments, the glen was empty again, except for Mally. She stuck her hat back on her head, tapped a pair of fingers against its brim in a salute to the standing stone, then slipped in among the trees on the side of the clearing that was closest to Lewis's cabin.

The Toyota's engine had developed a knocking noise by the time Earl turned onto the dirt road that led to his friend's cottage on the southeast shore of Calabogie Lake. The car rattled along in the ruts, trees scraping its sides for at least half a mile, before the square glow of a lighted window appeared ahead of them. Earl steered the Toyota in beside a Dodge van and a Honda Civic, then cut the engine. Going around to the passenger's side, he opened the door and hauled Howie to his feet.

"Oh, Jesus!" Howie cried.

"Take it easy, man. We're here now."

Supporting the smaller man, Earl helped him to the cottage door. An old Charlie Daniels LP was playing at full blast, so Earl didn't bother knocking. Keeping one hand close to the weapon stuck in his belt, he opened the door, then half-carried Howie inside.

The cottage was almost all one room with a couple of doors leading off on the far side to smaller bedrooms and the can. Sitting on floor pillows and a beat-up couch were two men and three women. They all looked up when the door opened. The cottage was warm with a good-sized fire in the hearth. The smell of marijuana was strong in the air. One of the men reached over to the stereo and took the needle off the record, dragging it across the grooves.

"Who the fuck are you?" he demanded, coming to his feet.

Earl left Howie propped up against the door. "Steve," he said. "How's it hanging?"

The man who was standing peered closer, then a broad grin cut across his features. "Hey, hey, hey! Fercrissakes, Earl. What're you doing up here?"

"Looking for a party—what do you think, Steve?"

Steve Hill nodded in appreciation—there wasn't a better reason to be doing anything. He was a tall thin man, wearing a faded Grateful Dead T-shirt and cut-off jeans. He didn't bother introducing his friends.

The other man looked like a biker—long black hair pulled back in a ponytail, a silver swastika hanging from one earlobe. He was wearing cowboy boots, greasy jeans, and a plain white T-shirt with the arms torn off. The three women seemed all of a kind—one blonde, two brunettes, but all three were sleepy-eyed and stoned. One of the brunettes was only wearing a pair of bikini briefs. The other two women wore shorts and halters.

"You want a toke?" Steve asked, offering Earl a joint.

"Thanks." Earl took a long drag, then held the joint up to Howie's lips. "We had us a little . . . hunting accident," he said as he handed the joint back. "You got a first-aid kit, man?"

"Hey, we got a fucking nurse here tonight." He nodded to the women and the topless brunette looked up. "See what you can do for the man, Sherry."

Unselfconsciously, Sherry stood up and approached Howie. She took in the amount of blood that his shirt had soaked up, then crooked her finger at him. "Let's go to the can," she said. "What's your name, tiger?"

Even through his pain, Howie had trouble keeping his gaze from her breasts. He glanced at Earl.

"Go on," Earl said. He waited until Sherry led Howie away, then looked back at Steve. "You got a phone in yet?"

Steve shook his head. "I come here to get *away,* man. What's up?"

"I got some serious business that can't wait."

Steve glanced at the butt of the gun sticking up from the belt and thought for a long stoned moment about Howie's shoulder. "You need reinforcements or something?" he asked finally.

"No. But I got to make a call to a certain man—the sooner the better, if you catch my drift."

"Where's the call going?"

"I'll make it collect."

"Hey, Lisa," Earl said. The blonde looked up. "You want to take my friend here up to your place so he can use your phone?"

Lisa's gaze ranged up from Earl's shoes to his face. "Sure."

"Wait a minute," the other man said. "You're with me toni—"

"Cool it, Max—okay?" Steve grinned at the bigger man and tossed him a small glass vial. "This is strictly a phone call, nothing else. Right, Earl?"

"You got it."

Steve nodded. "So check out the nosecandy, Max. Talk to Pam here and Lisa'll be back quicker 'n she can shake her ass."

Lisa sauntered over to the door where she put on a jacket and a pair of leather thongs. "Have you got wheels?" she asked when Earl and Steve joined her outside.

"Not so's you'd notice. We drove up in the Toyota—it's on its last legs and it's hot."

"Steve?" Lisa asked.

Steve tossed her a set of car keys. "Take the Honda." Then to Earl: "You bringing anything down on us?"

Earl shook his head.

"Anything in it for me? Can you use a couple more bodies?"

"I'll know more after I make this call."

Steve grinned. "All right. I owe you one anyway."

"I know," Earl said.

The smile faded on Steve's face, but Earl didn't notice. He'd already turned to follow Lisa to the car. Steve waited until the Honda's taillights were out of sight before going back inside. Maybe he could get some information from the guy Earl had left behind. Sherry was coming out of the washroom as he stepped inside.

"How is he?" Steve asked.

"He'll live. The bullet went through muscle tissue—missed the bone. He should go to the hospital for stitches, though."

"I've got a needle and thread."

"Gimme a break, Steve. That's not the kind of—"

"No hospital, Sherry. Too many questions—understand?"

"Yeah. Sure." She didn't look happy about it.

"So you gonna sew him up?"

"Here, Sherry!" Max called and tossed her the glass vial of cocaine. "Maybe this'll steady your nerve." He and Pam laughed.

Steve took her arm and steered her back to the washroom. "I'll give you a hand," he said.

After leaving Mally by the stone, Lewis made his way home where he sat in the dark for a long while before finally lighting a lamp. He went to the bookshelves and walked slowly around, reading the titles. Yeats' *Trembling of the Veil* stood alongside theosophist classics like Annie Besant's *The Ancient Wisdom* and Mundy's *I See Sunrise*. There were books by Madame Blavatsky, Raymond Buckland, Israel Regardie, Robert Graves, T.C. Lethbridge, Eliphas Levi, W.B. Crow and Charles Williams. There were some contemporary writers represented as well, such as Colin Wilson and E.S. Howes.

The subjects ranged from Fiji firewalkers to the Order of the Golden Dawn, Freemasonry to the Rosicrucians, Jung to spiritualism. All of the mysteries were represented, but it was up to the reader to discover which, out of those thousands of volumes, held a kernel of truth, and which were out-and-out quackeries.

Lewis stopped in front of the shelf that held Aleister Crowley's books. He thought of the stag and its mystery and tried to compare its wonder with Crowley's poor showing. "Do what thou wilt shall be the whole of the Law." That was the fundamental assertion of the self-confessed Beast. He had borrowed it by way of Rabelais and William Blake, but given it a new resonance, a Nietzschean morality. Only the strong should survive. Wasn't this nature's way? The natural way?

Lewis sighed. He took down a volume by Ackerly Perkin and brought it over to the table where he sat down, the book lying unopened before him.

Perkin had been a contemporary of Crowley's—the original owner, in fact, of much of this library. It was he who had first caused a shadow to fall on the stag, on the piping, on the rites that bound the two to New Wolding.

"Man needs illusion," this particular volume of Perkin's journals opened with, "for without his illusions, man is nothing. The strength of your illusions is dependent upon the strength of your will. The stronger your will, the more you will rule, for other men will always flock to him whose illusions are the most potent."

It was a circumspect approach to Crowley's assertions, but where the Beast had gone on to the magical uses of sex and the use of drugs like mescaline, Perkin withdrew from the world, seeking his illusions in microcosm, rather than the world at large. What he found merely intensified his belief in the need for illusion.

When he became aware of the piping and the stone, of the rites and the dancing and what they were calling to, he used what influence he had to evoke his own illusions to counteract the one he believed the villagers upheld. For while he would allow all men their illusions, he would not allow those illusions to manifest themselves in this world. Such a thing should not be possible. If, however, such a thing *was* somehow possible, then he was determined that the only illusions that would be manifested would be his own.

When Lewis tried to find out why Perkin would have done this, the only reason the journals gave him was that Perkin did what he did simply because he could. Because he believed it all to be illusion.

"Which is more illusory?" he asked in one entry. "Illusions built upon belief, or those built with reasoned disbelief?" Around this point the journals ended and Perkin returned to the wandering life he'd known before moving to Lanark County, leaving the library in his old house.

Mally had first appeared around this time and it was she who had helped a younger Lewis transfer all those books to his cabin in New Wolding. "The dark man won't be back for them," she told Lewis. "He's found his god in war now. He thinks it to be a reasoned exercise, or the greatest of all illusions, but whichever he decides it is, he won't be back."

Lewis often wished that he had never read any of Perkin's books—especially those that Perkin had written himself. Before them, Lewis had been a simple man, content with what he had. But when Vera died and Edmond fled, the books were all he had left to sustain him. They filled the emptiness inside him with questions until sometimes he no longer wanted the answers.

He longed then to return to the simple belief that he'd once shared with the other villagers, but it was far too late for that. Just as it was too late for the village to survive. There were only four of them under the age of twenty now. The old folk had died; the younger ones gone, out into the outside world seeking . . . illusions, he supposed.

When he had asked his own son why he was leaving, Edmond had replied, "There's nothing for me here." Lewis hadn't had an answer for that then. He didn't have one now.

Lewis flipped through the pages of the book, then let it close with a thump. If the hounds that chased the stag were Perkin's creations, if they were his illusions, then why were they still here, fifty years after Perkin had left?

Lewis was afraid of the answer to that question. He was afraid that by taking Perkin's books, by following the hundreds of threads that ran through them, the wisdoms along with the foolishness, that it was he himself who was now sustaining the hounds. That they crept out of the darkness of his own soul to chase the stag. For was that not what all the writers of these books sought? Not the mystery itself, but some method to hold it, to control and measure it, to dissect it to see what made it tick. He'd asked Mally about it once, knowing that his own search made him no better than those writers.

"You're not alone in what you do," she'd replied, as though confirming his worst fear.

"Then I *am* responsible?"

"How should I know, Lewis?"

"Did I make you? Are you one of my illusions? Or should I say delusions?"

"Does it matter?"

"Of course it matters!" he'd cried. "What are you?"

"I'm a secret, Lewis," she said. "That's all."

And that was no comfort at all.

"This is a nice place," Earl said as Lisa led him into the cottage and flicked on a light. "You had it long?"

"It belongs to my parents."

"Are they around?" His hand drifted towards the butt of his .38.

"No. They're in Europe."

Earl nodded. "So where's the phone?"

"In the bedroom—through there." She indicated a door, then drifted into the room after him. "So are you one of these tough guys that Steve uses on his jobs?"

Earl turned to her and laughed. "Steve's told you he pulls jobs?"

Lisa nodded. "Sure. Where do you think he gets all his bread?"

"I'll tell you where. Steve's got himself a dead-end job in the government and the only way he makes do is by selling dope to the people he works with."

"That's not what he told me."

Earl shrugged. "I don't care what he told you. He's an asshole, plain and simple."

"Well, then how'd you get to know him?"

"Even assholes come in handy sometimes. You ever try to take a shit through your nose?"

Lisa pulled a face.

"This is a private call," Earl told her.

For a moment it looked like she was going to say something, but then her gaze met his and a weak smile touched her lips. "Sure," she said. "No problem. I'll wait out there on the couch."

Earl waited until the door closed behind her, then picked up the receiver and placed his call. Collect.

"I'll take it," the voice on the other end said when the operator explained the nature of the call. Then to Earl, "This better be good. You know what time it is? You got a clean line?"

"Yeah. This won't take long, Joe. Think of it as me doing you a favor."

"I'm listening," Broadway Joe said.

"Tony Valenti."

"What about him?"

"Are you still looking for him?"

"What kinda game you playing, Shaw?"

Earl leaned back, stretching his legs out on the bed. "No game. I can give you Valenti, but you've got to move fast."

"Gimme me your number," Broadway Joe said. "I'll call you back in twenty or so."

Earl read off the number from the phone and smiled as he hung up. "Hey, Lisa!" he called. When she opened the door, he patted the bed. "We've got twenty minutes to kill before I get a return on my call. You want to get it on?"

Lisa stared at him for a long moment. "You've got some nerve, you know that?"

"I got more 'n' that if you look in the right place, babe."

"I'll bet you do." She studied him for another moment, then reached up behind her back to undo the clasp of her halter, freeing her breasts. "I must be crazy," she said as she stepped out of her shorts and got onto the bed beside him. "I don't even know you."

"I bet you say that to all the guys," Earl said as he grabbed her and pulled her in close.

Lisa just laughed.

Broadway Joe Fucceri hung up and looked across his desk to where his boss was lying stretched out on a leather couch. Ricca Magaddino had one hand behind his head, a cigarette in the other. He was a lean, dark-haired man, handsome with a Mediterranean cast to his complexion. He took a drag on his cigarette, blew a wreath of blue smoke up to the ceiling, then looked at Broadway Joe.

"So who was that?"

"That little punk Earl Shaw—the one with the coke deal."

"Oh, yeah. What's he want?"

Broadway Joe leaned back in his chair to put his feet up. He was in his late fifties now, ten years older than Ricca. His hair was going silver at the temples.

"Shaw says he can finger Valenti for us."

Ricca sat up and put his feet on the floor. "Do we still want him?"

"You, me, and Louie—that's all who know what really went down," Broadway Joe said. "Tony's not gonna talk. Shit, who's he gonna talk to? First cousin that sees him's gonna blow him away."

"You still got some feeling for him, hey, Joe?"

Broadway Joe shrugged. "You're the boss, Ricca. You know that. The old *padrone,* he wasn't changing with the times. But Tony— Christ, he was always so fucking loyal, you know what I'm saying? It's hard to get dedication like that now. I mean, so far's Tony saw it, the family was his career."

Ricca nodded. "Yeah. I know all that. But I think maybe we should send Louie out to see what Shaw's got. I never did like loose ends, *capito?"*

"Too bad we can't just use Shaw," Broadway Joe said.

Ricca regarded his *consigliere.* "Why not?" he asked. "I like that—keeps us right out of it."

"He's crazy," Broadway Joe said. "We used him once in that Miami deal your old man was running through Tony, and we're using him now for the coke thing, but I don't want us involved with his kind of killing. He does it for fun, Ricca. And he does it messy. If we were to get fingered, just saying he got busted—"

"Nothing can hold up in court," Ricca protested. "I mean, he's not even one of our own people."

"But say the story gets loose how the *padrone* really died? Say Tony says something and Shaw repeats it? The families wouldn't like that. If we still want Tony, we'll send my boy. That way we'll know what's going down. And besides, Louie's still hurting from that Malta deal, you know?"

Ricca grinned. "Hey, there's a reason you're still *consigliere,* Joe. You handle this shit, okay? Any way you think is best."

"I'll set up a meet between Shaw and Louie," Broadway Joe said. He pulled the phone closer and direct-dialed the number he'd gotten from Earl.

He was running, the hounds so close now he could hear the click of their claws on the asphalt. He turned to look back at them, wanting to stand and fight, antlers sweeping down, hooves flashing, but he knew there were too many of them. He could run, and that was all he could do. Run, with his heart pounding in his chest. Run, until his leg muscles ached too much to take him any further. Run, with the burning in his tissues and the sound of the dogs' cries ringing in his ears until he fell.

His flanks were streaked with sweat. Froth foamed around his mouth. The highway snaked on, deeper into the countryside. Then suddenly he stumbled. The asphalt tore at his skin. The dogs were on him in a flash, teeth ripping at his skin as he flailed his hooves. But it was too late. One dog, bigger than the others, sank its teeth into his throat and he—

—woke screaming.

He sat bolt upright in his bed. Brenda fumbled with the light switch beside her.

"Lance, are you—"

"Fine," he said, swinging his feet to the floor. His pajamas clung damply to his back and chest. "I'm fine. No problem." Except those fucking dogs had gotten him this time.

"Where are you going?"

"I've got a little unfinished business outside," Lance said. He shoved his feet into his workboots and went to the closet where he pulled out his shotgun. He cracked it open, checked its load. Empty. Opening the top drawer of the dresser, he pushed around his socks and underwear until he found the box of shells. He loaded the gun quickly, snapped it shut.

"Lance, *what* are you doing?"

He turned to look at her and she froze back against the headboard. His eyes were seeking more than just her and the bedroom.

"Lance . . . ?" she said softly.

He looked away, still hearing the howls of the pack, and went downstairs, boots clattering. Brenda stayed in bed, clutching the sheets with whitening knuckles. She heard the back door slam shut, imagined Lance's boots scuffling in the dirt around back. Then she buried her face in the pillow, scared again. She was always scared now, it seemed.

Lance walked slowly over to where Dooker lay sleeping. The German shepherd woke as Lance drew near and made a questioning sound in its throat. Lance only heard claws clicking on pavement, the howl of a pack hunting. He lifted the shotgun, the ends of the barrels just inches from Dooker's head, and pulled both triggers.

The roar of the shotgun's double blast shook him from his trance-like state. He looked at the weapon in his hands, at what was left of Dooker, and the tears started in his eyes. He threw the shotgun aside and cradled the bloody mess of the dog against him.

"Crazy," he sobbed. "Jesus . . . going crazy . . . Oh, Dook. I'm so sorry. . . ."

He bowed his head, sobs shaking him. That was the way that Brenda found him when she finally dared go outside. For a long moment she stood there by the back door, staring at him, afraid to move or call attention to herself. Then slowly she crossed over to where he was and laid a hand on his shoulder.

"C-come on, Lance," she said. "You'd better . . . better come in now."

He shook his head. "Got to . . . got to dig a hole for ol' Dooker, Boo. It's . . . I got to do it. . . ."

Brenda nodded. "I'll get the shovel," she said.

She left him there and went to the shed to get the tool, wondering just what she was going to do with Lance. He was definitely getting scary now. But he was still Lance, too. He needed help. She had to get him to go see the doc again, get him to recommend a psychiatrist—that was all there was to it.

As she returned to his side with the shovel, as she stood over him and poor dead Dooker, she realized that that was what she was going to have to do. Lance needed help and he sure wasn't going to look for it himself.

Please, Lord, she thought. Let me be strong. Let me be strong enough for both of us.

THE HUNTSMAN'S GUILE

lady, accept these words
I have lost the huntsman's guile
following that which is lost. . . .

—ROBIN WILLIAMSON,
FROM *"SONG OF MABON"*

The woods of Arcady are dead,
And over is their antique joy;
Of old the world on dreaming fed;
Gray truth is now her painted toy. . . .

—W.B. YEATS,
FROM *"THE SONG OF THE*
HAPPY SHEPHERD"

1

The sun had been up for a couple of hours and it was getting on to six-fifteen when Valenti heard the sound of an engine coming up his road. He'd been listening for it. Laying down his book, he went into the kitchen area where he got the UZI submachine gun from the small broom closet where he'd hidden it. He slipped out the back door.

He circled around behind the house and barn, moving quickly through the woods toward the front of his property. By the time the white Mazda had pulled into his drive, Valenti was approaching the vehicle from the road. He ducked behind the hedge as the Mazda's door opened.

A lean, wiry-looking man got out of the car and stretched, his attention on the house. He was dressed for the country in jeans, hiking boots and a light cotton shirt, with a dark blue wind-breaker overtop. Running a hand through his short blond hair, he turned to give the yard and road a quick lookover before starting for the house. By the time he reached the porch, Valenti had left the hedge and moved in closer.

He stood up behind the man's car, the UZI held down out of the man's view.

"How's it going?" he called softly.

The man turned, quicker than Valenti had expected, and took a smooth step to the side of the porch where he was half-screened by a cedar. His gaze locked on Valenti, one hand moving under his wind-breaker, until Valenti lifted the UZI. The man let his hand drop.

"I think you're expecting me," he said.

"Could be." Valenti came around the car, holding the UZI in both hands now, his finger taking up the slack against its trigger. "Where're you from?"

"T.O. Listen. I can understand your—"

"How'd you find the place?"

"A friend in Malta sent me."

"Oh, yeah? So how *is* Tony?"

A brief smile touched the man's lips. "You're Tony. Mario sent me."

"Okay," Valenti said. "Maybe I am." He lowered the UZI. "You had breakfast yet?"

"I stopped at a truckstop an hour or so ago. I could use a coffee, though."

"You got it."

"Do you want to fill me in on the situation?"

Valenti nodded. "Sure. Let's go inside. One thing, though."

"What's that?"

"I've got a couple of civilians inside—an upfront lady and her kid. I'd appreciate it if we didn't talk too loose in front of them."

"No problem. I'm Tom Bannon," he added, holding out his hand as Valenti mounted the steps.

Valenti took the hand. "Thanks for coming."

"You can't be sure he made you, then?" Bannon asked as Valenti fin-ished sketching out the problem for him. The UZI was back in its hid-ing place and they were sitting at the kitchen table, the coffee pot on a warming plate between them, each with a half-drunk coffee at hand. Valenti had kept the story simple. Things were going to get weird enough without his bringing up the business with the stag and Ali's wild girl.

"Oh, he made me all right," Valenti replied. "The thing is, what's he going to do with the information? To tell you the truth, I was expecting some trouble by now, but maybe he hasn't got the word out yet."

"Maybe he's sitting on it."

"What for?"

Bannon shrugged. "Christ, who knows? There's some talk on the street about him—he's supposed to have some big deal going down. Maybe he can't afford to get mixed up in family business right now."

"I don't think so," Valenti said. "Him and me—we never hit it off, you know what I mean?"

"With what I know about Shaw, I'm not surprised. He's got to be the main man in the deal or he gets antsy."

Valenti nodded. "That's the feeling he gave me."

"So how do you want to play this?" Bannon asked. "Are we going to wait them out, or do we take it to them?"

"Wait them out for now. I wouldn't know where to start looking for—" Valenti broke off as he heard a door open and close upstairs.

"Who'm I supposed to be?" Bannon asked in a whisper.

"Friend. Up for the week on holiday."

"Okay. Anything else I should know?"

Valenti shook his head. "Hey, Ali," he said as he saw her coming down the stairs. "C'mon in here. I got a friend I want you to meet."

Ali woke from a dream in which she was mediating an argument between Tony, the stag and Earl Shaw as to which of them was her real father. The stag had a man's body in the dream and was wearing denims and a T-shirt that said "Have you hugged your child today?"

Coming out of that dream in a strange bedroom, it took her a few moments to figure out just where she was and why. She sat up abruptly, her chest tighting with sudden fear. Her mother . . .

She got up and dressed, then padded out of the guestroom. She peered down the stairwell, but the house felt empty. Had her mother even arrived last night? Or had Earl Shaw caught her on her way home and . . . and . . .

She couldn't finish the thought. Stepping quickly to Tony's bedroom, she cracked the door open. She'd ask Tony because Tony'd know. He wouldn't have gone to sleep without making sure Mom was okay. When she saw her mother asleep on Tony's bed, a breath she hadn't been aware of holding left her in a long sigh. She hurried across the room and knelt by the bed, putting an arm around her mother. If anything had happened to her . . .

The sound of a car's engine came to her, the engine dying, then the slam of a car door. Ali tensed again. Too scared to move, she pressed herself closer against Tony's bed, holding her mother. Frankie moved in her sleep but didn't wake. Ali heard Tony's and another man's voice drift up from downstairs. Relief loosened tense muscles once more.

She gave her mother a kiss, then went back out into the hall. She opened and closed the door to the guest room, loud enough so that Tony would know she was awake, then headed down the stairs.

Tony introduced her to his friend while she poured herself a coffee. She added lots of milk and a couple of spoons of sugar, then sat down at the table with the two men.

"Tony," she began hesitantly, shooting Bannon a quick glance. "Did you talk to my mom last night?"

Tony nodded.

"How is she?"

"Not so good. But we talked a bit and I think she was feeling better by the time she went to bed. She had a rough day so maybe we should let her sleep for a bit longer." He paused, then added, "How are *you,* Ali?"

Ali thought about last night, about what would have happened to her if Tony hadn't shown up. . . . It didn't make for pleasant thinking. Given her druthers for a father, she'd take Tony over Earl Shaw any day. And the stag? She wondered as the dream flashed momentarily before her eyes.

"Ali?"

She looked up. "It's really scary, Tony. Why can't he just leave us alone?"

"Some guys . . ." Tony began, then he sighed. "I don't know, Ali. The money your momma's got left after rebuilding that house . . . That's a lot of money we're talking about. Some guys'll do anything for money, step on anyone."

Ali nodded glumly. She toyed with her coffee cup, wishing she knew more about who Tom Bannon was so that she'd know what they could and couldn't talk about.

"Tony tells me you read a lot," Bannon said.

She glanced at him. "I guess."

"I like to read, too, but I wasn't thinking when I packed to come up here and didn't bring any books with me."

"What kind of stuff do you read?"

"Mysteries, thrillers—anything with a bit of bite to it."

"I can lend you some books if you want," Ali said, interested despite herself. "Did you ever try Tony Hillerman?"

Valenti nodded to himself as Bannon kept Ali talking. It was a good move. Keep her mind off all the shit that was piling up around them. But meanwhile, he realized, he was going to have to come up with something. First off he had to get Ali and her momma out of here. And then . . . then he had to deal with the trouble Ricca was going to dump on their heads.

"No," Frankie said.

They'd all had breakfast once she'd gotten up. Now Ali and Bannon had gone down to the Treasure house for some books, leaving Valenti to try to talk Frankie into taking a short vacation. Frankie was having nothing to do with the idea.

"You don't really understand," Valenti began.

"Oh, I understand," Frankie said. "God, I lived with the man, didn't I? But I swore I wasn't going to run anymore. I've been scared of Earl for too many years, Tony. It's time I stood up to him once and for all."

Now what could he say? That it wasn't just Shaw? He decided to take a different tack. "What about Ali?" he asked.

"It's . . . this is something that we're both going to have to live with," Frankie said after a moment. "I wasn't in the best of shape last night, so when you offered to put us up, I have to admit I jumped at the chance. I was scared—mostly for Ali, but for me, too. But I don't want to always be turning to a man for help. Can you understand that, Tony? I have to make it on my own—and Ali's going to have to learn to do the same."

Valenti shook his head. "People got to help each other, or what've we got? Maybe it's a man helping a woman, maybe it's a woman helping a man—what's the difference?"

"There shouldn't be any, but there is," Frankie said.

She ran a hand through her hair. Valenti wondered what it'd feel like to touch that hair, all those curls. . . . Frankie's clear gaze settled on him.

"I've been dependent on men for my whole life, Tony," she said. "Even after I left Earl, there were always men in my life that I was leaning on—emotionally dependent on, even if they weren't supporting me in the traditional sense of the word. I'd probably still be going on like that—not wanting to, but needing to—but then I won that lottery and everything changed. It wasn't just the money, you see. It was the chance to go anywhere I wanted and start over again."

"And you picked Lanark."

Frankie smiled. "I guess it seems a little weird, doesn't it? But I used to live in that house, Tony. That's where I grew up. When I was a little girl, my father used to beat up on my mother and the thing I learned was that the man runs the family. That what he says goes.

"I left Earl, sure, but I don't think I ever got away from that lesson, so going back was my way of learning things over again. My mother ran away, just like I did from Earl. That showed me one way of dealing with the problem. But now I've come back and I'm not running away again. I might move away someday, but it'll be because I want to—not because I've been chased away."

"Well, I can understand that," Valenti said, though he was a little uncomfortable with the idea that a man wasn't the head of his own family. The wife and the husband, they each had their role, didn't they?

"Do you believe that men and women are equal, Tony? That they should have the same rights?"

"What? Oh, sure."

Frankie nodded, missing his hesitation. "But the woman's side of that balance has got a long way to go before the scales start weighing out even. It's funny, but Ali's the one that's made me see a lot of this—this whole idea of not only talking about equality, but doing something about it. She reads up on it." Frankie laughed. "Lectures me when she figures I'm stepping out of line. She's good for me. God, I love her."

"She's a good kid."

"She's a dynamite kid," Frankie said. "She's luckier in some ways than the women of my own generation, too. We were growing up when this whole thing came to a head—when Women's Lib was like a swear word and any woman involved in it had to be a lesbian."

Valenti shifted uncomfortably. He'd been guilty of that kind of attitude himself, when he'd bothered to think about it at all. He looked at Frankie, but she didn't seem to notice his discomfort.

"I worry about what all this is doing to Ali," Frankie finished. "Sometimes I feel that living the way we have has made her miss out on her childhood. She doesn't hang around with other kids a lot and she talks and acts like a little adult half the time. Sometimes I think she's got a better handle on things than I do. Like women's rights.

"Ali's grown up with the whole concept being a part of everyday life. Not that the battle's won—not by a longshot. But at least *something's* being done. Maybe it'll be easier still for my grandchildren. God, I hope so. If all of Ali's generation were more like her, I wouldn't have any worries at all. But then I have to ask myself—is missing out on a normal childhood going to hurt her in the long run?"

"Ali's the kind of kid who'll do good no matter what she sets out to take on," Valenti said.

"Oh, I don't doubt that. I just worry about not being a good mother, I guess."

"I don't think that's anything you got to worry about," Valenti said. "Ali talks about you all the time—you're number one in her book."

Frankie smiled gratefully.

"I've got to be honest with you," Valenti went on. "I never thought a whole lot about what you're talking about with this women's rights stuff, but listening to you . . . well, it makes you think."

"All men aren't to blame," Frankie said. "A lot of them are just victims, too. It's hard to get away from sexual stereotyping when our whole society is based on it."

Valenti nodded. He was going to have to think about this some more. "So you're not going?" he asked then, taking the conversation back to its beginnings.

Frankie shook her head.

"I've got to tell you something else then," he said, "while we're . . ." He searched for the word.

"Baring our souls?"

"Yeah. I haven't always been what you'd want to call a good man. I've been involved with some . . ." Again he searched for a word. "Some guys who aren't on the up and up."

Frankie leaned forward. "What are you saying, Tony?"

Valenti sighed. Christ, he didn't want to get too deep into anything, tell her things that would scare her off. He liked Frankie. He was comfortable with her and had to admire her for wanting to make her stand. And he really didn't want to lose his friendship with Ali. If things worked out, if he could deal with Ricca and Shaw and maybe hold on to what he had here, he didn't want to have Frankie telling him to stay away from the kid. So what could he say now?

"What I'm saying," he said finally, "is that I've run into your ex before, and he's a—pardon the language—but he's a piece of shit. That you already knew. But what you maybe don't know is that he's tight with some pretty heavy people. I mean, the usual case you get where the man's hassling his ex—it's not good, but it can usually be handled just like you're planning to. But your ex . . . He's into guns, Frankie, and he wasn't alone when he came looking for you and Ali."

"You're scaring me."

"It's good that you're scared," Valenti said. "This is a scary business."

"God. If anything ever happened to Ali . . ."

Frankie leaned weakly back in her chair, feeling her resolve drain away. She looked at Tony's serious face. He made it hard, too. There was something about him—not just the secrets she could sense in him, but some inner strength he had that she envied. She was attracted to him because of who he was and how he carried himself, because of his relationship with Ali, too. But what if that attraction was just her reaching out to lean on someone again?

"How . . . how involved in this scary business stuff were you?" she asked.

"Whatever I was into, I'm retired," Valenti replied. "Believe me, Frankie. But I will tell you this: What I learned in that business kept Ali from being snatched last night."

Frankie nodded. Neither Ali nor Valenti had been forthcoming about the details of what had taken place last night. Frankie meant to get to the bottom of it—only now didn't seem to be the right time. But there was more than just Earl involved. Of that she was sure.

She sat up straighter. "I'm still not going," she said.

"Will you let me help you?" Valenti asked. "As a friend helping a friend, or a neighbor helping a neighbor? No strings."

"But I'm not staying up here. We're going back to our own house."

"Fair enough. And you'll call if anything comes up?"

"God! Of course I'll call. We should call the police as well—now, before Earl comes back."

"And what are they going to do?"

Frankie thought about that. Unless they caught Earl in the act, the most that could happen was that she might be able to get a restraining order from the court, but she knew from past experience just how much use that would be.

"But if Earl *does* come again . . . ?"

"Call me," Valenti said. "I'm two minutes away and my friend Tom's staying up for the week. By the time the police answer your call, God knows what'll have happened."

Frankie nodded slowly. "Okay. I'll call you."

Valenti held back a "that's a girl." He didn't think Frankie would appreciate it. But come to think of it, who the hell was he to talk down to her like that? She was making a stand, wasn't she? And willing to do it on her own, too. You had to admire someone who was willing to do that, man or woman.

"Things are going to work out," he said.

"God, I hope so," Frankie said. But she knew she had a lot to think about. Just then Ali and Bannon returned, Bannon loaded down with a half-dozen books that Ali had lent him.

"You going to stay for lunch?" Valenti asked Frankie.

Frankie nodded and found a small smile with difficulty. Just looking at her daughter as Ali bounced happily about the room, talking up a storm with a somewhat bemused Bannon, she felt a stab of fear so sharp that her chest hurt. If anything happened to Ali . . . No, she told herself. Don't even think about it.

2

Broadway Joe Fucceri didn't much like the idea of the meet. He liked it less when he stepped into the restaurant with two of his boys and spotted at least three hired muscles inside, with another hanging around outside. It was easy to spot them—but then he was supposed to. What bothered him was that he couldn't make any of them. The fact that the meet was in the area of a lot of off-Broadway theaters hadn't escaped him, either. The message was: Play it cool.

The Silver Fox was waiting for him in a booth at the rear of the restaurant looking the same as always. The big smile, the silver hair. Broadway Joe motioned his bodyguards over to the counter and walked down to the Silver Fox's booth.

"Hey, Mario," he said as he slid in across from him. "Immigration know you're in town?"

Mario shrugged. *"Come te la sei passata?"* he asked. How's it going?

"Not so bad," Broadway Joe said, waggling his hand. "We got a

few problems, but there's always problems. Nothing we can't handle."
He picked up the menu and studied it for a moment. "You wanted to
talk?"

"I got a favor I'd like you to think about."

"Must be a pretty important favor to get you to fly in, considering."

"For me, it's important," Mario said. "For you, it's nothing."

"So tell me about it."

Mario studied him for a moment. He'd wanted a face-to-face meet,
because that was one thing he was good at. Reading faces. "It's about
Tony," he said. "Tony Valenti."

"That's old news now," Broadway Joe said.

"Old news in you don't want him, or old news in you've got a line
on him?"

"I'll tell you the truth, Mario, it's a little of both, you know what
I'm saying? Now I know you're not stupid enough to come in here
carrying a wire, so between the two of us, I know Tony had nothing
to do with the Don getting hit, so what do I want with him?"

"Word on the street says the open contract on him's still standing."

"That's just business—we're not looking for him."

"Not even if someone fingers him?"

"I never figured the Silver Fox for a snitch," Broadway Joe said.

Mario's eyes narrowed to slits. "I didn't fly three thousand miles
to listen to this kinda shit."

"So what *did* you come for?"

"I want you to call off the contract on Tony," Mario said. "As a
favor. You can say he was hit—I don't give a shit how you put it—
just so's you call it off."

Broadway Joe shook his head. "I don't like what I'm hearing,
Mario. I don't like your muscle, I don't like this 'off-Broadway' shit,
I don't like threats."

"I'm asking you for a favor, Joe."

"Yeah. But I'm hearing 'or else' behind your asking."

Mario shrugged.

"We were friends once," Broadway Joe said. "We were family,
Mario. But I don't know who you are anymore. You told me you were

retired, but the word comes from overseas that you're connected with some of the old families now. Now, I got as much respect as anyone for them, but this is America, and what they say don't mean shit here—you understand what I'm saying?"

"We'd still be working together if the family hadn't let me be deported."

"Well, I regret that," Broadway Joe said. "I really do. But that's the way of the world, *capito?* Not much we can do about that anymore."

"I'm not asking for that."

"I know. You're asking me for something that's not so easy for me to promise—not when I got to think about some of the old families trying to throw their weight around over here. What you're asking for is a little thing—but if I give it to them, what're they gonna ask for next?"

"This is personal—you know that."

Broadway Joe nodded slowly. "Between you and me, then?"

"Between you and me," Mario agreed. "And I *am* retired now, Joe. I've done the old families a favor or two, but shit, I got to live with them. It's better to be owed than owing."

"I can understand that," Broadway Joe said. "Okay. As a favor to you, I'm calling off the contract on Tony."

Mario regarded him for a long moment. You lying sonovabitch, he thought. But he'd had to try. "This's one I owe you," he said softly.

Broadway Joe smiled, taking the words at face value and missing the irony behind them. "I'm glad we had this talk, Mario," he said. "It's been too long. Maybe we can pull a few strings, get you back into the country legally—what do you say?"

Mario shook his head, matching Broadway Joe's smile with his own. "I'm too settled where I am now, Joe. But I appreciate it."

"You want to order now?"

"No. I've got a flight to catch." Mario stood up and offered Broadway Joe his hand. *"Ciao,* Joe."

Broadway Joe rose as well and shook. "May we all live long and prosperous lives," he said.

Mario nodded. When he left the restaurant, only one of the men

Broadway Joe had spotted as his muscle left with him. The other two sat, watching Broadway Joe and his bodyguards.

Now's not the place, Broadway Joe thought. But as soon as Valenti was hit, something was going to have to be done with the Silver Fox. It would be very carefully arranged, for although the old families didn't have the control that the media thought they did here in America, they still had a long arm. And Mario himself would be dangerous as soon as he learned about Tony being hit. Broadway Joe knew he'd feel a whole lot better once both of them were out of the way.

As the meet was going down in New York City between the Silver Fox and the *consigliere* of the Magaddino family, Earl Shaw was meeting a plane at the Ottawa International Airport. He drove a new Buick that he'd rented from Hertz under false ID. After leaving the lot with it, he'd taken the extra precaution of switching its plates with another Buick in an underground parking lot downtown. Leaving the car at a meter when he reached the airport, he drifted inside to wait for the most recent New York flight to disembark. He wondered who Broadway Joe had sent.

I'm gonna enjoy this, Earl thought. Ever since he'd worked with Valenti on that Miami deal, he'd had an itch for the guy. He was just too old-world Mafia for Earl's tastes. When he'd heard that Valenti had hit old man Magaddino, he'd had to laugh. Just goes to show you, he'd thought. Don't trust no-fucking-body.

The passengers were coming through now and Earl gave them the once over. When his gaze fell on Louie Fucceri, a smile came to his lips. Well, that figured. Who better to send after their old chief enforcer, than their new one? He caught Fucceri's gaze and nodded outside. When Louie nodded back, Earl ambled out the front door of the terminal and went for the car.

"He made you?" Louie repeated.

He sat in the front seat with Earl. He'd brought only one man with him, Johnny "Three-Fingers" Maita, who was sitting in the back.

When they'd stepped out of the terminal, looking for his car, Earl had trouble keeping a straight face. They were both in their three-piece suits, with their slick wop hair and dark complexions. It was just too much.

In the back seat, Fingers was now taking apart some aerosol shave cream and spray deodorant cans. Fitted neatly inside them were the makings of two small .22 pistols, complete with silencers. Putting aside the cans that had gotten the weapons in through customs, Fingers put the guns together. When the first was done, he passed it over the front seat to Louie, then went to work on his own.

"Yeah," Earl said in reply to Louie's question. "He made me. So what?"

Louie shook his head. "So what? He's going to be long-gone, that's so what."

"Where's he going to go?"

"Anywhere but where he was. I mean, think about it for a moment. Would you hang around?"

"Well, that'd all depend on who made me," Earl said. "Valenti knows I'm not connected. Christ, I've only done one deal with you guys before, so what's the problem?"

Louie didn't bother answering. If he'd known this before, he wouldn't have bothered flying in. "Well, we might as well check it out, now that we're here," he said.

Earl grinned. "Sure. Why not?"

Not for the first time, Louie wondered about his father's wisdom in trusting Earl with this Colombian run. Sure, he had some good connections in Bogotá. But he didn't have much in the way of brains.

"Did you get the artillery we're going to need?" he asked.

Earl shook his head. "I got that deal going down this afternoon." The reason he hadn't set it up sooner was that he was running drastically low on funds. Frankie-baby, he thought. You and me, we've got to talk. Real soon.

Coming off the Airport Parkway onto Bronson Avenue, he glanced at Louie. "You guys want to get set up at the hotel first?"

Louie nodded. Earl looked in the rearview mirror to see Fingers staring off out of one of the side windows. Nice suits, he thought again. Wonder how pretty they were going to look if they had to chase Valenti down through the woods. He grinned at the thought of the two big city gunmen floundering through the bush. The image kept him in good humor all the way to their hotel.

3

Frankie turned off the ignition after pulling into their drive. She didn't get out of the car right away, turning instead to look at Ali.

"What do you know about Tony?" she asked. "I mean, about what he did before he came to live up here?"

Ali regarded her mother and thought for a moment. She had a good idea why Frankie was asking this question, but she wasn't sure how much Tony had told her. Some, at least, or she wouldn't be asking what she was now.

"Not a whole lot," she said finally. "I get the feeling from stuff he's said that he was involved with some sort of law enforcement agency—something to do with studying organized crime."

Frankie's eyebrows went up. "Well, that explains a lot."

"What do you mean?"

"He knows things about Earl that I didn't think he could know without being involved in some sort of criminal activity himself. But now that you mention it, a policeman would know the same things— or at least enough to know what kind of a man Earl is." She shook her head slowly. "God, when I think of what he was like when I first met him . . ."

"What *was* he like, mom?"

"Different. Very different. Kinder. Or maybe he just seemed kinder. Not always concerned with making money any way he could. I'm not even sure when it all started to change."

"Do you think he's going to come back?"

Frankie nodded. "It's the money, Ali. He wants the money we won in the lottery and I don't think he'll stop at much to get it." She leaned back against the headrest, tapping her fingers on the steering wheel, then sat up abruptly. "We should get a move on," she said, getting out of the car.

"Are you going somewhere?" Ali asked as she joined her mother on the driveway.

"Not me—we. I promised Joy I'd be her moral support at the funeral home this afternoon and this evening, though God knows it's the last thing I want to be doing after all we went through yesterday."

"Mom, I don't want to go."

"You have to, Ali. I'm *not* leaving you here on your own again— not with Earl out there somewhere, just waiting for the chance to hurt us."

"I can go up to Tony's. . . ."

Frankie shook her head. "We've imposed on Tony too much as it is."

"He won't mind, mom. I *know* he won't."

"Ali, he has a friend staying with him. Do you really think they want to have you hanging around all week?"

"I got along really well with Tom," Ali protested.

"Yes, and he was nice to me as well, but let's not wear out our welcome, okay?"

"Tony said I could come up anytime I—"

"Ali, I said no."

"I'm not going," Ali said. "I'm not going to spend all day hanging around some yucky funeral home. I won't even *know* any of these people, Mom."

"Ali, please don't argue."

"I'm not arguing. I just don't want to go. Can't we at least call Tony and ask him to be really honest about whether or not I could come up? I could bring some of my studying and a book. I'd just stay up in the guest room and not bother them at all."

Frankie rubbed her right temple. She understood exactly how Ali felt. She wasn't particularly looking forward to the rest of this day, either. But she didn't want to impose on Tony any more than she already had. They were going to have to learn to face this problem with Earl on their own, even if it meant that she wouldn't be able to leave Ali home by herself for awhile. It wasn't fair to Ali—but it wasn't fair for her, either. God damn you, Earl. Why did you have to come back?

"Mom . . . ?

Frankie sighed as she turned to her daughter. The conversation she'd had with Tony went through her mind—all those reasons why it was so important that they faced up to their problems by themselves.

"I promise I won't be any trouble or get in their way or anything," Ali said.

"What if they have plans to go out?".

"Then I won't go up—I'll come with you. But can't we at least *ask?*"

Frankie hesitated a moment longer, then nodded. "All right, Ali. We'll ask, but I'm going to make the call and if he says no, there'll be no more discussion—deal?"

"Deal."

"Sure," Valenti said. "It's no problem at all."

"I hate to ask, only—"

"No, really. I'd love to have Ali come up. Tom likes her and we weren't going anywhere anyway."

"Well, if you're sure . . ."

"I'll tell you, Frankie, if it was going to be a problem, I'd say so. You want me to come pick her up?"

"No. I can drop her off on my way to town."

Ali was beaming when Frankie got off the phone. "I *knew* he'd say it was okay," she said.

"Well, I've got to change," Frankie said, smiling at her daughter's infectious good humor. She gave Ali a once-over. "And you could do with a wash-up and change of clothes as well."

"I'm on my way."

Frankie shook her head. "Uh-uh, kiddo. I've got first dibs on the bathroom."

"Tom's here to help me with the problem we were talking about last night," Valenti said to Ali.

The three of them were sitting around back of his house. The sky was heavily overcast, but so far the rain had held off. Valenti and Bannon were sitting in lawn chairs, while Ali perched on the stairs. Ali gave Bannon a quick look, while Bannon frowned at their host.

"It's okay," Valenti said. "Ali and I don't have too many secrets, right?"

Ali nodded.

"But the thing is, Tom, there's more going on here than just who Magaddino's going to send or the problem we got with Ali's old man." He let that hang in the air for a moment as he looked from Ali to Bannon.

Ali shivered thinking of last night.

"Like what?" Bannon asked finally.

"Well, it's not so easy to explain."

"We could play him the tape," Ali said.

Valenti nodded. "But I don't think it's going to do the same thing for him as it does for us. I think you got to hear the real thing first and then the tape just sort of helps you remember."

"I suppose," Ali said. "All I know is that the thing we should really be concentrating on is who Mally and Tommy are, and how we can find them."

Bannon looked at Ali as she said the name Tommy.

"Not you," Valenti said. "This is some guy who's playing a flute or something in the evenings and lives back there." He nodded toward the woods behind his house.

"You're losing me," Bannon said.

"So we'll fill you in," Valenti said. He explained about the music and the feeling of being watched. For the first time, Ali heard about what Valenti had seen the first night she'd seen the stag and then it was her turn to describe her meeting with Mally. Valenti covered the events of last night. When they were done, they both studied Bannon for his reaction.

"I don't know," he said, shaking his head. "You're putting me on—right?"

"I know the feeling," Valenti said. "But there's something going on back in there and I think it needs checking out."

"Maybe. But it seems to me that you'd want this problem with Magaddino straightened out first. I mean, so someone's playing music back in the woods. So what?"

"You haven't heard it yet," Valenti said. "And until you do, it's going to be hard for us to explain why it's so important for us to find out what it means. See, last night that buck deer saved us—Ali and me both."

"That doesn't make sense. It's just a deer. . . ."

Valenti nodded. "That's the thing. It's just a deer. A big one. So maybe someone trained it, but I don't know. If I hadn't seen what it did to Shaw's car last night, I'd have had to say it might not even have been real. I mean, I saw these things chasing it the night it was out behind Ali's place, but she didn't see anything but the stag."

"So what are you saying?" Bannon asked.

It was Ali who answered. "We should go up that track," she said, pointing to where the road petered off into the forest, "and see where it takes us."

Bannon glanced at the sky, then back to them. "It's going to rain."

"Probably," Valenti said. "But I think it'll hold off for a couple of hours still."

"What about your leg?" Bannon asked.

"It'll be okay—so long as we take it easy. I've been looking at a map of the area and there can't be more than about four square miles back in there before you run up against the Clyde River to the north and the county road that runs between Poland and Joe's Lake on the east. We'll follow the track—for an hour tops—and see where it takes us."

"You're the boss," Bannon said.

Valenti looked at him for a moment, then nodded. "Only problem I see," he said, "is Mario said he was sending somebody else to help us, but he wasn't going to be here till later today. I don't want to miss him."

"That's no problem," Bannon said. "What he told me was, the guy was going to hang back and keep a lookout from a distance. We don't make him, but then neither do Magaddino's people. When we need him, he moves in close."

"I don't like that. I don't want to have to be thinking that one of the people out there's on our side, you know what I'm saying? It's going to make me hesitate—maybe at the wrong time."

"Whoever Mario sends, he's going to be a pro."

Valenti nodded at length. "There's that." He glanced at Ali. "So what do you say, Ali? Do you want to go for a hike?"

Ali had been following the conversation between the two men a little nervously, realizing that she hadn't really taken Tony's background and current problem as seriously as she should have. Talk, like she and Tony had done about it before any of this began, was one thing. It was sort of romantic, like in a Bogart movie or something. But this was the real thing they were talking about now.

Maybe so, she told herself, but if she backed out of it at this point, she'd never find out a lot of things. About the stag, about the music . . . And besides, Tony was her friend and you didn't back out on your friends when the going got tough.

She found a smile for him. "What are we waiting for?" she asked.

"Would you believe a rabbit that can read?"

Ali held up a hand. "Please, Tony. Spare us the bad jokes."

"Okay, okay. Let me go inside and pick up a couple of things and then we'll go."

"All right," Ali said. "But if you're not back in five minutes, we're going without you."

Valenti gave Bannon a "what do you do without someone like that?" look as he went inside, but Bannon just laughed.

"C'mon," he said to Ali. "Let's wait for him at the end of the road."

Ali followed him. Anticipation of what they might find once they entered the forest was too strong to keep her natural good humor down. By the time Valenti joined them, she'd already begun to bounce back into a less introspective mood and forget her fears.

4

Howie Peale woke with the sun shining in his eyes. He turned over, onto his wounded shoulder. The pain made him roll quickly onto his back again.

Above him was a low plaster ceiling. He moved his head so that he could see the rest of the room. Where the hell . . . ? The fake wood panelling, the bookshelf stuffed with old Reader's Digest books, the mounted carp on the wall, the dresser with its cracked mirror and top laden with deodorant, make-up and panty-hose—it all served to disorient him. Especially coming out of the dream he'd just had.

He'd been in an old beat-up Ford in the middle of the bush somewhere. The car had been abandoned, didn't even have an engine, but he was sitting behind the wheel, acting like he was driving it. There'd been a car like it in the wood lot behind his parents' place and he'd often sat in it, daydreaming that he was everything from Al Capone to a driver in the Grand Prix. But that was years ago, while in the dream he was an adult sitting in that old car, his nostrils filling with the smell of mouldering leather and the tang of old metal.

Still, that was okay. He could have handled that, no problem. Except that the big buck deer that had attacked them last night was standing in front of the Ford, staring at him through the cracked windshield. He saw violence in the creature's eyes—the same kind of look that he saw in Earl's when he'd wasted that guy the other night.

The stag circled round until it was facing the driver's door and Howie remembered stepping on the gas pedal, as if that old Ford, without an engine and up on blocks, was going to take him away from the deer. He stomped and the buck came at him, head lowered, galloping, getting bigger and bigger until it hit the side of the Ford with a jarring crash.

Howie just sat there, clutching the steering wheel, watching it back up for another run, then suddenly he wasn't in the car anymore, but on a freeway. Coming at him, out of a low ground fog, was a pickup truck. It had a set of antlers attached to the hood, the headlights shining like some huge monster's eyes.

Howie ran for the woods, the pick-up chasing him. When he got in among the trees, he chanced a look back to see that the truck was gone. The stag was in its place, bearing down on him, antlers lowered. It was about then that he woke up.

He remembered it all now, the dream and the reality of last night. The sense of dislocation left him and he sat up, gingerly feeling his shoulder through its bandage. It hurt like hell. That wop who'd shot him was going to get his, damn straight. Howie started to lower his feet to the floor when the door to the room opened and the brunette who'd taken care of him last night came in.

"Uh-uh," she said, wagging a finger at him. "Doctor Mallon says plenty of rest, buster."

"Doctor . . . ?"

Sherry grinned. "Me, dummy. I'm Sherry Mallon—remember?"

Howie nodded. "Yeah. The nurse. Sure I remember—I just didn't know your name."

The blonde woman named Lisa came to lean against the doorjamb. They were both wearing snug-fitting jeans today—Sherry with a sweatshirt overtop while Lisa had on a lacy white blouse.

"So how are you feeling?" Sherry asked.

"A little woozy. Had some weird dreams."

"Well, that's to be expected. I went to the drugstore this morning to get some antibiotics and gave them to you earlier."

"What . . . what time is it?"

"About eleven-thirty," Lisa said from the doorway.

"Where's Earl?"

"He had to meet someone in Ottawa, he said." Lisa moved to sit on the edge of the bed as she spoke. "And everyone else is gone to work—except for us."

"You don't work?"

Lisa smiled. "I wish. No, I'm on holidays—great time of year for them, don't you think? But I had to use 'em or lose 'em. Sherry's got the day off."

"Would you like something to eat?" Sherry asked.

"Can I get up to eat it?"

"Well . . . just so long as you don't do anything strenuous."

Howie shook his head. "I couldn't do anything strenuous if my life depended on it."

"What time did Earl say he was coming back?" Howie asked after a breakfast of bacon and eggs.

"He didn't," Lisa said from the sink.

Howie thought about that. Christ, he hoped Earl hadn't dumped him. "Listen," he said. "I really appreciate you folks looking after me and everything."

"Do the same for a white man," Sherry said. She was sitting across the table from him, a crossword puzzle book open in front of her. "What's a six-letter word for 'more profound'?"

Howie shrugged. "I was never much good with that kind of thing."

"Wiser," Lisa said.

"*Six*-letter."

"Wisest, then."

"Oh, never mind. I'll look it up." She flipped to the back of the book and wrote "deeper" in the appropriate squares.

"Are you guys from around here?" Howie asked.

Lisa turned from the sink to look at him. "Us *guys?*"

"No. I mean—"

Lisa laughed. "That's okay—I was just teasing. I grew up in Perth, but Sherry's from out west."

"Where the buffalo roam," Sherry said. "Fear and loathing on the great plains."

The Hunter S. Thompson references were totally lost on Howie. "Perth's south of here, right?" he asked.

"Just a few miles down the road from Lanark," Lisa said. "Why?"

Howie thought for a moment, wondering how to frame his question. He didn't want to come off like an asshole in front of them—it wasn't often that he had a couple of good-looking broads like this, just shooting the shit with him. But there were things he wanted to know.

"Did you see the car we came in last night?"

Lisa nodded. "It's still out there. What hit you—a Mac truck?"

"No. A deer."

Sherry looked up. "A *deer?* C'mon. Get serious."

"No. Really. The biggest buck deer I've ever seen." And he'd seen so many, Howie thought. At least in the zoo. "It was the size of a moose."

"Maybe it *was* a moose," Sherry said.

Howie shook his head. "No, it was a deer all right. It just hauled off and hit us while we parked on this dirt road somewhere south of here. Does that kind of thing happen a lot?"

"What?" Lisa asked. "Deer attacking cars?"

Howie nodded.

"This is the first time I've heard of it."

"Up in the Rockies," Sherry said, "I've seen bighorns crowding a car, but not attacking it."

"And there was this music," Howie went on, wondering how to explain just what it had sounded like. "It was . . . eerie. . . ."

The two women waited for him to go on. When he didn't, Lisa gave a little laugh.

"Do you do a lot of drugs?" she asked.

"What? No. I mean, I wasn't high just then." What he was trying to say was that somehow the music had seemed connected to the buck's attack. He just didn't know how to come out with it and not sound stupid.

"Well, maybe we should do some now," Lisa said. "What do you think, Dr. Mallon?"

"I would prescribe a few good solid hits of a hash joint," Sherry said.

Lisa looked at Howie. "What about you, sailor?"

"Sounds great," Howie said.

He'd been dumb to bring it up, but at least he hadn't done it with Earl. Christ knows what Earl might have done because, now that Howie thought about it, it did seem to be a pretty dumb thing to be talking about. But the memory of that music bothered him and he was determined to go back and listen for it again. There was something in it that had wanted to hurt him, that still wanted to hurt him. He didn't know how he knew it, but he knew it was true. But he had to go back all the same.

"Here, Howie," Sherry said, passing him a joint. "Have a hit."

He smiled and took it from her, pushing his strange thoughts away. Fuck it. He'd worry about it later. Right now he had a couple of beautiful broads for company, dope to smoke, and some R&R due him. The buck and the music could wait. And so could Earl, as far as that went.

He sucked on the joint, drawing the smoke deep into his lungs and looked at his companions. Maybe he'd luck out and get a blow-job from one of them. Christ, maybe he'd really luck out and get one from both of them. He grinned, feeling himself get hard under the table, and took another toke before passing the joint on.

5

"You've got to be nuts talking the way you do in front of that kid," Bannon said.

Valenti glanced ahead to where Ali was almost out of sight because of the undergrowth. They were following the track which had dwindled into a footpath. Somebody used that path regularly, Valenti thought, because it was relatively clear. Who, exactly, he didn't know. The only people he'd ever seen using it were a couple of times when an old beat-up touring car parked across from his driveway while its occupants trudged off up the track for the day. There was an older man, a younger couple, and three or four kids—dressed in shabby clothes, but clean looking.

The last time they'd come had been in the fall. Valenti just assumed they were picnicking, loaded down as they were with backpacks and parcels, but now he wasn't so sure. Could be they were delivering staples to whoever lived back in there. This Tommy who made the music. Or Mally.

"I'm telling you," Bannon said. "It's just asking for trouble."

"Ali's a good kid," Valenti said. "She won't be no problem."

Bannon shook his head. "Right now it's not real. It's like a game or a movie or something. But what happens when it sinks in just what you really were in the family—Christ, what the family really is?"

"I think she understands."

"Bullshit. She's just a kid."

"I was thirteen when I did my first hit," Valenti said.

"Thirteen?"

"Yeah. There was a guy moving into the neighborhood—not connected or anything—who was trying to get a concession started. Drugs, you know what I'm saying? Well, the *padrone* he doesn't like this so he sends a cousin to talk to the guy, only the cousin doesn't come back. A couple of days later we find what's left of him hanging in one of the *padrone's* warehouses. Guy was skinned alive, fercrissakes. Mario told me he was still warm when they cut him down—guy was hanging there still alive for all that time . . ." Valenti shook his head.

"Anyway, this is serious business now. Trouble is, the guy—this pusher—he doesn't go anywhere without a lot of muscle and the *padrone,* he doesn't want a bloodbath taking this guy out. So someone gets smart and says, "Hey, he's on the street, there's lots of kids around—who's gonna think twice about a kid?' "

Valenti glanced at Bannon, who nodded to show he was listening.

"Nobody," Valenti said. "That's who. Not the guy, not his muscle. So I get my first contract. Mario sets it up. I got the gun in my pocket, and I'm running with a bunch of kids, you know, throwing a ball around. The ball gets near the guy's car, I run over to get it. The muscle's not paying any attention to me—Christ, I'm just a kid, right? So I get right up to the car, fire twice at him, and then I'm gone."

"Hell, of a thing—sending out a kid like that."

"Hey, it was the only business I was going to know." Valenti paused to make his point and Bannon stopped with him. "I'm not some cowboy," Valenti said, "notching my gun or something stupid. I never even used the same piece twice. But I was good at what I did and with the *padrone* there was never any bullshit—no fooling around, *capito?* Things had to get pretty bad before he called a hit."

"That's not what I heard," Bannon said.

Valenti nodded. "Yeah. Things started to change. The *padrone* got old—maybe he wasn't seeing so clearly anymore. I don't know. But most of the business I did with the Magaddino family, it was just talking, you know? I'd go talk to a guy—maybe he owes some money, maybe he's got to come up with a favor he promised and he's trying to welch on it. Whatever. There weren't that many hits—not in the old days. It wasn't good for business."

"Who needs trouble?" Bannon said.

"Exactly. Who needs it? But the way things are now . . ." Valenti shook his head. "I'm telling you, I look at the paper or catch the news and I can't believe what I'm seeing. Not just all this Middle East bullshit—it's all the weird guys out there. Serial killers, they're calling them. What kind of a guy does that, just killing for kicks? I mean, I can understand a guy getting angry, getting a little crazy, and I can understand when it's business—but what kind of a guy does it for fun?"

Bannon shook his head, then tapped a finger against his temple.

"You got it," Valenti said. He looked up ahead, not seeing Ali. "Hey, we better get a move on or we'll be meeting Ali on her way back."

Bannon let him set the pace.

Ali had been like a young pup, straining at its leash, until Valenti had waved her on.

"Go on," he said. "Scout things out. We'll catch up."

So she ran on ahead, enjoying the sense of freedom that being in the woods gave her. She slowed down after her first sprint, stopping to poke into holes and peer about and explore. Something shiny caught her eye on the trail, but it proved to be only a bit of foil from a cigarette pack, rolled up into a tight little ball. Far more interesting was the row of ants that moved steadfastly across the trail. She pushed aside some underbrush to see where they were coming from, then wrinkled her nose when she saw it was the body of a small dead chipmunk. She let the boughs slap back in place and headed on down the path.

It took a circuitous route through the trees. Approximately a mile from where the road ended by Tony's place and the track started, the path ran into a stream. Ali paused to dubiously study the scatter of rocks that could serve as stepping stones.

The trail continued on the other side of the stream, which was at its narrowest point here—at least so far as Ali could see. It was seven feet wide, tops. Further up and down the stream, the water broadened out to eight or nine feet, and there were no stones. She wondered if Tony was going to be able to cross, then decided to cross first herself to see how hard it would be.

The stones turned out to be laid down in what was almost a pattern. You stepped on one and as you swung your foot in front, there was another stone just waiting for it. In moments she was across.

That's funny, she thought as she sat down to wait for Tony and Tom. When you looked at the stones, it didn't seem like it would be so easy to cross. It was almost like an optical illusion. She leaned forward to have a closer look at them, then heard the bushes rustle behind her. Fear went through her as she turned. It didn't entirely go away when she saw Mally's thin features peering out at her from between the branches of the willows that grew on this side of the stream.

" 'Lo, Ali," she said. "What are you doing?" She stayed where she was, the low brim of her hat hiding her eyes, the willows all around her.

"Mally!" Ali said, finding a smile. "I was hoping to find you. I wanted to see where you lived."

"I live here."

Ali looked around, then past Mally to where the forest started again with a rank of cedars first, then a hodge-podge of birch, maples, pine and oak. "Here?" she asked.

Mally smiled. "In the forest—in all of it." She shook her head as though it were very hard to understand why such a simple explanation should prove so hard for Ali to grasp.

"Yes, but . . ." Ali began.

"Where are you going?" Mally interrupted. "To the stone or to the village?"

"Well, I didn't even know there was anything out here—I mean, besides the forest and you. And your friend Tommy."

"I don't really know Tommy," Mally said. "I belong to the moon, you see, while a mystery has him."

"A mystery?"

"The stag. The music."

"Oh," Ali said, although it didn't really explain anything. She was about to say more, when Mally's head lifted like a startled deer's and she peered down the trail.

"Men are coming," she said, moving a little deeper into the willows.

"It's okay," Ali said. "It's just Tony—you've already met him, sort of—and a friend of his named Tom Bannon."

"Can't stay."

"No one's going to hurt you," Ali promised.

Mally smiled, showing her teeth. "I know. It's just that until I see how the music touches the stranger, I'd rather not meet him."

"But—"

"When the trail forks, go left if you want to get to the stone, right for the village."

"But what are they, this stone and village?"

"Bye, Ali."

"Mally, wait!" But the wild girl was already gone.

Ali was all set to chase after her, then thought better of it. Sighing, she turned around to watch Tony and Tom approach.

"I don't know," Valenti said as he looked at the stepping stones. "Walking's one thing—if I take it easy, I'm okay. But jumping's something else again."

"Just try it, Tony," Ali said. "It's weird how easy it is."

"Easy for you to say."

"Baby."

Valenti looked at Bannon but found no sympathy there. "Okay," he said. "I'll give it a try already."

Ali watched his face as he stepped on the first stone and went for the next. The look of concentration was quickly replaced with enjoyment and in moments he was across. Bannon followed, his features also reflecting surprise.

"What did I tell you?" Ali asked.

Valenti smiled. "Okay. So, for once, you're right."

Ali punched him on the shoulder. "You just missed Mally," she said.

"Your wild girl?" Bannon asked. He looked around. "She was here?"

Ali nodded. "But she's gone now. She said that this trail can take us either to a stone or a village. Does that make any sense to you, Tony?"

Valenti shook his head. "I had a good look at the maps before we set out. This is Black Creek. What we've got is hills to the southeast, Snake Lake Mountain up that way, and marsh to the north. But I didn't see any houses marked."

"How long have we been walking?" Ali asked.

"About thirty-five, forty minutes," Bannon said. He glanced at Valenti. "You want to go a little further?"

Valenti nodded. "Sure. I'm doing fine. A stone or a village. Fercrissakes, what'd she mean by that?"

"Well," Ali said. "There's only one way to find out."

"So let's go," Valenti said, "and cut out all this gabbing."

Ali and Bannon exchanged grins. This time Ali stayed with the men.

It was almost another forty minutes before they reached the fork in the trail. The path had continued to wind, doubling back on itself, it seemed at times. The trees were almost all cedar here, with big junipers in the few clearings they came across.

"Left is the stone," Ali said. "Right takes us to the village."

"I'm for the village," Valenti said. "I want to meet this Tommy."

Bannon nodded in agreement. That was how Ali felt, too, though she did want to know just what this stone was. They took the righthand path. After about five minutes, it gave way to an open field. When they reached the top of the field's gradual rise, they were suddenly looking down into a small valley.

"Jesus Christ," Valenti said.

The other two were silent, but equally amazed. Below them lay a cluster of cottages that seemed to come right out of a picture book of the British countryside. They were made of fieldstone and wood, with thatched roofs, all except for the barns and one cabin that was closest to the higher slopes on their left, which had to be Snake Lake Mountain.

"This doesn't make sense," Ali said. "How can this place be here and nobody know about it?"

"How do we know that nobody knows about it?" Valenti asked. "How many people have we talked to about it?"

"There's that," she said.

They stood awhile longer looking down at the tiny village. There was motion around the buildings—people working in their gardens, Ali thought. She saw sheep dotting the slope on the other side of the valley.

"Well," Bannon asked. "Are we going down?"

Valenti and Ali exchanged glances, then the three of them started down the gentle slope toward the village.

6

When Brenda Maxwell woke on Monday morning, Lance was no longer lying beside her. She thought of last night, digging Dooker's grave in the darkness, Lance standing over it. Lance would probably never have gone to bed if she hadn't taken his arm and steered him toward the house and upstairs.

Sitting up, she had a pretty good idea as to where he was now. She got out of bed, wrapped a bathrobe around herself and went downstairs. Through the kitchen window she could see him at the edge of their property, standing over the freshly-turned mound of earth that lay on top of Dooker.

Eight years Lance had had that dog, she thought. And the two of them had been inseparable. The kind of work Lance did, when he could get it, hadn't interfered. Hauling, clearing land, working on houses—unskilled labor, but at least it brought some money in to help stretch the welfare check. The farmhouse they were living in used to belong to Lance's father. Now they rented it from the bank.

The rest of the land had been sold off, but no one wanted the old farmhouse. Just like no one wanted the Maxwells.

It hadn't always been that way, but things changed and what could you do? They had their problems. Money troubles. Looking for work. Making ends meet. But this new change in Lance didn't fit any of that. She'd read in her magazines how stress could make people go a little strange, but Lord, she'd never read about anything like this. Killing Dooker just didn't make any kind of sense.

And what would? a voice inside her asked. Would it make more sense if he turned the shotgun on her? Or on himself?

Brenda shivered. Get out or get help, she told herself. And do it now. But as she moved toward the phone, she saw Lance walk away from the grave. For a moment she thought he was coming back inside, but he walked around to the side of the house and was lost from view. She hesitated, heard the pickup start up, heard it back out of the lane. As it drove off, all her resolve drained from her. She sank into a chair at the kitchen table and stared wearily around the dingy room.

Lord, they had so little as it was—just their health and making do. Why did that have to be taken away from them, too?

It didn't seem right to Lance that Dooker should be lying under that pile of dirt in the backyard. It just didn't make sense. Dooker wasn't the kind of dog to lay around. He was a doer. Damn dog was never still, always checking out this, checking out that. Chasing rabbits and groundhogs. Catching 'em by the neck and giving them a quick shake that broke their necks, killing 'em fast and easy.

No way a dog like that was dead. Dooker'd just run off somewhere—playing a game. Looked like it was up to Lance to find him.

He nodded to himself as he drove to a special spot where the two of them had spent a lot of time. It was off a backroad, with a stream running by. Trees hung low over the water and there were lots of fields nearby, full of slow groundhogs just looking to get their necks snapped.

A cloud of dust spun up from Lance's wheels that took a while to settle after he'd passed. That was the trouble, Lance thought, watching the dust in his rearview mirror. Times like this a man left no more trace of himself than a dust cloud like that. Five minutes later, the dust settled down, and who the hell knew you'd been there?

When he reached the turnoff, he turned into a rutted road that was more pasture than road, the pickup shaking and rattling all the way. At the end of the road, he shut off the engine. Stepping out of the cab, he walked down to the stream and called for Dooker, waited awhile, called some more. After a time, he just sat down on his bumper.

Christ on a cross, that dog had really taken off this time. Where would he go? Lance thought about that, then found himself thinking about Buddy Treasure and the music he'd heard back when he'd gotten the flat in front of the old man's place. That's where Dooker would go. Chasing that music. Chasing the stag that made the music.

Lance nodded. Turning the truck around, he headed back toward French Line and the Treasure place. That's where he'd find Dooker. Chasing the music. Just like the music chased him. Lance gritted his teeth. He didn't want to think about that, about what the music did to him, about how it made him feel, about what chased him through his own dreams. He didn't want to think about that at all.

Lance stopped in front of the Treasure house and looked it over. Really looked at it, instead of giving it the quick nervous glances that he usually did when he drove by. It looked good. Fixed up real nice. He noted the debris in the front lawn. At another time he might have thought of offering to haul it away for a few bucks. At another time. If it were another place.

He got out of the pickup and stood listening to the silence. There was no sign of Dooker, no sign that there was anyone or anything around at all. Returning to the truck, he sat there studying the building, the wreck of a barn behind it, the woods behind that. In the early afternoon, even with the overcast sky above, the property didn't seem much different from any other place. Hell, why should it? It wasn't the house, but something in the woods behind it that was playing on his nerves.

He thought about what was back there. He'd lived his whole life in this area and never heard a whisper of talk about there being anything strange back there. It was just bush and marsh. But he couldn't shake the feeling that something was waiting for him in those woods.

He sat there for a long while, listening to nothing, just staring. Nobody passed him on the road. Nobody moved inside the house.

There's nothing here, he told himself. Reaching over, he turned over the ignition. The pickup started up with a cough, loud in the quiet air. He'd come back, he thought. But first he'd find Dooker. A man shouldn't go messing around in the bush without his dog. Christ on crutches, but there was nothing Dooker liked better than a good run through the woods.

Lance drove away, heading back for that special place that he'd already checked out once this morning. Dooker had to be there by now. But when he arrived, there was no sign of the dog. He beat the bush and called until his voice began to go hoarse.

That dog's just not here, he told himself. And that was because the damn dog was dead. He'd shot the poor bugger himself last night.

He lay down on the grass by the stream as a blur of tears clouded his eyes and his chest tightened with pain. The criss-crossing branches above him moved with the wind in a hypnotic pattern and then sleep crept up on him like a sly thief. He slept dreamlessly, one hand clenched in a tight fist on his stomach, the other stroking the grass at his side where Dooker would have been lying if he were still alive.

Lewis was expecting them, having been forewarned by Mally. She stopped by his cabin with a cryptic "They're coming," before vanishing into the forest again.

Who was coming? he wondered as he left his cabin. Jango Gry and his people? It was a little early for them. He looked up to the hill where the trail from the outside world left the forest to come down to the village. When he saw the three figures up there, he knew that Mally hadn't meant the Gypsies. Taking off his glasses, he shaded his eyes and peered up at the strangers. He had never seen any of them before, but he knew who two of them were all the same.

He waved to get their attention. When he saw that he had succeeded, he sat down on his chopping stump to wait for them to come down to talk. He wondered what they thought of what they had found.

"Somebody's trying to get our attention," Bannon said as they started down the hill.

Ali squinted, but all she could see of the figure by the cabin was that he was white-haired. "I wish I'd brought my binocs."

"What do you think he wants?" Valenti said.

"Maybe he's Tommy," Ali said.

Bannon nodded. "Could be. Could be anyone. But whoever he is, it looks like he was expecting us."

They followed the trail on down to the village. Just before it reached the first buildings it forked again, one path leading in among the cottages, the other swinging to the left where the figure had signaled to them. There was only one cottage between them and the old man's cabin. A middle-aged woman sat on its stoop and regarded them expressionlessly. A teenaged boy who was hoeing the garden paused in his labor, also to watch.

"Friendly, aren't they?" Ali whispered when they'd gone by.

Valenti nodded. Neither woman nor boy had responded to their friendly greetings.

"Did you take a good look at what they were wearing?" Bannon asked. When Ali and Valenti shook their heads, he went on. "The old-fashioned style of their clothes. I can remember my grandmother wearing one of those old black cotton dresses and the kid was wearing woolen trousers and a collarless shirt, both of which looked too big for him."

They reached the front of the last cabin. The trail went on, inclining more steeply as it entered the woods once more. That'd be Snake Lake Mountain, Valenti thought. Remembering his map, he was about to turn to see if he could catch a glimpse of the lake that should be over to his right when the old man who'd signaled them came around the side of the cabin.

After what Bannon had pointed out, Valenti took note of the man's clothing. Like the boy's, his trousers were woolen and he had a collarless white shirt on as well. Overtop was a tweed vest. His shoes were scuffed and old. Looking at him, taking in the creased face and snow-white hair, Valenti realized that everything about him was old.

He glanced at his companions, but they seemed to be waiting for him to make the first move. Valenti nodded and smiled at the old man. He took a couple of steps closer and held out his hand.

"My name's Tony Garonne," he said. "Are you Tommy, uh . . ." Christ, he thought. They didn't even have a last name for him. That bothered Valenti. He liked to treat older people with the respect he felt was their due and that included no familiarities that weren't okayed first.

The old man smiled as he took Valenti's hand. "I'm not Tommy. My name's Lewis Datchery. Welcome to New Wolding." His handshake was firm.

Bannon stepped forward and took Lewis's hand in turn. "Tom Bannon," he said.

"You're new to the area, aren't you?" Lewis asked.

Bannon glanced at Valenti, then nodded. "Yes. I'm just visiting Tony for the week."

"And who are you?" Lewis asked, looking at Ali.

"Ali. That is, Alice Treasure, only everybody just calls me Ali." She shook the old man's hand as well. His skin felt dry and leathery to the touch. "You knew we were coming, didn't you?" she added.

"Yes—yes, I did."

"Was it Mally who told you?"

"Ah, yes. You've met the little bandit, haven't you?"

Ali nodded. There was a moment's silence then that began to lengthen uncomfortably. Neither Ali nor Valenti knew quite how to begin, while Bannon stood back, just along for the ride.

"Do you all drink tea?" Lewis asked suddenly. After nods all around, he smiled. "Well, then why don't we step inside while I put the kettle on and we can find out what brought the three of you here today."

He moved to the front door as he spoke, ushering them all inside. Ali took Valenti's free hand as they went through the door, her mouth shaping a silent "Wow" as she took in the walls of books.

"How long have you lived here, Mr. Datchery?" Valenti asked.

"A very long time. And please—call me Lewis. We don't stand much on formality here."

He busied himself, filling a kettle from a water container, checking the stove for fuel, then setting the kettle on top. Adding another log to the stove, he sat down at the table and waved them all to seats.

"So what *does* bring you to New Wolding?" he asked.

"Well, that's kind of hard to explain," Valenti said. He paused to think about where he wanted the conversation to go, then decided to take a different tack. "You're sort of off the beaten path here, aren't you?"

Lewis nodded. "We don't have much commerce with the outside world. We grow what foodstuffs we need and the few staples we require beyond that are brought to us by the Gypsies."

Valenti thought of the touring car and its occupants. That explained the way they'd looked. He should have known. He'd run into Gypsies in New York, but he'd just never put it all together.

"Why?" he asked then.

Lewis looked puzzled. "Why what?"

"Well, what're you doing here? Are you folks, you know, Mormons or Amish or something like that? I mean, do you live here because of . . . religious differences or . . ." His voice trailed off as he realized what he sounded like. "Look. I'm sorry. I don't mean to come off all heavy with the questions or anything. I know it's none of our business what you're doing here, but living close like we do—like Ali and I do, anyway—we've been hearing things and . . ." How did he explain the stag? "It's the music, you know what I'm trying to say? We hear it and it makes . . . it makes a difference. So we're curious about it—like where it's coming from, who's making it, and why. Mostly why."

Lewis smiled. The kettle began to rattle on the stove and he glanced at Ali. "Would you mind seeing to the tea?" he asked.

"I'll get it," Bannon said.

"Thank you." Lewis regarded Valenti and Ali. "It's a long and not altogether interesting story what we're doing here. We are most of us originally from Wealdborough in England, from a small village named Wolding for Wold Hill, which stands above the village. Around the turn of the century, we turned our backs on what was then the modern world and returned to . . . older ways, including older ways of worship.

"It was Tommy's piping that was the initial catalyst for the change—not the Tommy that pipes for us now, but his grandfather. Again, our only contact with the outside world was with the Travellers—the Gypsies—and it was they who told us about the great forests of this continent.

"A number of us wanted to come here. We felt that in this land we would be closer to the mystery that the pipes called up, and so we came, a dozen families in all, to build a place for ourselves here. We named it New Wolding, to remind us of the land that we had left behind, and here we have lived ever since."

Bannon rolled his eyes, but Valenti and Ali leaned closer to the old man.

"What is this . . . mystery that you're talking about?" Valenti asked.

"In Gaul and Britain, he was given the name Cernunnos. In Wales, he was sometimes called Mabon. The Germanic people knew him as Uller, the winter bowman. The Greeks and Romans knew him in various guises: as Apollo and Orion; the Egyptians as Amen-Ra; the Hindus as Surya. He appears in the bible as Nimrod—Genesis describing him as a 'mighty hunter before the Lord'. He is a solar god, a huntsman and the lord of animals, and he has been both the pursuer with his own pack of hounds, as well as the pursued, with the hounds chasing him.

"The various descriptions of him become confusing when you try to put them all together, but I suppose that is a part of his mystery— just as the moon's White Goddess has her own secrets. I like to think of him as the Green Man, an earthier view of the legendary Robin Hood—a Trickster figure, if you will—but I think the name that best sums him up is Pan."

There was a moment's silence as they all digested that. Ali and Valenti remained fascinated. By the stove, Bannon shook his head. Tony was taking all this too seriously. And talking the way he did in front of the kid who . . . well, sure, she was a good kid, but come *on* . . .

Bannon wondered when was the last time that Mario had spent some time with Tony Valenti. Everything Bannon had ever heard about the man was good, but maybe, since the Magaddinos got on his case, something had happened to him so that he wasn't operating with quite a full load anymore. The way he just sat there, taking in all this bullshit about gods . . .

"But you said he was a sun god," Ali said. She knew her mythologies, even if the others didn't. "That the Greeks knew him as Apollo and Orion. Wasn't Pan a Greek god, too?"

Lewis nodded. "I told you that it becomes confusing. But the reason that Pan serves best, I think, is that he is so adaptable. There is something of Pan in each of the gods I named. And he has always been a reflection of what one brings to him."

"I don't understand," Ali said.

"I don't like to throw semantics around, Ali, but if you did understand, he wouldn't be a mystery."

"Yes, but—"

"That's what the native people of this land call the little spirits of the wood—manitous. Little mysteries. And Kitche Manitou is the Great Mystery."

"But Pan . . ." Ali frowned. "You said he's a reflection . . ."

"That is his Trickster aspect. He becomes what you bring to him. If you approach him with fear, he fills you with panic." Lewis smiled as he used the word. "If you approach him with lust, he appears as a lecherous satyr. If you approach him reverently, he becomes a majestic figure. If you approach him with evil, he appears as a demonic figure."

"You mean like Satan?"

"Exactly. The Christians weren't stupid. They borrowed what they could, from wherever it would be useful. They frowned on merriment and dancing, so they made Lucifer over in the shape of the Pagan Pan who embodied—at least for them—all that they stood against. But what can you expect from a religion that is based on so much suffering? It's little wonder that faerie couldn't abide the sight of their crucifix with the son of their god nailed to it. Did you know that the cross originally stood for the Tree of Life—for nourishment and life-giving? They turned it into a symbol of death."

Ali shook her head. "It doesn't stand for death—it stands for rebirth. Christ died so that our souls could be saved."

"But it is still a symbol of suffering. A symbol that man must suffer the trials of this world before he can reap the benefits of the one thereafter. In Heaven. I don't perceive life as something that must be suffered through for some dubious reward in the hereafter. Life can be and should be a joy right here and now!"

"It just means you're supposed to be a good person," Ali said.

"I can agree with being a good person, but Christianity doesn't espouse that—at least not by its actions. Are you a Christian?"

"Yes. Well, that is, I don't go to church, but I believe in God, I guess . . ."

"We're getting a little off-track here," Valenti said.

No kidding? Bannon thought. It wouldn't surprise him if what they'd stumbled onto here was some out-of-the-way asylum for the terminally strange.

"Just what exactly is it that's running out there in the woods?" Valenti wanted to know. "Pan? The devil? What?"

"We saw him as a stag," Ali added. "Not as a goatman."

"He's been known to wear both those manifestations . . . and many more," Lewis explained. "And as I said before, I prefer to think of him as the Green Man—a brown-skinned man, tall and antlered, wearing a mantle of green leaves."

"But what does he do?" Valenti asked.

"He doesn't do anything. He simply is. We are the ones that do, depending on our nature."

Valenti studied the old man. "And you folks worship him?"

"Not in the way *you* mean the word." He looked them over, one by one. "What you should do," he said finally, "is stay here this evening. Come to the stone with us. Hear Tommy's piping close at hand. Follow the steps of the dance. Perhaps the mystery will manifest, perhaps not. But you'll be closer to understanding then."

There was a long moment's silence.

"My mom's not going to be back till late," Ali reminded Valenti.

He nodded. He didn't want to say it out loud, but what he was worrying about was that maybe this was some kind of a cult and he didn't want Ali mixed up in it. On the other hand, he'd heard the music, and whatever else it was, it wasn't evil. It wasn't wrong. The mystery is what you bring to it, he thought, repeating what the old man had told them. What the hell did that mean? He looked over at Bannon, who was finishing up with the tea, pouring them each a mug. Bannon met Valenti's gaze but gave him no indication of what he thought.

"Okay," Valenti said. "We'll stay and check it out. Why not?"

"Why not indeed?" Lewis said and smiled.

Valenti looked sharply at him, trying to read something in the old man's features, in his eyes. Lewis returned his gaze. Humor crinkled his face with laugh lines, but it wasn't a mocking humor. Valenti wasn't sure what it was. It made him feel a little strange, one step out of kilter, like he did when he listened to the music. It wasn't unpleasant, he just didn't feel in control.

At home, sitting on his steps, he didn't mind that feeling. It promised him things—solace, peace of mind. Here, it would be sharper. Here, he wouldn't be able to just shut it off and walk back into his house. He heard a pitter-patter of rain on the roof and realized that the storm had finally come.

"Is the rain going to postpone this . . . whatever it is tonight?" he asked.

"The rain will stop before too long," Lewis said with the authority of one who lived more by the weather than by a watch on his wrist. "You'll see."

"Here," Bannon said, putting a mug in front of Valenti. "Have some tea." His eyes said, you and me, we've got to talk.

Valenti got up and went back to the stove with Bannon as Lewis began to show Ali around the bookcases. "What's the problem?" he asked in a low voice.

"This is crazy—you know that? Gods running around the woods and all this shit. The only thing we've got to worry about out here is the Don's boys tracking us down."

Valenti glanced over at Ali. She looked eager and ready for the evening, excitement barely under control.

"I know this doesn't mean anything to you," he said, "but it's something we've got to look into. It's important for us—Ali and me."

"And that's another thing," Bannon said. "I tell you, you're too free and easy in front of this kid. You've got real problems, Tony, and you're not helping yourself going on nature hikes while Magaddino has all the time in the world to set things up out there where it counts."

Valenti shook his head. "I know what I'm doing," he said. And added, I hope, to himself. "Besides, you think any of Magaddino's people are going to find us back here in the bush? We're probably in the safest place we could be right now."

"Just saying this whole village doesn't go weird on us and try to take us down."

Valenti touched the gun in his pocket. "We'll just keep our eyes open going in," he said. "That's all."

Bannon sighed. "You're the boss."

"It's going to be okay," Valenti said. He picked up a tea mug and brought it over to Ali, who'd returned to the table. *"Salute,"* he said, raising his mug to her.

Ali grinned at him and took a sip from her own.

8

Earl watched Fingers take the weapons out of the suitcase, one by one, and lay them on the bed. He glanced at Louie, standing by the window, then back at Fingers. What they had here was a fucking arsenal. His man hadn't believed it when Earl had put the order in earlier today. "What're you going to do with all this?" the man had asked. "Start a war?" Earl had simply shaken his head, unsure.

He still wasn't sure. He could understand the handguns—anything had more punch than those two little peashooters that Fucceri and Maita had smuggled in through customs. It was the heavy-duty artillery that had him puzzled. A 9mm Ingram submachine gun. A .30 calibre Browning automatic rifle. A sawed-off shotgun. An auto-reload shotgun. Together with the pair of Smith & Wesson .38s, they really did have enough here to set up their own army.

"You figure we'll be needing all this?" he asked.

Louie turned from the window. "It's nice to be prepared," he said. "What we'd like is to knock him down a flight of stairs, run his car off the road—something simple. But if it comes right down to it, I'm ready to shoot him into little pieces. Be my pleasure."

Fingers grinned. He was taking apart one of the .38s. When he got back to what he was doing, the grin was replaced with a frown. "You got burned," he said as he sighted down the barrel.

"What do you mean, I got burned?"

"Check the calibration on this—it's going to throw off your shot. The breech is worn, too." He spun the cylinder and shook his head. "I hope the rest of these are in better condition."

"Hey, what do you expect on short notice? This isn't the U.S. of A., pal. We got handgun laws here like you wouldn't believe."

"I'm familiar with Canadian regulations," Fingers said.

"I'll bet you are."

"Okay," Louie said. "Let's take it easy. Earl here's doing the best he can for us, Fingers. Aren't you, Earl?"

"You bet," Earl said. What a pair of fucking monkeys. "So are we hitting Valenti tonight, or what?"

"The way I figure it," Louie said, "if he's not gone, he's going to be expecting us tonight or tomorrow, so what we're going to do is lay off for a couple of days. That gives us a chance to set things up right."

"What if it's taking him a couple of days to get out of there?" Earl asked. He waved a hand at the weapons on the bed. "With all that shit in our hands, he won't be going nowhere if we hit him now. Wait too long, and all you've got is an empty house."

Louie shook his head. "If he's going, he's gone now. Maybe we'll take a quick spin round there later tonight—check it out. But if he's there, he'll be holing up tight. The thing we got to do then is keep him on edge. He'll be sitting in there, waiting for us, knowing he fucked up, knowing we're coming. I don't care how cool he used to be, he's carrying lead in his leg now and he's lost his edge. The man just won't be able to move fast."

"Yeah, but . . ."

"Look," Louie said. "We're doing this my way and we're doing this right. Any dumb ass could blow his ass off. I want him taken out clean. So clean, the police won't be looking for anybody even when they figure out who he really is."

"Okay," Earl said. "You're calling the shots."

Louie nodded. He didn't bother explaining that he'd already tried the frontal approach on Valenti that time in Malta—hit him two, maybe three times, and the guy still disappeared like a ghost. It hadn't done a whole lot for Louie's rep. So this time he wanted it to be perfectly planned. He wanted to work in so close that he could tap Tony on the shoulder just before they blew him away. *If* they blew him away.

Louie also liked the idea of taking Tony out without any evidence that it was a hit. In a way, Tony was an example. For two years or better he'd been thumbing his nose at the *fratellanza* and getting away with it. That wasn't good for business. Other people might think they could get away with it, too. But if he took Tony out without making it look like a hit and let the word go out that Louie Fucceri had been in the area, it wouldn't take too long for those who had to know to put two and two together.

It made a nice example. Told them Louie Fucceri worked clean, and he always finished a job he started. That had been one of Tony's own specialities, before he fucked up. Louie liked the idea of using it on him.

"So who's going to check the place out tonight?" Earl asked.

"We'll work that out later." Louie paused as a thought came to him. "What happened to the guy you were with last night? Did he know we were flying in?"

Earl shook his head. "He doesn't know dick about you being here. He got hurt last night so I left him at a friend's place."

"What kind of place?"

"A cottage—maybe a twenty-minute drive from Valenti's."

"Maybe we should work out of there—what do you think?"

Earl nodded. "Sure. But you'll have to ditch those suits. People up here don't wear many three-pieces in cottage country."

"That's not a problem," Louie said. Though Earl was. He was getting on Louie's nerves. Maybe when this Colombian deal that Earl was setting up was done . . . maybe the *padrone* would give Earl to Louie as a favor.

"I'm going to enjoy seeing you guys in T-shirts and cut-offs," Earl said.

"You talk too much," Fingers told him.

"Is that true?" Earl asked Louie.

Broadway Joe's son just smiled.

Late Monday afternoon, a black van, splattered with mud, pulled over to the side of the road just before the turn-off to Tony Valenti's property. The driver carefully checked the road both ways to make sure he was alone, then backed the van off the road.

The bed of the van rode high and there was no ditch, so the driver had little trouble squeezing his vehicle in among the trees. Branches scraped its sides and it drove right over saplings. When he got it far enough from the road, the driver killed the engine and disembarked. He moved quickly forward and began to straighten saplings that hadn't sprung back on their own, moving on to do the same with the grass and weeds. These latter didn't fare quite as well as the more resilient saplings, but by the time the man had brushed away the van's tracks from the mud on the side of the road and had thrown a camouflage net over the van itself, the vehicle was barely visible from the road.

The man stood for a few moments in the misting rain, regarding his handiwork. He had short dark hair and a day's worth of salt and pepper stubble on his cheeks and chin. His complexion was dark, made more so by his black water-repellant clothing and the shadows of the trees.

Going back into the van, he returned a moment later with a self-cocking commando crossbow in his hands. It was fitted with a scope that he checked out, sighting it on a nearby blackbird taking shelter in a cedar from the rain. The scope brought the bird in startlingly close.

"Bang," the man said.

Laying the crossbow down for a moment, he attached a belt around his waist. A small quiver of crossbow bolts hung from it. Then he picked up his weapon once more and slipped off into the woods, moving back toward Tony Valenti's house. His passage was silent in the wet forest.

9

"You understand what the old man was talking about in there?" Valenti asked Ali.

The two of them were sitting on the top step of the stairs going into the cabin, watching the rain. A small overhanging roof kept them dry. Inside the cabin, Bannon was reading while the old man sat at the table, doing what, Valenti didn't know. He just sat there. Thinking maybe. Valenti and Ali had come out to get a breath of air.

"How's your leg?" Ali asked.

"It's okay. It always aches a bit in this kind of weather." He turned to look at her. "You didn't answer my question."

Ali glanced at him, "Jeez, Tony. I'm just a kid. What do I know about this kind of stuff?"

"Don't give me that."

"Okay." She spent a moment picking at a thread on her jeans, then looked out into the rain. "The things he was saying confused me. I mean, all these old gods he was naming—some of them are sun gods, some of them are sort of hunter figures, some are a bit of both. But they come from all different kinds of mythologies and cultures."

"You figure they can't all be the same?"

Ali shrugged. "I don't know enough about it. I really am just a kid, Tony. The kind of stuff Mr. Datchery talks about—that's for scholars to figure out."

"Yeah, but you've read a lot. You're smart."

"And you're not?"

"I'm just a dumb Italian," Valenti replied, mimicking her. "What do I know?"

"Okay. I get the point already."

"So what do you think?"

"Well, I know there are similarities all around the world. And when it comes to Christianity—well, they did borrow a lot from other cultures. Easter comes around the same time as the vernal equinox— that's the Spring equinox when day and night are the same length— and even the whole business with Easter eggs is based on pagan fertility rites. In fact, even Christ's being crucified has parallels in other cultures. The Norse god Baldur was nailed to a tree as well."

"You're kidding."

Ali shook her head. "So I understand what Mr. Datchery was getting at, but at the same time I find it confusing. And then . . ." She looked at Valenti. "Then there's what I feel inside. About the music and the stag. When I think about just that, not about things that I've read or stuff that you learn in church, then it all starts to make perfect sense. Maybe I'm going a little crazy—I don't know."

"I don't think so," Valenti said. "I get the same feeling. And I've been hearing that music a whole lot longer than you have. But then I talk to Tom and he just says it's all a load of crap and that makes sense, too. I mean, how can any of that stuff Datchery's talking about be real?"

Ali sighed. "I don't know. What do you think'll happen at this stone tonight?"

"I'm still trying to figure that out."

"You don't think these people belong to a . . . well, a cult or something?"

Valenti shrugged. "The thought's crossed my mind."

"My mom used to know this guy who claimed he was a witch—not like riding a broomstick and casting spells and stuff like that, but it was some kind of religion. I talked with him about it a couple of times, but I was pretty young and I didn't understand a lot of what he was saying. Then Mom got mad 'cause he was telling me all this stuff."

"What kind of stuff?"

"Well," Ali said. "I read up on it after he stopped coming around—Mom didn't make him too welcome. Anyway, one thing I remember is that they had two gods instead of one—the Moon Goddess and her consort, the Horned Man—and that's . . ."

"Just like what we've got going on here."

"Or so Mr. Datchery says."

"But we've seen the stag, Ali. We've heard the music. And ordinary deer don't come to people's rescue like some kind of cavalry—not like the stag did that night."

Ali nodded. "Yeah. Only why did he do that?"

"That's the thing, isn't it?" Valenti said. "Maybe we'll find out tonight."

"I suppose." Ali thought about it. She wanted to go to the stone tonight—to hear the music right up close, to see what Lewis Datchery was talking about, but at the same time she found the whole idea a little scary. At least Tony was going to be there. And Tom. They'd make sure that nothing happened to her. Only, what if whatever took place happened inside her? The music hadn't made her look or talk any different, but ever since she'd first heard it, she'd felt different inside. She wondered if Mally would be there tonight, then realized that that was something else they hadn't talked to Lewis about.

"Rain's letting up," Tony said. "Just like the old man said it would."

"Tony," Ali said. "We never asked him about Mally."

"That's right. We never did."

"She says she's always been here," Lewis said, "and while she seems to know the mystery better than any of us, it doesn't affect her the way it does us."

"She told me she was a secret," Ali said.

Lewis nodded. "The Moon's secret—but I don't rightly know what she means by that."

They were all sitting around the table. Bannon had a poetry collection of Padraic Colum open in front of him and was obviously more taken by the book's contents than their conversation. Glancing at him, Ali wondered at the incongruity of someone involved in Tony's old business being interested in early twentieth century Irish poetry.

"You have to understand," Lewis went on, "that Mally's as much a riddle to me as she is to you. I've known her a great deal longer, of course, but while she lets enticing snippets fall my way during our conversations, she's never really come out and spoken plainly to me about anything."

"I know that feeling from just seeing her a couple of times," Ali said.

Lewis smiled. "And yet I trust her. She's been very good to me—kept me company through many an evening. She likes to have me read to her and brings me the odd book from time to time that she 'finds.' "

"She brought you all of these?" Bannon asked, looking up from his book.

"Oh, no," Lewis said. "But some of them. Others my friend Jango searched out and brought me—knowing my interest in such things. The greater portion of them, however, made up the library of the man who built the house you now live in, Ali."

She remembered something Mally had told her. "The 'dark man'?"

Lewis nodded. "That's what Mally calls him. His real name was Ackerly Perkin. He left this area well over fifty years ago."

"Mally . . . she's been around that long?" Ali asked.

"I've known her that long. I have the feeling that she's been around forever."

"But she looks my age." Ali couldn't believe the wild girl was fifty years old, if not older.

"She hasn't aged a day since the first time I met her," Lewis said.

"That's not possible," Ali said.

Still not looking up from his book, Bannon nodded in agreement.

"There's a great deal about Mally that doesn't seem possible, I'm afraid," Lewis told them.

"What about this Perkin guy?" Valenti asked. He was getting uncomfortable with the direction the conversation was going. Unlike Bannon, he'd heard the piping and seen the stag, so he knew that there was *something* odd going on around here. But people didn't just stop growing older. Not unless they'd died. "What's the story on him? And why does Mally call him a dark man?"

"She saw him as something dangerous," Lewis said, "though I'm not sure what the exact danger he represented was. Either he was capable of showing the mystery to be an illusion—which would, you'll have to agree, take a great deal away from its power to move our spirits—or the mystery was real, but Perkin was capable of creating illusions that could chase the mystery across the world like the legendary Wild Hunt chased the souls of the dead. What's even more curious, however, is that there was another Perkin in Wealdborough who was—in his own way—as mysterious as Ackerly Perkin as well as his exact opposite. We're back to illusions again—the original Perkin in England had none, while Ackerly Perkin had too many."

He regarded the confused looks on the faces of his guests and shrugged apologetically. "I'm sorry if I'm not explaining this very well, but the whole problem has been a source of much personal confusion and soul-searching and I still don't quite have it set in my own mind. My research has led me down too many false trails—so many, in fact, that I'm not quite sure myself as to which are the illusions and which not."

"You mean the stag's not real?" Valenti asked.

"He seems very real," Lewis said.

Valenti thought about it attacking Shaw's car last night. "I'll say."

"But something pursues the stag—and that's what confuses me the most at the present time. This Hunt—is it a natural phenomenon? By which I mean, if the stag exists as a mythical being, does it always follow that the Hunt will pursue it? Or was the Hunt created out of Ackerly Perkin's illusions and set upon the stag's trail? Or is it my own questioning as to what exactly the stag is that has set the hounds upon it—are the hounds my questions?"

"I thought the stag *was* the huntsman," Ali said.

"Some cultures have depicted him so," Lewis replied.

Valenti remembered what he'd seen the first night he saw the stag. There'd been shapes following it, looking first like hounds, then like monks or priests. . . . "Why's it so important to figure this all out?" he asked. "I mean, either something's real, or it's not—right?"

"But it's not so simple as that," Lewis said. "We've contained the mystery to some degree—kept it from roaming beyond the confines of these forests, because if it was to run free in the world . . ." He paused, looking for a way to phrase what he wanted to say. "There's too much wrong in the world now," he said finally. "And if you remember what I said about the mystery reflecting what it finds in the hearts of those who come into contact with it. . . ."

There was a moment's silence as his guests followed his train of thought.

"Boom," Valenti said.

Ali shook her head. "I can't accept that. What if you're wrong, Mr. Datchery? What if the stag's presence would be enough to just mellow everyone out?"

"There is no power in the world, not that of *any* religion's god or mystery, that can change people from being what they are. The world's history—what little we have recorded of it—proves that beyond a doubt."

"But—"

"And if you need further proof," Lewis continued without letting Ali speak, "then remember this: The mystery once had free run of the world. Were there no more wars? Did people help each other in times of famine or plague?"

"So you have to keep it trapped?" Bannon asked, interested despite himself.

"A better way to put it would be that we're keeping him alive," Lewis said. "He wouldn't survive very long in the greater world by himself. Unfortunately, our numbers have dwindled here in New Wolding. We are no longer enough to keep him here. The mystery speaks through Tommy's music and reaches out farther and farther each time it sounds. The mystery needs the rebounding echoes that come when the music touches the soul of a man or a woman and then returns to him. The echoes that come back to him now aren't always so good. They make the mystery wilder, driving him further from his aspect of the Green Man and more to that of a dumb beast. And at the same time, the Hunt grows stronger, feeding on those echoes. It becomes a downward spiral. . . ."

"Maybe it's time for him to go," Ali said. "You know. The circle turns and all that? Maybe he's got to go, so that he can come back stronger."

"That's the Christian in you talking. The miracle of Christ's rising from the dead and His subsequent ascension into Heaven."

Ali shook her head. "I think it's more pagan," she said with a small smile. "I mean, reincarnation and that sort of thing."

"I think I'm getting a headache from all of this," Valenti said. "The more you talk, the more confused I get."

"My own years of research and study have left me no better off," Lewis replied. "Sometimes I think that only Mally has the right of it. She says to just let things flow. What comes will come."

"She seems more active than that to me," Ali said.

Lewis smiled. "Well, she also says that it's better to do and experience, than to peck and worry at the workings of a thing."

"There's just no straight answer, is there?" Valenti said.

"Wait until tonight," Lewis said. "Maybe *you'll* find an answer."

"Will Mally be there?" Ali asked.

"Perhaps. She doesn't always go."

"Whatever happened to Ackerly Perkin? Bannon asked.

"The world went to war and he went to experience it." Lewis shook his head. "We've never heard from him again."

"What about the other Perkin?" Ali asked. "The one in England?"

Lewis sighed. "I don't know. It's getting late. Perhaps we should have some dinner and save the rest of your questions for another time. Wait until after tonight."

"Okay," Ali said. "Do you want some help with dinner?"

"I'd like that very much," Lewis said.

Valenti glanced at Bannon, but Bannon merely returned to his book as Lewis and Ali began to make a salad. Lewis already had a stew on and there was freshly raised dough ready to go into the oven. As the scent of baking bread filled the cabin Valenti returned to the door and studied the view.

Somewhere up on that hill, in among the wet trees, that was where the stone was. Somewhere in the forest, the mystery was walking . . . like a stag, or a goatman, or a man with antlers and a mantle of green leaves. Valenti wondered for a moment, before he went back to sit at the table: Did the mystery ever appear as a wild-haired girl with burrs and twigs in her curls who called herself Mally? Or maybe as an old man who lived by himself in a cabin in the forest, on the edge of a village that wasn't marked on any map?

Just what the hell were they going to find out tonight? He glanced at Ali, who was happily chopping up cabbage and carrots for the salad. Maybe coming out here today hadn't been such a good idea after all. If anything happened to her . . . Fercrissakes, he told himself. Don't even think about that.

10

By six o'clock Monday evening, Howie came to the conclusion that Earl had dumped him. He felt a curious mixture of relief and regret. On the one hand, this was going to be the big score. Earl wanted to just work his way deeper and deeper into the big money rackets, but Howie hadn't quite decided what he was going to do with the cut Earl had promised him. All he knew was that for the first time in his life, he was going to have enough money to do what *he* wanted for a change. People were going to listen to what he had to say. Women were going to want him in their pants.

The thing that balanced all that slipping away was the fact that he wouldn't be around Earl anymore. Earl with his crazy eyes. Earl who, if you said the wrong thing maybe, would just as soon blow you away as not. Howie didn't dislike Earl, but he'd learned to be more than a little afraid of him. His relationship with Earl had become a little like a big cat act in the circus, except the lion was in charge, and if it jumped through a hoop, it was only because it wanted to.

Howie shifted uncomfortably in his deck chair. What the hell was he going to do now? How long were Lisa and Sherry going to take care of him before they, too, picked up on the fact that Earl probably wasn't coming back to collect him? As though summoned by his thoughts the screen door banged open behind him and the women joined him on the porch. Lisa had a joint burning between her fingers.

"Want a toke?" she asked, offering it to him.

"Yeah, sure. Thanks."

"We," Sherry announced, "have got the munchies. What do you say to pizza?"

Howie's little fantasy of the two women both going down on him hadn't come about, but Sherry kept giving him considering glances like she was interested in him. It didn't make sense to Howie—women never wanted him unless they were going to get something out of it—but he sure wasn't going to complain if something started. He found himself wishing that Lisa would make herself scarce.

"Pizza?" he said. "Sounds good."

"So what don't you want on yours?" Sherry asked him.

"The works."

Sherry giggled. "Right, you don't want anything on yours."

"No, no. I meant—"

Howie never finished as the two of them exploded with laughter. Sherry and Lisa had been smoking all afternoon and were both flying high. Howie had smoked about one joint for every three of theirs— enough to keep a buzz on and dull the ache from his shoulder, but not too much so that Earl would come back and find him blasted. He grinned at the women now and took a long toke, holding the marijuana smoke deep in his lungs. Fuck Earl. He'd waited around for Earl long enough.

"Okay," Sherry said when she caught her breath. "The works for you, Howie." She started to giggle again but held it in.

"I've got it," Lisa said. "We'll get one large—mushrooms and green peppers on half, the other half with the works—and one small ham and pineapple." She retrieved her joint from Howie. "Anybody want to come along for the ride?"

Howie glanced at Sherry. She gave him a look that made him feel a little weak-kneed, so he shook his head.

"Okay. I'll be back in half hour or so. Don't get into trouble, kids."

When Lisa was gone, Sherry knelt down beside Howie's deck chair. "You're a funny kind of a guy, Howie," she said.

He cleared his throat. "Uh, yeah?"

"Mmmm. You're quiet—but nice quiet, not creepy quiet, you know? How's your shoulder?"

"It's okay. Pretty good, considering."

She leaned forward, resting her arms on the chair by his leg. "You know what I think would be really therapeutic?" she asked. She reached out with one hand and ran her fingers along his thigh. Even through his jeans he could feel each individual nail. "Can't you even guess?"

Howie shook his head. He didn't want to break the spell. Christ, he thought. This can't be happening to me.

"Well, speaking as your personal doctor," Sherry said, "I think . . ." She paused and started to pull down his zipper, slipping her hand in to grasp his hardening penis. "I think you need a little therapeutic loving—just to give you back your will to live. What do you think?"

Howie swallowed and nodded.

"Of course," Sherry said as she lowered her head, "this means you're going to owe me, and I'll warn you right now, I always collect on my debts. . . ."

Howie leaned back in the deck chair. Maybe she was feeling sorry for him, maybe she liked him, maybe she was just high—he didn't care which. He just couldn't believe this was happening. He didn't want it to ever stop.

Two empty pizza boxes lay on the ground. Nursing beers and sharing a joint, the three of them watched the dusk settle on Calabogie Lake. Howie was just flying. He kept glancing at Sherry, remembering, then looking away. The twilight reminded him of last night, chasing Earl's kid and the stag and everything, but mostly the music.

"The guy who owns this place," he began.

"Steve?"

"Yeah, Steve. When's he coming back?"

"I don't think he's coming back tonight," Sherry said, looking to Lisa for confirmation.

Lisa shook her head. "He's got something up tonight—him and Max. Pam said she might be coming by later with Eric. He's got some dynamite weed that he scored off of Johnnie Too-Bad—do you know him? He's one of those Rastamen with the snakey hair."

"I know a couple of those guys in T.O.," Howie said. "But I was thinking, do you girls want to go for a drive?"

Lisa smiled. "To see your big buck deer?"

"How'd you know that I was talking about that?"

"I know all and see all," Lisa replied. Sherry started humming the theme to *The Twilight Zone* and all three of them laughed.

"But I'm serious," Howie said after a few moments. "I don't know if we'll see the buck—Christ, I don't know if I *want* to see that sucker again—but that music. It was something. It was really something."

Sherry and Lisa exchanged glances.

"Why not?" Sherry said.

Lisa grinned. "Sure. Why not? It'll be good for a laugh."

A half hour later they were on the road to Lanark, Howie concentrating on where to turn off. He was flying high, but he was pretty sure he could find the place again. They hit a bump that he felt in his shoulder and he reached for the joint that was smoldering between Sherry's fingers. A couple more tokes wouldn't hurt at all. They missed the turn-off and ended up in Lanark village. It was almost full night by the time they retraced their route, coming from the south this time so that Howie could recognize the landmarks.

"This is it," he said. "Turn here." He smiled at Sherry sitting beside him. "You're going to love this," he added.

"I wouldn't miss it for the world," Lisa said with mock seriousness, but Sherry just smiled back at him.

Christ, Howie thought. He didn't know what he was doing, but he was sure doing it right, whatever the hell it was.

11

As dusk drew its veil across the day, Lewis led his guests outside. None of them spoke. Mosquitos hummed by their ears. The twilight air was heavy with the scents of meadow and forest. The chorus of frogs and cheeping crickets was occasionally punctuated by the sudden whirring sound of a June bug.

Valenti began to fidget as it grew darker. He leaned heavily on his cane, wondering again at how smart they were to go through with this. The coming of night had unsettled something in his soul—an anticipation of the piping, but also a vague uneasiness at what might be revealed tonight.

When he thought about what Lewis had said—how the mystery reflected what you brought to it—his uneasiness grew. Whatever it was going to find inside him, wasn't going to be peaceful. He'd been through too much. He had too much crap kicking around inside him. The scars that his years in *fratellanza* had left him weren't healed yet. They might never be healed. Not when he had to live with an armory in his home and an automatic in his jacket pocket.

He touched the gun's cold metal, then withdrew his hand from his pocket. He wished he hadn't brought it, but he was comforted by its presence all the same.

"It's an old stone," Lewis said suddenly. His voice was soft, but it startled them all in the quiet of the dusk. "It's been here for longer than we've lived in this land—maybe longer than the Native Peoples have been here, too. It's not like any stone in the area. What it's doing here, not even Ackerly Perkin knew. Maybe the Vikings who the historians now admit were here before Columbus—maybe they raised it to Thor or Odin. Maybe it was done by Celts. They were supposed to be here around that time, too. Or maybe it was raised by some people that came before either of them, that came before the Native Peoples as well. I don't suppose we'll ever know."

"Another mystery," Bannon said.

Lewis nodded. "Or part of the same one."

"The Indians had stone works," Ali said. "I've read about them— big stone circles and standing stones."

"But not this far north," Bannon said. "And it still hasn't been proven that they actually constructed them."

Both Ali and Valenti regarded him with new consideration. They really didn't know much about him, Valenti thought.

"That's true," Lewis said. "But this stone is different. You'll see."

Before they could talk any more about it, there was movement on the track leading up to the stone. A wolfish-looking dog gamboled by, trotting up the path, pausing to smell something before racing back to make sure that its master was following, then taking off again. Lewis's guests studied the boy that followed the dog. In the growing darkness they could only make out general details. He was plump-faced with an unruly thatch of hair. He ambled by them, obviously in no hurry to get to wherever it was that he was going. When he glanced at the four of them standing in front of Lewis's cabin, Ali nudged Valenti with her elbow.

"That's the boy from the garden," she whispered.

Valenti nodded. He'd recognized him as well.

"His name is Tommy Duffin," Lewis said.

"Tommy . . . ?" Ali frowned. "You mean the one who plays the pipes?"

When Lewis nodded, she tried to get a better look at the boy, but he was already too far up the track. He didn't seem much older than she was, Ali thought. And from what she remembered of him earlier this afternoon, he didn't seem to be exactly the brightest of people. Or at least not the friendliest. *He* was the one that made the uncanny music?

"He doesn't . . . you know . . ." Ali hesitated, not really knowing how to say what she wanted without it coming out all wrong.

"He doesn't seem like much," Lewis said for her. "I know. It's a curious thing. I've never understood why it's always been one of the Duffins who's been the piper. It's just another facet of the—" he glanced at Bannon "—mystery, I suppose. But Tommy changes when he begins to lip the reeds. His eyes lose their vacant look, his features seem to become thinner, more intense. It's something like the village itself. There's something about it . . . some air that keeps strangers away. They might be walking along a direct line that would take them straight through New Wolding, but somehow their feet are led astray and they never quite reach us."

"We got here," Valenti said.

"Ah, yes. But you've heard the music."

"What about aerial photography?" Bannon asked.

Lewis looked confused.

"Photographs," Bannon explained. "Taken from airplanes." He pointed to the sky. "When they were photographing this area for regional maps, the village should have shown up in the photographs, but according to Tony, New Wolding's not marked on any maps that the Department of Energy, Mines and Resources made from those pictures."

Lewis nodded, understanding now. "I can't explain that," he said. "There's so much that's not clear that I can't even begin to . . ."

His voice trailed off as a liquid spill of reed-pipe music came gliding across the quiet night air. It touched each of them with its plain and simple beauty. Lewis smiled, his heart opening to welcome an old friend, but his guests stood transfixed. Ali and Valenti had never heard it so clear and pure. It resonated inside them, waking yearnings and needs that they couldn't explain. Bannon, virgin to the music's spell, lifted his head, nostrils widening as though to take the music in with every sense he had.

"Madonna mia," Valenti breathed. "It . . . it's . . ." But he had no words to describe what he heard or what he felt.

The villagers were walking by Lewis's cabin now, heading for the stone where Tommy played. They were old and middle-aged for the most part, with a few teenagers in their ranks, but no young children. As a woman in her sixties paused at the end of Lewis's path, the four of them joined her and took up the rear of the ragged procession.

"Who are your friends, Lewis?" Lily asked.

Lewis introduced them, but they were too entranced by the music, by its closeness and clarity, to do more than simply nod. Lily smiled and took Ali's hand.

"Is this your first time to the stone?" she asked.

Ali nodded.

"Well, you'll have to dance with me—will you do that?"

Ali glanced at Valenti and Bannon, but they were both looking ahead. She felt the tug of the music, too, and was eager to reach its source, but she nodded again to the woman holding her hand.

"I . . . I think I'd like to try," she said shyly.

"Oh, you'll do very well," Lily told her. "Won't she, Lewis?"

"I gather she will," Lewis replied.

Mally was perched high in a tree overlooking the glade and its stone as the villagers trickled in. She'd arrived before anyone. She'd watched Tommy come, slow-footed and heavy-jowled, saw him put the reeds to his lips, watched him change as he woke the music from them. A smile glowed deep in her eyes at the sound of the reed-pipes. Oh, it was good and strong tonight, the music. Strong enough to call the mystery—maybe strong enough to keep the hounds at bay.

She settled more comfortably in her perch as the villagers continued to arrive. Tommy quickened the music so that it went from a slow air into a dance tune, and then Kate and Holly Skegland were swaying back and forth on the damp grass. Martin Tweedy soon joined them, but Mally no longer watched them. Her gaze was now on Lily and Lewis, and the three outsiders they were bringing to the glade.

" 'Lo, Ali," Mally said as she saw the teenager step onto the grass, her voice so soft that only she herself could hear it.

Lily was holding Ali's hand, drawing her out toward the dancers. The two men stood with Lewis, watching the piper and the moving figures. Mally nodded to herself as she judged the effect the music was having on Bannon. There wasn't exactly a fire in him—not like there was in the other two—but maybe something better. A deep stillness.

Old Hornie liked that. He needed the fires—like the bonefires on the hilltops on the merry eve and midsummer night and ghostnight—but he liked the quiet too. You could hear things in the quiet. The drumming of hooves and the whisper of the music. The dawn chorus when the feather-throated sang his praise.

Mally smiled. She wanted to go down and dance, especially with Ali, but she wanted to see their faces when the stag came, too. So she stayed in her perch, fidgeting and eager, waiting, smelling the air, watching their faces.

It was the stone that drew Bannon's gaze first—the dark bulk of it lifting skyward, moonlight on quartz veins that spiralled up and down its length like ancient runes. Then he saw the boy. Tommy was transformed—physically transformed. He wasn't the same boy at all as the one Bannon remembered seeing in the garden earlier that day.

Bannon hadn't known what to expect—either with the music, or what would take place at this stone. It had all sounded too spacey, too crazy. But now . . . hearing it, feeling the sense of mystery that deepened in this glade . . . he could understand what it was that neither Tony nor Ali nor the old man had been able to explain to him before.

It was magic, plain and simple.

That such music could come from that backwoods hick of a boy. That this place could remain hidden from the world. That there might even be some enormous buck deer that was a manifestation of . . . of whatever it was that set the heart apart from the actions of the body . . .

It was magic.

Bannon could feel a grin stretching his face. He understood why the villagers stayed on, and, in some way, why Lewis Datchery felt it was so important to know just what it was that happened when the music sounded. But for himself, it seemed more important to just go with the flow. Not to question, but to experience.

He had questioned. He had scoffed. But he knew now that those who questioned, those who took it all apart trying to find out what it was and what made it tick . . . they lost out in the end. The magic would always elude them. The mystery would only deepen. Because if it lost its secret, it just wouldn't be the mystery anymore. It would rob the experience of its potency. All you'd have left would be dry dust and the voices of men discussing what it was all about. The quiet, the music, the *magic* would be gone.

Valenti watched Ali dance, feeling like a doting father seeing his first born take her first step. A rush of affection went through him. In his mind's eye, he added Ali's mother to the scene. He imagined her standing here beside him, holding his hand maybe, the two of them watching Ali move to the music. Or maybe Frankie would dance with her daughter. Maybe she'd look at him from among the dancers, her gold hair spilling down in tangles and the music draining away all her worries and fears, making her strong, like she really was, even if she wasn't ready to believe that yet. Maybe if she could hear this, she'd believe it. Then he shook his head.

Yeah, he thought. She'd believe it. But it'd never be him with her. He had too much unfinished business hanging over his head and what the hell would someone like her want with the kind of guy he was anyway? She'd already gone through all that shit with Earl Shaw, fercrissakes.

He was surprised at how much that hurt—that he felt like that about Frankie in the first place, that it hurt so much that there was never going to be anything between them.

What kind of a guy made a living the way he had anyway? And for what? As soon as they had no more use for you, the *pezzi di merda* just dumped you. Didn't matter how loyal you'd been. Didn't matter what kind of shit you'd done for them.

The music played, a jiglike tune that only exaggerated his regret. Not for what had been, but for what might have been. For all the things he'd lost because of the business he'd been born into. He'd trade all that shit—the money, the respect, everything—just to have a kid like Ali to call his own. A woman like her mother to call his wife. He'd work as a fucking ditchdigger, fercrissakes, he didn't care.

But it was too late. He'd been what he'd been and now the debts were being called in. The Magaddinos were going to get him, one way or another. Either they'd kill him, or they'd keep him boxed up in a life where he was always looking over his shoulder, where he could never get close to anyone, because he'd never know when the *bastardi* would be there, just waiting to get him.

The music seemed to hold a personal message for him. Go ahead, he thought it was saying. Feel sorry for yourself, regret the things you've done and the things you'll never get to do. But just remember that you aren't what you were, but what you are now.

Sure, he thought. Tell that to whoever the new *padrone's* sending after me. But the music wouldn't let him hold onto that. It drew his gaze to the dancers, his heart to the music. The fires inside him muttered and burned, but danced in time to the piping notes.

Of the three of them, it was Ali who first spotted the stag soft-stepping from the forest behind Tommy's shoulder. It towered over the boy like a twin to the old stone, eyes gleaming, antlers smooth, head lifted high as it gazed into the glade.

Ali faltered in her steps. She let go of Lily's hand and stood still, staring at the enormous beast. She thought of everything that Lewis had told them, but realized as she looked into the stag's liquid eyes that none of it mattered. It didn't matter who or what the stag was, or where it had come from. All that mattered was that it existed. But still, she could understand the legends and myths that had grown up around this majestic being.

It was no longer a stag, the longer she watched it, but a man. He stood as tall, his antlers branching high into the sky, but on two cloven hooves now, not four. A cloak was thrown over his shoulder, matted with leaves and burrs and twigs, some green and growing, some dried to an autumn brown. His face was angular like a roughly chiseled statue—a wise face, and a sad one, but there was joy in it, too, and a sense of wildness, a sense of humor and fun. Only the eyes stayed entirely the same, dark and liquid.

Ali took a step toward him and then he changed again. Now the antlers were a ram's horns, lifting from his brow in two ridged sweeps. The cloak fell to the grass to become a carpet of mulch that he trod on with goat legs. His chest was hairy and muscular, his face a triangular shape that was accentuated by the tuft of a goat's beard that dangled from his chin.

Pan, Ali thought. She wanted to speak his name, but her muscles were too numb, her throat too tight to shape its sound. The music dipped and soared around her as she took a second and a third step, drawing ever closer to the magical apparition. And then she heard the other sound—distant at first, but growing louder. It was like the baying of dogs on the hunt, the howling of wolves. She remembered what Lewis had said about the Hunt and shook her head. They couldn't have him. Not this being.

The sound of the Hunt grew louder now, cutting across the music. The other dancers faltered. The goatman grew indistinct around the edges. He was the stagman again, taller, broad-chested, and then the stag. He pawed the ground with a hard hoof, spraying grass and clods of dirt. The dogs could be heard louder still.

"N-no," Ali said.

She started to turn around. She'd stop them. She'd give the mystery time to escape. But then a familiar figure was at her side, floppy hat covering the tangled and matted hair, teeth showing white as she grinned.

"Come on!" Mally cried as she took Ali's hand.

"No!" Ali protested. "The Hunt—"

"Stuff the Hunt!" Mally told her. "Tonight we're going to drink down the moon!"

They were directly in front of the stag now. Mally grasped Ali around the waist with both hands and with a cry of "Ali-oop!" flung her up onto the stag's back. Ali clung to its neck, stunned as much at where she found herself as at the wild girl's startling strength. A moment later Mally was up on the stag's back behind her, straddling the wide girth, her arms around Ali's waist.

"Run!" Mally cried to the stag. "Let's show them the night as they've never seen it before. We'll run them into their graves and then run some more. Hoo-*hey!*"

She kicked her heels against the stag's sides and it leapt high into the air, over the dancers, circling on prancing hooves in front of Valenti, Bannon and Lewis, then back toward the stone. There was a sound of snarling in the air as the Hunt drew close. The stag jumped toward the stone. Valenti took a few running steps after them, then his leg gave out and he stumbled to the ground. He watched the stag leap, its riders clinging to its neck and each other, and then it was gone.

He blinked. For a moment he'd thought it had disappeared right into the stone, but he knew that couldn't be right. It had entered the forest behind the stone. But why couldn't he hear it in the underbrush? And Ali . . . It was taking Ali away!

Bannon was at his side, helping him to his feet. Valenti shook off his hand and stared wildly at where the stag had disappeared. It was gone. *With* Ali. Oh, Jesus. What was he going to tell her momma?

"C'mon," Bannon started to say, but suddenly the glade was filled with dark shapes. The Hunt was all around them.

The dancers had fled to the shelter of the trees with the other villagers. Tommy stood up, back against the stone's rough surface, his dog Gaffa crouched snarling at his feet. The reed-pipes hung from Tommy's hands. His face was vacuous again, stripped of its inspiration. He stared at the two men and the shapes that surrounded them.

The shapes were dogs, then men, cowled and robed, then animals again. They milled around the circle, snarling. When one of them snapped at Valenti, he dug out his automatic, thumbed the safety off, and fired point-blank into the creature's face.

The explosion of the gun was loud. A deep silence followed the sound of its sharp report. The beast Valenti had shot didn't appear to have been affected at all by the bullet, but it backed away from him, as did the rest of the pack. Valenti took aim at the biggest one of them, but Bannon touched his arm.

"No," he said. "They're going."

Still silent, the pack flowed around the pair and ran for the stone. They split up, half passing it on one side, half on the other. Not until they were in the forest did they begin to howl once more.

"Oh, Jesus," Valenti said. The automatic hung at his side now and he leaned against Bannon. "It took her," he said. "Ali's gone. What the Christ are we going to do?"

Bannon turned to look at where they'd left Lewis standing. The old man came out from the shelter of the trees and walked slowly toward them.

"You!" Valenti said, lifting the gun.

"That won't help," Bannon said.

Valenti looked at the weapon, then slowly nodded. He flicked the safety back on and thrust it into his pocket. "Where did they go?" he asked Lewis. "Where's that thing taking her?"

"I don't know," Lewis replied. "This has never happened before."

"Great." Valenti studied the circle of villagers who were slowly emerging from the trees. They all appeared frightened. He turned to look at Tommy. The boy was still standing by the stone, the reed-pipes silent in his hand. "What about the pipes?" Valenti asked. "Can't you use them to call the stag back?"

"We don't command him," Lewis said. "All we do is celebrate him."

"Yeah. But the pipes call him, right?"

"Sometimes he comes—more often not. And never twice on the same night."

"Fercrissakes!" Valenti shouted. "Then what're we going to do?"

Bannon stopped to pick up Valenti's cane and handed it to him. "We'll find her," he said.

"How? Christ, what am I going to tell her momma?"

"C'mon, Tony. We'll—"

"It's that wild girl," Valenti said. "She grabbed Ali. She's going to be the one that pays if anything happens to her." He swung around to look at the villagers again. "And that goes for all of you—you hear what I'm telling you? Anything happens to Ali, and you're all paying."

"Please," Lewis said. "We meant her no harm. This has never—"

"Happened before," Valenti finished. "Yeah. I know. I heard you the first time. Well, it's never going to happen again, *capito?* This *babau* of yours—this bogeyman's not going to steal another kid, not if I've got anything to say about it."

As Valenti started for the stone Bannon caught him by the arm. "What are you planning to do?" he asked. "Chase after that thing?"

"You got a better idea?"

"The way I see it is, we've got two choices. Either we wait for it to come back here, or we head on back to your place. If Ali gets off that thing, I'm betting she'll head for your place. All we're going to do if we start running crazy through the bush is get lost ourselves."

"Yeah. But what if she falls off it somewhere back there? What if she's lying there hurt?"

"The girl's with her," Bannon said.

Valenti shook his head. "I don't trust that girl."

"I can't believe anything bad's going to happen to Ali," Bannon said. "Not while she's with the stag. Didn't you *feel* anything when it showed up?"

"I'll stay here—all night if necessary," Lewis offered, "and if she returns here, I'll bring her to your house."

"You're just a part of all this shit," Valenti said. "If it wasn't for you, we'd—"

"C'mon, Tony. You're talking crazy. No one here wants to hurt Ali. If you'd think for a moment, you'd see that."

Before Valenti could reply, the sound of the pipes started up again—softly, not a rallying call, or a celebration, just a sad series of notes that didn't quite make a melody. But it was enough so that Valenti remembered what he'd been feeling when the music had been going full tilt. It was enough to take the sharp edge off his fear for Ali. He turned to look at Tommy as the sound of the pipes faded away, but there was nothing in the boy's eyes at that moment. Nobody home, Valenti thought. He took a deep breath.

"Okay," he said. "Let's go home."

Bannon nodded. He turned to Lewis, but before he could say anything, Valenti spoke.

"Listen," he said to the old man. "Maybe I got a little carried away, but I'm worried about the kid, okay? She means a lot to me."

"I understand," Lewis said. "If I'd had any way of knowing this would happen, I would never have asked you to come to the stone."

Valenti nodded.

"If she comes back here, I will bring her to you," Lewis said.

"Thanks. And we'll send you word if something breaks on our end." Valenti glanced at his companion. "Let's hit the road, Tom."

Behind them, the piper by the stone began to play once more. The music that came from his reed-pipes was not the same as it had been earlier. It sang of regret now, and of things lost, rather than in celebration of the mystery. The sad strains followed the men as they took the path back to Valenti's house.

12

Frankie was exhausted by the time she turned off the highway to finish the last leg of her drive home. Exhausted and depressed. Funeral homes, hospitals, graveyards—they all left her emotionally drained.

She felt sorry for Bob's parents, and especially for Joy, but she couldn't have lasted another minute in the company of any one of the three without screaming. It wasn't their fault. It was just that the hours in the funeral home, on top of the scare she'd had last night, had not left her in the best of shape. Her nerves were so worn they were ready to snap. All she wanted now was to collapse on her bed and sleep it all away: Her fears about Earl, the jangling of her nerves, the depression . . . Hopefully, everything would look better in the morning.

She drove by the road that went up to Valenti's house and was about to turn into her own lane when she remembered Ali. God, she was in worse shape than she'd thought. Already slowing down, she suddenly slammed on the brakes when she saw the old pickup truck sitting in her lane. The seatbelt caught her shoulder, then whipped her back against the seat. The car's engine stalled, but she just turned off the ignition and lights, and stared at the truck.

Twilight had become night while she was driving home from Ottawa. The house was dark. Everything was dark—and quiet, too, now that the car engine was still. Her breathing was loud in her ears. She lost the outline of the pickup until her eyes adjusted to the lack of light.

It's Earl, she thought as she made out the truck's bulk in her lane once more. God damn him! She thought of what Tony had told her this morning, thought of what she knew of Earl from her own experiences with him, but she was so angry at the moment that she forgot to be scared. He was *not* going to move into her life again. Nor into Ali's. And he was definitely not getting a cent of the Wintario money.

She unclipped her seatbelt, opened the car door, and stepped out onto the road. Its uneven surface made it difficult to walk in her pumps, even though the heels weren't all that high. It wasn't until she neared the truck and its dark shape bulked beside her that she had to wonder just what in God's name she thought she was doing.

She was going to stop Earl? She put a hand against the side of the truck's bed for balance as a tremor of fear went through her. This was not smart, she told herself. Not smart at all. She ran a hand nervously through her hair, tugging at a knot in the curls. The smart thing to do would be to go up to Tony's and come back with him and his friend Tom.

She started to turn, then heard something move near the front of the truck. A shadow pulled away from the wheel, rose to its feet to become a man. Everything went tight inside Frankie's chest and she found it hard to breathe. She backed away, but the shadow followed her. There was a ringing in her ears, and something else as well. It took her a long moment to realize what it was: the music from Ali's tape, but the real thing this time, not information stored on magnetic tape.

"I want my dog, lady."

The man's voice startled her. She knew a momentary relief that it wasn't Earl's voice, then the fear came clawing back. Who was this?

"Y-your . . . dog . . . ?" she asked.

"I'm looking for him, lady. His name's Dooker. You better give him back. . . ."

Frankie continued to back up. "Look," she said. "I don't know anything about your dog. Does it look like I've got a—" She bumped into the hood of her own car and there was nowhere left to go. The man continued to advance until he stood over her.

"I want him, lady."

His breath was stale in her face. A small cry escaped her lips as he grabbed her by the shoulders.

"Please . . ." she began.

He shook her roughly. "I want . . . I want . . ."

Frankie tried to break his grip on her, to no avail. She could still hear the eerie music spilling out of the woods, low and distant, but immediate at the same time. It made her feel weak and strong, all at once, but while one part of her was falling under its spell, her fear of the man and what he was doing was stronger.

She lifted her knee, but the skirt she was wearing was too narrow to give the blow much power. Where it should have connected with his groin and doubled him over, all it did was make him grunt. His grip tightened on her shoulders. Suddenly he half-lifted her and threw her down on the hood of her car. Holding her down with one hand, he started to tear at her skirt with the other.

"Want you," he growled.

Lance was in that special place by the river where he and old Dook used to go when it came to him that Dook wasn't dead—he was going to shoot his own dog?—and he hadn't run off. Not Dooker. He'd been stolen. Old man Treasure's daughter—she had his dog, no ifs, ands or buts about it. That's where he'd first heard the music. She'd used the music to trap old Dook, just like she was trying to trap him. Filling his head with crazy shit.

He got up from the riverbank and into the truck. Turning the pickup around, he headed back along the dirt roads to the Treasure place, only when he got there, the place was empty.

He parked in the lane and walked around the house, peering into the windows and muttering to himself. Every once in a while he'd start calling for Dooker, but then he'd stop right away, the loudness of his voice startling him. When it started to rain, he hunched in the cab of his pickup, staring at the house through the rain-splattered windshield, wiping the glass every time the condensation built up too much. When the rain stopped, he went back to prowling the grounds, keeping a wary eye on the woods behind the house.

He checked the barn calling softly for the dog. The need to see Dooker, to know the old feller was okay, kept building up in him. His head ached as the pressure increased until he finally had to sit down again. He leaned back against the front wheel of his pickup and closed his eyes.

He had to have open ground around him. Even the familiar interior of the pickup's cab made him claustrophobic. At some point he realized that he must have dozed off—dreaming of shotguns and Dooker dying, but—Christ on a cross—there was no way that was true. The next thing he knew it was dark.

He heard a car engine sputter and die. Turning, he saw its head-beams on the road just before they winked off. A door opened and then he listened to someone walk across the road and onto the driveway. He waited until whoever it was had come too close to run away before he could talk to them, and then he stood up.

He was feeling a little better now. His head didn't hurt so much, and while he still wanted to find Dooker, the need to do so was no longer burning so painfully inside him. His eyes were well adjusted to the dark by the time he got up to look at the blonde woman that was standing by his truck.

He couldn't tell a whole lot about her face in the poor light, but the shape of her looked real good in the narrow skirt and top she had on. He started out asking her about Dooker, but then he heard it coming— first on the edges of his consciousness, then building up, louder and louder. That music. He should've run, he thought. He should've just taken off when he had the chance, but now it was too late. And in another moment, it didn't matter anymore.

He felt the hotness in his groin and when he followed the woman as she backed out of the lane, he wasn't seeing her the same anymore. She was a field that needed ploughing now. A bitch in heat. He could smell the blood on her. And Lord, oh, Lord, he needed to ride her.

Her skirt tore like paper and as she lifted her hands to claw at him he just grinned and bulled his face in against her breasts, away from her nails. With his left hand, he loosened his grip on her shoulder and grabbed her neck. His other hand tore at her undergarments. The music continued to burn in him as he bared her womanhood to the night air.

Her smell was so strong he could hardly breathe. She wasn't struggling so hard now, so he let go of her neck and tore at her blouse. Lifting his head, he arced his head back as far as it would go and let out a howl. Right about then, a car came around the curve and stabbed him with its headlights.

The man in the van was just getting ready to leave his vehicle for another circuit of the house and its grounds when he heard the music start up. Closing the rear door, he hefted his crossbow, head cocked as he listened. What the hell was that? He started through the trees, heading for Valenti's house, when he heard overtop the soft piping first a man howling like some kind of animal, then the sound of a car.

He doubled back, crossed the road that led up to Valenti's place at the same time as a car went by the turn-off, slowed and came to a halt. By the time its doors opened and the occupants were getting out, the man with the crossbow had entered the trees on the other side of the road and was working his way closer to where the car had stopped.

All of a sudden, he thought, the night had gotten interesting.

Howie knew a moment's panic when the car's headlights caught the two figures struggling on the hood of the car that was stopped on the road in front of them. All three of them saw the man raping the woman, but only Howie thought that it might be Earl.

"Don't—" he began, then shut his mouth. Don't stop, he was going to say. Don't get involved. But Lisa was already standing on the brake. "Don't let him get away!" Howie finished.

As soon as the car came to a halt, he opened the door on his side. Sherry pushed past him. Lisa was already on the road. When Howie glanced at her, he saw that she had something in her hand. It looked like a tire iron.

"You bastard!" she screamed.

The rapist lifted his head. For one moment, Howie thought the guy was going to have a go at all of them, but then he bolted and ran for the pickup that was parked in the lane. The woman he'd been abusing started to roll off the hood of the car. Lisa, faced with the choice of going after the man or catching the woman, opted for the latter. Sherry stopped to give her a hand. Howie, after taking a few steps towards the pickup, stopped as well when the truck's engine turned over, then caught. Weaponless, there wasn't much he could do but watch the pickup bounce across the lawn, dip into, then up out of the ditch, and finally tear off down the road. Once it hit the road, he turned back to the women.

The rapist's victim was having some trouble breathing. He had tried to choke her, Howie thought. Then as he moved in closer he saw enough of her features and that spill of blonde hair to know just who it was that they'd rescued tonight. Earl's ex! Jesus H., wasn't that just too fucking weird?

"For God's sake," Sherry told him. "Don't gawk at the poor woman."

Howie quickly shifted his gaze away from the woman's breasts.

"Don't try to talk," Lisa was saying to her. "Just take it easy. We scared him off. He's not going to hurt you now." She glanced up at Sherry. "Should we take her to the hospital?"

"Jeez, I don't know. Is she badly hurt?"

"I . . . I'm okay now," Frankie managed. She tried to sit up and fumbled at the ruin of her blouse. Lisa helped support her.

"Are you sure?" Sherry asked.

Frankie nodded slowly. "I live . . . I just live over there." She pointed at the dark house.

"Well, we'll get you inside," Lisa said. "Is there anyone we can call for you? There doesn't look to be anyone home."

"My daughter's staying with a neighbor—just up . . . just up the road."

"We'll get you inside first," Sherry said, "and then we'll see about your daughter. How old is she?"

"Fourteen."

Sherry put her arm around her while Lisa supported Frankie from the other side. "We should probably get you cleaned up first—before we get her. What do you think?"

Frankie nodded gratefully. When Sherry turned to Howie to ask him to put the cars in the lane, she saw he was just standing there in the lane, head cocked.

"Howie . . . ?" she asked.

"Listen," he said. "can't you hear it?"

"Hear what . . . ?" But then she didn't have to ask anymore, they could all hear it now. It was a plaintive lost sound that they could easily have missed if Howie hadn't pointed it out.

Listening to it, tears welled up in Frankie's eyes and she was surprised to realize that they weren't for herself, for what she'd just gone through, but for the sheer beauty of the music itself. The soft piping went through her, casting light on the tattered shadows that lay inside her.

"What is it?" Lisa asked softly. She glanced at Frankie, saw the tears in her eyes glistening in the moonlight, but saw also that Frankie was smiling at the same time.

Howie got nervous when he first heard the music. He was worried about the stag showing up, worried about the feeling he'd had this morning about being hunted. But then he started to really listen to it and he found himself sympathizing with the rapist's victim and pissed as hell with the rapist.

It was a weird feeling for Howie. He'd always sort of figured that what went on between a guy and a girl, well, that was their business. Maybe things'd get a little rough on the broad sometime, but hell, they all wanted it, didn't they? Only now . . . The music was so sad. His chest felt tight. He glanced at Sherry and wondered what it'd be like if she was his girl, say, and some guy tried to stick it to her. Sherry chose that moment to look at him. She couldn't read his face, but she reached out and gave his hand a squeeze. That only confused Howie more.

He shook his head suddenly, clearing it. "Maybe I should move these cars," he said.

His words broke the spell. While his two companions helped Frankie into the house he got into her car and started it up. What's Earl going to say? he wondered as he pulled the car into the lane. Jesus, things were really messed up. But then, he thought, why the fuck should I worry about what's with Earl? Earl wasn't here and maybe, just maybe, it was time for Howie Peale to do something for himself for a change.

The man waited until they were all inside the house before he rose from the cedars where he'd been hidden and started up the road to Valenti's house. He wasn't sure what to make of what he'd just seen. His mind was still filled with the strains of that soft and distant music he'd heard.

It had done something to him, that music. He'd felt something wake inside him in response to it. What, he wasn't sure. But something.

Cradling his crossbow, he continued up the road, forcing himself to concentrate on the business that had brought him here in the first place. It was time to check and see if Tony Valenti had returned home yet.

13

"You say the road just stops at Valenti's place, right?" Louie asked, as Earl turned off Highway 511 toward French Line.

"You got it," Earl replied.

"Well, let's just take a spin by the end of his road for starters," Louie said.

"I don't see why we don't just—"

Louie cut Earl off. "This is my baby," he said. "You don't have to understand shit, you understand what I'm saying? Now you can just point out the spot to us and then blow, or you can hang in and maybe—if you do what I say—earn yourself a little bonus."

Earl didn't bother correcting him. Louie could think Earl was working for him all he liked. He could throw his weight around, mouth off—no problem. But Earl wasn't going to forget. And when this Colombian deal he'd set up with Louie's old man went through . . . well, maybe he and the wop could repeat this little conversation. Only this time, Earl would call the shots.

He made the turn that would take them to Lammermoor instead of French Line if they went far enough. "It's coming up," he said, slowing the car.

They passed by the road and came up on Frankie's place.

"Is this the closest neighbor?" Louie asked.

Earl didn't answer right away. He was looking at all the lights on in the house. His bucks were sitting in there, just waiting for him. All he needed was Frankie's signature. The second car in the driveway bothered him.

"Hey—are you listening to me?"

Earl glanced at Louie. "Yeah, sure. Valenti's place is maybe half a mile up that road on a dead end. Other than that place we passed a mile or so back, the next closest people are living just outside of Lammermoor."

"How far's that?"

"We're talking maybe two miles."

"What about this place?" Fingers asked from the back seat. He indicated a rundown old log cabin that was coming up on their right.

"It's deserted—like the other place just before we got to Valenti's road."

"Okay," Louie said. "I'm getting a feel for the area. Turn us around once and then drop me off at the end of Tony's road."

Earl glanced at him. "Listen," he began. "If you're—"

"Just get this shitbox turned around and drop me off, okay?"

"Sure," Earl said. "No problem."

He turned the car and headed back the way they'd come, slowing as they drew near to Frankie's house once more. The drapes were drawn, but he could see figures moving inside, silhouetted against the interior lights. Party while you can, he thought as he pulled over to the end of the road leading to Valenti's.

"You want me to come?" Fingers asked.

Louie shook his head. He picked up the Ingram that was lying on the seat between himself and Earl. "I can do it. I'm just going in for a look-see. You drive on, Earl, and come back and pick me up in a half hour or so. Think you can handle that?" He stepped out of the car before Earl could reply and closed the door.

"You heard the man," Fingers said.

Earl nodded. He drove off. Maybe he'd made a mistake, calling Broadway Joe. All this Valenti shit was slowing down his personal business. Who cared if Valenti bought it or not? What was important right now was the bread Frankie had. Once the money was in hand, there'd be plenty of time to deal with Valenti. It wasn't like Louie had a monopoly on wanting to pay the guy back.

He glanced in the rearview mirror. Fingers was resting easily. Wonder what he'd do if we just left his boss back there? Earl wondered. Maybe when he took out Louie, he'd put a bullet through Fingers' head while he was at it. Fucking wops.

"Pull over," Fingers said suddenly. They weren't more than a mile and a half from where they'd let Louie off.

"What for?"

"We'll give him his twenty minutes or so," Fingers said, "but I want to be close in case something comes up."

"He isn't exactly gonna phone or anything," Earl said as he pulled over.

Fingers leaned over the seat and killed the engine. "I want to be able to hear," he said. Hefting the Browning automatic rifle, he stepped out of the car.

"Somebody drives by and sees you standing there with that, they're gonna wonder why," Earl said as he joined Fingers on the road. He swatted at a couple of mosquitos. Of course they went for him instead of the wop.

"You let me worry about who sees what," Fingers replied. He walked a little way down the road.

Earl trailed after him, hands in the pockets of his jacket when he wasn't swatting bugs. The fingers of his right hand closed around his .38. Bang, he thought. I should just blow the both of you away right now and tell Big Daddy Broadway Joe that Tony Valenti hasn't lost his touch yet. But maybe, as a personal favor to Joe, Earl would see what he could do.

Earl grinned. If it wasn't that it'd probably fuck up the dope deal, he was real tempted. He'd show these wops that he didn't have to belong to no fucking "family" to get ahead.

"What's Louie's problem with Valenti?" he asked as he came up beside Fingers.

"Goes back a way. You know Louie's got Tony's old job, right?"

"Sure. First deal I ran by you boys was through Valenti."

"Yeah, well, when Tony hit the *padrone,* he tried to disappear. Trouble was, he went to the first place we thought of looking—Mario Papale's place in Malta. The guy they called the Silver Fox."

"Before my time. I never heard of him."

"Yeah, well, he was one of the best. Anyway, Louie went to Papale's place to hit Tony—it's like his first hit on the job, you know what I'm saying?"

Earl nodded. "Only he blew it."

"It don't look so good. Well, Louie's made things up, but this's always been a little piece of unfinished business. He's got all the respect a man can get, because when he does a job, it gets done, and no one's holding the Malta deal against him because he was up against both Tony *and* the Fox, but it's still eating at him, you know? So he's got to do it right this time—up close and personal."

"Yeah, but dead's dead."

"Sure it is," Fingers said. "But it's a matter of honor for Louie now. He wants to do it himself—with Tony looking him in the eye and *knowing* what's going down—and he wants it clean, too. That's going to give him a lot of respect, if he pulls it off right. Any asshole can do a hit. It takes a guy with something special to do it just right. Clean. No connections. Just the right people knowing what went down."

"I guess," Earl said. If you're a wop and not too bright. Fercrissakes. Honor. Respect. Who the hell did these guys think they were anyway?

"You've got to be family to understand what I'm telling you," Fingers said.

"Hey, I understand," Earl said. "I gotta lot of respect for your boss. He's some kind of guy, let me tell you. We don't get his kind up here."

Fingers nodded, pleased with the response.

Lap it up, Earl thought. Christ, Howie should see these guys. Thinking about Howie, he realized that he really should do something for the guy. He was a little worm, but he could be useful. He should get Howie back to Ottawa, keep him out of sight of these Italian clowns. It was always good to have some backup that nobody but you knew you had. Earl always liked the idea of having an edge.

An edge was what Louie was looking for, too. He'd talked to his father just before they'd left for Lanark and learned about the meet with the Fox. That complicated things, made it even more important that this hit didn't look like what it was. At least not until they'd done something about Papale.

He followed the road, keeping to the side where his shoes made just a rustle of sound in the grass. Mosquitos hummed around his head, but few landed. He heard a soft sound like a birdsong coming from deep in the woods, but it was almost gone before he could place it. He wondered about what kind of bird would make a sound like that, then turned his thoughts back to the business at hand.

Before they planned anything, they had to know if Tony was still hanging around. Louie wasn't really expecting it. Tony'd never been stupid. But he might not have made Earl. Or maybe he wouldn't figure that Earl would go to the family with what he had even if Tony *did* think he'd been made.

Until they knew for sure, there wasn't a whole hell of a lot they could do. And for this kind of thing, Louie liked to do the job himself. If you were going to do the hit, then you should be the one to case the area. Get the feel of things. Figure out who was where, what they'd do. Being careful kept you alive after the job was done. And the less people involved, the better.

Every since the fiasco in Malta, he'd worked pretty much just with Fingers. It'd be easy to load the area with *soldati,* but that didn't look good—not if word got out to the other families. He could just hear the talk. "Hey, didja hear the Magaddinos finally got Tony Valenti? Took twenty guys under Fucceri, but what the hell, they got the job done."

No, Louie thought. That wouldn't look good at all. And besides, too many men got in each other's way. Like in Malta. Well, Tony wasn't going to have the Fox to pull him out of this one. If he was still in the area, it was just going to be the two of them.

He could see the lights of the house now. He got the Ingram ready for use and moved in closer, through the hedge and out onto the lawn. He saw a man he didn't recognize sitting by the window at the front of the house. A few moments later, Tony walked by and sat down beside him.

Louie grinned when he saw Tony limp. Guess you haven't forgotten me yet, huh, Tony? He made a circuit of the house. When he was sure that it was just the two men, he started back down the road. It was starting to come together now—how he was going to play it.

Halfway back to where he was going to meet Fingers and Earl, he paused to listen. There it was again. Had to be some kind of bird. But what kind of birds were out at night? Didn't they sleep or something? The sound was eerie, but he shook off the feeling he got from it. He knew shit about the woods, but he wasn't about to let some little birdie get him all jumpy. Sure as hell was a strange sound, though.

He continued on his way.

The dark-haired man had followed Louie up from the road. He'd recognized Fucceri right off, finger tightening on the trigger of his crossbow, but he knew that by the time he fired and started to reload, the two men in the car would take him out. As the car drove off he realized that this probably wasn't the hit yet.

He followed the lone man up the road, finger tightening again as Louie stood outside Valenti's house, studying the two men sitting by the window. When Louie made a circuit of the house, the man stayed on his trail. He was still undecided as to what to do with Fucceri as Louie made his way back down the road.

When Louie stopped suddenly, the man froze. Had he been heard? He stilled his own breathing, then understood what Louie was hearing. It was the music. This is just one busy area, he thought as Louie continued on his way. The scene with the woman down by the road. The music. Fucceri showing up. Not to mention what had brought him here himself.

The car returned then, making his decision for him. He melted further back into the trees and watched Louie get in. The car turned around and drove off, and the man returned to his van, listening to the quiet until another spill of eerie music slipped across it, fey and distant.

Cradling the crossbow, he leaned against a tree. That music . . . There was something in it . . . something . . . He shook his head. He could almost understand what it was saying to him, but he wasn't sure he really wanted to know. It was like it was talking to him personally, and while he'd never had any second thoughts about who he was or what he did with his life, he had the feeling that the music was trying to tell him that he should.

14

Lily stayed to keep Lewis company by the old stone after the other villagers had left the glade. Lewis wasn't surprised. They were old friends and he appreciated her presence. It helped him concentrate on something other than the downward spiral of his thoughts that tonight's events had set into motion, making him feel his years more than usual. What did surprise him, however, was that Tommy Duffin had stayed as well.

Tommy sat, half-hidden by the base of the standing stone, Gaffa lying near his knee. He would have been invisible, and then forgotten, if he didn't lip his reed-pipes from time to time, sending a few bars of a sad air across the glade that lingered, faded and then were gone, until he started the cycle over again.

Such a sound, Lewis thought, hearing the piping tonight as though for the first time again. It was this that they had heard in Arcadia, a music like this, when the world was young, but the forests already old. The mystery seemed close when the music played. Surely he was hidden by the low-hanging branches of the nearest trees, or in the spill of briars and bushes that grew thick on the slope behind the stone. He'd be a Green Man, a stag, a goatman, a boar . . . whatever shape he chose, or in no shape at all . . . but he was near. Or was it just the music? Lewis wondered. Just the glade that knew him so well, some trick of the stone, or was the mystery returning? Had he lost the hounds and was now bringing Mally and the girl back . . . ?

Lewis was held by the hope in the music, the promise of it, until Tommy brought the pipes away from his lips and laid them on his lap. Then the ghost of Ackerly Perkin returned to torment Lewis with its talk of illusions and lies, all tied together with just enough truth and a certain logic to make it difficult for Lewis to decide what was real and what was not.

Do what you will shall be the whole of the law. When Crowley spoke the words, they contained too much self in them. There was not enough thought of the world as a whole. And yet, an individual was important, as an individual. Lewis believed that. It was what an individual brought to the world, what an individual gave to the mystery that mattered. But if it was all illusion—

Lily laid her hand on his, bringing him abruptly from his thoughts. "He seems near, doesn't he?" she said. "That special presence of him is so close."

Tommy was playing once more—only breathing across the pipes, but it was enough to send a soft thread of sound across the glade and out, beyond its boundaries, into the forest and the night. This had to be real, Lewis thought. It was no illusion that had leapt off into the darkness, bearing away Mally and the girl. If something had substance, then it couldn't be illusion, could it? But where did it start? the pinprickle whisper of Ackerly Perkin's voice asked, harsh in Lewis's ear. If it all began with illusion, what was it now?

"I love it when it's like this," Lily said. "I love to feel his mystery without that pack of black monks snapping at his heels."

Lewis regarded her. "That's how you see them? As monks?"

"As monks . . . or as priests." Lily shrugged. "The Hounds of God. I can remember the first time you told me about what the Church did to the mystery. The one they called Jesus—the Green Man they hung from a tree in the desert. How St. Paul took the mystery and twisted it to make a religion of intolerance and self-torment. That's how I still see the pack. As St. Paul's dogs, still trying to trap the mystery with their lies."

"I said that?" Lewis asked, remembering the conversation he'd had earlier that day with his guests. Had his questioning and confusion driven him so far astray that it took someone else to remind him of what he'd once believed without questioning?

"Yes, you did, Lewis," Lily said. "Don't you remember?"

"Are they real, then?"

"What? The hounds?"

Lewis nodded.

"Hate's still real, isn't it? And intolerance?"

Lewis nodded again.

"Well," Lily said, "so long as they exist, there will always be hounds. Something will always chase down the Green Man. You told me that, too."

"And the mystery?" Lewis asked. "What of him?"

"I don't know what you mean, Lewis."

"Is he still real?"

Lily tried to study his features, but it was too dark to make them out. "What are you saying, Lewis? That we've imagined the mystery?"

Lewis sighed. "I don't know anymore. I think I've filled my head up with too many words. I've learned too much, tried to capture with logic something that only exists outside of it."

"You always told me that it was how we took our knowledge from the world that shaped us," Lily said. "That there was a glory in reaching out to touch the mystery with our minds as well as our spirits."

"But it *can't* be understood."

"That doesn't make trying to a waste of time." Lily smiled and took his hand. "Isn't this strange?" she said. "Here I am using your own arguments against you. But then I don't think this is between you and me at all, Lewis. It's between the man you once were and the man you are now."

"Which one is right?"

"I don't know, Lewis. All I know is that the mystery belongs to everyone."

Lewis nodded. "I agree. But there's no other place for him except for here. And maybe not even here anymore."

"Then we've got to make a place for him."

"And if we fail to do that?" Lewis asked. "Then what? What's he going to do out there in the world? Nobody wants him out there."

Lily smiled. "I think you've got to give him more credit than that," she said. "We're not talking about some buck deer, Lewis. We're talking about something that makes the forests shiver when he walks by."

"Now you sound like Mally. She thinks we should have more people in New Wolding if we want to keep him nearby. And if we don't, that we should just let him run free."

"I don't think that's our decision to make," Lily said. "We may think we're deciding what to do with him, but I'm sure the mystery just does whatever he does."

Do what you will, Lewis thought with a shiver. He didn't like the way this conversation was going at all.

"I don't know what's right or wrong anymore," he said.

"You shouldn't worry so much," Lily said. "You didn't used to worry so much, Lewis. Don't you remember how much happier you were then?"

"Everything seemed simpler then."

"Things haven't changed, Lewis. The outside world's still outside, and we're still here. The dogs chase the stag, and then the stag chases them. It all balances out in the end."

She couldn't see it, Lewis thought. Something was changing the stag. It was drawn to outsiders—like Tony Garonne and the young girl that it had borne away with Mally tonight. Things *were* changing. But maybe it wasn't fair of him to point that out to Lily. Maybe they were just changing for him.

He turned to try and explain himself one more time, but then Tommy began to play. As the music filled Lewis it drained away his questions and worries, left room inside him for the mystery and nothing more. When Tommy laid the pipes aside again, Lily squeezed Lewis's hand.

"He'll come back," she said. "And he'll bring both Mally and the girl back with him. You might ask him, straight out, Lewis. Or you might ask Mally."

Lewis nodded. Or he could ask the girl. Would she know? Whatever the stag and Mally saw in her, she was still a young girl. Brighter than average, though he was judging her by New Wolding's standards. Maybe they were turning them out smarter in the world beyond the village. But she didn't talk in riddles. Maybe she'd be able to explain it to him when she returned. If she returned.

"He'll bring them back," Lily said again, as though reading his thoughts. "You'll see."

Lewis looked from her to the shadow that was Tommy Duffin, sitting at the base of the old stone. Although he wasn't playing the pipes just now, Tommy looked thin and fey-eyed in the moonlight, as though he weren't Tommy Duffin yet, but still the Piper. He met Lewis's gaze and a smile flickered in his too-bright eyes. Then he lifted the pipes once again.

15

Bannon settled on one of the sofas by the window when they got back to Valenti's place and watched Valenti pace restlessly back and forth across the room.

"C'mon," he said finally. "Settle down. You're going to burn yourself out and then when we need you, you won't be there."

Valenti frowned, but he came to sit down. He *was* burning up energy. Angry, worried, he just couldn't sit still.

"The leg giving you problems?" Bannon asked.

Reflexively, Valenti rubbed his leg. "Yeah. I got a couple of steel pins in there holding some of the bones together. The leg was a real mess by the time I got it to a doctor. He did what he could, but . . ." Valenti shrugged. "It aches in the damp, and sometimes when I overdo things it starts to act up, you know what I mean?"

Bannon nodded. They sat quietly for a long moment, then Valenti spoke again.

"What am I going to tell her momma, Tom? Fercrissakes,

she's going to be here any minute to pick her up, and then what?"
The phone rang before Bannon could reply. "I'll get it," he said.

Howie walked slowly around Frankie's living room, taking in the furnishings, the books and knick-knacks. The place'd look a hell of a lot different if it was his and he had her kind of money. That was for sure. He wondered what Earl would think if he could see Howie here in his ex's house—being asked in, being one of the good guys, fercrissake. Maybe he could go pick up the kid from Valenti's, snatch her, make a play for the money himself.

Howie could just feel that things were turning around for him. He had a woman being nice to him and it wasn't costing him a cent. He was on his own and no one was sniggering behind his back. He could do it. He could snatch the kid, if it wasn't for Valenti. Valenti would recognize him from last night. Howie didn't doubt that. Too bad, though. Wouldn't it be a laugh, maybe handing Earl some of the money, because—well, hell—it had been his idea. Then he thought of Earl, of how his eyes got, the way he just blew away that Goldman guy . . . Howie's pleasure ran from him.

Just then Sherry came down the stairs with Frankie.

"How are you feeling?" Lisa asked, standing up from the couch.

"A lot better," Frankie said. "But if you hadn't come when you did . . ."

Lisa smiled and waved a hand breezily between them. "That's just the kind of people we are," she said. "Scouring the backroads, looking for people in distress." The shock of breaking up the rape and the subsequent excitement had brought them all down, but while Sherry was cleaning Frankie up, Lisa and Howie had gone outside for a joint. They were both buzzed again.

Frankie lifted a hand and gingerly touched her throat. "Still . . ." she said. Her voice was a little husky.

"You're going to be all right," Sherry said. "But once we pick up your daughter . . . well, I don't think it'd be such a good idea for you to stay here on your own. If that guy comes back . . ." Frankie shuddered and Sherry took her by the arm. "C'mon. You'd better sit down. Now what's the number where your daughter's staying?"

Christ, Howie thought. I hope they don't want me to go pick up the kid. He looked at Frankie, really looked at her for the first time since he'd seen her on the hood of the car. She was sure some looker. He wondered why Earl had ever dumped a woman that looked that good. If she was his, he'd never let her go. No way.

Feeling his stare, Frankie's gaze lifted to meet his just then. Howie started to look away, then found a smile instead. What did he have to be nervous about? He just wished she wouldn't look at him with that hurt look. Christ, it wasn't like he'd tried to jump her or anything. Maybe she just didn't like men or something. He wanted to look away but found himself caught by her gaze. Then Sherry made the connection and Frankie looked over at her as she began to speak into the phone.

"Hello? Yes, I'd like to speak to Alice Treasure please. No. I'm calling for her mother. My name's Sherry Mallon. Just a minute." Sherry put her hand over the mouthpiece and looked at Frankie. "He wants to talk to you. He sounded sort of . . . I don't know. Strange."

Frankie shook her head. "Oh, God. He probably thinks you're involved with my ex. He tried to kidnap Ali last night."

Sherry's eyes widened. "Was that him again tonight?"

"Oh, no. That's one thing Earl's never had to do—force a woman. They usually crawl all over him." She reached for the receiver. "Here, let me talk to him."

Sherry handed her the phone, but her gaze went to Howie who looked guiltily away.

"Hello, Tony?" Frankie said into the phone. "Oh, it's you, Tom. I was just— No, I'm fine. Well, there was a little bit of trouble. . . . No, please don't. There are some people here who helped me out and are willing to go pick up Ali. No, it's really not necessary. No, it was no big thing. Please. Well, all right. Yes, thanks." She looked at Sherry as she hung up. "He's coming down."

"Who is?" Howie asked, a little sharply. That drew another look from Sherry.

"Tony's friend Tom," Frankie replied.

Sherry patted her shoulder. "Sit back and relax a bit," she said.

"You're going to find these waves of feeling weak coming on for awhile, but don't worry. It's just your body's reaction to what you went through earlier. You're going to be fine."

Frankie nodded. "I know. But thanks. When I think about what he almost—"

"Don't think about it," Sherry said. "Not right away."

"But knowing he's still out there . . . Maybe I *should* report it."

Lisa shook her head. "You don't want to go through that kind of circus," she said. "I've been there and, believe me, what the cops put you through is way worse than anything the fucker that tried to rape you would have."

"She's right," Sherry said. "They'll treat *you* like the criminal, like it was *you* egging him on."

"I suppose . . ."

"Believe me," Lisa told her. "You don't want to go through it."

"Try to rest a bit," Sherry said. Then to Howie, she added, "Do you want to get a bit of air?"

Here it comes, Howie thought. "Sure," he said. Fuck it. What could she do to him?"

"Something's wrong down there," Bannon said as he hung up.

"What do you mean?"

"I don't know. But I'm going to find out."

"Well, I'm not waiting here."

Bannon shook his head as Valenti started to get up. "Someone's got to stay here in case Ali shows—remember?"

"Yeah, but—"

"Let me handle this, Tony. I mean, what did I come up here for? To take hikes in the woods?"

"Sure. It's okay. You're more mobile than me—I can understand that."

Bannon smiled. "Hey, I know how you feel about this woman, Tony. I'm not going to put the make on her."

"What do you mean you know how I feel?"

"Hey, if you don't know, you must be the only one."

"C'mon," Valenti said. "What am I doing—mooning over her?"

"No. But you get a soft look in your eye whenever she's in the room."

"Fercrissakes, the next thing is you'll have me married off like some kind of—"

"I've got to go," Bannon said. "We can talk about this later, if you want."

Valenti nodded. He watched Bannon check the clip on his automatic, then thrust the gun back into his jacket pocket. "Take care," he said.

Bannon glanced at him. "Always," he said, then the door closed behind him.

Jesus, Valenti thought. The whole world was falling apart. He got up to stand at the window, but then the phone rang again. He started for it, favoring his bad leg.

As soon as they were outside, Sherry turned to Howie. "Okay. What's the story?"

"What's your problem, Sherry? All of a sudden you're—"

She cut him of. "Look. Hanging around with Steve, I've run into a few things. Some dope dealing, sometimes things that get a little heavy and someone's got to get patched up, but I don't want to be any part of this shit—do you understand me?"

"Sure. But—"

"This Earl she mentioned—is that the same guy that came by with you last night?"

Howie nodded. "Yeah. But it's not like what you're thinking."

"No? What do you call snatching somebody's kid?"

"She *owes* him fercrissakes. She's sitting on so much money. . . ." His voice trailed off as she shook her head.

"You just can't leave her alone, can you?" she said.

"What're you talking about? You don't even know this fucking woman!"

"But I know this old story, Howie. How come the woman always owes something? What's with you guys anyway? Where do you come off thinking that anything with breasts and a vagina automatically owes you *anything?"*

"Hey, now wait a minute. This afternoon . . . it wasn't me that started, you know . . . fooling around."

Sherry regarded him steadily. "What's the matter, Howie? You can't even come out and say it?"

"Well, sure. But—"

"This afternoon was a bit of fun. I was in the mood to make somebody happy, and that's all. It sure as hell didn't mean that I'd stand around while assholes like you and Earl take Frankie for a ride."

"You don't want to shoot off your mouth like that," Howie blustered. "Earl hears you, he'll . . ."

"He'll what?" Sherry asked.

There was a moment's silence. This wasn't going right at all, Howie thought. He looked at Sherry, thinking about how it had been this afternoon. Now she was saying it was like she'd been feeling sorry for him or something. Like he couldn't get himself a piece of tail whenever he wanted. And she didn't know Earl. Earl'd just punch out her lights before listening to her lip.

"What'll Earl do?" Sherry repeated.

"I'd be real interested in hearing about that, too," a new voice said.

The two of them stared at the newcomer. He'd come so silently across the lawn that neither of them had heard him coming.

"Who the fuck are you?" Howie demanded, trying to cover his nervousness with bravado.

Bannon studied the two of them. He'd come in at the end of their argument, but he'd caught enough to get an idea as to who and what they were talking about.

"I'm here to see Frankie," he said. "The name's Tom Bannon. What happened here?"

"It's a little complicated," Sherry said.

"Well, how's Frankie?"

"She's fine. No, that's not right. She's taking it pretty good, but she's still suffering from a mild state of shock."

"What happened to her?"

"Someone attacked her. We were just driving by and scared the guy off, but she's still a bit shaken up."

Bannon's gaze went to Howie, but Sherry shook her head.

"No," she said. "That's one thing I doubt he had anything to do with."

"Hey," Howie said. "I don't need to take this kind of shit. If you—"

"Get out of my way," Bannon said as he mounted the stairs. "I want to see Frankie."

Howie moved aside. He glared at the man, then at Sherry. The fuckers. He was getting sick and tired of being pushed around. You took a whole lifetime of it, but you had to stand up sometime. Maybe now—what with his shoulder hurting and the fact that he'd lost his gun—maybe he had to hold off for now. But he was going to get even. With all of them.

He met Sherry's gaze before she followed Bannon inside. Especially with you, sister, he thought. Christ, he wished Earl was here. Earl'd show them all. They wouldn't be talking like this if Earl was around. They'd all be standing in a line, waiting to suck his dick. They'd do whatever Earl told them to do.

The door closed behind Sherry, but Howie didn't bother following them in. He stood outside, listening to the night. He kept thinking that he was hearing snatches of that weird music, but just when he'd start to listen for it, it would disappear like it had never been.

That music did something to him. It made him feel strong and scared at the same time. Like something was going to hunt him down, but like he could be the hunter if he just stopped being so shit-assed scared of his own shadow. He wondered if he could find the spot where he'd dropped his gun last night. He wondered if it'd still be there.

Glancing at the house, he strode off into the night. He'd feel a lot better with that hunk of steel in his hand.

"Tony?" a man said when Valenti picked up the phone. There was something odd about the voice, like it was being run through electronics to disguise it.

"Yeah. Who's this?"

"That's not important. Thing is, Mario wants to know—what's the bottom line on this deal? Someone comes sniffing around, do we send them home in a box, or what?"

"No one's got to die on account of me," Valenti said.

"Yeah, but if it comes down to it . . . Say the Don sends in Fucceri or one of the other heavy guns. There's not going to be much chance for conversation, you know? What do you want? Just some time, or are you staying here?"

"I'm staying."

"Then it's going to be a war—you know that, don't you?"

"Sure," Valenti said. "But I don't feel good about it."

"Yeah. Who needs it?"

"Did Mario have his meet with the Magaddinos?"

"Yeah. He talked to Broadway Joe."

"And?"

"Joe said he was calling it off," the voice said. Before Valenti could relax, it added: "But he sent in his kid Louie and Johnny Maita."

"Shit. So that's it then."

" 'Fraid so, Tony. Listen, I'll be in touch. You had visitors tonight, by the way. I caught Louie Fucceri casing the place, but I let him go till I had a chance to talk to you. So maybe you better be careful."

"I get the picture."

"Glad to hear that. *Coraggio,* Tony."

"Sure."

Valenti cradled the phone. Christ, they'd already been here. That fast. So what had stopped them? What were they waiting for? And who the hell did Mario have out in the bush watching out for him?

Howie couldn't believe his luck. First pass out, taking an easy amble along the road leading up to Valenti's, sticking to the grass verge and trying to remember where the stag had hit the car, and then he just about kicks his piece into the woods. He bent down and picked the gun up. The weight in his hand made him feel better immediately. That was the thing about a gun. When you carried one, people respected you. They just didn't fuck around when they were looking down that metal bore.

He'd have to be careful firing the sucker, seeing's how his shoulder wasn't in any shit-hot shape yet. Maybe he'd be better off using it left-handedly. He transferred the gun to his left hand. It felt a little awkward, but nothing he couldn't handle. It wasn't like he was going target shooting. Anything he'd be firing at would be just a couple of feet away from him.

Unloading the gun—two spent shells and four unfired that he didn't want to take a chance on, seeing how they'd been lying out in the rain—he tossed the contents of its cylinder into the bush and loaded it with some fresh shells he had in his pocket. All right, Mr. Cool-talking Tom Bannon. And you, too, Sherry. Time for you to kiss the gun.

Grinning, he started back for Frankie's place.

Bannon nodded a greeting to Lisa, then went down on one knee in front of the chair where Frankie was sitting.

"How're you doing?" he asked.

"Okay, I guess."

"Tony wanted to come down, but I talked him out of it. His leg's giving him some trouble."

"He's all right, though?"

"Oh, sure."

Frankie looked past Bannon's shoulder, then her gaze returned to his face. "Where's Ali?"

"Well, you know, we weren't sure what was going down so we didn't think she should come. Besides, with what your friend here tells me, maybe it'd be a good idea if you spent another night up at Tony's." Right now, Bannon didn't trust anyone. There'd be time enough to tell Frankie about Ali once she was up at the house.

"I'm so tired of having to always depend on somebody else," Frankie said.

"I know what you mean," Bannon said. "But what the hell—it's just for the night. Until we can figure out what went down and what we can do about it."

"I wanted to call the police."

"Well, I don't know what they could do for you at this point, but maybe it's not so bad an idea."

"But Lisa and Sherry said I shouldn't—that they'd just give me a hard time."

Thank you, ladies, Bannon thought. "Listen," he said. "Why don't you just grab a few things and I'll walk you up to the house, okay? We can talk it all out there."

"Sure."

"I'll give you a hand," Sherry said.

Lisa shook her head. "My turn."

Sherry turned to Bannon after the two women went upstairs to pack some toothbrushes and the like. "Want to split a joint?"

"No thanks. I don't smoke." He followed her outside and stood on the porch while she lit up, wrinkling his nose as the sweet marijuana smoke drifted toward him.

"You disapprove?" she asked.

"No. I'm just not big on sucking any kind of smoke into my body." He paused a moment, studying the dark lawn and the road beyond. "What happened?" he asked finally. "How bad did it get?"

Sherry explained briefly, but with enough detail to make Bannon's eyes flash with anger.

"Wish I'd been here," he said. "I'd have . . ." He shook his head. Tony was going to be pissed. Christ, *he* was pissed. "So she didn't know the guy?" he asked.

"Nope. He was driving a beat-up old pickup, but none of us was together enough to take down the plates."

"And you folks were just driving by?"

Sherry nodded. "Maybe you should know something else. Howie—the guy that I was talking to when you arrived? Well, he's involved with Frankie's ex. He got shot last night. I think they were trying to snatch her kid."

Who got snatched by a buck deer and a girl with horns instead, Bannon thought. "Where do you fit in?"

"Earl and Howie showed up at a little party up near Calabogie—

that was the first time either of us met them. It's beginning to look now
like it was a mistake."

Bannon nodded. "You'd better watch out for them—especially
Earl. From what I hear, he doesn't mess around. He plays for keeps."

"Oh, that's just great." Sherry studied him for a moment, then
took a long drag from her joint. "I think we're going to split—
Frankie's going to be all right with you, isn't she?"

"Yeah. Thanks for what you did."

"Sure." Sherry looked over to Lisa's car. "Wonder what happened
to Howie."

"Maybe he went for a walk."

Sherry smiled humorlessly. "Maybe we'll just leave without him."

The door opened behind them and Lisa and Frankie stepped outside. Lisa shut off the lights and locked the door while Bannon took
the small Adidas bag from Frankie.

"If we don't see you again, take care," Sherry said as she started
for the car.

"We'll do that," Bannon replied.

"Hey, what about Howie?" Lisa asked as she followed Sherry.

"Fuck him."

"I thought *you* were going to."

Sherry didn't bother to answer as she opened the door and got in.
Bannon waited until Lisa was inside as well and the engine had turned
over before he took Frankie's arm. The car's headbeams stabbed the
darkness, lighting up Frankie's car and the side of the house near the
lane.

"C'mon," Bannon said.

He led her down the steps and started for the back of the house,
waving to Sherry and Lisa as their car backed out of the lane. They
were plunged into darkness when the car headed down the road, but
Bannon knew where he was going. He'd been this way in the daylight
already and he had an eye for detail. He'd automatically filed a picture
of the area away in his head so that he had no trouble leading Frankie
across the backyard to the road that would take them up to Valenti's.

"I can't believe this is happening," Frankie said as they neared the road. Her voice was quiet, almost natural, but Bannon could hear the tension in it. It sounded huskier than usual, too. "I thought Earl was bad enough, but this . . ."

"Everything's going to work out," he replied. "You'll see." But he wasn't looking forward to telling her about Ali's disappearance.

"God, I hope so. Because right now . . ." She turned to look at him, but the darkness hid his features. "It's like winning all that money included a one-way ticket into a soap opera. Thank God Ali was staying with you and Tony. If she'd been at home by herself . . . That guy was just waiting for me in the driveway, Tom. And he was crazy. He started off telling me he wanted his dog back—as though I'd stolen it or something—and then he just . . . then he just jumped me." Bannon felt her shudder. "And there was nothing I could do. Nothing! He was so strong . . ."

"He's dead meat if he shows his face around here again."

"Are you . . . ?" She hesitated. "This business that Tony used to be in—are you a part of it, too?"

"What kind of business is that?"

"Some kind of study group on the mob."

"Tony told you that?"

"No, Ali did."

Bannon nodded to himself. Smart kid. "You could say so—though I didn't have the same connections that Tony did."

"He's pretty hard on himself, isn't he?"

"Who—Tony?"

"I know the look—God knows, I've worn it often enough myself. There's things he's done that he's not too proud of now. That's how I felt when I first realized what I'd gotten myself into with Earl."

"What do you mean?" Bannon asked, happy to keep the conversation going in the direction it was. If it kept her mind off what had happened tonight, if it helped to distance her a little bit from the immediacy of it, it could only help.

"I found out he was dealing drugs," Frankie said. "Not just a little bit of weed like everybody was into smoking back in those days, but hard stuff. I thought he was cleaning offices at night—can you believe it? Talk about innocence. Instead, he was setting up these parties

where they'd turn on kids who were twelve or thirteen—Ali's age—
selling dope, selling sex. . . ."

"But you weren't a part of it."

"No. I thought I was pretty together, but I found out I didn't know
a thing."

"Yeah, but—"

"Why do I feel so bad about it?" she said before he could ask.
"How about the fact that everybody knew it was going on but me.
People I thought were my friends—I couldn't figure out why they
were all drifting away. It got so I never left the apartment because I
didn't have anywhere to go."

"Still," Bannon said, "that's all in the past now."

Frankie shook her head. "It doesn't feel like that—not with Earl
being back."

"You don't have to worry about Earl," Bannon said. "He's going
to be taken care of."

"Maybe—but not by you, blondie."

Bannon and Frankie froze at the new voice. Bannon started to
reach into his pocket, but the barrel of a gun was thrust roughly against
his back. Jesus, he thought. How goddam stupid could you get? He
should have realized when Sherry told him who Howie was that
Howie wouldn't just take off.

The lights of Valenti's house could be seen in the distance, but they
could just as well have been on the other side of the world for all the
good they were going to do. A hand went into his jacket pocket and
came out with his automatic.

"Well, look at this," Howie said. "What a pretty little gun."

Bannon felt Frankie trembling beside him. "Tom," she asked.
"What does he want?"

Howie grinned, feeling strong. "Maybe I just want you, babe."

The words were just too close to those of the man who'd attacked
her earlier this evening. The tension that had been slowly draining
from her caught her with a snap. Her chest felt so tight she couldn't
breathe. She smelled the other man's stale breath again. Felt his hands
on her. Heard his voice.

Want you . . . want you . . .

Tearing free of Bannon's arm, she bolted.

"No!" Bannon cried and turned, striking at the gun.

The .38 bucked in Howie's hand. Its discharge sounded like an explosion as it went off. Shrill against the echoes of the gunshot, Frankie screamed.

16

Riding the stag.

It was the most glorious thing that Ali had ever experienced . . . and the most frightening. The wind rushed by her ears, making a sound like music; hooves drummed its rhythm. She could feel the stag's powerful muscles moving under her legs. Mally held on to her, laughing, while she clung to the stag's neck, wanting to laugh, but wanting to cry as well.

There had been that moment of shock when Mally threw her up onto the creature's back, the look on Tony and Tom's faces as the stag pranced in front of them, and then it was off and running and the shock gave way to wonder. The stag moved in long graceful leaps and bounds, never jarring them when it landed, never throwing them from its back when its powerful leg muscles bunched and then lifted them all into the air again.

The old stone was gone, Tommy's pipes and the dancing villagers with it. The night seemed to belong only to the three of them and that was when the shock wore off and Ali's fears rose front and center in her mind. She was alone in the night with some mythic creature and a wild girl. Abducted. And she—

For the first time she realized that they'd been running for too far and too long without crossing a highway or seeing the lights of a cabin or a house. The trees they were moving through seemed different from those of the forest behind Tony's house. The pines were almost like redwoods, impossibly tall. Between each pine stand was a wild jumbled bushland of cedar, oak, maple, birch and elm. The air had grown colder. If Ali turned her head, she could see her breath frosting in the air.

She looked up as they went speeding through a clearing. A swollen moon hung low in the sky. The stars seemed too close—the sky too dark, the stars too bright. She had only a moment for this to register before they were in the forest again.

The ground was no longer on an even keel. The stag took them up a gradual incline that was spotted with the stone fists and gnarly knees of stone outcrops. The sound of the stag's hooves was louder, as though the ground had become the resonating skin of a huge earthen drum. Where were they? Ali wanted to ask someone, but there was no one to hear her. Mally was still laughing and shouting something that was either in a foreign language or made up of nonsense words, for it didn't make any sense. And how did you talk to a stag? She leaned closer against its neck.

"Stop!" she cried. She tried to make her voice as loud as she could so that it would ring above the sound of the stag's hooves and the noise Mally was making, but all that came out was a soft whisper. "Please stop."

The stag turned its head slightly and Ali stared into one large liquid eye before her mount looked ahead once more.

"I'm scared," she said.

She knew this wasn't Lanark County. She didn't know where it was, but it wasn't any place she knew of. They didn't have trees this big anywhere in the Ottawa Valley. They didn't have this kind of a forest. It was too . . . primal. This wasn't a place for mankind—or for girls, either, she thought. It was a wild place.

The ground inclined sharply now and suddenly they burst out of the forest. The stag's hooves clattered on rock, but it never slowed its pace. The huge moon was very close now, and the stars . . . This wasn't the night sky she knew, Ali thought. Oh, jeez. What was happening to her?

As they continued to climb at a breakneck pace, she could see the countryside for miles around. There were no lights, no sign of houses or men anywhere. Just the big moon shining down, the stars hanging so low she felt she could reach out and catch them, and the dark forests stretching out as far as she could see, off into invisible horizons that were swallowed by the night.

She couldn't look anymore. Instead, she burrowed her face against the neck of the stag. The clattering of its hooves and Mally's wild singing combined with the pounding of her heart until she got so dizzy she knew that any moment now she was going to fall off the stag's back. She was going to fall and smash her head open on those rocks. She'd roll and bump and spin all the way back down the steep incline that the stag had so effortlessly climbed. But then the stag slowed and Mally suddenly broke off her singing.

Ali opened her eyes to see that they were approaching a summit. Her teeth chattered from the cold and the stag's breath billowed around her like clouds. She was thankful now for the warmth of it on one side, Mally behind her. The stag slowed to a walk. There were shapes outlined against the sky before them. Ali thought of pictures she'd seen in travelogs of Ireland and Britain, and then they were in among the stone formations and the stag came to a halt. Mally slid down from its back and landed sure-footed on the ground.

"Come on, then!" she called to Ali.

Ali just stared around herself. The formations of the stones were like some primal Stonehenge—not raised by men, but by some freak of nature. Or by the gods. Is *that* what the gods are? she wondered. Are they what's responsible for all the oddities and impossibilities to be found in nature? Maybe those things were their signatures. The stones towered three times Ali's height—and she was still sitting on the stag. The big moon, looming close, appeared to be impaled on their peaks.

"Ali, Ali, in free!" Mally sang.

Ali turned to look down at the wild girl. Mally had lost her hat and her hair was a bewildering thicket that stuck up every-which-way all around her head. She was hopping about from foot to foot, dancing to her own inner music, and for a moment the chorus from Cyndi Lauper's "Girls Just Want to Have Fun" ran through Ali's head . . .

Mally held up her arms to Ali. Praying to whatever god who would listen that she didn't fall and crack her head on the stones, Ali slid down from the stag's back. Mally caught her.

The stag immediately paced away from them. It stood between two tall rock formations and stared eastward, its antlers like the bare limbs of a tree thrusting up into the night sky. Ali moved carefully to see what it was looking at, her legs feeling a little rubbery. Before she reached the stones, Mally bounded ahead of her. The wild girl scrambled carelessly right up to what Ali discovered was a sheer drop of hundreds of feet when she finally stood beside her.

"What a night," Mally murmured. "What a magic night!"

Ali shivered. Her breath was wreathing around her face, and while she was wearing jeans and a windbreaker, they weren't enough for the chill that the night air held.

"Here," Mally said, offering her own jacket.

"But you—"

"—Can run naked in a snowstorm and not be cold. Don't you know me yet?"

Ali shook her head. "A secret," she muttered under her breath. But she took the proffered jacket and did feel warmer with it on. "What are we doing here, Mally? Where *is* here?"

The wild girl shrugged. "Don't really know."

"But we must be somewhere."

"Maybe we're inside the old stone," Mally said with a grin. "I really don't know, Ali. This is a place that Old Hornie comes to when he wants to be close to what he used to be a part of."

"I want to go back," Ali said.

Mally turned slowly and studied her face. "Truly?" she asked.

"Well . . ." Her mother's face reared in Ali's mind. Frankie would be worried sick when she found out. And Tony, too. And she was scared anyway, though not so much, maybe, now that the wild ride was over. Did she really want to go back? Because this was it. This was her big chance—her big adventure. This was what she'd always wished would happen to her. Going through the wardrobe into Narnia. Down a rabbithole. *Doing* something, like Enid Blyton's Famous Five. She'd devoured tales of adventures and the fantastic, from Joy Chant to Caitlin Midhir, and had always longed to be the kid that that kind of thing happened to. To hold the Weirdstone of Brisingamen like Alan Garner's Susan . . .

"Can . . . *can* we go back?"

"Go back?" Mally laughed. "It's easy to go back. The getting here's the hard thing. I can only come when I ride the stag and then I always mean to stay forever, or at least a week, but I'm always drawn back. To my own forests, I suppose, thin as they are. Or maybe it's Tommy's piping . . ."

"Why are we here?" Ali asked.

"For fun!"

Girls just want to, Ali thought. "No," she said. "I mean, I understand that, it's just . . ."

"Not reason enough? Then look around you, Ali. Breathe the air. This is beauty. This is a place that still has its heart."

Ali turned to look out over the darkened forest again. The air was cold, but it *was* invigorating. It went down into her lungs and woke every cell in her body as the chill pure oxygen rushed through her bloodstream. And she wasn't all that cold anymore. Maybe she was adjusting to the temperature drop.

"It is beautiful," she agreed.

Mally grinned back at her. "It's beauty. Wonder. Magic. Enchantment. Mystery." Her voice hung onto the last word, instilling it with something that sent a thrill running up Ali's spine. "Lewis talks about Old Hornie as though he was the whole of mystery," Mally added. "As though whatever wonderful beings, from his Green Man to ancient Pan, were all wrapped up in this one being, but it's not so. This—" she swung her arm in a wide circle "—is the mystery.

"We catch peeks of it, little whiffs of its scent, a breath of its air, a whisper of its sound, and it sets our hearts a-tremble. That's why Old Hornie's magical. He's a part of all this. But only a small part. He's a bit that came loose, and while he can return here, he's no longer a part of it. So he roams our world, looking for the other bits that've come loose over the years. They're the mysteries of our world."

"That's it?" Ali asked.

"No. It's not so simple. Men have wonderful minds—they can imagine. They can do something wonderful that no beastie can. When some of this magic comes loose and drifts into our world, men's minds give it its shape. They make a Pan, an Odin, a Jesus. Did Lewis tell you how the mystery reflects—*becomes*—what you yourself project?"

Ali nodded.

"This is why."

"But . . ." Ali shook her head slowly. "Religions are based on these things, people live by them, *believe* them. . . ."

"Religions are based on mysteries," Mally replied. "They always have been."

"But if they aren't real, then—"

"No!" Mally cut her off. "They *are* real. Faerie lies in our minds, but it's made real by this place. From this place. Gods and demons and the magics that witches and enchanters use—it's all real. And all from here. Don't you see? This place is the lifestuff of beauty. Of Magic."

"But when you talk about God and Heaven and everything . . ."

"You talk about it. You and Lewis, and the dark man did—but I don't." She frowned, looking for the most precise way to tell Ali what she meant. "All those gods and prophets," she said finally, "they were given their lifestuff from this place, but they were their own being. Men might have imagined them, but once they existed, they became what they had to be, not always what men wanted them to be. It's like the dark man's hounds."

Ali looked nervously around. She'd forgotten about them.

"You'd do well to beware of them," Mally said, "but there's no need to worry right now. It always takes them longer to reach this place than it does the stag."

"Well, that's a relief."

"Yes. The dark man made them, Ali. He made them just to see if he could—out of his disbelief. He didn't want something like Old Hornie to be in the world. Men made him up, the dark man said, so he'd make up something to hunt Old Hornie down, but he never really believed that he could. And when he did, he never really believed they were real. And when he finally realized they were real, he discovered that he couldn't control them because such beings are always true to themselves."

"That's awful," Ali said.

Mally nodded. "But it's always been that way. The leaders that men follow must always do away with the leaders that went before. 'Great Pan is dead!' they cried—not because he was dead, but because they wanted him to be dead. Him and all his kind. Yet you've seen his cousin here tonight, you've ridden on his back, and I don't doubt that in some old glade in Arcadia the old goat's still piping, still making the nights merry with his magic—or his panic—depending on how you approach him. It was only the Christians that wanted him gone."

"Lewis doesn't like Christians much either," Ali said.

"Oh, but they're not the worst, you know. Neither the first, nor probably the last. Only the most successful—so far. What's most amusing is that they made Pan into their devil, but it's their own god's son who's more the old goat's cousin."

Ali shook her head. "I'm not too clear on whether gods are real or not, but I can't see that. Pan used to, you know, drink a lot and chase the ladies."

"He'd catch them, too!" Mally said with a laugh. "But he wasn't evil. It's just that the Christians made him so."

"But Jesus—"

"Preached love, not hate. Spoke of a heavenly kingdom on earth. People changed what he said to suit themselves, Ali. And even Christianity's not the same now as it was back then. When it was growing, it took a bit of this, a bit of that, and made one thing out of it all until it began to split apart again—only from the inside out. Those gospels of theirs—if you look hard enough through them, you can find a passage to forbid anything you want, and another to condone the same thing."

"I never thought of it like that."

"Neither did I. But I talked to the dark man a lot. To Lewis and others. I learned how to read the truth between the lines they spoke. I think I would have liked Jesus. The man—and the mystery."

"What about you?" Ali asked. "Are you a mystery, too?"

Mally smiled. "Oh, no. I'm a secret—it's not the same."

"I wish you'd stop saying that. Why can't you just tell me who you are?" Or what, she added to herself. "Lewis said you were young when he was young—but you never changed. You never got any older."

"Is it so important to know everything?" Mally asked.

"The more you know, the better you can understand. How can I make decisions if I don't have all the facts?"

"What decision is there for you to make?"

Ali didn't have an answer for that.

"I think the world needs its mysteries and its secrets," Mally said. "Without us, it wouldn't be such a merry place."

"The world's not all that happy," Ali said.

"I meant merry as in 'fey.' Without the mystery of what men call faerie, the world loses its depth. The resonating of our secret music. The glamor that we lay upon the wild places. There are mysteries and secrets living in the places that men have built, too, but they aren't so merry."

"So magic?" Ali asked.

Mally shook her head. A smile that was more bitter than sweet touched her lips. "No—this time I meant happy. They're not so happy. Sometimes I'm not so happy."

"Why did you bring me here?" Ali asked. She was no longer so scared—well, at least not very scared—but she was puzzled.

"Because of the fire in you—like the one in Tony." She pronounced his name "Too-nee."

Ali frowned. "Fire . . . ?"

"A brightness—like a fire of bones." At Ali's confused look, Mally tried to explain. "On midsummer's night when the bonefires are lit by the people of the hills to give their greeting to their mother moon."

"A bonfire?" Ali asked.

"That's what I said. A bone—fire."

"You mean they burn bones?"

"Some—to return a bit of the world's marrow to its mother." She took Ali's hand and led her back into the middle of the rock formation's circle. "This is where they light their fires on that night," she said, indicating a dark ring burned into the stone. In the moonlight, it stood out dark against the lighter stone.

"Who are these people?" Ali asked.

"Faerie. Secrets."

Ali smiled. And was it so important to know everything? Maybe not, but that wouldn't stop her from trying. She glanced at where the stag had been, but he wasn't there now. The stone circle seemed empty except for the two of them.

"The stag . . . ?" she began.

Mally pointed to where they'd entered the circle. A tall figure stood there overlooking the forest that they had travelled through earlier. The Green Man, Ali thought, in his cloak of twigs and leaves. His antlers gleamed in the moonlight.

"Lewis wants to keep him in New Wolding," Mally said, "but there's not enough people there for him now. Tommy calls him up, and he ranges too far, picking up the reflections of minds that don't celebrate him—minds that don't know him, minds that can't conceive of him. What they reflect back hurts him. It changes him—makes him wilder than he would be if he were free."

"Where do I come into it—and Tony?"

"You both have the fire in you—only in you it burns brighter and you are . . . purer. More innocent to the darkness that men add to their souls when they leave their childhood behind."

"But what is it that you expect me to do?"

"You could free him."

Ali looked from the Green Man to Mally. "Me?"

"You could do it. It's not that you're the only one who could, but you're the one that's here, you're near him. So you could do it. It needs doing. Signal to him with a fire of bones—call him with the light inside you, rather than with music, and you can free him."

"On Midsummer's Eve?"

"That would be the best time," Mally said, "but it can be done any time. I'd do it as soon as you could. Tomorrow night. He'll hear Tommy playing, but he'll hear you, too. If you call to him strongly enough, he'll choose you and then you can set him free."

"How?"

Mally shrugged. "I don't know exactly. You'll know. With the moon and the twin fires, inside and out, you'll know."

"Lewis said that if the mystery was to be freed into the world that it'd be a disaster. He would take all the bad things in the world and project them back. Everybody'd go crazy and destroy everything."

"That could happen," Mally said. "If all the world were like New Wolding. But there are mysteries everywhere and the world, while it totters one way and another between wars and disasters, it still survives. No, Ali. It's very simple. If the stag stays in New Wolding with only a few to celebrate him, he'll no longer be a positive force. He'll break free and do great damage. If there are enough people in the village to celebrate him, then all will be as it had been."

"But you think he should be freed."

"I think you could free him," Mally said—which wasn't really a reply to what she'd asked, Ali thought. The wild girl studied her for a moment. "You've ridden him," she said finally. "You've had your legs wrapped around his belly and felt the thunder of his hooves in the forest. What do you think?"

"You said earlier that you expected me to free him, but now you're hedging your bet."

Mally shook her head. "I only said that you could do it. It's not for me to say what you should do."

"I think I want to go home. I'm getting confused and people will be worrying about me."

"Needlessly."

"But they don't know that."

"That's true. Anyway, the hounds are coming—listen."

Ali could hear them as soon as Mally pointed the sound out. She'd been hearing it for a while actually, but it had seemed more like the wind and she'd been concentrating on what Mally had been saying. The baying of the Hunt was like the pipes in that way, she thought. It just kind of crept up on you until it was too late.

"Does he ever get to rest?" she asked, looking at the Green Man.

"Oh, yes," Mally said. "Some nights the hounds don't chase him at all. They're not clever creatures—just persistent."

The sound of the pack was bringing back Ali's fear. Her throat went dry and it was hard to breathe. She cleared her throat nervously.

"Can—can I talk to him—to the Green Man?" she asked. "Is there time . . . before . . ."

"Before the pack gets here? Probably. But mysteries don't talk much—not to those like you and me, Ali. I think it would be better if we returned. Do you want to go to the stone, or to Tony's house?"

"Oh, the stone. That's where Tony will be, don't you think?"

Mally closed her eyes for a moment, then shook her head. "No. He's at home."

"What did you just do?"

"I peeked—from here to there. It's much easier to catch a glimpse of there from here, than the other way around, though poets and bards and the like—they can see from there to here. It's part of their art."

"Can I do it? Can you show me how?"

"I could, but I won't. Not right now. Come, Ali. We should go. If the pack catches our scent . . ."

Ali regarded her, nervousness growing. "What would happen? I thought they only wanted to chase the stag."

"Yes," Mally said. "But if they catch our scent here, they'll think we're from here as well. The dark man set them on the trail of any mystery, you see. We can't escape them as easily as the stag, so it's time for us to fly."

She took Ali's arm, but Ali shook herself free of the grip. Trembling, she moved closer to where the Green Man stood. As she drew near he turned, and she was lost in those eyes again, liquid and dark, wise and foolish all at once. She tried not to blink, nor to look away, though she wanted to do both. Just being this close intimidated her. But she wanted to see if there were a need to be free in him. The kind of look some animals had in the zoo. The look the fieldmouse she'd caught one year had had—the year she'd decided she wanted to be like Gerald Durrell and thought she'd better start early learning how to collect wild animals as he had. Only she let the fieldmouse go after only keeping it for a night. She couldn't bear the look in its eyes, the way its little body never stopped trembling.

So she searched the Green Man's eyes, met his gaze for as long as she dared, but finally had to turn away, the question unanswered. Looking into his eyes, she felt something grow hot inside her, a burning. The fire that Mally had been talking about, she thought. It followed her nerves, sparking along their lengths like an electric shock. Not until she looked away did she realize that she was holding her breath.

She let it out, drew in a lungful of cold air, then another. Slowly the burning cooled, but she didn't look back at the Green Man. Was it so important to know everything? Maybe it was impossible to know anything, little say everything, about some things. But if she had to make a decision about the stag, she had to know what *he* wanted, didn't she?

The sound of the hounds, much closer now, drew her away from the Green Man's presence. Be a mystery then, she thought. She rejoined Mally, who was regarding her with a curious expression in her catlike eyes.

"What did you see?" the wild girl asked.

"I don't know. I'm not sure. Maybe it wasn't so much seeing something as *feeling* it. But I don't think he needs me, Mally. I don't think a being like that needs anything or anybody."

Mally nodded, though whether in agreement or understanding, Ali couldn't tell. "He knows how to keep a secret," she said.

"I suppose. Only how am I supposed to—"

The baying of the hounds was suddenly very close.

"We have to go now!" Mally cried.

She caught Ali by the hand and ran toward one of the stone formations. It reared above them, its base dark and shrouded in shadow as the tall heights blocked out the light of the moon. Ali tried to draw back as they neared it, but Mally raced on as though she meant to run right into it.

"Mally!" Ali cried, digging in her heels.

The wild girl didn't reply. Instead she scooped Ali up in her arms. Undaunted by the weight, she sprinted for the stone. Ali shut her eyes.

She expected them to hit it with a jarring impact, but in the next instant they were tumbling across grass. Mally landed like a cat, on her feet and running, but Ali sprawled in a tangle of limbs. She opened her eyes and saw that they were in Tony's front yard.

A surreal mood fell over her. She'd been dreaming, she was sure. She'd wandered out of Tony's house and dreamed it all. The hidden village in the forest, Lewis and the old stone and the dancers. The stag and the wild ride and that place that the mysteries came from.

She looked at Mally. If she'd been dreaming . . . Shouldn't Mally disappear, now that she'd woken up? Or maybe she was dreaming Mally, dreaming this, too.

The wild girl stepped close and offered her a hand up.

"Thanks," Ali said, determined to be polite even if she were dreaming.

Mally regarded her, a half-smile on her lips. Her hat was still missing and her hair was a wild nest of burrs and twigs and bits of leaves. It wasn't a dream, Ali realized as she took in the two small horns poking out of that thicket of hair. There were a hundred things she wanted to ask Mally right then and there, but before she had a chance, the quiet of the night was broken by a sharp gunshot. Right on the heels of it came a woman's scream.

Ali and the wild girl turned as one to look down the road leading up to Tony's. They saw figures on the road, the blonde hair of two of them highlit by the moon. Ali recognized the one closest to them just before that figure went tumbling to the side of the road.

"Mom!" she cried and started to run.

Mally sprinted ahead of her. With a shock, Ali realized that the wild girl was growling as she ran.

"That's my mom!" she cried after Mally.

Another gunshot stole away her words with the volume of its report.

17

The gunshot lifted him from the captain's chair in the front of the van. He was out the door, crossbow in hand, before Frankie's scream tore across it.

He didn't think about where he was going. Automatically, he'd started for Valenti's house. The sound of the second shot confirmed the direction and he ran all out, cursing himself for being so complacent once he'd let Louie Fucceri drive off. Christ, he could be stupid. Louie could've spotted him, or the van, and doubled back. Or he could've just sent another team in once he'd confirmed the target was in place.

He was getting too old for this kind of shit and that was all there was to it. A man should know well enough when to leave it alone. Let the young bucks take the risks. It wasn't like he needed this.

Expecting the trouble to be up at the house, he wasn't prepared for the struggling figures that suddenly appeared on the road in front of him. There seemed to be four or five figures in or around the action. How big a team had Louie sent in? This many men, it wasn't going to look good to the families. How many men could it take to hit a limping ex-enforcer? they'd be asking.

As he closed in he tried to pick out a target, but it was too dark and he couldn't make out who was who. A third shot rang out.

When Frankie screamed and fell, Bannon couldn't tell if she'd been hit or not. The gun went off close enough to momentarily deafen him. He turned, trying to hit Howie's gun arm, but was thrown off by the fact that Howie was using the weapon lefthandedly. Before he could compensate, Howie fired again.

Something punched Bannon in the side. The force of the bullet half-lifted him an inch or so, up onto his toes, and then he was falling backwards. The left side of his torso went numb. A burning sensation spread from the wound. The whole scene took on a preternatural clarity as though he could suddenly see in the dark. He thought he heard a kid's voice—Ali's voice. He saw Howie taking careful aim at him, a gun in each hand. No way the bastard would miss at this range.

He hit the road hard enough to knock the wind from him. The wound in his side throbbed as though someone had kicked it. He tried to reach the knife that hung between his shoulder blades, but he had landed on his right arm and his left wouldn't do what he told it to. The strange clarity of sight that had come over him let him look right into Howie's eyes. He knew the exact moment Howie was going to fire— telegraphed by a certain look—but then Howie aimed at a new threat. The .38 in Howie's left hand went off, the shot going wild, as something attacked him.

Bannon couldn't make out what it was. Some kind of animal, he thought. Growling deep in its chest like a panther. He saw whatever it was bowl Howie over, then his vision began to blur. Got to hang on, he told himself. This was no time to be wimping out. He had a job to do. Tony was depending on him to . . . He passed out, face turned into the dirt, before he could finish the thought.

Howie felt good. Even when Bannon was turning—the move quick and sure like he knew what he was doing—Howie wasn't bothered.

He kept a grip on the stolen automatic, but used his .38 to shoot. His first shot was a clean miss, but the second caught the fucker and blew him off his feet.

He gave a quick glance in the direction that Frankie had fallen, saw she wasn't going nowhere fast, not that babe, and turned back to Bannon to finish him off. What do you think fuckhead? he thought. Still going to brush right by Howie Peale like he didn't mean shit? You got about two seconds to feel sorry for yourself, but don't bother apologizing.

He tightened his finger on the trigger of the .38, then some sixth sense warned him that he was blowing it. He lifted the gun to meet the new threat, thinking it was Frankie, maybe, except whatever it was attacking him now, he didn't even think it was human. He had just a momentary view of it in the dark. Wild hair, teeth white in a dark face. He pulled the trigger of the .38, missed, and then it was on him, bearing him to the ground with the force of its rush.

He lost both guns. He cried out when his shoulder hit the ground. There was no time for another sound. A small fist drove into his solar plexus, and then his pain and the need to vocalize it was gone.

Ali had forgotten how strong Mally was. And how fast. She ran at the wild girl's heels, meaning to go to her mother, but then she saw Bannon get shot and Mally attack his assailant. When the guns flew out of Howie's hands, she pounced on the nearest. By the time she had it in her hands, Howie was dead.

She started to lower the weapon, then saw a shadow coming toward them from down the road. When the crossbow registered, she didn't even think about what she was doing. She just held the gun out with both hands and pulled the trigger.

The .38 bucked in her hands and she dropped it, the shot going wild. The man with the crossbow dove for the verge. When he sat up, he laid his weapon down on the grass and lifted his empty hands.

"I'm with Tony!" he cried.

Hands still stinging from the recoil of the .38, Ali found the gun again and lifted it, trying hard not to shake. "H-how do we know that?" she asked.

Mally crouched over Howie, her cat's eyes gleaming as she studied the stranger.

"Fercrissakes, you can ask him. I'm here to help him—not make
war on little girls."

Ali frowned. She didn't know what to do. "Mally?" she asked
softly.

The wild girl shrugged, her gaze never leaving the man. He looked
at the two of them, wishing he knew how to handle this. In another
minute the blonde kid might pull the trigger again and this time she
might get lucky and actually hit him. As for the other one . . . she was
the size of a kid, too, but he'd seen the way she'd taken out the guy
she was crouched over.

"Look," he said soothingly. "Why don't you just ask Tony, okay?"

"Ask him what?"

All three of them turned at the sound of the new voice.

When he got off the phone, Valenti had taken the UZI and a flashlight
and gone outside to make a sweep of his property. He took his time
about it, walking with the flashlight off and stuck in his back pocket.
He put as little pressure on his leg as he could.

The information he'd received about Louie Fucceri—that he'd
been within yards of the house, fercrissakes!—settled in with numb-
ing force. He'd thought himself very capable, able to go up against
anything the Magaddinos threw at him, but now he realized that he'd
lost touch with it all over the past couple of years. Lost that hunter's
instinct that had kept him alive for so long.

He had to get it back if he wanted to survive, but he didn't know
if he could. Because it wasn't just being out of touch that had let him
lose it. Something had change inside him as well. Changed forever.

He'd been a hard man. A hunter. Now he was something else. He
could still get angry, he was still tough, he supposed, but it wasn't the
same thing anymore. Before, the *padrone* had pointed him where he
had to go. He'd been like a weapon in the Don's hand. And he'd gotten things done. But now he was thinking about it, and thinking
slowed you down.

He didn't want to go back to what he'd been. He preferred what he'd become—was still becoming. But he had some unfinished business. He didn't want to deal with it, but he had to. Trouble was, he didn't even know if he could anymore. He'd been following something else now—following the mystery.

That was what it was, he realized. The mystery. The music started to heal him, but it was the mystery that was finishing it. The mystery and the Treasures. It wasn't until he'd met Ali that he'd understood what he was missing. She'd made him feel whole again— just like that. And her momma . . . Well, maybe Frankie wasn't for him, but just knowing a woman like her made him feel good.

So he was going to stay. And he was going to help Frankie, too. He'd get Ali back from whatever had stolen her away—from whatever the mystery really was—and then he'd make sure that nothing hurt either her or her momma again.

Oh, yeah, Tony, he thought. You're talking the talk, all right. But what're you going to *do?*

He came around to the front of the house, keeping close to the woods. He used his cane with his left hand. The UZI hung from his right shoulder by a strap, his hand on its pistol grip. He had a 32-round box in it, ready to go. Two more were in his jacket pocket along with the automatic.

Come on, Louie, he thought. Let's stop fucking around. You had me in Malta, but you blew it. So either do it right, or step into my sights and let me show you how it's done. No *pezzo di merda* like you's going to keep me on the run. Not no more.

He was looking right across his front yard when suddenly two figures appeared on it as though they'd fallen right from the sky. Valenti's finger tightened against the UZI's trigger, then relaxed when he saw who it was. He was about to call out to them, when the gunshot split the night, Frankie's scream following hard on its heels.

Jesus, no! Don't let the Magaddinos make their play now—not with Ali in the middle of it.

Before he could move, Mally and Ali were on their feet and running for the source of the gunshot. A second report followed the first as Valenti hobbled across his lawn, making for the road. He saw figures struggling there. Bannon had to be the blond.

Damn this leg! Valenti cried soundlessly as he saw the man he figured was Bannon go down. He was still too far away to do any good himself. Mally and Ali had both reached the scene as a third shot rang out. He saw the wild girl leap onto whoever had cut Bannon down. He tried to put on more speed.

By the time he'd halved the distance, there was a fourth shot. Then he was close enough to her them talking and he moved in, ready for anything. When he spoke, they all turned to him. He kept the UZI ready for action.

"Christ, Tony!" a familiar voice said. "Is that you? What do you say you call off your little Amazons and give an old man a break?"

Valenti tucked his cane under his arm and took out the flashlight. The beam stabbed the night. He moved it to the man's face, then let the UZI hang from its strap as he moved forward.

"What the hell are you doing here, Mario?"

"Helping out. Look, Tony. We got no time for talk. Tom got hit bad and I think maybe the woman did, too."

Valenti thought his heart would stop. He'd forgotten the scream he'd heard earlier. Christ, it couldn't be Frankie.

At the same time as he turned, Ali bolted for her mother. Frankie was sitting up and the beam of Valenti's flashlight caught her face. He quickly pointed it away.

"Mom! Are you okay?"

Frankie nodded slowly. "I can't take much more of this," she said, her voice still husky. Ali knelt down beside her, and rather than speaking, she put her arms around her, holding her close. Valenti started for them, but Mario caught his arm. "We got other problems right now," he said. He plucked the flashlight from Valenti's nerveless fingers and played its beam over Howie's face. "Do you know this monkey?"

Valenti started to shake his head, then looked closer. "He might have been with Shaw last night. It's hard to tell, though."

"Okay. Fuck him. We got to look after Tom. You want to get something on that wound of his while I get my van?"

"Sure."

Valenti went down carefully beside Bannon and pulled the blond man's jacket away from his chest. Jacket and shirt were soaked with blood. Mario handed him the flashlight.

"Hang tight," he said. "I'll be right back. I got a kit in the van— but then I got to take him to get patched up."

"Do it," Valenti said.

He noted that Mally had pulled another of her vanishing acts, then turned his attention to the immediate problem. He looked up when he sensed motion close at hand. Frankie and Ali had approached him and were standing by.

"Oh, jeez," Ali muttered and looked away.

Frankie swallowed painfully, then knelt down beside Valenti. "Can I . . . can I help?"

"Yeah. Could you hold the light?"

It was easier to work with both hands free. He peeled Bannon's shirt back, sopping the blood carefully with his own jacket. The wound was a mess, but he figured the bullet had gone right through. Bannon was going to need a lot of blood. He was going to need a helluva lot better attention than what they could give him, or he wasn't going to make it.

"Any idea who that guy was?" he asked as he worked, nodding toward Howie's body.

Frankie cleared her throat. "Tom said he worked with Earl. That he was with Earl when he tried to grab Ali last night."

Valenti nodded. "Yeah, I thought it was the same guy."

Ali was looking at the dead man, fascinated and repulsed at the same time. Then she realized that Mally was gone. Down at the end of the road Mario's van started up. The engine's revving was followed by the sound of wheels spinning. A few moments later the van's headlights appeared and caught them in its glare. Mario pulled over to the side of the road, then backed up so that they wouldn't have far to carry Bannon.

"We'll put him on the bed," he said as he opened the back door.

With Frankie and Valenti's help, he got the wounded man inside. Grabbing a first-aid kit, he crouched beside the bed and started to work on the wound.

"He's gonna need blood," he said.

"Is he . . . is he going to be all right?" Ali asked.

"Christ, I hope so. Tony, I got to go. I can't help him here."

Valenti nodded. "You want me to handle that?" he asked, indicating Howie's body.

"No. Haul him up here. Then you got to go, Tony. I don't know when Louie's coming back and I don't know how many *soldati* he's bringing, *capito?* You can't stay."

"I've got to stay."

Mario studied him for a moment, then nodded. "Okay. But then we got to play this at both ends, you know what I'm saying? If we get rid of Louie and his boys, they're just gonna send more."

"What're you saying, Mario?"

"I'm going to New York after I take care of Tom. Can you hire any local talent?"

"Fercrissakes, Mario. I don't want you involved anymore."

"Too late. Broadway Joe gave me his word and he broke it. He owes me now. So are you gonna be all right? I'll try to send someone, but my connections aren't what they could be this side of the Atlantic. I had a hell of a time just outfitting this van."

Valenti glanced inside. There was a small arsenal in there. It was outfitted for camping, but besides the weaponry there was a great deal of what looked like sound equipment. Valenti recognized a sonar device and a couple of listening hookups for taps or long-range microphones.

"You'd better get going," he told Mario. "We'll work things out here."

Mario glanced out the back door to where Frankie and her daughter were standing off to one side. "You sure?"

"Yeah."

"Okay. *Coraggio,* Tony."

Valenti shook his head. "So that *was* you on the phone, wasn't it? What were you playing at?"

"I didn't know who was listening—if anybody was, you know what I'm saying? Louie thinks it's just you with maybe some muscle, he's not gonna play it the same as he would if he knew it was you and the Fox."

"There's that."

"Okay. I'm going. You sure you don't—"

"You handle New York," Valenti said, "but no big show, okay?"

"I've got some ideas—nice and simple ones. You take it easy." Mario tipped his finger against his forehead. "Nice to meet you, ladies," he added to Frankie and Ali. "I wish it could've been under more pleasant circumstances."

He got into the captain's chair on the driver's side. Valenti stowed Howie's body in the back, then slammed the door shut. Mario drove up toward the house where he turned the van around. As he passed them heading back he blinked his headlights. They stood, watching until his taillights disappeared, then slowly regarded each other.

"How're you holding up?" Valenti asked them finally.

"I think I need a few things explained," Frankie said.

"We can do that," Valenti said. He collected the various weapons, including Mario's crossbow. "Let's talk about it up at the house— okay?"

Frankie nodded. She really looked beat, Valenti thought.

Ali slipped her arm around her mother's waist, and he followed at a slower pace. Christ, he wished things'd slow down a little. But he had the feeling that they were just going to get worse.

He paused at his front door, letting the other two go on inside while he turned back to look out across his front lawn. They had just appeared there, he remembered. Ali and the wild girl had just appeared on his lawn as though they'd tumbled out of thin air.

"Tony?"

He turned to find Ali standing by the door. "Are you okay?" he asked.

She nodded. "How about you?"

"I'm handling it."

"I don't think my mom's doing too good. Are you coming in?"

He followed her inside to find Frankie curled up on one end of the couch furthest from the door. Ali sat down beside her and took her hand while Valenti settled in the couch opposite them. Frankie held Ali's hand gratefully and gave them both a wan smile.

"Busy night," Valenti said.

Frankie nodded. "Will your friend be all right?"

"Yeah. I think so. He seemed like a tough guy." Valenti regarded her, hearing again the touch of hoarseness in her voice. Then his gaze settled on her bruised throat. Oh, Christ. "Frankie, what happened to you?"

She took a deep breath and let it out slowly. "I . . . I was attacked when I got home. There was this man in a pickup . . . waiting for me. . . ."

Ali's hand tightened on hers.

"Jesus," Valenti muttered. "That Howie guy?"

She shook her head.

"You mean it was some guy that had nothing to do with your ex?"

"Not that I know of."

"Fercrissakes. What's going on around here?" Valenti shook his head. "It's like the whole world's gone crazy all of a sudden. Did this guy tell you what he wanted?"

Frankie swallowed. "Me," she said in a quiet voice.

There was a long moment of silence, then Ali moved closer to her mother and put her arm around her. "It's going to be okay, Mom." She looked at Valenti. "Isn't it, Tony?"

"Well, we're sure going to give it our best shot."

Silence fell between them again. Ali just held her mother. Valenti sat uncomfortably watching them, wanting to comfort them both while trying to fight the anger that was rising in him. Frankie's eyes held a distant, hurt look. When they finally cleared, she looked at Valenti.

"That man with the van," she asked. "Is he one of your old business associates—from when you were doing the study on the mob?"

Valenti blinked. "Who told you that?"

"Ali did."

"Oh." He glanced at Ali, who shook her head slightly from side to side. Right, kid. Maybe we'll leave it like that for now. But you and me, we've got a long talk coming to us. "Yeah," he said. "Mario taught me everything I knew about the mob. He was sort of my . . ." He searched for the word.

"Your mentor?"

"Yeah. That's close enough."

"Well, he certainly seemed to know what he was doing. And all that equipment."

"Yeah. Mario's always been good with toys—gadgets, that kind of thing. Listen." He looked from Ali to her mother. "Maybe we should be thinking about getting some sleep—what do you say?"

"I'd like that—oh, my bag! I had some things in it. . . ."

"It's by the door," Valenti said. "I brought it up. Look, you know the way upstairs. You take my bed, Frankie, and Ali can have the guest room again."

"What about you?"

"I'm going to be fine down here—don't worry about it. Besides, somebody's got to keep an eye on things in case, well, you know. I'll sleep lighter down here."

He got the Adidas bag. As Frankie started up the stairs he caught Ali's arm. "We've got to talk," he said.

"I know. Tomorrow—okay? I'll get up early. Mom's a pretty heavy sleeper."

"Okay. You got a date."

"She's going to be okay, isn't she, Tony? I mean, she looks so . . . I don't know. Sort of washed out."

"She's been through a lot of crap. She's not young and resilient like you, and she hasn't been through it all before like me. But she's going to pull out of it fine, Ali. Trust me. She's a tough lady—she just don't know it."

Ali nodded. "G'night, Tony."

"Yeah. *Buena notte.* You call me if you start feeling weird or you hear anything, okay? And tell your momma the same thing."

"I will."

He watched her go up the stairs, then headed back to the couch. He sat there for awhile, massaging his leg, thinking. Then he got up and took all the weapons into the kitchen. The .38 Howie had used was the only one that had been fired, but when he had finished taking it apart and cleaning it, he started on the others. With his hands busy, it was easier to think.

* * *

Considering how little time they'd spent in their own house, Ali was already beginning to feel as comfortable in Tony's guest room as she did in her own bedroom. Once she was washed up and had tucked her mother in, she sat on the bed in the nightie that Frankie had brought up for her and stared out the window.

She was young and resilient, was she? She wasn't so sure about that. She was dealing with it all by pushing it aside and filing it under "Handle This Stuff Later." She'd had a lot of practice with that kind of thing. Previous problems hadn't been quite as stunning as what she'd experienced over the past forty-eight hours, but she was finding that she could deal with them in the same way. It hadn't been easy moving around as much as she had, always having to fit into a new school, a new neighborhood. That was why she'd learned to depend on herself first. She could handle herself. Hadn't tonight proved it? But when she really thought about it all . . .

Strangely enough, it wasn't the mystery, as either stag or Green Man, that came to the fore of her thoughts, but wild-haired Mally. The riddle of just what she was and what she really wanted nagged at Ali. Lewis had been very eloquent in explaining how things should be, even if he wasn't working with the whole story, while Mally had an offhand manner about her that gave her reasoning a little too much patness. But Mally had taken her to that other place. Ali still didn't really know where or what it was, but it had been something that couldn't be faked.

So should she do what Mally had said, call the mystery to her with a bonfire and set him free? But what if that was a mistake? She just couldn't know what to do until the mystery told her what *he* wanted and she supposed the only chance she'd have of finding that out was by calling him to her. The idea both excited and frightened her.

Talk to Tony, she told herself. Maybe even to Lewis, though she'd have to be careful with what she said to him. And what about her mom? What should she tell her? Jeez, it was all so confusing.

Something disturbed her thoughts then. It was a sound—not Tommy's piping—but it sent a similar shiver up her spine. Moving from the bed to the window, she opened it and leaned close to the screen. She could her it more clearly now. It was the pack. Hunting. Still chasing the stag, she supposed. But the sound grew closer and closer, and as she watched they came out of the forest, dark shapes on the lawn, now dogs, now hooded monks. She wanted to draw back from the window, but their gazes locked on hers, holding her in place with the sheer force of their wills.

If they catch our scent here, she remembered Mally saying in that other place, *they'll think we're from here . . . the dark man set them on the trail of any mystery, you see. We can't escape them as easily as the stag. . . .*

Oh, God. Was that why they were out there now? Did they think she was another loose bit of mystery in the shape of a teenager?

Uneasily, she watched them moving back and forth at the edge of the trees. Call Tony, she told herself. Though what was he going to do against things like these? Shoot them? She remembered the men trying to shoot the stag a few nights ago. They hadn't had much luck. Why should these creatures be any different?

She opened her mouth to call to Tony anyway, but her throat was so tight that the sound only came out as a squeak. She swallowed drily, went to try again, but then saw the pack slip back into the forest, one by one. When the last of them was gone, the spell holding her in place was gone. She closed the window quickly and lay down on the bed, all her muscles feeling like jelly.

If the stag was set free, what would happen to the Hunt? God, never mind that. If the pack was really after her, what was she going to do? Lying on her back, she stared up at the dark ceiling and wished that the world would slow down. This is what happens when you think an adventure would be fun. You forget about the scary parts, but by then it's too late. You're stuck right smack dab in the middle of it.

She didn't think she'd sleep, not wound up as she was, but as she started planning how she'd try to find Mally tomorrow, her eyelids began to droop and she fell asleep right in the middle of a thought.

Frankie didn't find sleep as easily. The shakes hit her soon after she lay down and nothing seemed to ease them. She grabbed a fistful of sheet with each hand and twisted and turned and then the cramps started. No matter how she lay, she couldn't alleviate them. They were like menstrual pains, only far more severe. The muscles of her abdomen seemed to knot in a series of muscle spasms that left her weak and teary-eyed from the pain. This was the second time they'd hit tonight.

The first time had been when Sherry had taken her upstairs at her own house and was helping her from the shower. If she'd been alone, she would have collapsed right there in the bathtub, but Sherry had seen the problem immediately and helped her into the bedroom and onto the bed.

"Do you have any Valium?" she'd asked Frankie. "Any kind of muscle relaxant at all?"

Mutely, Frankie had shaken her head.

"Okay. Just lie still. Your body's having a reaction to what you went through. Sometimes it takes a little while to hit, but nobody gets off clean. Try to straighten your legs. That's right. Now lie still. Don't breathe too quickly—you're going to hyperventilate. Just take it a breath at a time. In. Hold it. Okay, now let it out. Hang on. Now in again . . ."

The pain had eased after awhile, and as Frankie followed those instructions now, the new knots began to slowly unravel. These cramps were longer in leaving, but they'd been far more severe. She wondered if she should ask Tony if he had any Valium but didn't dare get up. What if she collapsed at the top of the stairs and fell right down them? Or . . . If she stumbled at all . . . She couldn't bear the thought of him helping her up, of him touching her. It wasn't Tony personally. She couldn't stand the idea of any man touching her right now.

In and out. She went back to the slow breathing as her panic fed new torment to her abdomen. God, why did her body have to be so weak? Why couldn't she step out of this . . . this memory? For that was what it was. She felt unclean—even after two showers, one at home earlier, another here before she went to bed. But no matter how hard she had scrubbed, she still felt soiled. In. Hold it. Let it out. Wait a moment. In.

What if this feeling never went away?

Stop it, she told herself. In. Hold it. Out.

She was going to pull out of this. She was going to rise above Earl and this goddamn rapist. That's why she'd moved back to Lanark. Not to find someone new to lean on, whether it was Tony, some other man, or even Ali. She was here to stand on her own two feet and nobody was going to stop her. In. Hold it. Let it out. It was hard to maintain the slow-breathing as her anger grew, and finally she just let it wash through her. The cramps didn't get worse. Instead, the anger seemed to clean her. If only she wasn't so goddamned useless!

No. There was a big difference, she told herself, between leaning helplessly on someone and letting someone be a friend, helping out like a friend would. That's what Tony was doing. Being a friend to both her and Ali. Like she had been a friend to Joy Goldman. That wasn't giving up control to someone else. That was just doing what everybody was here on this earth to do. Not just looking out for number one, but doing what they could to leaving the world a better place than it was when they came.

God, that was such a sixties ideology, she thought. But then she was a child of the sixties. Those years had shaped her, leaving a far more lasting impression than the subsequent decade and a half. So she had to follow it. She had to go on. Deal with Earl, deal with the bastard who'd attacked her, but then go on. Just because they were dead to what was around them, didn't mean they were going to leave her feeling the same. She wouldn't let them win.

But she couldn't help wondering, as she looked around the shadowed corners of this strange room, what that man in the pickup was doing right now. What kind of thoughts were going through *his* head? How could he just go out and do what he did to someone he didn't even know? Or had he driven by her house, seen her working out in the yard perhaps? Or spotted her in Perth or Lanark and followed her home one day to see where she lived? What hole did people like that crawl out of?

She got up as the last of her cramps eased and went to look out the window. I'm not going to let you win, you bastard, she thought out into the night. Not you in your pickup and not Earl. This is it. I've run as far as I'm going to run. The next time you come for me, remember that. Because if hurting you is what it's going to take to leave the world a better place, then that's what I'm going to do. Believe it.

She felt strong for the first time in days. Just standing there, the floor cool under her bare feet, her arms wrapped around her flannel-clad body, she felt as though she really *could* deal with things.

She thought about the walk up from her house, the sudden violence, a man dying, Tom Bannon hurt, the guns . . . Surprisingly, she wasn't disturbed by that aspect of what she'd gone through. Maybe it was because she'd still been in a state of semi-shock. It had all happened around her with a certain blur. All she could think of was that in the morning she was going to ask Tony for one of those handguns. She was going to ask him for it and get him to show her how to use it. How to take it apart and put it back together. How to do whatever it was you did to things like that to keep them in good working order.

When she finally turned from the window and climbed back into bed, she fell asleep as soon as her head hit the pillow.

18

"Hey, don't take it so bad," Lisa said as she pulled out onto the highway. "It's not like you had an investment in the guy or anything."

Sherry nodded. "I know. But it still pisses me off. I should have
gone with my gut feeling when I first saw him. The guy's a worm."

"Ah, but a poor hurt worm," Lisa said. "That's the trouble with
you, Sherry. You're a sucker for anything that's feeling a little pain."

"I should have become a vet then. At least animals don't turn
around and burn you."

"I suppose. Frankie seemed pretty nice, though—don't you think?
What pisses *me* off is what she had to go through. But that guy that
came to pick her up—now he was something else."

"Don't you ever think of anything else, Lisa?"

"Once in awhile—but I'm working on cutting it out. You want to
light up a joint?"

"Sure."

Lisa laughed suddenly. "Christ, I'd like to see little Howie's face when he finds out he's got to walk back to wherever it is that he came from."

Sherry smiled. "Let's hope he's got a long way to go."

By the time they got back to Steve's cottage, the joint had done its trick and they were both feeling better. The lights were on inside, but except for Steve, no one else was around.

"Christ!" Steve said when they came in. "Where the hell've you been?"

The two women looked at each other, then back at him.

"What's your problem?" Lisa asked.

"What's my problem? I'll tell you what's my problem. Earl Shaw's called three times looking for his little buddy, *that's* my problem. What happened to him?"

"He wanted to go for a drive," Lisa said. "And then once we got to where we were going, he wanted to stay there. What difference does it make?"

"Look. You don't know Earl. The fucker's insane. He left his buddy here and now he wants him back. When he finds out that you've dumped him somewhere, there's going to be hell to pay."

"Come on, Steve," Sherry said. "What's he going to do—sue us? If he tries to get tough, just sic a couple of your biker friends on him."

Steve shook his head. "This guy kills people."

Sherry blanched. Lisa patted her shoulder. "Don't worry, Sherry. I'll talk to him. Did he leave you a number, Steve?"

"It's by the phone. Listen, Lisa. Don't expect any favors from him just because you balled him last night."

Lisa gave him a withering look as she went to use the phone.

Lance took the first corner past the Treasure house in a skidding slide, his rear tires spitting dirt and gravel. He almost lost the pickup right then and there, but the sound of the engine's roar and the wheels bouncing in the potholes, the lack of shocks that made the whole truck rattle, it all served to bring him back to his senses. He slowed down a little but pointed the pickup on down the road. He'd really done it now. Christ, that woman would have the police on him. . . .

He couldn't face that. Couldn't face the idea of being booked, of the time in court, but most of all he couldn't face Brenda. What could he tell her? That was the hardest thing. Because he didn't regret the deed itself. That was something he'd always imagined doing, just grabbing some good-looking high-class woman and tearing into her. Yessir. But he'd never had the balls to actually do it—not until that goddamn music egged him on. And it had felt good, too.

For once he'd been in control. If he'd had the time, that woman would have done anything he told her to, just to keep on his good side. *Yes*sir. A moment like that balanced against all the bowing and scraping for welfare checks. It didn't make things better. It didn't ease the pain and confusion of the bank taking his house and land and then renting the suckers back to him. Talk about a kick in the balls. It didn't make the little bit of money stretch any farther. Didn't make damn near begging for make-work feel any better. But goddamn, for one moment there he'd really been in charge. And that had been great—though it would have been even better if he hadn't got caught.

How long would it take for the police to get out to her place, listen to her story, then come to get him? He slowed down and pulled over to the side of the road. Christ, what was he going to tell Brenda? She'd stuck by him through a lot of shit—a hell of a lot more "for worse" than "for better." But she wouldn't stand by him on this.

He closed his eyes, but all he could see against his eyelids was the woman's frightened face, the white of her flesh in the moonlight as he tore at her clothing. Buddy Treasure's little girl, all grown up and his for the taking. If only that other car hadn't shown up.

Christ on crutches. But if he was going to pay for it anyway. . . . He was almost tempted to go back and see if those people were gone, maybe finish the job if the police weren't there guarding her. If they hadn't taken her away. But what if she hadn't called them? Hell, what if she didn't know who he was? Just because he knew her didn't mean she'd remember him. It had been years since her mother ran off with her. Why the hell should she remember Lance Maxwell? She could be just lying there alone in her house right now, thinking it was over. . . .

He shook his head, trying to get it to clear. Christ, but it ached. It was just filling up with a kaleidoscope of images of the woman and him. Riding her wouldn't be like doing it with Brenda. Hell, no. This one was young, smooth like a doe, and he could be her buck deer, yessir.

He blinked his eyes open and stared through the windshield into the night. What the hell was he doing? Thinking of going back? Christ on a cross, she'd be talking to the police right now—giving his description, maybe even remembering his name from when he used to do some odd jobs around her old man's place.

Panic reared in him again, but he shoved it roughly down. Ease up, Lance, he told himself. Only one thing you can do now. The decision came hot and hard, like the way the music put the fire between his legs.

He shifted the pickup into first, turned on the headbeams and headed down the road again.

Louie and Fingers were sitting on the bed. Between them was a suitcase. Louie was drawing a map on a piece of paper, using the case for a flat surface. "Okay," he was saying. "There's a door here. Window. Window. This might've been a cellar door—maybe just a root cellar. I don't know."

Fingers nodded. "Simple's the best way. One of us in a side window, then go in the front and the back. If we do it quick and easy—"

"I don't want the place to look roughed up," Louie said.

"Yeah, but this other guy—you couldn't make him?"

"Must be local talent."

"Okay," Fingers said. "But you've got two of them to worry about now—no way you can do it clean."

"I got an idea you're gonna love," Louie said.

Sitting by the window, watching the pair of them, Earl could only shake his head. Christ, had they been watching too many caper movies or what? Looking at them, you'd think they were planning a major heist, not just knocking off a couple of jerks—even if one of them *was* Tony Valenti. Listen, he wanted to say, just let me handle it, but then the phone rang.

"Yeah?" he said in the mouthpiece.

"Hi, Earl. Lisa here. Steve says you're looking for Howie."

"That's right. I thought he needed some rest. What did you do with him—take him out bar-hopping or something? Listen, put him on, would ya?"

"I can't. He asked us to drive him down to Lanark—over to your ex-wife's—and we left him there. We just got back."

"You did *what?*" Earl looked up to find both Louie and Fingers watching him. He tried to compose his features.

"I said we just got back," Lisa repeated.

"No. What I want to know is where did you take him?"

"What do you mean?"

"What the fuck was he going to see her for?"

"Well, he wouldn't tell us," Lisa explained. "He said you'd be mad, but he did mention something about fixing things up between you. Hey, I didn't know you had a little girl, Earl. You never told me that last night."

"How long ago did you leave him?"

"Oh, I don't know. An hour maybe?"

"Right. Thanks for calling."

Earl hung up, thinking: And maybe we'll talk some more, depending on how much Howie told you. He shook his head. Christ, Howie. You fuckup. He'd had to tell the wops about him, once he realized Howie was gone, losing the edge of having a hole card on them.

"Who was that?" Louie asked.

"Just one of the girls that I left my partner with."

"What happened—he take off?"

"Something like that."

"Who'd he go see?" Louie wanted to know.

"Look, that's my problem," Earl said. "You stick to Valenti and let me worry about what's my business."

Louie glanced at Fingers, then back. "Was it your ex-wife he went to see? The one with the money that you're hoping to use to finance your deal with my old man?"

Earl stared at him, stunned. "What the fuck would you know about that?"

"You don't think we check into people we do business with?"

"Cute. Who'd you check me out with? The Better Business Bureau?"

Fingers stiffened, but Louie shook his head. "Don't play the smart-ass, Earl," he said. "Maybe you're big stuff up here, but in the circles we run in, you're just a small-time hood, *capito?*"

"Sure," Earl said. This wasn't the right time for him to make his play.

"So your wife—she knows Tony?"

"Now how—"

"Think about it," Louie said. "What else are you doing up in the bush where you just happen to run into Tony, but sniffing around her? So answer the question. Does she know Tony?"

"Looks like."

"This complicates things," Louie said.

"What the problem?"

"First off, we don't make war on women and kids."

"Sure," Earl said. "But that's only in the family—right?"

Louie shrugged. "Maybe so. But it's never good business."

"Look, like I said. You let me handle them, okay? What've you got to lose, fercrissakes? It's not like—"

He broke off as a sharp rapping came at the door. Fingers moved silently from the bed and took up a position by the wall near it. He drew his gun and attached its silencer. Louie nodded to Earl.

"Open it," he said.

Earl crossed to the door and jerked it opened. A large wheeled laundry hamper stood in the hall in front of their door. "What the fuck?" he muttered and looked both ways down the hall, but it was empty so far as he could see. As he started to reach for the cloth that was covering the hamper Fingers stopped him.

"Easy," he said. "That could be—"

"Oh, fercrissakes," Earl said. "This isn't some fucking movie. What do you think? There's gonna be a bomb or a stiff in there?"

He laughed as he caught hold of the edge of the cloth and flipped it aside. The laughter died in his throat as he looked down into the pasty-white features of Howie Peale's corpse.

"Oh, fuck," he said.

Louie and Fingers looked inside. Fingers reached down and plucked a silver stick pin from the front of the corpse's jacket. The head of the pin was a small sculpted fox's head.

"Papale," Fingers said. "He's warning us that he's in."

Louie nodded. "Get rid of that thing," he told Earl, indicating the hamper. "Then we've got some serious thinking to do."

Lance turned off the ignition after pulling in beside his house. He sat in the truck for a few moments, then got out and slowly walked around to the front. Standing near the road, he looked back at the building.

There was a light on in their bedroom—that was where Brenda would be. Another light on in the kitchen and on the front porch. For him. That's how it was when he was coming in late. She always left those two lights on for him. What was she going to think when she found out what he'd been doing while she left those lights on for him tonight? He'd taken off this morning without a word and then tried to hump Buddy Treasure's little girl, only she wasn't so little anymore, was she?

It was Brenda's disappointment that was going to be the hardest to take. She'd stood by him through a lot of hard times. Losing the farm. Losing both the boys—the one in an accident with a thresher, the other to drunk driving. And his ma and pa. What were they thinking when they looked down on him now, when they saw what he'd done to the Maxwell farm—six generations it'd been in the family—when they saw what he'd done to the Maxwell name.

It wouldn't matter, probably, except that he got caught.

Time's wasting, he told himself. You know what you came here to do. He headed for the house, wishing he could hear that music one more time.

"What did you tell him that for?" Sherry asked when Lisa got off the phone. "Now he's going to take it out on Frankie."

Lisa shook her head. "He can't do that. He knows that we know now—so what can he do? If anything happens to Frankie, he knows we can go to the police."

"What makes you think that'll stop him? Maybe he'll come after *us* now."

"I know this kind of guy," Lisa insisted. "He talks big, but—"

"You're wrong," Steve said. "Earl Shaw's one crazy mother-fucker. Believe it. If I were you, I'd be planning a long vacation somewhere until this all blows over. That's what I'm going to do. I like having my balls all in one piece."

"C'mon, Steve. What can he do?"

"I don't know, but I'm not hanging around to find out. It's going to take him forty-five minutes or so to get out here, if he comes here first, and I plan to be long gone in the next five."

"Where are you going?"

"I've got a friend who's got a chalet up in Wakefield—someone Earl doesn't know."

Lisa glanced at Sherry. "You're scared, aren't you?"

Sherry nodded. "You're not?"

Lisa thought about that for a moment, about the kind of man Earl had appeared to be last night. A little rough, full of himself, sure. But crazy?

"I saw him take a tire-iron to a guy once," Steve said. "You want to know what for? The guy was leaning against Earl's car."

"For real?" Lisa asked.

Steve nodded. The two women exchanged glances, then Lisa turned to him. "Take us with you?"

"If you're ready to leave in four minutes."

"You're on."

Brenda Maxwell was lying in bed when she heard her husband's pickup pull into the lane. Thank God. He was finally back. She'd made an appointment with Dr. Bolton for him for tomorrow morning. Now she just hoped she could get him to keep it. She listened to his footsteps in the lane, heard them fade. He's gone to the grave, she thought. She'd stood over it herself earlier today, thinking about poor old Dooker, of how things had changed. Whatever demons were driving her husband, she just hoped it wasn't too late to drive them away.

She was about to go downstairs and call him in when she heard the front door open and his workboots clomping down the hall to the kitchen. Should she get up and fix him something to eat? He'd missed breakfast, lunch and dinner, unless he'd eaten out. Where in God's name *had* he been all day? Before she could get out of bed and go downstairs, she heard the back door open and the screen door creak on its hinges, then slam shut. Now what was he doing?

Her feet found their worn slippers and she put an old housecoat on. It was dark in the hallway and on the stairs going down, but she decided not to turn on a light. Lord knew what was going through his mind at the moment. She didn't want to spook him. Not with the appointment set for tomorrow morning. Not when she'd have somebody to help her deal with this thing.

She went down the stairs slowly, fingers trailing along the banister. Keep remembering those good times, she told herself. So times have been rough. They'll get better again. She muttered the words to herself, using them as a litany as she practiced them. She had to convince him.

Her foot was just leaving the last stair when the sudden report of the shotgun being fired sounded like an explosion outside. She jumped, almost falling from the stairs, and recovered only by clutching the banister.

She knew before she reached the kitchen and flicked on the backyard floods what she was going to see. But she went through the motions all the same. It wasn't until she stood on the porch and could actually see him sprawled across Dooker's grave, the shotgun lying nearby and the ground splattered with his blood, that she slowly sank to her knees. Leaning her head against the support pole of the porch, she tried to pray, but all she could find were tears.

19

" 'Lo, Lewis—Lily."

Lily looked up sharply as the disheveled figure swung down from a tree above them and settled on her haunches to stare at them. There was no hat hiding her matted curls tonight, and for the first time Lily saw the small horns lifting from Mally's brow. Her eyes widened slightly, but then she nodded. She should have guessed that the wild girl was more kin to the mystery than to the village.

Lewis had always talked about her as though he'd known her for years, but since it was only fairly recently that Mally had been seen around the village and joined them in the dance, Lily had never really put a great deal of mind to what Lewis had told her about the wild girl. Lily had just assumed that this Mally was a daughter or granddaughter of some other Mally that Lewis had known.

"You're back," Lewis said.

"That I am. What a night it's been."

"The girl you took?"

"I brought her to her home."

"Why did you take her, Mally?"

The wild girl shrugged. "I wanted to show her a thing or two before you filled her head with too much bookish nonsense."

"Nonsense? You little scamp! You're the one that started me on all those books in the first place."

"But only because you'd never stop asking questions," Mally replied with a grin.

Lily laid her hand on Lewis's arm, calming him. "So Ali's safe with her family?" she asked. "We heard some gunfire, you see. . . ."

"It had nothing to do with us," Mally assured her.

"Well, that's a relief. We were very worried, what with Ali disappearing and those men that came with her being so angry."

Mally nodded. "Well, I've got to go now."

Movement by the stone caught their attention. Tommy stood up and thrust his pipes into his belt. He looked at them, a grin resembling Mally's touching his lips before his usual vacuous look came over him and he yawned. Whatever possessed him when he piped was gone and he was just plain Tommy Duffin again. He walked slowly by them without a word, Gaffa at his heels. They took the path down to the village.

"How old are you?" Lily asked. Lewis looked over at Mally, very curious as to how she would answer.

"Don't know," Mally replied. "I lost count a long time ago."

"Fifty years old?" Lewis asked. "A hundred?"

Mally laughed. "Oh, much older than that, Lewis!"

It was hard to tell if she were joking or not. Finally Lily asked, "What sort of being are you?"

"Just me." Her gaze caught Lily's. "I'm a secret—that's all." She laughed again and stood up. "But I'll tell you this, tomorrow you'll see some moon magics and won't they be fine! Your piper can pipe the whole night long, but tomorrow old Hornie will be jumping a fire of bones and too busy to pay your dancers a call. See you then!"

"Mally!" Lewis cried, but she had already melted into the forest without a sound.

"What did she mean, Lewis?" Lily asked, taking his hand.

"I don't know," he replied. "I never know what she means. But sometimes I think that if I ever do, I'll wish I had never wanted to know in the first place."

"Now what do *you* mean, Lewis?"

He shook his head. "You know I've told you about the mystery and how wild it could get if we didn't take care of it the way we have for all these years?"

"Yes. But . . . ?"

"I think Mally might be wilder yet."

He rose to this feet, joints cracking, and helped Lily up. When she seemed as though she were going to talk some more, he laid a finger against her lips and shook his head.

"Let's just walk," he said.

A FIRE OF BONES

Beloved Pan and all ye other gods who haunt this place, give me beauty in the inward soul; and may the outward and inward man be one.

—PLATO,
FROM *DIALOGUES, PHAEDRUS,*
sec. 279

"This is the place of my song-dream, the place the music played to me," whispered the Rat, as if in a trance. "Here, in this holy place, here if anywhere, surely we shall find him!"

—KENNETH GRAHAME,
FROM *THE WIND IN THE WILLOWS*

1

Ali woke early on Tuesday morning. Neither the late night nor the excitement of the past few days could keep her in bed. She felt invigorated and alive. There was so much to *do* today! The house was quiet as she dressed. By the time she came downstairs though, Valenti was making a pot of coffee in the kitchen.

"Hey, kid," he said as she took a seat at the kitchen table. "How's it going?"

"Okay. My mom's still sleeping."

"Gives us a chance to talk, then."

"I guess. Have you heard about Tom yet? Is he okay?"

Valenti shook his head. "I'm still waiting for Mario to call."

"But he's going to be okay, isn't he?"

"I sure hope so, Ali. You want some of this?" Valenti tapped the coffee pot.

"Sure."

He brought milk and sugar to the table, returning to the stove for the coffee. Ali filled her mug about a third full of milk before pouring her own coffee. Valenti laughed as she began to spoon in her sugar.

"Having a little coffee with your milk and sugar?" he asked.

She stuck out her tongue. Valenti fixed his own coffee and the two of them sat in a companionable silence, sipping the hot liquid and enjoying the moment of peace. It was Valenti who finally spoke.

"So what happened to you last night?"

Ali frowned, playing with her spoon. "It's sort of hard to explain . . ." She looked up, caught his gaze for a moment, then looked away. "It doesn't make a whole lot of sense."

"Try me."

She took a quick breath and glanced at him again. He smiled.

"Take your time," he said.

"Okay. When the stag took off, it didn't just go into the woods behind the stone. It went . . . someplace else—maybe even *into* the stone, for all I know. . . ."

"So what do you want to do?" Valenti asked when she finally ran out of words.

Ali liked that about him. Unlike most adults, he talked to her as though she might have an idea or two of her own and he was willing to listen to them.

"I don't know," she replied. "I feel like I should do what Mally says—or at least call the mystery to me to see if I can get him to talk to me, or communicate what he wants in some way. If it's what he wants, I guess I'll do it. I'll set him free. If I really can. But what if Lewis is right? What if letting him go really *would* be a danger?"

"I guess it comes down to which of them you trust the most," Valenti said.

"I suppose. Lewis makes sense because everything he says is pretty well based on what we know the world to be. The mystery's the only magic thing with him. It's different with Mally—everything's magic around her. I mean, jeez. Just *look* at her. But I don't know if I really trust either of them. I get the feeling that they're both looking for something for themselves out of all this. Lewis wants everything to fit into a neat little box and he wants to control when to open it and when not to."

"And Mally?"

"I'm not really sure what she wants. She's *so* different. Sometimes she acts just like another kid—but sometimes she acts like she's a thousand years old."

"Maybe she is," Valenti said. "Considering what she told you."

Ali regarded him sharply. "You don't really think that, do you?"

"I guess not," he said with a laugh, but he didn't sound all that sure.

"What would you do, Tony?"

He thought for a moment, then shook his head. "That's not for me to say. You and me, we come from two different directions, you know what I'm saying? If Mally wanted my decision, I figure she'd have come to me. I think this is something you got to decide for yourself." Just like your momma's got her own things to work out for herself, he thought. "But I'll tell you this, Ali. Whatever you decide, I'll back you all the way."

"Even though I'm just a kid?" She couldn't help asking that. For all that she was happy that he treated her like an equal, she still couldn't shake that little nagging doubt that maybe she was too young for some things.

"Just a kid, just a kid. Fercrissakes, Ali! Don't lay that on me. You got more smarts than most adults—understand? Don't you ever let nobody tell you different. Stuff you've gone through—most people I know would've just folded a long time ago."

"I'm not that brave," Ali said. "And it wasn't really scary."

"Bullshit it wasn't."

"Well, maybe a little at first . . ."

"So I'll say it again: What are you going to do?"

Ali sighed. She put off the moment by concentrating on fixing a new mug of coffee. Valenti didn't push, but she knew he wasn't going to let her leave the table without a decision.

"Okay," she said finally. "Here's what I'm going to do. First I'll try to get hold of Mally—talk to her some more. But while I'm doing that, I'm going to go see Lewis again. I've got a little more background now and I think I'll be able to make more sense out of what he means than I could before."

"What about the mystery?"

"I'll call him with the bonfire. But it's got to be up to him what happens from there on."

"What if he can't tell you? You know, what if he's mute or something?"

"I don't know, Tony. Maybe I'll have made a decision after talking to Mally and Lewis so I'll know what to do if that happens."

"That makes sense," Valenti said. "You talk to your momma about this yet?"

Ali shook her head. "And there's no time to now, Tony. I've got to go right away if I'm going to get everything done by tonight."

"I can't let you go by yourself."

She met his gaze and held it. "You can't stop me, Tony."

"Your momma—"

"Look," she said. "Mom's going to need someone around her in case my—" she stumbled over the word "—in case my father comes back. He'll look for her at our house, and maybe up here, but there's no way he'll be tramping through the bush looking for me. I mean, get real. So she'll be safe with you, and I'll be safe in the woods."

"Why don't you just wait for her to get up—or go wake her and talk it over now."

"She'd never believe me. I hardly believe any of this myself, and I've *seen* Mally and the mystery. Besides, I think she needs to sleep, Tony. You've seen how rough things've been for her. I'll talk to her when I get back."

"She's going to kill me."

"She doesn't have to know. Just tell her that I've gone for a walk in the woods—along the trail, you know? Tell her that it's perfectly safe."

Valenti sighed. "Okay. But I don't think this is such a good idea."

"You told me it was something I had to decide for myself," Ali said, throwing his own words back at him.

"Yeah. I said that all right. So go. But have something to eat before you take off."

"I'll make a sandwich that I can eat on the way."

Valenti shook his head and smiled. "You got an answer for everything, don't you?"

Ali grinned back at him. "Somebody's got to—right?"

"Right."

Valenti thought about giving her a gun—one of the small automatics—but in her inexperienced hands it would be more dangerous than helpful. People who didn't know weapons figured that a gun could solve any problem, but sometimes it just made people too cocky. Ali would be better off hiding her ass if trouble came. He wondered about a knife, then knew what he could give her.

"I want you to take one of my canes with you," he said. "The Alpine one with the spike on the end. It's got a good solid handle, too."

Ali looked at him. "You're joking, right?"

"I'm serious."

"Come *on,* Tony. What am I going to do with a cane. Whack somebody with it?"

"Maybe. Just let me get it."

"Yeah, but—"

"As a favor, Ali—okay? I let you go and get into all kinds of mischief, you take my cane. Fair trade. Deal?"

Ali shrugged. "Deal."

She made herself a peanut butter and onion sandwich while he fetched the cane. He looked at the sandwich just before she closed the halves together.

"You're going to eat that?"

"Sure."

"It's your stomach. Here."

Ali liked the cane. It had a T-shaped handle, a wicked-looking four-inch spike on the end, and a number of small silver crests nailed into the wood near the handle. She looked more closely at them and saw that they were little engravings of castles and cottages with the names of German-sounding places written underneath them.

"I got this from a friend in Austria," Valenti said. "They use these for climbing mountains or something—I don't know."

"I like it," Ali said, thinking, it'll be great for whacking weeds with, if nothing else.

Valenti walked her to the back door and waved her off. He watched her until she reached the forest, then the phone rang and he went back inside. Ali paused, looking back at the house. She swung the walking stick experimentally and sent a satisfying cloud of dandelion seeds into the air. Whack. Whack. Then she entered the forest and started off down the path at a jaunty clip, swinging the stick with one hand while taking bites out of the sandwich that was in her other.

She had the forest to herself today and enjoyed the feeling. It was so nice a day today, compared to yesterday's overcast skies, with the sunlight coming through the overhead boughs in bright beams. She listened to squirrels scolding her and each other, finches, sparrows and robins in the trees; red-winged blackbirds as she got near the stream. A perfect day, she thought. She wasn't really surprised to find Mally sitting on the stones by the water, waiting for her.

" 'Lo, Ali," the wild girl said. "Looking for bones?"

"Maybe. I'm going to talk to Lewis first."

"Lewis knows books," Mally said, "not mystery stuff."

"I still want to talk to him."

Mally shrugged. "Okay. Let's go. I'll show you a short-cut—right through the forest—that'll drop us out almost on top of Lewis's cabin."

"You don't mind my talking to him first?" Ali asked.

"Mind?" Mally shook her head. "I *like* Lewis, Ali. He's my friend. Just like you are—though I've known him longer."

"But . . ."

"Friends don't always have to be right," Mally said with a grin. "C'mon, now. I'll race you to that birch tree."

"No fair. You're quicker than me."

"I'll just hop then—on one leg."

Before Ali could answer, the wild girl lifted a leg behind her, caught its ankle and started hopping madly for the tree. Laughing, Ali set off in pursuit, but even with the handicap, Mally got there first.

Valenti was just hanging up when Frankie came downstairs. Her hair was all tousled and she had a sleepy look in her eyes, but she still found a smile for him. She was wearing a baggy sweatshirt and a pair of loose cotton tie pants. To Valenti, she looked like a million dollars.

"Is there any coffee left?" she asked. "I could smell it in my sleep."

"Plenty," Valenti assured her. "How're you feeling?"

She thought about that for a moment. "Good," she said finally. "Surprisingly good, all things considered. Is Ali up yet?"

"Yeah. She just went for a walk in the woods back of the house."

"Will she be safe?"

"Oh, sure. She's a smart kid—she'll keep her eyes open. If something comes up, she'll come running back."

"I wish she hadn't gone."

"She'll be fine."

Frankie nodded. "Well, I'm glad we've got a few moments. I wanted to ask you a favor, Tony."

"What's that?"

"I want you to give me that gun you took from the man who shot Tom last night. I want you to teach me how to use it."

Valenti hadn't known what to expect from her, but this hadn't been it. "You want a gun?"

"Is that so surprising after all I've been through?"

"But you can't use it—you're not licensed to carry one. If you'd shot that guy who attacked you last night, you'd be up shit creek right now."

"Look at me," Frankie said. "I'm not a physical match for either Earl or that man. But I am *not* going to be a victim anymore. What other choice do I have?"

"Yeah, but the law—"

"Don't tell me about the law, Tony. I wasn't so out of it last night that I didn't see what you were carrying. That was some kind of machine gun, wasn't it? I suppose you've got a license to carry it?"

"Well, now . . ."

"So what's the difference, Tony?"

Valenti thought about how he'd considered giving Ali a gun earlier in the morning. The same rules applied here, but when he thought of what Frankie'd already been through . . .

"Okay," he said finally. "But I'll tell you straight off that a gun's not going to solve anything. It's just a tool. Don't think you're going to be a different or tougher or better person just because you've got one in your hand. If you pull it out, you got to be prepared to use it. If you use it, you got to be prepared to hit somebody—you know what I'm saying? And you can't let yourself get cocky because—especially when we're dealing with your ex—he's going to be carrying a piece, too. You got to be prepared for the fact that whoever you're shooting at is going to be shooting back."

"I've thought about it," Frankie said. "Believe me. I've gone over and over it. This isn't something I'm looking forward to. I don't want to be some gun-toting moll like you used to investigate. But I've got to do something. I won't be a victim anymore. And I've got Ali to think of. I can't expect you to stand guard over us twenty-four hours a day. I don't want somebody doing that. I appreciate the help you've been so far, Tony, but I *have* to be able to stand up for myself."

"Yeah," Valenti said. "That's what you moved back here for."

"As soon as this is over—one way or another—I'll get rid of that gun so fast it'll make your head spin."

"I believe you." He hesitated for a long moment, fiddling with his coffee mug before he looked at her again. "Listen, I got to tell you something. I was never investigating organized crime. I want to be straight with you. I respect you and I don't want to have lies and bullshit lying between us. I never told Ali that stuff she told you. That's just something she came up with because she—I don't know. Wanted to protect you, maybe. I think she was afraid maybe you wouldn't let us be friends if you knew the truth."

Frankie's fingers tightened around the handle of her own mug. "What . . . what are you trying to say, Tony?"

"I used to be one of those guys—part of the families, you know? But I never made no war on women or kids and we didn't deal in dope or prostitution, neither. Not when the old Don was *padrone*. But I was in the business all the same."

Frankie didn't say anything immediately. She just sat there, looking at him, wondering why this revelation wasn't bothering her more than it should. Was it because she'd already known Tony, and for all that he seemed very capable when it came to guns and trouble, he just didn't strike her as a gangster?

"What happened?" she asked finally.

Valenti give her a quick run-down of the events that had led to the *fratellanza* putting out a contract on him. He talked about Mario and the fumbled hit in Malta, about how he'd finally made it back here to Lanark and just wanted to disappear but her ex-husband had identified him and called down the cousins on him.

"See," he finished, "things were already different for me. Living here . . . I didn't feel like I was in exile. It was like I never had anything to do with the families in the first place. When I think of who I was, it's like I was a different guy. I was really starting to put it all behind me, but then all this shit came down on us. Now I don't know. It's all coming back to me and I don't like it, but I can't run away this time. Just like you." He glanced at her. "It's a funny thing, you know. I was all set to run again, but it was Ali who talked me out of it. She told me I had to make a stand." He shook his head. "Christ, she's really some kid."

The coffee pot was empty. Not trusting herself to speak yet, Frankie got up and put some more water on. She stood by the stove, warming her hands by the burner, though it wasn't cold in the kitchen. The chill she had was inside her.

What do I feel? she asked herself. This man's just like Earl—only he's the big time. Then she shook her head. No, Tony wasn't like Earl. Not by a long shot. From what he'd told her, he'd basically grown up in a family business. He'd just never known any better. If all your role models, your father and uncles and grandfathers, if they were all gangsters, how could a growing boy think that was wrong? It was a way of life.

She turned to look at him. God, a person could rationalize anything. What she had to figure out was, was she being understanding because she needed him right now, needed the skills and abilities he'd acquired from what he'd been, or was it because she really *did* understand him?

"I guess this changes things," Valenti said finally.

"It changes them," she agreed, "but I'm not sure how."

He regarded her with a puzzled frown and she found herself smiling.

"I liked you right off," Frankie said. "More importantly, Ali liked you right off, and I've learned from experience that she's a damn good judge of character. There's been a lot of times when I'd come home with some guy and she'd never say a thing, but I'd know she didn't think much of him. Unfortunately, she was usually right. I've never had much luck with the men in my life—not as lovers, at any rate. So now I meet someone that both Ali and I like and . . ."

"Hey, I'm not, you know—"

"Coming on to me," Frankie said. "I know that. But I do like you, Tony. Only right now my feelings are all confused. I'm still coming down from last night, I've got Earl to worry about. . . . I need you right now, for what you know, for what you are. It's your past that makes me feel safe, that makes me feel that things are going to work out, that Earl won't be able to just walk all over me again, that that guy, if he comes back, won't be able to . . . hurt me again."

She combed her hair with her fingers, nervously pulling at a knot. "I don't want to be dependent on anybody," she said. "I told you that. But there's something good—something *healthy,* I think—about having a friend that you *can* depend on."

"I can be a friend," Valenti said. "I know the kind of guy I was. Things won't go no further and when this shit's over we can just go our separate ways."

"I'm not saying that, Tony."

"Then what are you saying?"

"God, I don't know. It's in my head, but I can't put it into words."

The kettle began to boil and she turned thankfully to the interruption it offered. But once the water was poured and the coffee dripping through the filter, she came and sat across from him again.

"I got a call from Mario," Valenti said. "Just before you woke."

Frankie looked grateful for the change in topic. "Did he say how your friend was?"

"He's doing okay. He's in intensive care, but the doctors are pretty sure he'll pull through. I'd like to know what kind of a song and dance Mario pulled to stop them from calling in the police—I mean, it *was* a gunshot wound—but he says everything's cool. He was calling me from Ottawa."

"He's not coming back?"

"I don't think so. He said he was going to take care of some business in New York."

Frankie didn't ask him what *that* was supposed to mean—she didn't want to know. The coffee had finished dripping through, so she got up again to refill both their mugs.

"What do you think of me?" she asked when she sat down once more. "What do you see when you look at me?"

She didn't seem to be able to stop the conversation from returning to them. But the terror she'd felt last night was never far from her thoughts. Coupled with it was the old fear that all men just regarded her as an object, as something they could use however they wanted. The attempted rape was just an exaggeration of what usually went down in her other relationships. The men might take her out to dinner or to a movie or something, but it all boiled down to getting into her pants and getting *their* rocks off. Too many times she just didn't hear from them again.

So why did she attract that kind of a man? What was there about her that brought them to her? Or was there something more deeply wrong with her, some Freudian explanation that centered around the way her father had treated her mother—and even Frankie herself— so that she'd go out looking for men like him? It wasn't the first time she'd worried about this and it never ceased to confuse her.

"I got to tell you," Valenti said. "I've never been that good with women. I was never rough or anything, but I just never wanted anything longterm, you know what I'm saying? But last night I got to thinking about Ali. . . . I'd give up everything to have a kid like her. And I was thinking of you, too . . ." He paused to clear his throat. "I know I said I wasn't going to come on to you or anything, but I got to tell you, I was thinking about you and wishing I'd been a different kind of person so that I'd have a chance to be with someone like you—permanently, you know?"

"But why? There's nothing special about me, Tony. I'm just—"

"Bullshit, there's nothing special about you." It was like talking to Ali, he thought. "It's not just the way you look—which is sensational, I've got to tell you that, too—it's the way you carry yourself. It's what you got inside. And I'll tell you something else: You can tell a lot about a person by their kids. You raised Ali by yourself and you did one helluva job, Frankie. A person who can do something like that, she's special to me, let me tell you."

Frankie reached across the table and laid her hand over his. "You really mean that, don't you?"

"Yeah." He looked down at her hand on his, then back up to meet her gaze.

"I needed to hear that, Tony. I go through life needing a lot, it seems."

"I think we're all like that—needing reassurance. There's nothing wrong with it. The only thing wrong is when there's no one there to give it to you."

Frankie nodded. She squeezed his hand, then let go and reached for her coffee mug. Her hand was trembling slightly and she hoped Tony didn't see it.

"You and me," he said suddenly. "We're like hearts and flowers for two mornings in a row now. It's getting to be a habit."

"I'm glad we had a chance to talk."

"Yeah. Me too."

Valenti ached to see her sitting there across from him. There was a look in her eyes that promised him something, but there was no way he was going for it. Not now. Not today. Not so close on the heels of what she'd gone through and with everything that was coming up. But when it was over, when she didn't need him for what he'd been, then maybe he'd see if she'd take him for what he was now. He pushed aside their mugs and fetched Bannon's automatic and a cleaning kit.

"Okay," he said. "Before we start shooting up a tree trunk, you're going to learn how this little beauty works. Now this little thing—"

He broke off as she touched his hand again. "Thanks," she said.

Valenti knew what she meant. The promise was still in her eyes and it seemed warmer now. A hot flash went through him, just at the closeness of her. He cleared his throat again as she took away her hand. Brushing a strand of hair from her eyes, she leaned forward. He took a breath and started again.

"Okay. Now this is the safety. When it's on, the gun doesn't work. See, you can pull the trigger, but nothing happens." He snapped the magazine free of the grip and showed it to her. "This is your magazine. It holds twelve rounds. Now they called these self-loading pistols when they went on the market back around the turn of the century. You don't get the recoil on these, not like you do on a gun that uses a cylinder. That's because the same gizmo that ejects the spent round and brings the new one up absorbs a lot of the recoil. I'm going to let you fire both today, but I think this is the one you'll want to hang on to. It's lighter, easier to manage. . . ."

Ali paused when they came out of the woods above Lewis's cabin. She couldn't see the old man from where they were, but a trail of smoke rose up from his chimney, so she thought somebody must be home. Where would he go anyway?

"C'mon," Mally said.

Ali didn't move. "I was just thinking," she said. "Maybe I should talk to someone else—like the lady I was dancing with last night."

"Lily?"

"Yes. Her."

"What for?"

"Well, I know what you think and I know what Lewis has told me, but I don't know what the villagers themselves think. They're not all like Lewis, are they?"

Mally shook her head. "Lewis is different—just like Tommy is, but in another sort of a way."

"I thought so. I think I'd like to talk to her—just to get another perspective."

"You could try climbing a tree," Mally said with a smile.

Ali laughed. "But that won't tell me anything—not about this, anyway. Do you know where Lily lives?"

"Sure."

The wild girl angled off toward the village. After a last look at Lewis's cabin, Ali followed. Looking ahead, the brush grew so dense it seemed impossible to pick through, but Ali found that if she stayed right on Mally's heels, she had no trouble. The wild girl chose a winding way, bypassing the heavier thickets, until they were suddenly in a small pasture. Cows lifted their head to regard the two intruders, ignoring them once they'd passed.

"That's where Lily lives," Mally said as they reached the far side of the village. She pointed to a small picturesque cottage overhung with vines. Rosebushes clambered up the sides of its stone walls.

"Aren't you coming in?" Ali asked.

"No. I'll wait for you here."

Ali paused. "Don't you like Lily?"

"Oh, I like her all right, I just don't know her. You go on ahead."

Leaving her walking stick with the wild girl, Ali went on by herself. As she neared the door of the cottage, she began to feel a little shy, but before she could change her mind, the door opened and Lily was standing there, looking at her. A smile creased the old woman's face.

"What a pleasant surprise," she said. "Do come in."

"I don't want to be any bother."

"Nonsense. We see few enough new faces in the village—I'm happy to see you." She ushered Ali inside. The cottage was all one room, divided into a neatly kept sitting room, a kitchen and a sleeping area. The quilt on the bed was gorgeous, Ali thought, knowing that her mother would just love it. When she stepped closer to investigate it, she realized that the whole thing was hand-sewn.

"This is beautiful," she said.

"Well, thank you—Ali, wasn't it? That was a whole winter's project back when Jevon was still alive. Jevon was my husband."

Ali nodded. She glanced at a sepia-toned photograph on the mantle. "Was that him?"

"Yes, it was. Handsome devil, wasn't he?"

"Who took the picture?" Ali asked. She'd been under the impression that they didn't have much in the way of modern conveniences in New Wolding. Where would they even get the film developed?

"Lewis's son Edmond took it. Before he left the village for good he used to travel quite a bit between the outer world and the village. He left with the Gypsies one year and never did come back."

"Gypsies? You mean like *real* Gypsies?" She remember Lewis mentioning something about them.

Lily nodded. "They come once or twice a year—just one family, the Grys. Jango—he's a grandfather himself now—has been bringing his family for as long as I can remember. We get what we can't grow or make ourselves from them. Sugar, some teas and spices, that sort of thing. Lewis wasn't too happy the year Edmond left."

"Why did he leave?"

"Oh, you're young. You know how restless young people can get. The village wouldn't even have been settled in the first place if some of the young folk from the original Wolding hadn't been restless themselves. My own son Peter left—the year after Edmond did."

"Do you miss him?"

Lily looked at the photo of her husband and sighed. "Oh, yes. I miss him. More so now that Jevon's gone. I keep hoping that he'll come back one day, but I don't think he will."

"Why not?"

"Lewis says that if you stray a too long from the village, you lose the way back."

"There's less and less of you each year, isn't there?" Ali asked.

"I'm afraid so. But my Jevon saw it coming. We changed, you know. We've become, not so much lazy, as forgetful. All we do is dance at the old stone now. Sometimes the mystery comes, sometimes he doesn't. We used to sacrifice a bull there at that old stone—every year we did that." She didn't notice Ali's face go pale. "I think that's important—rituals and the like. Not this come-when-you-will attitude that we've slowly fallen into. I think if it weren't for the mystery—if he didn't still come to us at the stone—we'd all be gone now."

"You don't think he should be freed?"

"Freed? Oh, who's filling your head with such nonsense? There's nothing binding him here. Do you think something like him could be held captive by the likes of us?"

"But I thought—I thought it was the villagers who kept him here. Tommy's piping and all that."

"You've been talking to Lewis," Lily said, "and Lewis thinks too much. He has to have everything neatly explained, but it doesn't work that way. We're talking about a *mystery*. I love Lewis like a brother, Ali, but sometimes I just want to shake some sense *out* of that head of his."

"Mally says there's something keeping him here, too."

"Oh, yes. The wild girl. Where did you go with her last night, Ali? You made us all very worried."

Ali shrugged. "Just . . . away."

Lily's eyes went dreamy. "I always dreamed of that. Of the stag taking me away on his back . . ." She sat silent for a long moment, lost in her thoughts, then blinked and looked at Ali. "Not that I'm unhappy here, you understand. But there's a little bit of Lewis in us all, I suppose. I'd like to know where the mystery goes in that stag shape of his. It must be to some very special place."

Ali couldn't begin to explain that landscape of wild forest land and the circle of stone formations. "We went a long way," she said at last.

"I'm sure you did. But tell me. Do you long to be back there, wherever it was that he took you, or can you still be content here in this world of ours?"

"I . . ." She'd spent a lot of time being scared, Ali realized, and then a lot more talking with Mally. In the end, she hadn't really experienced very much of that other place. She remembered the moon— how big it had been and how low—and the stars so close you could almost reach out and touch them. The peace in among those stones. The very air . . . "I'd like to go back," she said.

There was a touch of yearning in her voice that made Lily nod her head. "I thought it would be like that," she said. "It's like the stories of Faerie, isn't it? Once you've been in their Middle Kingdom, you can never again be content in the fields of men."

"I suppose."

Lily nodded. "But I still think I'd have liked to have gone—just once."

It didn't seem fair, Ali thought. She'd gotten to go and she was just a kid with her whole life ahead of her, while this old woman . . . All those years and never once getting a glimpse of that place. Unless she saw it in Tommy's music, or felt it in the presence of the stag.

What would Lily do if the stag didn't come anymore? Would Tommy still play his pipes? Or would all the villagers move away? Maybe it'd be better if the villagers did go. She didn't know if the people of New Wolding were happy or not, but they had never really had a chance to see what else there was to see in the world. That didn't seem right either.

"I've got to go," she said suddenly.

"Oh, no," Lily said. "I haven't even had a chance to offer you some tea. And I was going to make scones, too."

"Another time," Ali said. "I've really got to run."

"You promise you'll visit again?"

Ali nodded. "Bye, Lily. And thanks."

"For what?" the old woman asked, but Ali was already at the door. She waved to Lily and went outside, softly closing the door behind her. Mally was right where she'd promised to wait, playing with the walking stick.

"Are we going to see Lewis now?" she asked.

Ali shook her head, "We're going to look for bones," she said. "Where should we build the fire?"

"There's only one place will do," Mally said, handing Ali the cane. "On the very top of Wolding Hill."

"Okay. Let's get to it."

A minute or two after she'd fired the .38, Frankie's wrist still hurt. Her ears rang from the loud report. Tony had warned her about the kick that the gun had, showed her how to hold it properly, left hand supporting the right, but it had still come as a shock.

"I think I'll stick to the other one," she said.

Valenti nodded and handed the automatic back to her. "Yeah, I thought it would suit you better, but I wanted you to try the .38 at least once—just to know what it felt like. Now you won't be wondering about it all the time."

Frankie looked at the cardboard target they'd set up about fifteen paces from where they stood. "I didn't even come close."

"You did better with the automatic. You did good, Frankie. You want to go in for a sandwich?"

"Sure. Tony, why don't you go after those men? Why don't you go into the city and stop them before they come out here?"

"Well," Valenti said. "First off, in the city, they've got the advantage. We can't go around packing a lot of artillery and then just blast away with it when and if we catch up to them. But they can just hang out wherever they are, pick us off and disappear. What would you say to the police if they stopped us to ask what I'm doing with my UZI and why you're carrying a piece?"

"You're right."

"And the second thing is, if they're willing to leave us alone, I'm happy to return the favor. I'm not gunning for them, Frankie. I want to leave that kind of shit behind me. If they force my hand, I'm going to meet them with all the firepower I can put together, but I'd rather be left alone."

"I'm glad to hear that," Frankie said. "Really."

Valenti nodded. "I'm not just saying it because it's something I think you want to hear. Believe that."

"I do."

"That's good. That's really good."

They left the weapons on the table and set about making some lunch. As she started to slice bread Frankie glanced at the clock over the stove.

"Oh, no!" she cried. "Look at the time. It's after twelve."

"What's the matter?" Valenti asked.

"It's Ali—she's not back yet. God, I feel terrible. I forgot all about her. If something's happened to—"

"It's okay," Valenti said. "Trust me. She's fine."

"But what's she doing out there?"

Frankie had turned to him and for a long moment she held his gaze. Valenti sighed. Maybe it was time to get the last of the lies out of the way. Well, not exactly lies, he corrected himself. Just the things that neither he nor Ali had bothered to expand upon.

"The thing of it is," he said, "she's got a friend in the woods—a girl named Mally. And there's this village back there that we visited

"It's not for a court," Mario said. "It's for the other families and whatever I decide to leave of the Magaddinos, *capito?*"

"Don't do this to me, Mario."

"Pen and paper. Get it." He watched the *consigliere* fumble for a paper and pen. "You should have known better," he said. "I took a fall for the family and I took exile for them. I could handle that. I saw how things were going. I could see the young blood coming up and that things were changing. But you should have remembered that I don't take shit from nobody, Joe. We had a deal."

"What was I supposed to do, Mario? The Don says—"

"Ricca's no Don—he's just a punk. Now you start writing. You put down on paper who called the hit on the old Don. You write down that Tony was set up to take the fall for it. You call off the contract on him. Simple."

"Nobody called a hit on the old Don, Mario. Tony just got—"

"Fuck you! Tony was loyal and you know it. Now you either write it or I'm gonna start taking pieces off of you with this." He moved in close with a sudden quick move and shoved the muzzle of the Ingram up hard against the *consigliere*'s side. Joe let out a gasp. On the couch, Dan was starting to stand, but Mario had already moved back to his earlier position. The muzzle of the Ingram settled on Dan.

"Don't try to be a hero," Mario told him. "You're way out of your league right now." He glanced back at Joe. "Write!"

"It's not going to change anything," Joe said. "Ricca's still the Don. The other families got to live with that. You think they give a fuck about you, Mario? You think they're all going to back you up? Wise up, fercrissakes."

"Ricca called the hit on his old man—right? Who did it? Louie?"

"It doesn't matter. The old Don's gone and—"

"Who did it?"

"Look, Mario. It was business, okay? The old Don was converting everything into legitimate businesses. He was going soft. We had to do something."

"Whose idea was it?"

"Ricca's," Joe said quickly.

yesterday. Let's finish fixing up these sandwiches and I'll tell you all about it over lunch." And I just to Christ hope you believe what I'm about to tell you, he thought, because I'm not so sure I do myself.

Frankie was puzzled, but she went back to slicing bread. "Okay," she said. "So long as you're sure she's okay."

"She's fine."

"I just wish you wouldn't sound so mysterious about it."

"There's the word," Valenti said. "You got it in a nutshell. Mystery's what this is all about."

2

Broadway Joe didn't recognize the intruder immediately. The shock of his office door slamming open and the man's sudden appearance held him motionless for a long moment. He saw a darkly tanned face with a couple of days' worth of beard smudging its outline; short dark hair above the face, a long raincoat below. Behind the man, Joe's bodyguards had already been taken out. Freddie was lying stretched out on the carpet, Dan leaning up against a wall doubled over. As the man brought an Ingram submachine gun up from his side and pointed its muzzle at the *consigliere* recognition finally dawned on Broadway Joe.

"Jesus Christ!" he cried. "What the fuck d'you think you're pulling, Mario?"

"Tell your boy to forget it."

Broadway Joe looked beyond Mario and saw that Dan was straightening up, one hand going under his sports jacket for his gun. The Ingram never wavered from Joe's face. Swallowing thickly, the

consigliere called out to his bodyguard: "Don't do it!" He laid his own hands flat, palms down, on the top of his desk.

"I want to hear the sound of a gun hitting the carpet," Mario said, "and then I want your boy to drag his pal in here and then go sit in a corner, nice and quiet—got it?"

"Sure, Mario. Sure. No problem. Do you want to put that thing away?"

Mario shook his head. He moved further into the room to where he could cover both the door and the desk. Dan Barboza, plainly unhappy, lifted a .44 Magnum from its shoulder holster, using just his thumb and forefinger, and dropped it on the floor. Grabbing Freddie under the armpits, he dragged him into Broadway Joe's office, dumping him in front of the couch on the far side of the room. He sat down then, glaring at Mario.

"Okay," Mario said. "Here's how we're playing this. I want you to get a piece of paper and a pen, Joe, take it out nice and easy, and then you're gonna write down a little confession for me, *capito?*"

"You think I'm crazy?" Broadway Joe demanded. "I'm not writing out nothing."

"Then you're dead."

Joe glanced at his bodyguards—you are fucking finished, his eyes told Dan—then back at Mario. "Come on, Mario. Let's be reasonable. What's this all about?"

"I tried reason, Joe. But you broke your word. I don't give anybody a second chance, you know what I'm saying?"

"I couldn't call back the hit. Christ, you think I didn't *want* to? But the *padrone* wants Valenti gone, so what can I do?"

"You should've told me that yesterday, Joe."

"Hey, yesterday I was sure I could talk Ricca into okaying it. By the time I find it's a no-go, it's too late to get in touch with you."

Mario shook his head. "That's not good enough, Joe." He made a small motion with the Ingram. "Pen and paper—let's get a move on."

"What am I supposed to write? Nothing you get from me's going to stand up in court, Mario. You know that. Anything I give you's under duress."

Sure, Mario thought. "And what about Tony taking the fall for it? Was that Ricca's idea too?"

Broadway Joe nodded. "The old man was trying to go legit, but we knew we could get to him with Eddie putting the squeeze on his girl-friend. And who else would the Don call in but Tony? Things just worked out, what with Tony having a hard-on for Eddie in the first place and everybody knowing that the Don had told him to lay off."

"So you take a guy who's been loyal his whole life—who's given you his whole life, fercrissakes—and you just dump him."

"It was business, Mario."

"Fuck you. We're talking loyalties here. You think you're gonna keep the old guard on if that's all they got to look forward to?"

"I know, Mario. That's why we've got to forget about this shit now or the whole business falls to pieces."

Mario glanced at the bodyguards. Freddie was sitting up now, but he still looked stunned. Dan had settled back in the couch. He wasn't so hot to trot now—not with what he was hearing.

"There's still a way out of it," Mario said.

"What's that?"

"It's like a disease," Mario explained. "You just cut out the sick part, you know what I'm saying?"

"We're talking about the head of a family here. No one's going to stand for—"

"Write," Mario told him. His voice went cold. Broadway Joe paled and set pen to paper. "Just put it all down there," Mario added, "just like you told me, and you let me worry about what comes after."

A tense silence fell over the room as the *consigliere* did as he was told.

"How long you been in the business?" Mario asked Dan.

The bodyguard started, then shrugged. "My old man stood for me—nine, maybe ten years ago."

"What's your name?" Mario nodded when Dan told him. "Jimmy Barboza—he's your old man? I used to work with him—Christ, that goes back awhile now. He was a good man. The Guicciones took him out over that warehouse deal, right?" Mario shook his head. "That was a fucking waste if I ever saw one."

Broadway Joe set aside the pen and pushed the sheet of paper over to Mario's side of the desk. Mario read it quickly, never taking his gaze from the *consigliere* for too long. "That's nice," he said. "What do you say, Dan? You gonna witness this for me?"

Dan hesitated, glancing at Broadway Joe.

"What we got here's not going to the law," Mario said. "It's just for the families, *capito?* You don't wanna sign, that's okay."

Dan looked at the *consigliere* again. "This shit's all true?" he asked. "You guys really set Tony up to take this fall?"

Broadway Joe wouldn't answer. Mario stepped close again, nudging him with the Ingram. "Man asked you a question."

"Yeah," Joe said. "It's true. But you think about it, Dan. You sign that, you're going against the family. The old Don, he was going soft—wanted to be legit before he died, fercrissakes. Where does that leave the rest of us? Without jobs—that's where. You think you can make the kind of bread you're pulling in now driving a fucking truck or working in a factory?"

"My old man drilled it into my head," Dan replied. "You do your part for the family, and the family'll take care of you." He looked at Mario. "Sure, I'll sign it."

Mario smiled. "Okay, Joe. One last thing for you to do. Get on the blower and have Ricca meet you here. Fuck this up, and you're dead."

"And if I don't fuck it up—what happens to me then? Who says I'm not dead anyway?"

"At this point, that's just the chance you got to take."

"Give me your word that I'll get out of this alive."

Mario shook his head. "I can't do that, Joe. We can't have deals between us—not after you screwed me once already."

"Fuck you, then."

Mario shrugged. "Then you're dead." He started to bring the Ingram up so that its muzzle was level with the *consigliere*'s head, but before he could pull the trigger, Joe picked up the phone.

"The thing we've still got to decide," Mario said as they waited for the connection to be made, "is who do we hand the family over to once Ricca's gone?"

* * *

Ricca came in with one bodyguard. Before either of them knew what was happening, Mario closed the door behind them and waved them to the couch with the Ingram. Dan, his Magnum back in his hand, went to relieve Ricca's bodyguard of his piece. The bodyguard was a tall blonde Swede named Lars Andersson. The kind of guy Ricca was, he didn't trust his own people, just like they wouldn't trust him if they knew him better.

"What the fuck is going—"

Ricca shut up when Mario waved the Ingram at him.

"This guy's not going to understand," Dan said as he relieved the Swede of his gun. "He's not family, you know?"

Mario nodded. "I know the kind—bought with money, not with blood. Okay, Dan. You and Freddie can blow."

"We'll wait for you outside," Dan said. "You're gonna need somebody to get you in to talk to the right people."

Mario nodded again. He waited until the door closed behind the two men, then studied his prisoners. Ricca, Joe and the Swede sat in a row on the couch. Joe was slumped in a corner, already defeated. Ricca looked scared and that made Mario shake his head. This punk just couldn't be the same blood as the old Don. The only one who didn't seem either defeated or afraid was the Swede. Just too dumb, Mario thought, meeting the big man's gaze. There wasn't a great deal of intelligence showing behind the Swede's glare.

"Look," Ricca said, licking his lips. "We can make a deal. I've got—"

Mario shook his head. "No deals," he said and opened fire with the Ingram.

It took the Swede the longest to die. He almost made it across the room before he sprawled at Mario's feet. Mario looked at the bodies, feeling nothing. No satisfaction. Nothing but a certain regret that things had had to turn out this way.

He put the Ingram back under his raincoat where it hung out of sight from a strap on his shoulder and picked up the paper he'd had the *consigliere* write out for him. He needed a photocopier now. When the door opened behind him, he turned quickly, the Ingram coming up again, but it was only Dan who held his empty hands up before him.

"We better split," he said.

Mario nodded. "You got any ideas who the best person is to take this to?" he asked, holding up the confession.

"Bennie LaFata."

Mario thought about that. He knew Bennie—he'd been a *capo* back before Mario had been deported. He was a good man and he knew about loyalties, only . . . "You think he'll do?" Mario asked.

"He's gonna listen."

"That's all we can ask for."

There was a lot to do, Mario thought as he followed Dan out of the office. By the time they reached the elevator, they could hear people's voices raised as they wondered what had happened. It wouldn't be too long before the place was crawling with the NYPD's finest.

Mario looked back down the hall just before he got into the elevator. He'd have to send Tony a clipping—once this hit the papers. He just hoped Tony could handle the problem of Broadway Joe's son on his own because Mario knew he wasn't going to be able to get back up to Canada before tomorrow at the earliest.

"We gotta *go,*" Dan said. He was holding the elevator door open.

Mario nodded and stepped inside, still watching the hall until the elevator's doors slid shut. Time to stop thinking about Tony, he told himself. If he didn't keep his mind on the job at hand for the next few hours, the whole thing could still blow up in his face. By the time the elevator reached the ground floor and the three men were on the street, he had his priorities straight. His worries for Tony went to the back of his mind and he concentrated on what came next right here and now.

"So now we set up a meet with LaFata," he said.

"I know just the place," Dan said.

Mario glanced at Freddie. "Are you in?" When Freddie nodded, he clapped Dan on the shoulder. "Then what are we waiting for?"

Dan stepped out from the curb to flag down a cab. As they were pulling away, the sound of sirens filled the street behind them.

3

Throughout the afternoon Frankie kept thinking: I dreamed about that stag. I dreamed that it was in Ali's room that night. But every time the image of it rose up in her mind, she pushed it aside. That hadn't been real. And what Tony had told her this afternoon—that couldn't be real, either.

She would have thought that he was putting her on, except he had told the whole story through so matter-of-factly, so very seriously. He had his own doubts, but he couldn't deny that there was *something* going on, that all this talk of mysteries and the like had some basis. And he'd seen the stag. He'd seen the wild girl.

"I don't like it any better than you," he had finished up with, "but my not liking it sure isn't going to change anything."

"But Ali—she could be in danger."

"She's in the middle of it—I'll give you that—but I don't think she's in danger. Do you think I would have let her go if I thought she was?"

Frankie had wanted to go looking for Ali right then—into the forest, to that village or to the stone—but Valenti had talked her out of it.

"She's a big kid," he said. "We got to give her a chance to work things out for herself."

"Tony, she's only fourteen."

"And going on thirty-five."

Frankie had to smile, remembering that. Tony was right. But then the image of the stag in her daughter's room came back. The smile faded, then was gone.

"What're you thinking about?" Valenti asked.

Frankie turned to look at him. They were sitting on lawn chairs behind his house. With iced drinks on the arm rests, the two of them looked as though they were simply soaking up the sun, domestic picture that was only flawed upon closer scrutiny. Frankie had a holster on her belt. The automatic was nestled in it. Balancing its weight on the other hip was a leather pouch with extra ammunition clips. Valenti had a .38 in a shoulder harness, the UZI hanging from the arm of his chair by its strap. He, too, was carrying extra clips for the UZI and rounds for his pistol.

After talking over lunch, they'd returned to Frankie's place so that she could get some clothes suitable for the bush. Valenti had decided to take to the woods near the house tonight, rather than wait inside where they could get bottled up, depending on how many men Louie brought with him. Outside, the advantage came back to Valenti and Frankie once more. When they'd returned from Frankie's they had made a number of circuits through the brush closest to the house to get a feel for the area. They knew the terrain now. Louie had only seen the place at night—and that was briefly. His men would only have what Louie told them to go on.

"I'm sorry," Frankie said. "What did you say?"

"You keep smiling, then frowning, then smiling again—I was wondering what you were thinking about."

Frankie sighed. "Oh, everything." She touched the handgrip of the automatic. "I feel like nothing's very real right now . . . or maybe it's too real. I don't know. Here we are with all these guns, waiting for either Earl or some extras from the *The Godfather* to show up. Meanwhile, my daughter is running around the woods with a stag and some girl who has horns growing from her head. Does any of it make sense to you, Tony?"

"Your ex and Louie—yeah, that I can understand. And I think I know what you mean about the rest. It's unreal and too real, all at the same time. But I'll tell you something: When that music comes drifting from the woods, or when I hear it close up like I did last night, I feel like I'm really close to something then, you know what I'm saying? It's like the answer to everything, not just what's going down now, but that *everything* is just out of sight and if I hang in for a couple of seconds longer, it's all going to be laid out in front of me."

"I'm really worried about Ali," Frankie said.

"Yeah. I know."

"I mean, I understand what you're saying, but I find it pretty hard to believe."

"Look." Valenti glanced at his watch. "It's going on four. Why don't we give her until four-thirty or five and if she's not back by then, we'll go looking for her, okay?"

Frankie wanted to go right away, but she nodded in agreement. She was always willing to give Ali a pretty free rein, mainly because Ali could handle it. Frankie could put her foot down when it was needed, but mostly it wasn't. Whatever her daughter was mixed up in now, she supposed she owed it to Ali to let her handle things her own way. Doing otherwise was a breach of the trust built up between them. But God, it was hard. If she could just *know,* instead of having—

"Heads up," Valenti said quietly.

Frankie turned to look at him, then caught motion out of the corner of her eye and saw what had prompted his comment. A bedraggled tatterdemalion of a figure had stepped from the forest and was approaching them. It was the wild girl, Frankie realized as the figure came closer. Mally. She took in the girl's pinched features, the thick tangle of hair with its twigs and leaves, the raggedy clothing, patched and burred, and there, rising up from her forehead just by her hairline, was a pair of small horns.

Frankie swallowed thickly. If this much was real, then what was to stop all the rest of it from being real? The stag . . .

The wild girl came to a few paces from where they were sitting, then sank languidly to the grass. She's like a cat, Frankie thought, taking in the unblinking eyes and the smooth movement that never wasted a motion. For a moment or two they regarded each other, then Mally laid an antler on the grass between them. There were feathers and beads tied to it by leather thongs, swirling patterns scratched into its beam.

" 'Lo," Mally said and smiled her Cheshire smile.

"Where's Ali?" Valenti asked, voicing the question that had been on the tip of Frankie's tongue.

"In the forest," Mally replied, nodding behind her. The motion hardly made her hair move at all, it was so tangled today. "But she sent me here with a message so you wouldn't worry. The message is: 'Not to worry—I'll be back later tonight.' "

"What is she *doing* out there?" Frankie demanded.

"She's planning to call Old Hornie—the mystery—to her tonight, but I also think she's learning how to be a secret like me."

"You're not making a lot of sense," Frankie said.

"She's like that," Valenti muttered.

"Please, Tony." Frankie looked back at the wild girl. "I'm Ali's mother, Mally, and I'm very worried. Why does she have to call this mystery to her? What's going *on* out there?"

"And why didn't she come and deliver the message herself?" Valenti added.

"Well, I'm faster in the forest than she is," Mally said, answering Valenti first, "and as to what she's doing and why, that's something she'll have to explain to you, if you can't riddle it for yourselves. I won't do it because some things can't be explained, some shouldn't be, and some lose their heart when they are."

"Is she in danger?" Frankie asked. "Will you at least tell me that?"

Mally met her gaze for a long moment, then she reached over and traced the curve of one of the antler's tines with a fingernail. She started at its base and circled around until the tine ended in a point and her finger was just touching air. Then she did it a second time. The third time she brought her hand toward the antler, she picked it up and shook it lightly. The beads made a little rattling sound against the bone as she handed the antler to Frankie.

"This is for you," she said.

Frankie took it gingerly. "This . . . ?"

". . . is special," Mally said. "The mystery shed them a year or two ago and I've kept them ever since. We're using one to call him, but Ali wanted you to have this one."

"But what does it—what is it for?"

Mally shrugged. "She said you'd like it. I did the carving and hangings and all myself."

Frankie glanced at Valenti, then back at the wild girl. "Thank you," she said. It was obvious that Mally was proud of what she'd done with the antler and it did have a certain primitive charm. In fact, Frankie thought as she studied it more closely, it radiated a certain feeling of goodwill. Her hand tightened around it.

"Please, Mally," she said finally. "Will my daughter be all right? This isn't a joking matter for me—I'm worried sick. I have to know that she won't get hurt playing . . . doing whatever it is she's doing with you."

"Will she be all right?" Mally repeated. "I don't know. She's calling the mystery to her. If it comes, she'll be . . . changed. But she's already changed some as it is. She's been to the heart of the mystery once already and if it speaks to her tonight . . ." Her thin shoulders lifted and fell. "Everything is dangerous. She won't be in any physical harm—not that I know of—but she'll have to be strong in her own heart so that she's not swept away by the wonder of what she'll meet tonight."

Valenti remembered the dogs that could look like men, or like both. "What about the pack?" he asked.

Mally turned to look at Valenti, but her gaze seemed to go right through him, as though she were seeing into some far distance. "I don't know," she said softly. "All I know is that the fire burns strong in both you and her—but it burns purer in her. If anyone can free the mystery—from ceremony, from worship, from disinterest, even from the hounds—it will be someone like her." Her gaze focused suddenly and settled on the UZI. "Besides, you face your own danger here tonight, don't you? Where do *you* think she'll be safer? In the forest, where the secrets will watch over her, or here?"

"Oh, God," Frankie said. "I don't know. What she's planning to do, what you're saying . . . it scares me."

"But only because you don't understand. The unknown doesn't have to be grim."

Valenti thought about what could happen here tonight. It was bad enough that he had one amateur around. Did he really need someone else to look out for?

"I think we should let Ali get on with what she's doing," he said to Frankie. "She's your daughter and it's your decision, but that's what I think. Things could get pretty hairy around here tonight."

"Maybe I should just take her and go," Frankie said.

"That's running again."

"I know that, Tony. But maybe I'm just not cut out for making a stand. I came back here to exorcise old ghosts, not take part in a gangster shoot-out."

Valenti nodded. "Well, it's your decision, Frankie. Either way, I'll back you. Just do what you think is right."

"But I don't *know!*"

"When all's said and done," Mally said, "all roads lead to the same end. So it's not so much which road you take, as how you take it."

That made sense, Valenti thought. We all got to die sometime. So it's the way you lived that you left behind. Beside him, Frankie nodded as she, too, thought it through.

"Tell Ali I wish her luck," she said.

"As she'd do to you," Mally said. "I think you made a strong choice. Whether or not it's the right one, I don't know. But it's a strong one."

Frankie found herself smiling.

"Listen," Valenti said. "Do you think you could take Ali to stay with Lewis for tonight? I mean, I don't know how long it's going to take you to do whatever it is that you're going to do, but I'd feel better if I didn't have to worry about her suddenly showing up in the middle of a firefight, you know what I'm saying? I'd like to think that whoever's moving out there in the bush around this place tonight isn't someone we got to look out for."

"She can stay with me," Mally said.

"I thought you didn't have a place," Valenti said.

"But I have the whole forest!" Mally hopped to her feet, grinning. She waved breezily to the pair of them. Before either of them could speak, she was moving off across the lawn, heading for the forest. In the blink of an eye, the trees had swallowed her and Frankie and Valenti were alone once more.

"Did I do the right thing?" Frankie wondered aloud.

Valenti didn't answer. He knew she didn't expect him to.

"God, I wish I knew what was going on there tonight," she added.

"I know what you mean," Valenti said. "But right now, I think I'd like to know what's going down with Louie more. He's playing this whole game too cagey for the way I like to do business."

"Maybe he's not coming anymore," Frankie said. "Maybe your friend Mario managed to talk some sense into the people in charge."

Valenti shrugged. And maybe Mario had declared open season on the Magaddino family and then there'd *really* be hell to pay.

"Of course," Frankie said, "there's still my ex . . ." Her voice trailed off.

"It's always something," Valenti said. *"Così fan tutti*—that's the way of the world."

4

"He *what?*" Louie growled into the phone. "You'd better run that by me again, Johnny—I don't think we got such a good connection."

Sitting by the window, watching him, Earl smiled. Aw, he thought. The big bad Mafia hitman's getting himself some bad news. Ain't that a fucking shame. He studied Louie for a moment, taking in the whitening knuckles around the handset and the strain that was showing in the man's features, then turned to look out at the view of Ottawa's skyline. This was Louie's seventh or eighth call—Earl had lost track after the first few—and the first one to give him some answers.

It had all started when Louie went to make his regular late afternoon call to his old man. For awhile there, he'd gotten no answer. When someone finally picked up the phone at the other end, it turned out to be a cop. Louie had hung up quickly, phoning around until he'd gotten hold of Johnny "Bomps" Bompensiero. Maybe he's gonna wish he never did, Earl thought.

"Bennie's doing what?" Louie demanded. "Hey, since when does

Bennie have anything to say about—I don't give a fuck, Johnny.
We're talking the Magaddino family here, or are you forgetting who
pays the bills? I answer only to the *padrone* and my old man—you
hear what I'm telling you? This bullshit you're handing me's pissing
me off. I'm in the middle of something important and I got to—"

Louie broke off and something dark passed across his face as he
listened to Johnny Bomps. Earl turned to see what was going on. He
glanced at Fingers who was watching his boss with a worried expression.

"You *sure?*" Louie said softly. "Okay. I hear what you're saying.
Tell whoever that I'm flying in tonight and I don't want nobody talking about this outside the family—not till I get back. Hey, they owe
me that much, Johnny. Just tell them that I'm calling in my favors. I
got a little thing to clear up here in the next couple of hours and then
I'm flying home. Right. This'll be one I owe you, Johnny. Yeah,
thanks."

Louie cradled the phone and turned toward the window, not seeing Earl or the view, his gaze fixed on memories.

Christ, Earl thought, looking at him. Ever since these wops blew
into town he'd been running around, wiping their asses like some
brown-nosing tourist guide. He had better things to do than get involved in some fucking mob soap opera. He should never have mentioned a word about Valenti—let the wops take care of their own
problems. He should have just grabbed the money and run. He could
have been in Bogotá by now, or at least on his way. First class—him
and Howie.

Earl frowned, thinking of Howie. Howie had been something of a
twerp, but he'd had his uses. What bothered Earl most about the fact
that Howie was dead, though, was how the little fucker'd bought it.
Somebody'd just punched a hole in him. Earl didn't feel any particular loyalty to Howie but you couldn't let guys go around wasting people that worked for you. It made you look like an asshole. Like you
were out of control. And nobody wanted to work for someone who
was out of control.

"What happened?" Fingers asked.

Earl looked at Louie. Fercrissakes, he looked like he was gonna cry.

"The old man's dead," Louie said. "Him and Ricca—they got hit this afternoon. Johnny don't know all the details, but there's some kind of shit going down. Bennie LaFata's waving around a paper that puts the finger on Ricca for calling the old Don's hit and the old guard's got some funny idea about backing him as the new *padrone*."

"Where'd they get hit?" Fingers asked. "Who did it?"

"Christ, I don't know. They were in the old man's office. Somebody just blew 'em away."

"Papale," Fingers said. "It had to be the Fox did it. Christ, I'm sorry, Louie. Broadway Joe was the best we had."

Louie started to nod. "You're right. It had to be Papale. That gives me two reasons to blow the fuck out of Valenti."

"What's going on?" Earl asked. "I had a deal and—"

"My old man's dead!" Louie shouted. "Can you understand that, you dumb fuck? You got nothing now—no deal, nothing!" He started to draw his gun, but Fingers got to him before he could pull it free. He held onto Louie's arm and turned to Earl.

"You better get out of here," he said.

For a long moment Earl was ready to face them down. With the deal going down the tubes he felt like showing these wops just where they could blow it, but then he realized that although they might just be a couple of assholes, they were a couple of assholes that were connected. No point in calling the mob down on his own ass. He could wait for a better time.

"Hey, I'm sorry about your old man," he said. "I just wasn't thinking. You say there's no deal, okay. There's no deal. But cut me in on this Valenti shit—I'll do this as a freebie with you, just to show my goodwill. What do you say?"

Louie stared him down, glared at him until Earl's gaze flicked away, then slowly he calmed down. He let go of his .38 and Fingers stepped quickly back, an apology on his lips that Louie waved away.

"That's okay, Fingers," Louie said. "You did good." He turned back to Earl. "So what's in it for you?"

"I told you straight—goodwill and that's it."

Louie shrugged. "I don't trust you."

"Okay. Then I'll stay out of it. Let me just ask you to do one thing—keep my family out of it, all right? I need the kid to hold over my ex's head and I need my ex to sign over her bread to me. After that, I don't give a shit what happens to them."

"Now that I can understand," Louie said. "See, I know you got no loyalty. You don't understand what we got in the *fratellanza*. But when I know it's your own profit you're thinking about, then I can trust you not to fuck up."

Earl couldn't believe what he was hearing. It was like these guys took all this bullshit seriously. What the fuck was the mob in business for if it is wasn't to turn a profit?

"So here's the deal," Louie said. "If Valenti's alone, we take him— me and Fingers. We're not going to play this pretty anymore. This time we're going in and we're going to blow the fuck out of him. If your old lady's around, we'll let you talk her out—but just long enough to sign over the bread. After that, she's got to go. We're not leaving any- thing of Valenti's standing. Not him, not his house, not his women, nothing. *Capito?*"

"That's fine by me," Earl said. And it was. The wops could take turns blowing the hell out of each other for all he cared—just so long as he got to walk away with his bread. "Are we going now?"

"We're going to need one or two more things," Louie said. "How long'll it take you to run us down a rocket-launcher?"

Earl blinked. "Hey, come on. What're you—"

"You don't understand, do you?" Louie said. "These fuckers killed my old man, not some asshole I never heard of, but *my* old man. I want Valenti and Papale in little pieces. I want to drop their ears on the old man's coffin when it gets lowered into the ground, you understand?"

"Right. A rocket-launcher. That's gonna cost."

"Money's no problem. Fingers give the man some bread."

Fingers pulled out a billfold filled with U.S. currency and started counting out hundred dollar bills into Earl's hand.

"That's enough," Earl said when he was holding twenty of them. "If I can't get it for this, it can't be got. You want anything else?"

Louie shaped a fist with his right hand and tapped it against his left breast. "Everything else I need's right in here," he said.

Earl looked into Louie's eyes and saw something in them that he found in his own reflection sometimes. It was a piece of madness—not fruit loops but the kind that could pass for sane, until you check out the eyes. It leapt like a spark from Louie to Earl and Earl grinned.

"I guess you're right," he told Louie.

Fingers Maita stepped back and regarded the pair with misgivings. There was something in the air and he didn't like it. He knew that neither man cared for the other, but right now it was as though they were brothers. He'd known Louie for a long time, and knew him to get like this once in a while. He was hard to hold down, then. He just went crazy until he leveled whatever was standing in his way. Fingers didn't give a shit about that—Louie was the boss and what he wanted done got done—but this way of doing it just made things too risky.

The air in the room almost crackled with whatever was passing between the two men. Then just before it broke off, Fingers thought he heard something, a sound like a flute coming from a long way off, but as soon as he started to listen to it, the vague music faded and he wasn't sure if he'd actually heard it or imagined it. As soon as it was gone, whatever it was that had linked his boss to the Canadian was gone as well. We're getting into some weird shit here, he thought.

"Give me a couple of hours," Earl said. "I'll be back so we can still make it out there before it gets completely dark."

Louie looked at his watch. "If you're not back by seven-fifteen, we're going on without you."

Not with the honeypot that was gonna bankroll him lying there right in the line of fire they weren't. "I'll be back in time," Earl said and headed out the door.

Jesus, Howie, he thought as he was waiting for the elevator. Too bad you're missing out on this. It's gonna be some party. He grinned. Anything'd be a party compared to the car trunk that he'd shoved Howie's corpse into, though he wouldn't mind being there to see the face of the dude who finally opened his trunk when the smell got to be too strong and he found himself staring face to face with Howie Peale and his amazing maggot show.

The elevator arrived with a *ping* and Earl got in, turning his thoughts to the business at hand. Who the fuck did he know that could come up with a rocket-launcher in the next hour or so? By the time he was out on the street, he had a destination in mind. He'd just check out the Ottawa chapter of the Devil's Dragon biker gang. If those suckers didn't have it, it probably hadn't been made yet. At least not when it came to hand-held weapons. Christ, he'd even seen a full-size cannon out there one time.

5

The top of Wolding Hill lifted a flat granite face from its wooded shoulders. It was a solid expanse of rock with little vegetation except for an old pine growing out of a fat crevice that time and the elements had filled with wind-gathered dirt. The pine grew in one corner of the summit and had shed a carpet of browned needles that had needed sweeping.

Using cedar boughs, Ali and the wild girl cleared the needles away from the area they were using. Throughout the afternoon, they lugged fuel for the bonfire up to the summit, laying it down on the rock. By the time they were finished, they had a tangle of windfalls, twigs and most of the bones from the skeleton of a deer that Mally had found, all piled up in a circle that was five feet across and almost four feet high at the tip of its cone.

Ali sat and looked at it now, poking at the wood with the metal-shod point of her walking stick. She still wasn't sure that what she was doing was right; she wasn't even sure exactly what it was that she *was* doing here. All she knew was that she had to see it through.

She stared at the antler that lay at the very top of the pile. This one was different from the small antlers that had been with the deer skeleton. It was carved with designs and hung with beads and feathers. "They were Old Hornie's once," Mally had informed her. The twin to the one in front of Ali should be in her mother's hands by now, she thought. She wasn't really sure why she'd sent it along with Mally.

She heard a sound, someone scrabbling up the last bit of bare rock, and turned, almost expecting it to be her mother or Tony, but it was just Mally returning from having delivered Ali's message. She had a paper bag in one hand, a leather water-bag slung over her shoulder.

" 'Lo, Ali. Come see what I found." She presented Ali with the bag that, when Ali opened it, proved to hold sandwiches. Ali's stomach grumbled as she smelled them.

"Where did you 'find' them?" she asked.

"At Lewis's cabin."

Ali started to tell the wild girl that just taking things wasn't right, but she was too hungry to carry the argument. Thank you, Lewis, she thought as she took the top sandwich out. "What did my mom say?" she asked around a mouthful of bread, sliced hardboiled eggs, cheese and watercress.

"Well, she started out saying no," Mally replied, taking the other sandwich, "but she changed her mind."

"What made her change her mind?"

Mally shrugged. "Don't really know. I think it's partly because she knows you have to do this and partly because they're expecting their own trouble down there and they want to keep you out of it."

Ali stopped chewing. Trouble. That meant either her father or the men that were after Tony—or maybe both. She wondered how much Tony had told her mother. He had to have told her about the stag at least and something about what Ali was doing up here, but what about the men who were after Tony? Had he told her about them and *why* they were after him?

Probably not. She couldn't see her mother accepting that very readily. It was too bad, though. Ali had been having hopes of maybe getting the two of them together when this was all over. But they were probably too dense to know that they'd make a good couple, and knowing her mother, once she *did* find out about Tony's past, all bets would be off.

"They both had guns," Mally said.

"They *did?* Both of them?"

Mally nodded. "Small ones." She mimicked a pistol with her hand. "And one that was neither small, nor big like a rifle."

Considering Tony's background, Ali thought, that could be just about anything. "You sure my mom had one?" she asked again. She just couldn't believe it.

"Oh, yes," Mally said. "I saw it, didn't I?"

Way-to-go, Tony. Turn my mother into a moll. But just remember—she's not Sybil Danning. Not by a long shot. And those were just movies, not the real thing. Ali wasn't sure if the idea that her mother had a gun comforted her or not. It was good to know that she'd be able to protect herself, but Ali liked her mother the way she was. She needed to assert herself a little more, especially around men, but this?

Ali sighed and took another bite of her sandwich. What a weird move this had turned out to be. We have to put down some roots, her mother had said. Find a place we can really call our own. But the peace and quiet they'd both been hoping for hadn't appeared. Ali thought about how their lives had turned topsy-turvy in the past few weeks. She didn't regret it—not exactly. Not when you weighed Tony and Mally and the stag—especially the way the mystery made her feel—not when you weighed not ever having known them against the trouble that had come with them.

"Did you have enough?" Mally asked.

Ali looked down and realized that she'd devoured her sandwich. "I guess so," she said with a rueful smile. "I'm not being very good company, am I?"

"What do you mean?"

"I've been moody—brooding all day."

Mally shrugged. "Talking's not everything, Ali. Sometimes just being together's enough. Didn't the mystery teach you that yet?"

"I'm not very good at lessons, I guess." Ali licked a crumb off her finger. "Are you sure my mom understood why I couldn't come home?"

"No. But I think she trusts you to know your own heart."

"That'd be the day," Ali said, but she knew she wasn't being fair. Her mother was pretty good when it came to disciplining her, but she gave Ali a lot of slack. Ali found that she didn't get into a lot of the messes that other kids did simply because she knew her mother trusted her not to and Ali didn't want to blow that trust. "I hope they'll be okay," she added.

"You can't worry about them," Mally said. "You've got to think about Old Hornie now."

Ali shot a glance at the unlit bonfire. "When do we start—you know, lighting the fire and everything?"

"When we hear Tommy's pipes—that'd be best."

Ali nodded. She looked away to the west. The sun was lowering steadily, turning into a deep orange ball as it neared the horizon. She hadn't brought her watch, but by the way the shadows were lengthening down below them in the forest, she didn't think it'd be too long until nightfall. Then they'd hear Tommy's pipes and light the fire and she'd call the mystery to her . . .

Thinking about the piping reminded her of last night and where Mally and the stag had taken her. That place was almost like the music itself—very real, very here and now, but unearthly, otherworldly, fey at the same time. She loved the sound of that old word. Fey. That's what people would say if she'd lived back then and they saw her riding the stag, with a horned wild girl for a companion. "That Ali," they'd say to each other. "She's so fey." Either that or they'd burn her as a witch.

Ali looked at the heap of wood in front of them and shivered. She turned to Mally.

"What about the Hunt?" she asked. She'd already told the wild girl about having seen them outside her window last night.

"Don't think of them," Mally said, "or you might call them to us. But if they do come—don't listen to them. Everything they tell you will be a lie. Logical, oh, yes, and persuasive, but a lie nevertheless."

334 / Charles de Lint

"I'm nervous."

Mally smiled. "Don't be. You rode on his back last night, didn't you?"

"Well, yes. But this is different."

"Yes," Mally said softly. "It *will* be different." She studied Ali for a moment. "Try to be a little merry," she added.

"I'm having enough trouble keeping my knees from knocking together, little say trying to wear a smile."

"But merry can mean 'looking for' as well as 'happy,' you know. Try to be a little of both—keep a balance and you won't do so bad. The merry poet searches for her muse, but she does so happily. Why don't you do the same?"

"I'm not searching for a muse," Ali said. "I'm calling the stag to me."

"Some people might say that's the same thing."

Ali frowned and looked away, first to the antler on top of the unlit bonfire, bedecked with its feathers and beads, then westward, to where the sun was just peeking above the horizon now.

"I just want to talk to him," she said. "I want to ask him if he wants to be free—that's all, Mally. I'm not looking for anything for myself."

Mally nodded. "I know. But you have to do something for yourself at the same time, or it's all in vain."

"I don't understand."

"I know," Mally replied. "But it doesn't matter. It'll happen just the same."

"You know more than you're telling me—don't you? What's in this for you, Mally?"

The wild girl shrugged. "I don't really know more," she said. "I don't know what's in it for me, or you, or even Old Hornie. I just know that some things must be done—the knowing just comes to me. I think it's because I'm a secret, that's why I know things, but I don't know why I know them."

"You're the reason Lewis's son left, aren't you?" Ali guessed. "And Lily's son and the others, too. You talked to them and showed them what lay beyond the village and these woods, and once they saw it, they just had to go. Isn't that so?"

"I talked to them. But I always said the village needed more people in it, not less. I didn't make them go."

"You wouldn't have to." Ali felt she was close to something now, but she wasn't sure what. It wasn't simply a matter of figuring Mally out—who she was and why she did what she did—but something more. "You gave Lewis the books," she went on. "Did you talk to Ackerly Perkin as well?"

Mally didn't answer.

"Are we freeing the mystery," Ali asked, "or binding me to it?"

Mally lifted her gaze until her cat's eyes studied Ali. "It's getting near the time," she said. "Best light the bone-fire now."

Ali didn't say anything for a long moment. Answer me! she wanted to shout. She wanted to grab Mally and shake the truth out of her, but she knew it wouldn't do any good. There was only one way to find out now and that was to see this thing through to its end. God, she thought as she pulled a pack of matches out of her jeans. I hope I don't regret this.

Lewis smiled when he saw that the bag of sandwiches and the water-sack were gone. He'd seen the two girls heading for Wold Hill and knew something was up. He also knew that they'd be hungry, and while Mally would never ask for something, she wouldn't find it at all hard to just 'find' the provisions and take them along.

I wish I knew what you were up to, he thought as he looked toward the hill now. The twilight was deepening. He stood, listening to the quiet, enjoying it. For a few minutes all the questions and riddles were held at bay by the simple beauty of the moment, then he heard a scuffle of feet on the path running by his house.

He looked over to see Gaffa bound by, Tommy following the dog at a slower pace, his pipes in hand. This wouldn't be a gather-up night, Lewis thought, but all the same he left his cabin behind and followed Tommy Duffin up the path to the old stone. He had a feeling that something was in the air tonight. He just didn't know what. He certainly didn't intend to miss out on it.

* * *

The kindling caught quickly and soon the flames were licking the bark of the larger fuel. One match, Ali thought. Not bad. And I've never even been a Girl Guide. The sun set as she watched the fire take hold. Soon it gave off more light than the graying sky. She glanced at Mally. The flickering light made shadows play across the wild girl's features. Then Ali's heart gave a little thumping lift as the sound of Tommy's pipes drifted up the hill.

"Call him to you now," Mally said softly.

Ali nodded slowly. "How?" she asked.

"Use the fire that burns inside you."

I don't have a fire inside, Ali wanted to say. All I've got is butterflies. But the sound of the music against the crackle of the bonfire woke something inside her and she thought that must be it. She concentrated on that feeling. Looking into the bonfire, mesmerized by the dancing flames, she tried to call the mystery to her.

"Use his name," Mally said.

"I don't know his name."

"Give him one then—one that you will know him by."

Old Hornie, Ali thought, then shook her head. No, that was Mally's name for him. Just like Lewis called him the Green Man. What did she think of him as? Just a mystery. A small smile tugged at her lips. Maybe as Bambi's father?

"Can you feel the night?" Mally asked. "It's listening. Call him."

Ali nodded. But I don't have a name, she thought. She had to back away from the fire a little as the flames continued to rise. People are going to see this for miles, she thought. What if they send in forest fire fighters? It was a beacon. To call the mystery, yes, but if he were real, then mightn't there be a whole realm of otherworldly denizens that it could call? Victorian elves and gnomes came to mind. Illustrations from dozens of children's books. Faeries and trolls and everything in between. She thought of the Hunt that had been watching her window last night, the pack of hounds that chased the stag. She shivered and put the image of them away.

Instead she tried to think of a name for the mystery. What came to mind was a chapter from an old friend of a book, *The Wind in the Wil-*

lows. Grahame's Rat and Mole and especially Badger all walked through her thoughts. She'd never been as big on Toad as most people. It was the quiet creatures she'd loved the best, the descriptions of quiet times. Picnics and Yule nights and rowboats on the river . . .

She remembered the chapter where Otter's son Portly was lost and all the animals went out looking for him. Rat and Mole in their rowboat . . . they found him, but they found something else as well. The mystery watching over the little otter. Grahame called him the Piper at the Gates of Dawn. Ali never thought of Pink Floyd when she heard that phrase—just of Grahame's book, of Rat and Mole's awe, and of the chill that ran up her spine whenever she thought of those few pages, or read them again.

That's who you are to me, she told the mystery. I just wish I knew your name.

She could see him if she closed her eyes. Not as a stag or a Green Man like Lewis did, nor as he'd appeared in the otherworld, but as the goatman he'd been for a moment last night. The long curling horns and the pinched features that reminded her a little of Mally. His reed-pipes were like Tommy's, but different, too. Because his music was different. What Tommy played made her want to move; it made her emotions dance until she just had to step her body to its rhythm. But the other music, *his* music, it would fill her with peace. She'd never heard it, but she knew what it would be like. She knew *just* what it would be like.

She tried not to hear Tommy's music, searched instead for the melody that she knew the mystery would play if he had the pipes instead of Tommy. Closing her eyes, she drew up the image of him in her mind. It flickered just at the limits of her grasp. His music was almost there, but then Tommy's piping stole it away and her memories went back to last night again. The goatman was a stag when it came to the old stone. There was dancing. She was moving to the music with Lily. Then Mally caught her up and tossed her onto the stag's back and they were off and away—away into some elsewhere.

She went with the memory, followed it on that wild ride through a forest that didn't exist in this world, to the summit of that other-worldly mountain with its circular stone formations. The moon hung low and full, the stars were so bright. Her breath frosted in the air. The mystery was a stag, then a man in his mantle of green leaves and she was standing in front of him, asking him what he wanted, asking him for a name. Again she was caught by his gaze—as powerful in memory as it had been last night. Something in their gazes connected and went on and on and on.

There's no name for something like you, she thought. No one can name you. All they can do is take an aspect that they can see and call you by that. Pan. Old Hornie. A Green man. Greenmantle.

Greenmantle.

That's what I'd call you, if I only knew you from last night. But I've known you all my life, haven't I? You're what makes the seasons change, the blood to flow. You taught me how to breathe when I left my mother's womb. You taught my body to grow and my heart to recognize you when I finally saw you. In the pages of a book. In the melody of a tune. In the spread of a branch against the sky. In the hop of a robin, the eyes of a cat, the scent of a blossom . . .

She watched herself turn away from him in the memory—because Mally was calling her. They had to leave that place in elsewhere. It was time to go before . . . before what? Then she heard the sound of their baying, and the warm feeling that the memory had left in her chilled in her veins. The Hunt. The pack. They had to hurry, because if the hounds caught their scent in that place, they'd chase her and Mally, just like they chased the stag. In her memory, she saw that they'd gotten away from the pack. But then she remembered later that night, the hounds at the edge of the forest, watching her as she stood by the window. . . .

Her eyes opened with a snap. The fire blinded her for a moment, and she blinked, looking away from it.

"Mally?" she started to say, but the wild girl was gone.

She stood up, shivering for all the heat that the fire threw off. Something was wrong. She couldn't hear the piping anymore. How long had she been away in her memories? It couldn't have been too long because the fire was still burning high. But where was Mally? Why did she feel so strange?

The sound of the pack came to her again, but very close now. She stooped and picked up Tony's walking stick, holding it with nervous fingers. Something was very wrong. She turned slowly, staring at the darkened forest, her night vision poor from looking into the fire. But when it cleared, she saw them stepping from the undergrowth. They weren't hounds now, they were men in hooded cloaks. The foremost held a crucifix between himself and her.

"M-mally . . . ?" Ali mumbled.

The fire was behind her, the pack fanned out in front of her. There was nowhere to go. The mystery hadn't come and Mally had deserted her. I didn't call you, she wanted to tell the hooded men, but the words choked in her throat. I wanted the mystery.

"Don't be afraid," the foremost man said. "We have come to save your soul."

Behind him, two of the other men shook ropes out of the folds of their cloaks and advanced on her. Ali held the pointed tip of the walking stick out toward them, but her hands shook so much that the stick fell from them and clattered on the stone. Her knees went wobbly and she sank slowly to the ground, staring at the hooded men with wide frightened eyes.

"P-please," she said. "I don't . . . I don't need to be saved."

The man with the crucifix shook his head slowly. "You will thank us when we are done," he said.

The men with the ropes leapt forward and caught her by each arm, then dragged her toward the old pine tree. Ali was so scared she couldn't even struggle. She just went limp in their arms. Please, she cried soundlessly. Mystery. It was just trying to help you. Help me.

There was no answer to her soundless call. The woods remained silent as the men bound her to the tree.

"There is a demon in you," the man with the crucifix said. "Through the power of God we will cast it from you."

The rope hurt her wrists and ankles as they tied her spread-eagled to the tree. Her strength came back to her in a panicking surge, but it was too late now. She strained against the ropes, but that only made them burn her skin as she struggled to free herself. Her blood hammered in her temples. The crucifix was thrust up near her face and the hooded man stared at her, but because the fire was behind him, all she could see was darkness inside his hood, as though he didn't have a face. Behind him, the other men went down on their knees in a half-circle.

"Oh, Lord, we beseech you," the man with the crucifix intoned. "Aid us to rid the world of this evil."

Not real, Ali told herself. This wasn't real. But the ropes were real. The bark of the tree was rough against her back. It was real.

"Who are you?" she cried, her voice going shrill with panic.

"Your saviors, child. Fear the demon inside you, not us."

He touched the crucifix against her forehead and a red hot fire went through her mind. Ali cried out again, but this time all that escaped her throat was a long wordless wail.

"Trust in the Lord," the hooded man said, but Ali was too far gone now to hear him.

6

In the flicker of the bone-fire Mally watched her companion, waiting for the tell-tale glimmer of the inner fire she hoped would wake in the teenager. The bone-fire continued to burn higher. Combined with Tommy's piping, it opened doors in Ali that even Ali couldn't be aware of. Mally nodded in satisfaction.

You'll heed this calling, won't you, Old Hornie? she thought. Listen to its pulse—see its brightness. How can you resist?

Mally could hardly contain her excitement. A moment like this was all too rare. The mysteries tended to roam a smaller and smaller area as they grew older, dwindling in stature, in magic, until sometimes they simply faded away. But tonight Old Hornie would be sent out into the world again like a gust of fresh air. He'd blow through the hearts of men and make them sit up and *see* again, even if only for a moment.

Mortals were such that just the smallest taste of that *sight* would send them questing the rest of their days to recapture it. And while that questing would remain unconscious in most, while it would be only a tiny part of their overall being, it would be enough to return a spark of old glory to hearts that were dimmed. It wasn't the magic of the mystery that was important, nor the finding of it, but the quest itself.

It might save a forest, it might save one tree. One man might be kinder to another, when he might otherwise have passed the need by. It was beauty that needed preserving, whether it lay in a forest, a field, or a city street. Whether it was the workings of a plant, from seed to new growth to mulch, or the workings of some complex machine. There was room for everything in the world, so long as men remembered the beauty. And once seen, as they would tonight when they brushed Old Hornie's thoughts as he chased the world itself in his freedom, they might not remember, but they would never forget. Some part of them would always recall what they'd only *seen* howsoever briefly tonight.

So call him, Mally thought, looking at Ali. Let him know the wider world again. Let him run free so that he doesn't just reflect what lies in a few minds, but encompasses the wonder of the world at large. A reflection that will be neither good nor ill, for it simply is.

She hugged her knees and rocked back and forth, delighted with what she was accomplishing. I needed someone like you, Ali, she thought. Oh, for such a long time. The winds of the otherworld blew through your soul long before Old Hornie took us there. Can you hear them now? Can you feel them on your face?

Ali's eyes were closed. Mally leaned closer to peer into the teenager's face. What do you *see* right now? she wondered. She felt a great affection for Ali and started to reach forward to brush her short blond curls with a brown hand when a sudden draft of cold air flickered across the summit of Wold Hill. Mally blinked, and between the closing and opening of her eyes, Ali disappeared.

Mally leapt to her feet, looking all around the summit. "Ali?" she cried. "Ali! Aliiiiii!"

Gone. Disappeared like a forgotten thought. Mally paced nervously around the fire, her nostrils flaring as she tried to pick up Ali's scent. Old Hornie hadn't taken her, because Mally would have sensed his coming, would have *known* he was here, long before Ali. But if Old Hornie hadn't taken her into that elsewhere . . .

Mally raced through the forest, making for the old stone. She ran at a breakneck pace, bounding from stone to fallen tree, dodging low-hanging boughs and deadfalls. When she burst into the glade by the old stone, just Lewis, Tommy and the dog Gaffa were there. No Old Hornie. No Ali, either—though Mally hadn't been expecting her here. Tommy broke off his playing at Mally's sudden entrance.

"Did he come?" she demanded, turning her attention to Lewis, rather than Tommy. "Was he here?"

"Slow down," Lewis said. "What are you talking about?"

"The mystery! Was he here?"

Lewis shook his head. "No. We've only just come ourselves. And anyway, it's not a gather—"

Mally turned away from him and glared at Tommy. By the piper's knee, Gaffa growled. "Play those pipes!" she cried. "Call him here! Now, now, now!"

Tommy looked at her dumbly, whatever spirit possessing him when he played, long gone now.

"What's the matter, Mally?" Lewis asked. "And where's Ali?"

"Gone!" she cried. "Stolen like smoke. Taken to . . ." And then she knew. "Did you hear them tonight, Lewis?" she asked. "The hounds? Did you hear them?"

"I thought I did—just a few moments before you arrived. But the sound of them was very faint."

"Oh, they've got her, then. They've got her!" The wild girl's eyes flashed with anger—as much at herself for not realizing this risk as at the pack itself. "I should have waited for Midsummer's night. I shouldn't have been in such a hurry." She looked suddenly at Lewis. "And see where it's gotten me? I'll be lucky to get her back now, little say set Old Hornie free."

"Set him—"

"I'll need the fire in the lame man to call him to me now. No time to set him free. All I can do is hope that he can take me to wherever the pack has her before it's too late."

"Too late for . . . ?"

She was off before Lewis could finish his sentence. He watched her bound into the woods, taking the trail that led to Tony Valenti's house. Lewis shook his head, then he looked up toward the summit of Wold Hill. He could see a glow there in the sky above the trees. What had they been up to? He glanced at Tommy, who sat with his pipes on his lap, staring off into nothing, then over to where the trees had swallowed Mally.

A cold chill went through him as he looked back up the hill. The feeling he'd had earlier came back stronger than ever. There *was* something in the air tonight, only he was no longer a part of it. But when he thought of that young girl that both the stag and Mally had taken such an interest in, when he thought of her in some danger . . .

Mally had mentioned the hounds. Lewis didn't know why they would be after Ali, but he knew he had to do something. What he could do, he didn't know. But he had to at least try. There'd be time enough later to find out what Mally had meant when she talked about setting the Green Man free. Didn't Mally know that men today had more dark than light in their hearts—that the mystery would reflect that darkness back into the world because of what men had become?

Giving Tommy and the old stone a last look, Lewis started up the hill, his aging heart filled with misgivings.

7

A half hour before nightfall, Valenti stood up from the kitchen table. He took out his .38, checked its load, then replaced it in its shoulder holster. Next he checked the UZI and the pouch of spare rounds. He put a windbreaker on, then slung the UZI from his shoulder by its strap. There was a small pack by the door that he slung over his other shoulder. It had a couple of thermoses of coffee and some sandwiches in it.

"Time to go," he said.

Frankie nodded. The automatic snug in the holster that hung from her belt was an unfamiliar, but somewhat comforting weight. Glancing at the table, she thought, we really should clean up the dinner dishes, then realized how ridiculous the thought was.

"Do you really think they'll come tonight?" she asked.

"Something's going down tonight—all my instincts tell me that. Better grab your jacket. It's going to be cooler now that the sun's down."

Frankie shrugged into her jacket. Now that they were actually going to go out into the night and wait for the attack, she had to ask herself again why she was doing this. It wasn't the kind of thing that fit into her life. What was happening now belonged on some cops 'n' robbers show, not real life. Practicing with the gun this afternoon, listening to Tony's strategies, hadn't prepared her for the reality that she had to face now. If Earl came, if Tony's enemies came, *could* she do anything?

Valenti could see what she was going through. "Look," he said. "You can still bow out of this. You don't have to be a part of it. I'll tell you right now that it's going to change you. If you come out of this tonight, you're never going to be the same after."

"I'm not sure I feel the same right now—I'm already not the same person I was a couple of days ago."

"You could go to the village, or you could take the car and get yourself to someplace safe."

Frankie shook her head. "Ali's still out there. I won't desert her. And I won't desert you. I'm responsible for part of what's happening tonight. If Earl comes, it's because of me. And those other men— they wouldn't even know you were here if it wasn't for me."

"They had to find me sooner or later, you know what I'm saying? I knew that."

"I'm not running again," Frankie said. "This is all crazy—the guns and everything—but I'm not running."

Valenti regarded her for a moment, then nodded. "You're going to do just fine," he said.

Frankie wasn't sure how she should take that. He meant it as a compliment, but she didn't see anything fine about carrying a gun, about maybe having to use it.

"C'mon," Valenti said. He picked up Mario's crossbow and started out the door, favoring his leg. He hoped it wasn't going to slow him down. Louie already had an edge with the extra manpower he could command.

Frankie gave the inside of the house a final look. In the warm interior lighting, the big room had a cozy look. Nothing about it suggested the violence that the night was going to bring.

"Coraggio," Valenti said. "That's what Mario'd say if he was here. Have courage."

"Coraggio," she said. "Like in 'don't let the bastards get you down'?"

"You got it."

"So let's do it," Frankie said. She followed him out into the night, scared but determined not to show it.

"So here's the plan one more time," Louie said—needlessly as far as Earl was concerned. Christ, these wops liked to hear themselves talk. "You and Fingers each take a side of the road and follow it up till you're flanking the house—one on each side. You got to get a position where you can watch both the back and sides at the same time, *capito?* Then when I let go with this sucker—" he patted the rocket launcher that Earl had managed to pick up from the Dragons "—and blow out the front of that fucking place, you can just pick off anybody who tries to make a run for it. And aim low, okay? I want a chance to look Tony in the face before I finish him—that's if I don't blow him to fuck with the first shot."

Earl shook his head. "We're gonna have to be in and out *fast,"* he said. "The noise that thing's gonna make, the place'll be crawling with cops before we know it—even out here in the sticks."

This was a case where Fingers agreed with Earl, but he didn't say anything. Louie wanted to use a rocket-launcher, then that's what they would do.

"You let me worry about the cops," Louie said. "Now get going. I'll give you ten minutes to get into position, then I'm hitting the front."

Earl picked up his .38 from the seat beside him and stuck it in his belt. Grabbing a rifle, he got out of the car. "I'll take the left side," he said.

Fingers nodded.

"Ten minutes," Louie repeated. "That's all you got."

Fuck off, Earl thought. What do ya think this is, the army? "You got it, Louie," he added aloud. And maybe, just accidentally on purpose, a stray shot might take your greasy little head off—you know what *I* mean?

He started off along the road leading up to Valenti's place, angling into the woods as soon as he was away from the car. He had something else he wanted to check before he played Louie's game. If Frankie was home, they just might be playing by a new set of rules. But the house, when it came into sight, was dark. Either Frankie had split, or she was up at Tony's.

He moved closer to check the lane, spotted the car sitting in it and nodded to himself. Okay. Tony's it was. That fucking Louie better not blow up his meal ticket, he thought as he hurried to get into position up by the Valenti place. Earl Shaw's had to wait too long to get on the gravy train again.

"Nervous?" Valenti whispered.

Frankie nodded, the movement almost lost in the darkness. They were in the woods in back of the house, right at the edge of the trees. Valenti still carried the UZI slung from his shoulder, but the pack with coffee and sandwiches had been stashed in a tree where no one would run across it. He carried the crossbow.

"I'm feeling a little nervous myself," he said. "There's something in the air—like the way it gets just before a storm, you know?"

"Coraggio," Frankie whispered back, liking the sound of the word.

Valenti grinned. He started to answer, then cocked his head. "Listen," he said, leaning close to breathe the word into Frankie's ear. "Do you hear it?"

At first Frankie didn't know what he meant, but then she heard it, too. The soft piping came drifting out of the woods behind them, a distant eerie sound.

"Makes me feel quiet and excited—all at the same time," Valenti added, before leaning away from her.

They sat and listened to it. Valenti remembered the slack-faced boy who changed when he brought the pipes to his lips. He thought of the dancers by the old stone and the stag when it came—biggest goddamn deer he'd ever seen.

Frankie thought about Ali and prayed that she was safe. The music helped ease her fears. There was something in it that told her that there were good things in life to balance the bad. A simple enough thing, but it was a real comfort at the moment. Wherever that music came from, it couldn't be bad, she thought. It couldn't hurt Ali. She reached out and found Valenti's free hand and gave it a squeeze.

Valenti started at the touch, then squeezed back. Simple thing that—a touch of hands in the dark—but it turned his determination to iron. Nothing was going to hurt this lady—not if he had any say in it. He felt good, holding her hand, knowing she was so close to him, but he had to wonder what kind of a stupid fuck he was, letting her get involved in what was going down tonight. Mary, Mother of Jesus, he prayed. Get us through tonight and I'll burn a hundred candles for you. I know I'm not much, but do it for her, okay?

It was a long time since he'd prayed or thought about the church. When he tried to picture the Virgin, he couldn't. He saw only Her Son, up on His cross, and damned if He didn't have the same eyes as the stag.

At first, Fingers thought the music was coming from the house. But then he was in position and he realized its source was deeper in the forest behind them. He didn't like that. It meant there were people closer than there were supposed to be and people always made trouble.

He didn't like this job. You do a hit in the city, it's no problem disappearing into the crowd. But out in a place like this, the cops'd be stopping anything that moved, fercrissakes. And there were only so many roads out of here—unless you wanted to try the backroads and that was just asking to get lost.

No, he thought. There was going to be shit flying no matter how you turned it. He checked his watch. The luminous digits told him he had a minute to go before Louie let loose with his rocket. Christ, he wished that music'd stop.

He started to count out the seconds and moved a little closer to the edge of the trees. The house was lit up like a Christmas tree, but he had the feeling there was no one home. He trusted his instinct—you had to in this kind of work—but he'd know for sure in a couple of moments.

Okay, Louie. Let her *go!*

Earl wanted to get closer to the house, but it was drawing too near to the zero hour. If Frankie was in there, he didn't want her blown to pieces before he got his bread from her. That fucking wop! What the hell did he have to blow the place up for anyway? By the time they were finished with Valenti it wouldn't make any difference to him if his house was standing or not.

Earl moved out of the woods to the corner of the old broken-down barn and studied the house. Nobody moving in the windows, but that didn't mean shit. They could be humping on the floor for all he knew. He glanced at his watch. No time at all to check it out now.

In the quiet as he counted down the remaining seconds, he became aware of the music drifting out of the woods behind him. That shit again. He had a nervous memory of that big buck deer suddenly coming onto him, but then he patted his rifle. Just try me tonight, you fucker. We'll see whose show it is. But he wished the music'd ease up. It grated on his nerves.

His fingers tightened on the trigger of the rifle. He'd like to have whoever was making that sound in his sights right now.

Louie Fucceri paid no attention to the music. He smiled humorlessly as he got into position. He could see the lights of the house from where he stood on the road. He edged in closer, then knelt in the dirt with the launcher balanced on his shoulder. He aimed through the break in the hedge where the walkway came down from the house to meet the road.

Nice of you to line things up like this for me, Tony. Time to say bye-bye now. This is for the old man, you hear what I'm telling you? You don't fuck with the Fucceris, Tony. It just don't pay.

He fired the weapon. The rocket roared from the launcher with a tail like a comet's trailing behind it. By the time it hit the house and took away most of the front wall with its explosion, Louie was running toward the building, the auto-reload shotgun in hand.

"Boom," he muttered. "Did you hear that, Papa? You show Tony a good time when he meets you in hell, okay?"

Fingers thought he heard something moving in the woods to his right. He began to turn in that direction to check it out when the explosion came. There was a moment of shocked silence, then before he could turn back to the house, he heard somebody cry out from where he'd heard a sound a moment ago.

He didn't even think. He just eased down the trigger of the Ingram and sprayed the area with bullets.

"Jesus Christ!" Valenti cried when the explosion came. "What the hell was that?"

He started to rise. They had to get out of here. It sounded like Louie'd brought in some full-scale artillery, fercrissakes. He turned to tell Frankie to just run, that they were getting out of here and never mind making a stand, when a line of bullets cut a swath through the bush. Valenti dropped to the ground, pressing Frankie down. A second line exploded, lower this time. It was only the trees between themselves and the gunman that saved them.

Frankie froze. She pushed her face against the mulch and panicked. When the bullets finally stopped and Valenti rose to his feet, she just stayed where she was, unable to move for a long moment. When she lifted her head, it was to see Valenti out on the lawn taking aim with the crossbow.

He was taking advantage of the time their attacker needed to change clips. She heard the wet thuck of the crossbow bolt as it hit its target, heard the man cry out, then the sharp crack of a rifle cut across the night and she saw Valenti lifted up onto the tips of his toes before he sprawled face forward on the lawn.

She stared numbly at him. Was he dead? Oh, please God, he couldn't be dead.

The rifle sounded again, kicking up sod a few feet from Valenti. She had to go to him. She had to drag him to the safety of the trees before they shot him again, but she just couldn't move. The rifle fired again. More sod flew up, closer again.

"T-tony?" she called in a hoarse whisper. Oh, Jesus. He *was* dead. "Tony?"

Then she saw his hand move, clenching at the grass and dirt. What was he doing? When she realized that he was trying to drag himself back into the trees, she knew she had to help him.

Coraggio, she could hear him say in her mind, remembering, but she didn't have any courage. Doesn't matter, she told herself. You've got to help him all the same. Swallowing thickly, she drew the automatic he'd given her and aimed it in the direction of the rifle fire. Then she crawled out toward Valenti.

Earl blinked when the rocket hit the house. Jesus. It had demolished the place. He aimed his rifle toward the back in case somebody came out, but he didn't see anybody surviving that. You can kiss good-bye to the bread now, he told himself. So much for Fucceri's promise that he could have Frankie for as long as it took her to sign the money over.

The chatter of Fingers' Ingram brought his attention to the woods in back of the house. He saw Fingers step from the trees, spraying the woods with bullets. When he paused to change clips, a figure moved onto the lawn and aimed something at Fingers—Earl couldn't make out what it was, but he saw Fingers take a fall and then he was firing his own rifle.

The figure went down and Earl grinned. Got one. Maybe the big Tony Valenti himself. He put a couple more shots around the fallen figure, then turned when he sensed he was no longer alone. Louie stood there, his face looking weird in the flickering light thrown by the burning house.

"I hit somebody up by the treeline," he told Louie, "but whoever it was got Fingers first."

Louie turned slowly from the house. "Fingers bought it?"

" 'Fraid so."

"Shit. Show me."

Earl pointed to where the men had gone down, then paused when he saw a blond-haired figure crawling to the man he figured was Valenti. Well-well, everything wasn't a total loss. He started to get out of the light thrown by the fire, realizing that if Frankie was around there might be others. Fucked if he was going to take a chance at getting hit at this point in the proceedings, but Louie just started across the lawn. He had the shotgun up and was ready to fire, not giving a shit who took a shot at him.

It was a real shame, Earl told the audience in his imagination. I mean, we took 'em out, but we lost both Fingers and Louie in the action. A crying shame.

He brought the rifle up to his shoulder and eased his finger on the trigger. The bullet caught Louie in the back of the head. Spread his face all over the lawn, Earl thought with a grin. He glanced over at Frankie and saw her head jerk up. His grin widened as he started across the lawn himself.

He worked another bullet into the chamber as he approached, frowning slightly when he saw she was holding a gun on him. Then he smiled again. Fucking thing was shaking so bad there was no way she was gonna hit anything, just saying she got it together enough to pull the trigger. Too bad it was her writing hand or he might have tried one of those fancy trick shots like in the movies—blown the sucker right out of her fingers.

"You better lay that thing down," he said as he got closer.

"B-back off," Frankie said. "Just leave . . . leave us alone."

Earl shook his head. "What we got here's a standoff of sorts," he said. "Except I can shoot you, but I don't think you got it in you to shoot me, Frankie. Now you can put that down and nobody else is gonna get hurt. I don't give a fuck about the wops—they've blown the shit out of each other now, so they're out of the picture. It's just between you and me, and you know all I want. Sign over your bread to me and everything's gonna be okay. All you got to do is spend from now till the bank opens in the morning with me, and then you're home free. Understand?"

He started to move closer, but Frankie waved the gun at him. "I'll shoot," she said. "I really will. Don't . . . don't come any closer."

"This is the wrong way to play it," Earl said. He tried to see who it was that he'd shot. "Is that Tony? Hey, he's still moving. Tell you what. I'll throw him in as part of the deal—what do you say?"

"G-go away, Earl. I don't trust you."

"Okay, Frankie. I hear you." He lowered the rifle. "See? I don't wanna hurt you. But you better think of Tony. Looks to me like he needs help and he needs it quick. Promise me the bread right now—throw away that gun—and I'll help you get to some place where we can call an ambulance for him. Is it a deal?"

Frankie was having trouble keeping the gun trained on her ex and trying to see how Tony was doing at the same time. She knew he was hurt, but she didn't know how bad. He did need help. If she could only trust Earl. He could have everything she owned, but she knew he wouldn't do what he said. He never had—why should he change now?

"Look," Earl said. "I'm showing my good faith by putting this down." He laid the rifle on the grass and held both hands up to her. "See? I got nothing now and you've got the gun. So let me help you with him."

Laying the rifle down brought him a step closer. Now as he spoke, his hands held casually in front of him, he managed a few more steps until only Valenti was between them.

"I'm not such a shit, you know," he said soothingly. "I mean, we had some bad times and you had to split—I can see that now. But we had some good times, too. So let's do this deal for those good times. I give you your man—you give me the bread."

He could see that she wanted to believe him. Her face was strained in the flickering light thrown off by the burning house. She still kept the gun on him, but it was drooping slightly. Earl knew he had to do something. That fire was gonna bring whatever fire department they had out here in the sticks and the cops wouldn't be far behind.

"Come on, Frankie. Put the gun down."

It drooped a little lower, wavered and she brought it up, dropped again. Earl pretended to look at Valenti. "Christ, would ya look at the hole in him!" he said.

Frankie's gaze went to Valenti and Earl lunged across the stricken man. He kicked the gun out of her hand. When she started to rise, he backhanded her across the face, then knelt down on top of her, pinning her arms and torso to the ground with his knees and the weight of his body. As she struggled against him he hit her again. Sliding off her, he grabbed her by her hair and hauled her to her feet. She threw a punch at him, but there was no strength behind the blow.

"You never learn, do you?" he said. "Look at yourself, fercrissakes. I could beat the shit out of you with one hand, so what're you struggling for?" He slapped her again, then grabbed her roughly by the arm and started to haul her across the lawn.

"Tony!" she wailed.

"Fuck Tony. Where's your bankbook, Frankie? Tomorrow morning, you and me've got an appointment at the bank, but until then we're gonna disappear."

"No!"

Frankie let herself go limp and sank to the ground. When Earl cursed and bent to lift her, she punched him in the groin with all her strength. He doubled over, still trying to grab at her, so she hit him again.

"You . . . you're . . . you're dead," he gasped.

She scrambled out of his way as he stumbled to his knees. Everything she'd been through coalesced into a burning need to strike back. She was *not* going to be the victim again. Tony was depending on her. On her hands and knees she covered the few feet separating Valenti from her, tugging at his UZI when she reached him. The gun came free. She turned with the weapon in hand to see Earl on his feet, still hurting, but drawing a handgun from his belt.

"Goddamn you!" she cried and pulled the trigger, only the trigger wouldn't move. Nothing happened. Moaning, she did the only thing she could think of and threw the useless gun at Earl's face.

8

It took him awhile—Lewis was feeling his age tonight—but he finally reached the summit of Wold Hill. He stood there, catching his breath, and stared at the bonfire. It reminded him of his boyhood. New Wolding was all new then—another steading carved out of the wilderness, differing only from a hundred other such places in Eastern Ontario by the beliefs of its people. Their beliefs and their insularity.

There had been bonfires then—down by the old stone. Once a year they offered a ram or a bull up to the spirit that spoke through Tommy Duffin's pipes.

Things had been simpler then. But the village lost its solidarity as the young ones began to move away and the old ones died off. And Lewis had changed. Mally had given him the dark man's books and he'd come to question as much as those who'd left had questioned, only he had stayed, searching for answers at the source of the riddle, rather than out in the world beyond.

He couldn't remember just when they had stopped the offerings or the bonfires. Green grass grew where once the charred circle had been black in the glade, where the red blood had flowed. Had there been a pack then? Lewis couldn't remember. If Perkin's hounds had been around at the time, they hadn't been quite so bold.

He wondered what Mally and Ali had been up to tonight. Neither of them was here now. He hadn't quite understood what Mally meant about Ali being gone. *Stolen like smoke,* the wild girl had said. By the Hunt. By Perkin's hounds. They might even be my hounds now, Lewis thought uneasily.

He moved closer to the bonfire and spotted Ali's walking stick lying where she'd dropped it. He bent down slowly and picked it up, hefting it in his hands.

There was something about this hilltop tonight, he thought. Something different. He could feel something in the air—a gathering of . . . intention, he supposed. He didn't feel alone. There was a charge like static electricity in the air, a heaviness like the forewarning approach of a storm.

He turned from the fire and looked out over the darkened forest. The sky was clear, the stars sharp and bright against the black sky. The smell of smoke mixed with the pungent odor of cedar and pine. If there was a storm coming, he thought, it wasn't a physical one. What had the girls been doing here? Calling the mystery—that was what. To set him free. That was enough to cause a storm, Lewis thought.

The dull boom of Louie Fucceri's explosion reached the summit where Lewis was standing and he looked skyward, thinking it was thunder. The sky was still clear. But then he made out the glow, far off in the woods where he knew Valenti's house to be. He heard the chatter of gunfire. He could *feel* the anger that was unleashed when men took weapons to hand.

Lewis had always been open to the flow of the woods, to the mystery's presence in the forest, to the way Tommy's pipes called the mystery and the way the mystery answered. So he felt the emotions coming from Valenti's house, but he felt stronger ones very close at hand. There was anger here, too. Fear as well.

He turned slowly, but he was still alone on the summit. When his gaze reached the old pine tree, he shivered, but he didn't know why.

He took a step toward the tree, then paused as he heard the sharp clatter of hooves on rock. He looked for the mystery, sensing his closeness, but couldn't find him—not as a stag, not as a Green Man.

Mally, he thought. What have you woken here? And where are you now?

Mally had reached the slow moving waters of Black Creek and was just starting to cross it by the stepping stones when she realized she was no longer alone. Something was out in the night with her. She paused on the New Wolding side of the creek and looked back the way she'd come, trying to pierce the gloom.

"Hornie?" she tried.

The willows rustled and the shadowy bulk of a boar stepped free of the slender trees, his tusks gleaming, his bristled hide swallowing the starlight where it touched him. Mally glided from the stones and knelt beside him, running her nails along his hide. The image of a burning fire slipped from his mind into hers and Mally nodded.

"Yes," she said. "Ali was calling you. But something's taken her and I think it was the Hunt. Will you help me find her?"

The tusker shook his head. Two images blossomed in Mally's mind, one following the other in quick succession. The first showed the boar returning toward the fire of bones, the other Mally going on across the stream.

"Oh, no," Mally told him. "I have to come with you."

She looked the solemn beast in the eye, surprised at how much he had communicated with her already. The mystery didn't concern himself overly much with the workings of the world. He simply went where he went, did what he did, amoral as a wind that is neither good nor evil, but simply is. And like a wind, the mystery could be channelled. By Tommy's pipes. By the chasing of the Hunt. By a fire of bones. By the moonlight. By a thousand and one things.

Mally was afraid that if she left him to himself, the mystery would simply wander off after a time, forgetting Ali—not because he wasn't intelligent, but because he had never given Mally any reason to suspect that he had much of a memory. Did the sun remember what it passed over during the day? Did the wind remember all its journeys?

She laid her hand on the boar's shoulder, then stepped hastily back as he began to change. The bristled hide became a cloak of leaves. The boar's head, a man's head with ram's horns tonight, rather than antlers.

He had a thousand and one shapes, Mally thought.

The mystery regarded her steadily and new images leapt from his mind to hers. She saw the fire of bones again, but it became two separate fires. In one she saw just Ali's face, frightened and desperate. In the other was a view of Tony Valenti lying still on the grass, his life's blood draining from his body. Ali's mother stood over Valenti, confronting a man that Mally vaguely recognized from a few nights ago. This was the companion of the man she'd killed last night.

"What are you trying to tell me?" she asked the man in his cloak of leaves.

"Who needs you more?" the mystery replied. "The lost or the dying?"

Mally took a few quick steps back, stunned at the sound of his voice. She'd never heard him speak before. The voice was resonant and low and sent shivers up her spine.

"You . . . you can talk?" she said.

She suddenly understood the wonder that Ali must have felt the first time she'd seen Mally's horns, the first time the stag had come to her, the first time her life had changed. Mally might have been less surprised if a tree had turned and spoken to her.

"No . . . no one needs me," she said when she realized that the mystery wasn't going to answer her.

"Every living thing needs a secret," he said. "You must choose whose you will be tonight. I will go to the other."

"I . . ."

Mally looked down at her hands, flexing her fingers. They were good for hitting and grabbing and "finding" and the like, but healing . . . ? She had heard the explosion that had come from the lame man's house. Right now, he lay hurt, dying. The mystery had shown her that. What could she do for him? Besides, she was responsible for Ali. But if Ali *had* been stolen away by the hounds, Mally knew she wasn't strong enough herself to deal with them. She could run, oh, very quick, and was good with tricks and such, but to rescue Ali that wouldn't be enough. Perhaps she *should* go to the lame man.

"Choose," the mystery said.

"I don't *know!*" Mally cried. "I'm just a secret—the riddle, not the answer. I'm not wise like you."

The mystery looked at her for a long moment, then turned and disappeared among the willows.

"You can't go!" Mally shouted after him. "I haven't chosen yet!"

But she already had, she realized. The mystery had taken it from her mind, knowing her choice before she did herself.

"If I'd *truly* been wise," she muttered, "I'd never have set any of tonight into motion."

She thought about what the mystery had shown her. She'd just have to trust him to rescue Ali while she tried to help the other. Turning, she bolted across the stream, taking the stepping stones two at a time. There'd be time enough to wonder about it all—the mystery talking, wisdoms and those which weren't so wise, who was free and who was not. . . . She'd puzzle it all out later. Now was a time for doing.

In the glade on the side of Wold Hill, watched over by the old stone, a man in a mantle of green leaves stepped from between the trees and out onto the grass. Gaffa whined and crawled forward on his belly, sniffing at the man's feet, puzzled at the lack of a scent. For a moment the man studied the stone, his ram's horns gleaming in the starlight, then he stepped toward it and disappeared inside.

Behind him, Tommy Duffin awoke to find himself standing with his face pressed against the cold rock, leaning there, his pipes half-held in a limp hand. All around him were green leaves, as fresh as though they'd just been pulled from their tree. They were thick around his feet and made a pillow of sorts for him as he sank slowly to the ground and sat in them.

Gaffa laid his head on Tommy's knee and Tommy began to stroke his pet, wondering all the while at the strange dream he'd just had. He knew he hadn't left the glade, but he felt as though he'd been walking, as though some part of him had come an immense distance and still had a long journey to complete before the sun rose.

Shaking his head slowly, he lifted his pipes to his lips and blew softly across them. Against his back, the old stone seemed to shiver in response.

9

"This is what you have worshipped, child," the hooded figure said.

Ali head his words through her pain, but they didn't immediately register. He held the crucifix against her brow and a white heat exploded from the contact, spreading through her nervous system like a brush fire. Incongruously, her thoughts went to the folk tales and fantasies she was so fond of reading. Elves feared iron and the symbols of Christianity. Did the hooded man's crucifix burn her because she was one of them? Earlier she'd been imagining herself as fey. Maybe she really was, and now she was going to burn for it.

In the instant it took for those thoughts to rush through her, the pain faded. She went limp in her bonds, hanging from the tree like a rag doll, while a wave of imagery flooded her mind. The hooded man filled her with what he wanted her to see.

"Look upon its evil," he said, "and repeat after me: 'The Lord is my rock, and my fortress, and my deliverer.' "

"N-n-nuh . . ."

Ali tried to shake her head, but the crucifix kept her pinned against the tree, immobile, while the flood of images went through her.

The goatman strode through her mind, his face twisted with lust, eyes rimmed red, his phallus standing erect between his legs like a tree. He fondled it as he stared at Ali. A long forked tongue slipped from between his lips and moved sinuously to the rhythm of a music that was like the sound of Tommy's pipes—that same kind of instrument was its source—but it was a discordant sound that came forth, a sound that raised her hackles and sent a shiver of repulsion through her. Her throat worked convulsively and she gagged.

"For *this* creature you forsook the Lord?" the hooded man demanded. "For this monstrosity?"

"N-nuh truh," Ali managed. She tried to focus on the shadows inside the man's hood, but the images he projected were too strong.

"Not true?" he shouted. "And what of this—is this not true as well?"

She saw a man in a field with a German shepherd. They were listening to the goatman's music, and like the goatman, the man began to play with himself. She saw him again, in bed with a woman, entering her from the rear, howling like an animal. She saw him shoot the dog. She saw him attack her own mother, throwing her up against the hood of a car, tearing at her clothes. She saw him place the barrels of the shotgun that he'd used to kill the dog in his own mouth and pull the trigger. And all the while that hellish music sounded, like nails dragging across a blackboard, and the goatman was standing there behind the man, grinning, grinning. . . .

"Nuh-nuh truh!" she cried.

But she knew it was. What the hooded man showed her now—this had all occurred. She could see the goatman laying his pipes aside, dipping his fingers into the man's blood, the forked tongue licking the red liquid from the fingers with obvious relish. . . .

All true.

"This is what Satan offers," the hooded man said. "This and nothing else. Torment and hurt. 'Resist the devil, and he will flee from you.' Believe in the Good Book, child. 'God is light, and in Him there is no darkness at all.' No room for such blasphemy against life."

Now she saw the old stone in its glade, the villagers capering around in a circle to the music that an older version of Tommy Duffin played on his pipes. She recognized Lewis and Lily—both younger than she knew them to be now. A man stood by the stone, holding a long-bladed knife. Two other villagers brought out a bull.

The man cut the bull's throat open and caught the gush of blood in a large metal bowl that he offered up to the stone, where the mystery stood again, but now he was an antlered man. His eyes still burned red. The nails on the ends of his fingers were long talons as he reached for the bowl. When he drank from it, streams of blood flowed around the edges of the bowl and dripped from his chin onto his cloak of leaves. And all the while the villagers danced and the piper piped his hellish tune.

True.

She saw a couple copulating in the forest, the goatman piping over them as they tore at each other in a frenzy. The lust in their eyes was just a pale glimmer of what she saw in the goatman's eyes as he ejaculated onto the couple.

True.

" 'Abstain from fleshly lusts, which war against the soul,' " the hooded man quoted. "Is this the monster you aspire to, child? Is it your innocent body you would have the creature penetrate with its godless lechery?"

"N-nuh . . ."

They paraded through her mind, hateful image following hateful image, until Ali choked on them. Repulsion filled her throat with bile. She struggled against the ropes in a sudden frenzy, but there was no escape, either from her bonds or the images that the hooded man poured into her mind by way of his crucifix.

"The scriptures ask, 'If God be for us, who can be against us?' and I answer you, Satan is. You look upon his works, child. Can you still embrace him? You sell your soul when you consort with him. Repeat after me: 'God be merciful to me a sinner.' "

Ali could barely hear him. The discordant music, the hellish images, were driving her further and further from sanity. You lied to me, she cried to the mystery, to Mally, to Lewis, as she plummeted into

madness. You lied to me. You said he was good, but you liedliedlied-
lied. . . .

"Evil is legion," the hooded man cried. "There is but one Son of
God. Child, accept Him as your Savior!"

A maelstrom of violent and lecherous images swirled around Ali
as she fell from sanity. She clutched at the hooded man's words, but
when he named Christ by name, the image he gave her was of Jesus
hanging on the Calvary Cross, His body wracked with pain, His eyes
full of hurt, the crown of thorns piercing His brow.

There was no comfort to be found there. It was all the same. Violence and hurt. If Christ was a Savior and men had done that to Him,
given Him so much torment, then what hope was there? They had
done this to Him and done, as well, so much evil in His name. They
had tortured and raped and killed, all for a man they had hung on a
cross, a man they would nail to a cross again if He returned to them
now.

Lewis had been right in that, she thought, as she started to let herself go. There was no more point in struggling. Better to just go away,
to give up life, if this was all it offered. If behind each smiling façade,
men had only hate and hurting to give each other. I guess you told me
one true thing, Lewis, she thought.

"If you would be saved," the hooded man told her, "then accept the
Lord. He is all that can stand between you and the monster that has
you in its clutches. Accept the Lord, child! 'His enemies shall lick the
dust.' Accept Christ as your Savior and you *will* be saved!"

But Ali wasn't listening. She had caught hold of a thought and
where nothing else had helped her, that thought did.

Lewis.

What Lewis had said about the mystery.

He has always been a reflection of what one brings to him.

So if you came to him with violence or lust in your heart, *that* was
what was reflected back. But if you came to him with goodness, without evil . . . Nobody was perfect, but if you really tried to be good and
approached him, then he'd be good for you—wouldn't he? She pic-
tured Jesus in her mind, not the hateful image of Him on His cross, but
others she had seen, of a gentle man, a kind man. . . .

A light began to blossom inside her, burning away the hooded man's images. Her tormentor had shown her truths, yes, but not the whole truth.

The light continued to grow inside Ali and the hooded man stumbled over his words. He took a step back, startled, perhaps even frightened, by what he saw in his victim's face. As the crucifix lifted from Ali's skin her head cleared. A different fire, her own fire, burned away the confusion, the fear. She saw Christ's face and smiled when she saw that He had the mystery's eyes.

It was so simple that she could have wept. The mystery was only what you brought to him.

The light inside her began to flow out of her pores until she was like a fiery statue. The ropes burnt away. Pushing herself away from the tree, Ali staggered toward the monks. Were *they* what you brought to them as well? They had chased her down because she'd carried the scent of the otherworld on her when she'd returned from that place in elsewhere. But when she'd confronted them, had it been her own fears and confusion that had put the words in the hooded man's throat?"

"I don't need to be saved," she said softly.

The light burned from her. Where it struck the hooded figures, they smoked. Their cloaks hung loosely on them now, and then they were a milling pack of hounds, whining with uncertainty, cringing as she stepped toward them, finally fleeing.

That's *it?* Ali wondered. That was all it took?

"Was it such an easy struggle?" a voice asked from behind her.

Ali turned to find the mystery standing under the pine tree, watching her. Ram's horns curled from his brow and a mantle of green leaves fell from his shoulders.

"You came very close to not surviving at all," he added.

Ali looked at him. The awe she'd felt the last time she'd seen him in that other place wasn't present now. This being that stood so quietly under the tree seemed like an old friend.

"I called you," she said, "but they came instead."

He nodded. "They were something you had to confront. I came to help you, but you didn't need my help after all."

"But you did help me. I'd given up, until I remembered what Lewis said, that you were what we brought to you. That's true, isn't it?"

The horned man nodded.

"Do you want to be free?" Ali asked. "That's what all this was about, you know. I had to know if you wanted to be free."

"Whether *I* wanted to be free, or you?"

"I . . . I don't know. I want to be free, sure. I just didn't know that I wasn't. What about you?"

"I can't be free until mankind is no more. But I can't be bound, either."

"What *are* you?"

"A mystery." He smiled. "As your friend Mally said, does everything need to be explained?"

"It'd help," Ali said. "But I suppose that would make things too easy."

"Just so."

"Why can't you help the others?" she asked then. "Like the man with the dog that the hounds showed me. Why does there have to be bad things?"

"I do try to help, but men will be what they must be; they reap what they sow."

"There's more than one of you, isn't there?"

He nodded.

"Is Mally one of you?"

"No. She is of your world. As I come from that otherplace to here to touch your souls, she is of your world itself, from the earth and the forest and the moonlight on them. A little mystery."

"A secret," Ali said. "Does she know what she is?"

"Do you know what *you* are?"

A dozen facile answers came to mind, but Ali shook her head. After what she'd learned tonight, she knew there was no easy answer to what she was. To what anyone was.

"I wonder where she went," Ali said finally. "When I was calling you, she was here with me, but then suddenly she was gone."

The horned man smiled. "Not she—you. You stepped sideways

into another place when the hounds came—a place akin to that otherworld that I bore you to last night, but another elsewhere again. The world and Mally are still where they were."

"Then how . . . how do I get back?"

He stepped closer to her, drew off his green cloak and laid it across her shoulders. The leaves rustled and she touched the edge of the cloak with wondering fingers.

"I will send you back," the horned man said. "Remember me. What I am, what I can be; what you are and what you can be."

He touched her brow, brushing the skin with his fingers. Ali blinked. She had the feeling that she was in an elevator, a quick lurch in her stomach. Then she was staring at the same tree, but the horned man was gone. She turned slowly to see the fire still burning and a figure beside it.

"Mally . . . ?" she started to say, then realized who it was. " 'Lo, Lewis," she said and smiled. She felt completely at peace, with herself, with the world.

Lewis looked up quickly. He heard Mally's familiar expression, but another's voice. "Ali?" he asked.

"It's me, Lewis." She fingered the cloak. The leaves were gone, the real ones at least, but by the light of the fire she could see that the cloak now appeared to be made of hundreds of pieces of cloth in the shapes of leaves, all sewn together. "I've had such a time," she said. "I've been all the way there and back again—just like Bilbo."

Lewis didn't catch the analogy, but he heard the dreamy quality in her voice. "Are you all right, Ali?" he asked.

"I couldn't be better. What are you doing here, Lewis? Where's Mally? I've such things to tell you, but first I should see my mom and Tony so that they don't worry about me. Boy, they're not going to believe what I . . ."

Her voice trailed off as she caught a look on Lewis's face in the firelight.

"What's the matter?" she asked. "What happened?"

Lewis pointed in the direction of Valenti's house where a dull glow still showed. "I think there's been some trouble," he said softly.

Ali's good feelings washed away in a flood of worry. "Oh, God!"

she cried and took a few little steps, but she was more worn out from the ordeal than she realized. She wavered and would have fallen if Lewis hadn't caught her. "I've got to go to them," she told him. "I've got to help."

Lewis helped her sit in front of the fire. "All we can do is wait and hope," he said. "Mally's gone to help them." I hope, he thought. "You're in no condition to go anywhere, never mind traipsing through the forest."

"But . . ."

Lewis took her hand. "Tell me where you've been," he said.

Ali wanted to argue, but she didn't have the energy. She leaned her head against his shoulder. "It . . . it's hard to . . . explain . . ." she began. Her eyelids fluttered and then before she realized what was happening, she was asleep.

Lewis eased her down so that her head was pillowed on his lap. He didn't know where she'd come from, out of the blue as she had, nor what had really happened here tonight, but he knew that something had. Something important. A change that would affect them all. He'd just have to wait until Ali woke to find out, he thought as he stroked her hair.

The poor child was worn right out. He would have taken her down to his cabin, but he didn't think he had the strength left in him to make the descent—not carrying her as well. They would just have to stay here until Mally came back. He hoped she wouldn't be long, but with all that was happening tonight, he wasn't raising his hopes. Just so long as she *did* come back—that would satisfy him at this point.

He let his chin rest against his chest and continue to stroke Ali's hair. If he listened carefully, he found, he could hear the sound of Tommy's pipes, though it was late for him to be playing them. The sound of them helped ease his worry. But only a little.

10

Earl dodged the UZI but lost his grip on his .38 in doing so. The handgun fell in the grass by his feet. By the time he had it in his hands again and had turned back to Frankie, she was kneeling behind Valenti, her automatic pointed at him.

"We already been here, Frankie," he said. "Remember?"

She stared at him, blinking back tears. Oh, she remembered. What Tony had shown her. What Earl meant to do to her. What he meant to do to Ali. He deserved to be shot. He deserved the worst that could happen to a human being.

"You ain't got it in you," Earl said. His teeth gleamed mockingly as he grinned. "So put that thing down and let's stop fucking around. You don't need your knees to sign over that bread. Either you get rid of the gun, or I'll blow 'em off, babe. Simple. Or maybe you're gonna get brave and pull the trigger. Well, I got news for you, Frankie. People don't just fold up and die when you shoot them. Look at your boyfriend, fercrissakes. He ain't dead yet. Shoot me, and I'll take you with me. But I don't think you're gonna shoot me, are you?"

She wanted to. God, she wanted to. It was self-defense. Killing him would be so justified that half the world would get up and cheer if she did. But she couldn't. Not because she didn't have it in her, but because it would take her down to his level.

She could care about Tony, even with all he'd done, but she knew she wouldn't be able to live with herself if she killed another human being, no matter how justified. God help her, she wanted to. But if she did, he'd win. Either way, he won. If she was going to lose anyway, she would it on her own terms.

She brought her hand down and tossed the gun on the grass in front of Valenti. His eyes were open, and in the harsh light from the burning house, she could see approval in them. Somehow he knew what had gone through her and he respected her choice. The difference between him and Earl was that what Earl saw as her weakness, Tony knew to be her strength.

"All right," Earl said. "That's playing it smart, Frankie. Come tomorrow morning when the banks open, we'll get the bread and then I'll be out of your life. It wasn't so hard now, was it?"

It was the hardest thing she had ever done, Frankie thought, but she knew he'd never understand.

"What . . . what about Tony?" she asked.

"We leave him."

"But he'll die without help."

Earl nodded, still grinning. "Yeah, I know."

Frankie looked down at Valenti, but there was no recrimination in his eyes. "I couldn't do it," she said softly.

"It . . . it's . . . okay. . . ."

"Oh, Christ," Earl said. "Why don't we get out the fucking violins? C'mon, Frankie. We got to blow. Cops'll be crawling all over this place. Maybe they'll find your boyfriend in time . . . maybe he'll live long enough for them to take him to trial. They'll lock him up and throw the fucking key away when they figure out who he really is. 'Course maybe I'll just . . ."

He started to aim at Valenti's head, when he heard something coming at them through the bush to their left. Oh, Christ, Earl thought. It's that fucking buck deer. He turned in that direction, aimed, but before he could fire, he heard a sharp report and something hit him in the side like a piledriver.

"What the fuck . . . ?" He looked stupidly down at his own gun, then slowly turned to Valenti and Frankie. Valenti fired his own .38 a second time. This time the bullet caught Earl square in the chest and lifted him off his feet before he slammed into the ground. He was dead before the impact.

"Maybe you . . . couldn't . . . do it. . . ." Valenti said to Frankie as he let the weapon fall from his hand. He didn't know where he'd gotten the strength to lift the thing. "But . . . but I could. I . . . I had to . . . Frankie. You understand . . . don't . . . you . . . ?"

"Don't talk," Frankie said. "Oh, Jesus. Don't move. I'm going to call an ambulance."

"You got . . . got to get out of here." Valenti said.

"He's right."

Frankie turned at the sound of the new voice. In the light from the burning house she saw the wild girl, thin and dressed in tatters, her hair a tangle of knots and twigs and leaves. Protruding from just above her hairline were the two small horns that Frankie remembered so well. She'd made the noise that had distracted Earl.

"Mally?" she said. She looked beyond Mally, hoping to see Ali, but the wild girl seemed to have come on her own. "You don't understand. We've got to get him to a hospital."

Mally shook her head. In the distance they could hear a siren.

"I don't want you here when . . . when the cops come," Valenti said. "Please, Frankie."

"I'm not leaving."

"You must," Mally said. "And we're taking him with us."

As the wild girl started for Valenti, Frankie blocked her way. "You *don't* understand! He's been shot. God knows what will happen to him if we move him. He's lost so much blood already. . . ."

Mally regarded Valenti and saw that the fire in him was dying down, but still there. "The mystery'll know what to do to help him," she said. "And Lewis will help us."

The sound of sirens was drawing closer.

Mally pushed Frankie aside. "I'm going to carry him," she said.

The strength in the wild girl's arms when she pushed Frankie aside should have told her that it wasn't such an impossible thing, but it wasn't until Mally gathered Valenti effortlessly up in her arms that Frankie realized that just maybe Mally could do it.

"I'll be going quicker than you," Mally said. "Follow the path and it will take you to where we're going. When you reach the stream, ignore what you think you see. Just take the stones across."

"But . . ."

"The . . . guns . . ." Valenti said weakly from Mally's arms. "Try and get . . . ours before the cops . . . before they come."

"But . . ." Frankie tried again.

"Just follow the path," Mally repeated, nodding with her head to where it began. Then the wild girl turned and the forest swallowed her.

Frankie stared numbly through the trees but couldn't see anything. She couldn't hear anything, either. Just the crackle of flames and the siren that was now coming up Tony's road. She took a deep, steadying breath and started to gather the weapons.

She slung the UZI over one shoulder, put the automatic back in its holster, Valenti's .38 in her pocket, counting the weapons to herself as she did it. Something was missing. Then she remembered the crossbow and fetched that. She was just entering the forest when the Ontario Provincial Police cruiser pulled up in front of what was left of Tony's house. By the time the OPP officers made their way cautiously around to the back of the house, she was gone as well.

She never once looked at Earl after Tony had shot him. She didn't even think about him.

Lewis lifted his head as the sound of Tommy's piping changed. The music grew bolder, more insistent. Almost as though it were summoning them. Ali stirred and sat up, rubbing her eyes. She heard it, too.

"We've got to go," she said. "To the stone. He's calling us this time."

Lewis nodded. He got slowly to his feet, joints aching. He used Valenti's walking stick for leverage. Ali let him keep it as they made their way down the hill, through the trees and then the bushes up behind the old stone. The music had grown louder, but it was no longer so insistent. Whatever possessed Tommy knew they were coming. As they stepped into the glade the piping quieted to a murmur.

" 'Lo, Ali . . . Lewis."

Mally was waiting for them. By her feet lay Valenti's still form.

"He needs help," the wild girl said. "I thought Old Hornie would help him, but he's just sitting there in Tommy's eyes, not doing anything. Will you help, Lewis?"

Lewis nodded. He knelt down beside Valenti, but the light was too poor for him to see what needed to be done.

"We'll have to get him to my cabin," he said, but Mally shook her head.

"He's got to stay here," she explained. "Old Hornie's all that's letting him hang on. Tell me what you need and I'll go get it."

"Well, a lantern for starters. Hot water. Clean cloth. We'll also need . . ."

As he listed off the items, Ali shut him off. She went down on her knees beside Valenti and smoothed his brow with her hand.

"My mom?" she asked Mally, interrupting Lewis.

"She's fine," Mally said. "She'll be along soon."

Ali nodded and went back to stroking Valenti's brow. "Don't die, Tony, I've got so much to tell you. I've talked to him—to the mystery."

His eyelids fluttered and he looked up at her, trying to smile. "Th-that's sen-sensational. . . ."

"Aw, jeez. What did you have to get hurt for?"

"It wasn't . . . wasn't my idea. . . ."

"That's what you say. Is it over now?"

"I . . . I think so. Depends on how . . . on how Mario did . . ."

Ali laid a finger against his lips. "You'd better not talk."

She looked over to Lewis and saw that Mally was already gone. By the old stone, Tommy continued to play.

The music kept getting louder, helping Frankie keep to the path. She had one bad moment, at the stepping stones, but she remembered what Mally had said and forged across. By the time she reached the glade, it was well lit by one of Lewis's lamps. She saw Mally and her daughter talking. A strange-looking boy was sitting by a tall stone, playing the pipes that were the source of the music. A dog lay by his knee. And then there was Tony, lying there, his shirt off. An old man was just tying off a bandage. Tony looked so pale in the light of the lamp that her heart gave a lurch.

"Mom!"

Ali had caught sight of her. Frankie let the weapons fall to the ground and drew her daughter into her arms. This was what mattered, she realized. It was for this that she hadn't let herself fall into the trap of doing things Earl's way.

"Thank God you're okay," she murmured into Ali's ear.

"Let's thank ourselves," Ali said. *"We're* the ones that did it."

Frankie hugged her tighter.

EPILOGUE

Et in Arcadia ego.
[I too am in Arcadia.]

—INSCRIPTION ON A TOMB IN A
PAINTING (C.1623) BY GUERCINO

Only to the white man was nature a "wilderness" and only to
him was the land "infested" with "wild" animals and
"savage" people. To us it was tame. Earth was bountiful and
we were surrounded with the blessings of the Great Mystery.

—LUTHER STANDING BEAR,
FROM *LAND OF THE SPOTTED EAGLE*

In the early hours before the sun rose, Ali sat outside Lewis's cabin. Lewis and her mother were inside, Lewis sitting at his kitchen table, half asleep, her mother sitting beside Tony, holding his hand and talking to him, though he couldn't hear her. He had passed out when Lewis began working on him, but though his breathing was ragged, he was still alive. Ali liked seeing them together, Tony and her mother.

" 'Lo, Ali."

She turned to find Mally standing by the corner of the cabin. The wild girl dug about in the pocket of her oversized jacket and came up with a paperback book that she gave to Ali.

"This is for you."

Ali held it up in the light coming from the cabin door. It was a copy of Thomas Burnett Swann's *Wolfwinter.*

"Jeez," she said. "How'd you know I was looking for a copy of this. . . ." Her voice trailed off as she realized that the only reason it had been missing in the first place must have been because Mally had "found" it earlier. "Thanks," she said.

Mally sat down beside her. "You talked to the mystery, didn't you?" she said.

Ali nodded.

"I talked to him, too," Mally said. "I never even knew he *could* talk. What did he say to you? Did you ask him if he wanted to be free?"

"He said that he already is."

"Then why does he stay here? Why does he let the hounds chase him?"

"I don't know," Ali said. "Maybe because he's not really free at the same time." She turned to look at the wild girl. "He's not really *the* mystery, Mally. He's just a part of a bigger mystery."

Mally nodded. "That other place."

"That place," Ali agreed, "but here, too. The mystery that's here, in *this* world—he's a part of it, too. There's more than one of him."

"I wonder why," Mally said.

"Everything doesn't have to be explained," Ali said.

Mally looked at her and a broad smile settled on her face.

Frankie had come to stand in the doorway and caught most of their conversation. The ordeal of the past few days rose in her mind, but then she looked out at the forest and thought of it, of that glade with the old stone that she'd glimpsed only so briefly, of the village and Lewis, of Tony. At that moment, from the forest, from the glade and the standing stone, the soft sound of piping drifted to them.

Frankie remembered some of what Ali had told her of her experience with the mystery in that place that wasn't here or now, but somewhere, somewhen else. A hallowed place, a peaceful place. What they had here, in one small pocket of wilderness in Lanark County, was just an echo of it. But if an echo was all they could have, then an echo would have to be enough.

Pan's pipes were playing, and if it wasn't the mystery himself playing them, it was still his music. She wanted to hear that music always, to hear it with Ali, and to hear it with Tony. It looked like the bad times were finally over and there were things unspoken between Tony and her that could be spoken now. Though there was one more thing that had to be done.

"Time to go, Ali," she said softly.

Ali turned to look up at her mother. "Go where?"

"Back. Someone's got to explain things to the police. With any luck we'll be able to convince them that Earl and those men had a falling out among themselves and keep Tony right out of it. We'll tell a half truth—that they were after the Wintario money."

She was no longer carrying the automatic, but she still had the .38 in her pocket. Now she picked up the crossbow from where it leaned against the wall by the door.

"We might be in for a bit of a rough time," she added, "because if I have to, I'm going to tell them that I shot Earl."

Ali swallowed, then nodded. "But they'll think it was self-defense, won't they?"

"I hope so, Ali. Come on, now. We've got to go."

"But we'll come back here . . . ?"

Ali regarded her mother, but Frankie had turned to look inside the cabin where Tony lay. "You can bet on that, kiddo. I don't know how things are going to work out between him and me, but if they don't work out, it won't be because I didn't try."

"What he used to be—it doesn't matter?"

"Does it matter to you?"

Ali shook her head.

Frankie smiled and stepped from the door. "Well, it matters to me. It's important to know what a person was. But it's more important to know what they are now. Does that make any sense?"

Ali nodded. She looked around for Mally, but the wild girl was gone. Frankie put her arm around Ali's shoulder, and after saying good-bye to Lewis, together they started down the trail that led for home.

"I'll be back to see you, Mally!" Ali called into the forest as they entered it.

A head hung down suddenly from a low branch above them. "I know you will," Mally said. Then she swung down to the ground and ran off laughing through the trees. The laughter faded, but the sound of Tommy's pipes followed them all the way home.

AUTHOR'S NOTE

The preceding novel is a work of fiction. All characters and events in this book are fictitious, and any resemblance to actual persons living or dead is purely coincidental.

While the *fratellanza* as portrayed in *Greenmantle* is based on an organization that had its origin in actual Sicilian history, this novel should in no way be taken as a disrespectful comment against anyone of Sicilian or Italian descent. Every race and culture has its bad element—if a finger needs to be pointed, it can be pointed at us all.

The slang references to racial and ethnic groups do not reflect my own personal viewpoint whatsoever.

Greenmantle had its roots in the same chapter from Kenneth Grahame's *The Wind in the willows* with which Ali Treasure was so enamoured: "The Piper at the Gates of Dawn." My own interest in moon and horn mysteries can be traced back to my reading that chapter as a child.

The real springboard, however, was Lord Dunsany's forgotten

fantasy *The Blessing of Pan.* Written in Dunsany's usual lyric prose, the book is set up for an atypical climax of the good vicar overcoming the heinous pagan rites of his flock, only to end with a complete turnaround. My sympathies, in such cases, often lie with the pagans, not because of any particular pagan leanings of my own, but because I dislike religious intolerance of any sort.

Since first reading *The Blessing of Pan,* I've retained an interest in that lost village of Wolding, visited only by the Gypsies and a horned mystery—hence this book. Had Dunsany survived to this day and written his own sequel to *The Blessing of Pan,* I find it highly unlikely that he would have come up with anything like *Greenmantle.* But I do hope that, here and there in a passage or two, some echo of the wonder I first found in his book has made its way into what I've written where it might touch someone else.

The above paragraphs come from *Greenmantle*'s original Author's Note, written in the summer of 1986, and still hold true as I read over the galleys for this Orb reissue of the novel.

Something I didn't mention in that earlier note was that another reason for my writing *Greenmantle* was an interest in exploring the place that Mystery holds in contemporary society—how we view it, how it affects us, who we become when it directly touches us. Today, some thirteen years after I first wrote the book, and with the millennium fast approaching, the questions seem perhaps even more pertinent, or at least they're being asked by a great many more people.

Greenmantle was never meant to answer those questions on its own. But I do hope the novel helps continue the dialogue: between ourselves, and between ourselves and the mysteries of the world.

On another note, I'd like to invite those of you who wander the Internet to come visit my home page. The URL (address) is: http://www.cyberus.ca/~cdl.

CHARLES DE LINT
Ottawa, Spring 1998